PRESIDENT ORANGEJOB
AND THE CRIMSON MARIPOSA

A NOVEL

BY

ROSEMARY LIGHTFOOT
NESS BITNER

This story was inspired by the spirits that visit with us and share our memories and look into the future with us. They are eternal beings that live in our consciousness and speak to us from time to time. They often reveal things to us while we sleep.

Book cover by Cheekycovers.com

Interior layout by Ebooklaunch.com

THE CHARACTERS

President Orangejob	President of the United States of America.
Sheila Carson	Genius woman from Milltown.
Bob Carson	Sheila's father.
Heidi Carson	Sheila's mother.
Donny	Sheila's older brother.
Adam	Sheila's younger brother
Cecilia or CC	Eccentric, clever, beautiful woman.
Old Yellow	Cecilia's Toyota Land Cruiser.
Johnny	Sheila's elementary school boy friend.
Ehud Burke	AKA Hud, prospector, pilot.
Gibby	Mountain man, Jo Anne's lover.
Jo Anne	Waitress, Gibby's lover.
Fat Sam	Proprietor, bartender.
General Porter	Conspirator.
Connie, Linda, Pattie and Sandra	BASE bank intern trainees.
Carlos	AKA Sebastian Carlos de Carmella, AKA Carlos, guitarist.

Tee O's	Upscale restaurant.
Mr. Howard Rockman	Connie's father.
Mr. Santifalo	Assistant Research Director at BASE.
Mole	Bond trader at BASE.
George	Stock trader at BASE.
Paul Wheeler	Research analyst at BASE.
Walter Black	CEO of BASE BANK AMALGAMATED, conspirator.
Sal	Operations manager at BASE.
Jack	Conspirator.
GRAB	Jack's company.
Mr. George Palmer	Co CEO of Bear and Otter Consulting, conspirator.
Mr. Henry Kelly	Co CEO of Bear and Otter Consulting, conspirator.
Mr. Rothstein	Banker, conspirator.
Mr. Won Low	Banker, conspirator.
Mr. Rawbone	Procurer of lethal materials, conspirator.
Rosemary	Recluse, best selling author, spirit medium.
Bud	Rosemary's tabby cat, exceptional mouser, explorer.
Spirit	The Great Spirit of all Living Things.
Marty, Marty's lovers, David, Big Chief, Big	Spirits.

Horse, Little Sparrow

Preface

What makes a genius a genius? Some would say it is a brain given to someone at birth. Others would say it is a DNA strand that was somehow modified by an intervening thing that is not of our world.

But genius is mostly like an exceptionally rare tasty grape. It may lie dormant until stimulated. What stimulates its awakening? Maybe it's a visionary dream that arrives like a thunderbolt in the night, but maybe it's something else.

Perhaps it's born in struggle, in its effort to overcome adversity, like an exclusive grape varietal must struggle for nourishment by pushing its roots deeply into rocky soil. Perhaps latent genius blossoms because its soul was stressed, tortured and pushed into the deep like the roots of a valuable Vitis.

• • •

The job posting that arrived at the MIT placement office sought a person with excellent qualities in both mathematics and theoretical physics, a willingness to work in secrecy for the U S government, and a willingness to work in isolation while rapidly defining multifaceted problems and solving them. It required that person to forgo any publishing about the research projects and to remain forever silent about the projects or the methods used to achieve the results.

That person would toil ceaselessly until a problem was defined, the answers discovered, and then that person would retreat into anonymity afterwards unless called upon once again by the U S government to solve yet another problem; and that person would agree to drop whatever other endeavor that person was engaged in after the project and disengage from that endeavor or career if called back to serve the U S government. That person would need to be a strong willed sort of person who relished challenges. The placement officer at MIT knew that person was Sheila Carson.

"Why me," asked Sheila. "Of all the PhD's in my class and your alumni data base, why are you recommending they hire me for this?" She preferred to stand when talking to the placement officer, or most men for that matter.

"They want a fresh look at this, Sheila. They've tried the math only and the physics only approach, they've tried different schemes with several of our brightest alums and they are essentially nowhere. They want a fresh mind to start over from scratch. I told them about you, about your ability to think about a problem and define it; then theorem test things in your mind, visualize the math needed and then derive the solution all in your head. I, I mean the school, doesn't have anyone else quite like you Sheila. I told them that I, I mean your faculty advisors, all consider you to be a promising genius. We told them your IQ tested over 200. They know that. I've already told them I would urge you to take this on for the good of our country."

"Okay, then I'll accept the offer."

"Just like that?"

"Yes, you said it was for the good of our country. I believe you are a man of your word and I love my country for the freedoms and opportunity it offers, despite its faults. I feel it's my duty to accept."

"Very good Sheila, then I'll confirm. I have here a sealed package for you about security matters. You'll need to take care of that before you leave Boston. And, there's one other thing, Sheila."

"Yes?" Sheila's voice revealed apprehension.

"You must leave your personal life behind. These people did their homework Sheila. They specifically said you could not tell Johnny where you were going or what you'd be doing. No further contact."

"Trust me sir that will not be a problem."

Thus, with no fanfare or ado to old friends Sheila Carson promptly met with the local FBI agents, completed her background questions, obtained her security clearances, packed her two bags with her necessary belongings, and purchased a one way train ticket to Plaintown, Colorado.

CHAPTER ONE

THE PRAIRIE DARKNESS

Sheila napped intermittently most of the night. When she woke between snoozes she stared out her window. The Silver Streak Amtrak hurtled relentlessly through the quarter moon darkness, an empty nothingness interrupted only by an occasional dim spot of light from a distant farm house. That occasional farm light defied the vast emptiness of the high plains. It reassured her that life was out there, that some isolated humans were anchored to these endless grasslands scratching their existence from them. As train wheels clacked over the rail joints speeding by beneath her, farms' lights appeared and vanished from her window. The prairie expanse engulfed the onrushing train like a whale swallowing a sardine. Expanses of darkness flew past her window and disappeared. It returned to the vast nothing nowhere from where it came, only to be replaced by more endless spans of prairie that hurtled towards the train from the vast nowhere ahead. All that night the train had closed the distance between its silver engine and Plaintown. But now the wheels of the train screeched and the brakes hissed a release of steam. The great silver beast rolled into Plaintown's Central Station. Sheila was ready for her ride to end.

Her last nap was different from her others. She wondered if it really was a nap. She didn't know what it was. It felt like deeper sleep than a nap for it to be a nap. It was more like a deep out to the world sleep, the kind of sleep that borders on being a diabetic coma. She wasn't dreaming though. She could tell when she awakened from her sleeps that she'd been dreaming. It was not a dream. That's what was so weird about it. It had to be something that actually happened. It occurred when the train was a half hour into Colorado after coming across Kansas. She remembered peering out her window and noting that she hadn't seen a farm house light for a really long time. Then the dark somehow got even darker if that was possible. It got soupy dark, and then thick and sticky densely dark before it became a kind of twisting roiling ominous dark; but the new kind of dark didn't act like it wanted to hurt her. It just wanted to show off its stuff to her, to impress upon her that it was out there waiting, just biding its time and waiting. And it seemed to be straining to tell her something.

She experienced a kind of nervous spasm body start. It was a jolt that shot through her entire body leaving her shaken and wondering about what she saw. Her spastic start woke the man in the aisle seat next to her. He was an old frumpy guy who wore a Black suit with no necktie. Black hair bushed out of his undershirt and open collar. He'd been sleeping and sometimes snorting with his mouth open. He rode the whole way with his shoes off and smelled like he needed a shower and a foot bath. She remembered that same smell coming from some of the men who were at Daddy's Grange meetings. It was old man's smell. The man frowned at Sheila in a stupor daze then turned his back to her and resumed snoozing.

Just when she thought the ride through Kansas and eastern Colorado would never end the screeching steel wheels against steel rails announced her journey was ending. She was groggy tired but ready to begin her new job and her new life.

She promised herself that she'd leave her emotional baggage back East. She'd stop dwelling on the tragedy that felled her father. She'd close the door on Mother's inconsolable screams from her whitewashed room in the asylum. She'd close the chapter on Johnny. She'd forget the humiliation and rage she felt after she caught him red handed screwing her roommate with his pants still around his ankles. Her roommate deserved that asshole. She'd block out his sweet promising words forever, those dreamy words that once sustained her emotions. She was finished thinking about him. Done! She now realized she imagined her hopes and plans for the two of them as an emotional escape from her family's misfortune.

In this next chapter of her life she would find a way to let go of her bitterness. She'd stop dwelling about the loss of their beautiful farm with its rich bottom land along Pennsylvania's spectacular Pohopoco. But she'd never let go of the distrust she felt toward the government and their empty patronage about how they were being a noble family getting gutted for the greater good. Those faceless impersonal bureaucrats killed her father.

She would *never* forget the lesson from that experience. The government doesn't care one iota about any individual. Your so called rights come from the Constitution and the Bill of Rights; but even then you can not have those rights respected by any government agency unless you are willing to fight tooth and nail to insist that your rights are respected. Poor Daddy, good Daddy, got worn down to a nub of his former self from all the fighting. After seeing what they did to him, after living through his indescribable anger and sorrow, she swore to herself that she would never allow any government bastards to steal from her again, no matter what. It was what she called her meaningless hostile attitude. She owned no land anymore so none could be taken from her. All she had left was her brains. She'd sell them to the highest bidder. Ironically that bidder was the government.

At last she was in the West where it was dry and sunny. She'd leave her Eastern sore throats and sniffles packed away in that same 'forget the mouse' jar as her emotional aches. She smiled a small inward thanks for the job offer that brought her to the dryness. Getting the best of her sinuses would be a good thing. Saving money on nose tissues was a small first happiness, a tangible good thing. She would be conscious about keeping her promise to self. She would cling only to the good things that happened in her life since she left Pennsylvania. She'd cherish her fantastic years at MIT and all the incredible mind stretching she experienced.

She always knew she could think well, but she only realized how widely encompassing her mind could become when she directed it to wrap around a problem. She never knew how to stretch it and push it like that before she went to MIT. She'd forever remember the quiet meditative times that she sat on the lawn before the Great Dome. She inhaled a breath of pleasure when she recalled her solitary walks along Charles River. She called them her theorem walks. Somehow her corollaries and proofs naturally fell into place while she walked and talked about them with her brain.

Between brain and her everything fit together perfectly. Her course professors threw math and physics at her like footballs. The assumption was no one was stupid and you needed to know how to use the different disciplines of math and physics to solve problems. She caught every football and she learned more than methods. She learned how to think about problems and how to draw upon those different disciplines to solve them. She learned how to derive answers and to not rely upon memorization. She sought out new challenges and relished opportunities to go where no problem had ever taken anyone before. She developed confidence in her own mind, and she confirmed what she always knew about herself. She valued her mind and the times she spent with it just thinking. She valued that much more than going on a date.

She was not the best looking woman or hottest sexpot in any of her classrooms, but she was darn good looking. She had a very nice body with eye catching legs. She was not quite magazine centerfold or model material, but she had a charming perky fresh faced look and a friendly personality. She wasn't a lanky slinky type who wore expensive clothes that screamed 'My daddy is richer than God! Nor was she a glitzy clothes horse at parties. She just fit in. And that's all she ever tried to do. Her body filled out very late, but when it did she noticed men giving her their 'I'd like to get me some of that' look.

Most of the men she knew at MIT appreciated her for her mind. A few seriously tried to make her, but the reserved part of her personality always put her guard up and pushed them away. She told herself she was saving her hymen and her love for Johnny. Johnny went to Harvard. But he was history now. In her new life out West she promised herself to ban Johnny from her mind time. She would be the consummate professional mathematician. If the right man came along and wanted her, she'd give him serious consideration. But, if Mr. Right never showed up that would be okay too. No matter what, she swore to herself she'd never throw herself at any man. But she secretly wished she knew what it felt like to be fucked.

She'd proudly wear her beavers, the Rat and Grad Rat, those misnamed school rings with beavers on them. She was not going to hide her brains to humor a man who acted like a jerk with her. She was proud of her Rats. She earned dual PhD's in mathematics and applied physics and deserved every measure of respect those rings represented.

The train hissed to a jerky stop. It was time for the devourer of prairie miles to disgorge its passengers and goods. The cushy leather pad which was stuck to her numb bottom for twenty hours was finally parting ways with her. It was time to leave her seat, gather her bags and leave the silver beast. She was anxious to stand and stretch and walk and inhale the not train air. Her eyes blinked happiness to leave the beast's nuisance cigar smoke and dull fluorescent lighting. She also wanted to stop thinking about that weird twisting dark something that revealed itself to her on the vast prairie. She was going to throw herself into her work at Bear and Otter Consultants, LLC.

A woman named Cecilia was assigned to be at the exit platform holding a sign with the name 'Sheila' on it. The company human resources man who hired her said Cecilia was kind of an expressive sweet hearted woman who dressed loudly. Cecilia was told to shout out the name 'Sheila' when she saw a tall dark brunette carrying two black suitcases. And so the cute long legged virgin with her bags and her brain walked off the train looking for a loudly dressed woman named Cecilia.

CHAPTER TWO

PIG TAILS AND TIE DOWNS

S heila trundled her bags after her, the smaller one piled onto the top of the big one with its rollers. Dutifully, obediently she pulled her belongings before her upward and forward, forward and upward, until forward was all that was left because upward had nowhere left to go. She inhaled deeply and looked about for Cecilia. Where was this woman described to her as loudly dressed and enthusiastic? Sheila peered at the line of locals waiting to greet the debarking passengers.

There she was! It was impossible to miss seeing her. She was a crazy looking wild geek girl-woman, well fitted to her description. Yes, Cecilia was definitely geek-looking, a ready to be committed to an oddity museum looking sort of geek. She wore pig tails with purple ribbons, a red calico skirt with a not matching green and blue sweater jacket. Her mustard and black stripped leggings disappeared into Marine Corps green wool socks stuffed into a pair of black thick soled Marine Corps combat boots. She was medium height, voluptuous, very well-muscled and physically toned. Her body complimented her striking face. Sheila was told about Cecilia's expressiveness when she accepted this job offer. She heard Cecilia was extremely bright, but that she carried some undefined emotional baggage. 'Don't we all?' thought Sheila when she heard that one. 'What man thinks there's some woman out there without emotional baggage?' Sheila tuned out as the contracting agent droned on about how Cecilia was very impulsive with a very sweet personality with boundless enthusiasm for everything; and above all else unabashedly forthcoming, direct and honest to a fault. All of that fit Cecilia all right.

The woman she noticed had to be Cecilia. Who else would jump up and down, wave a cardboard sign that said 'Sheila Carson,' and scream her name so loudly that everyone in the train station noticed? Sheila observed that Cecilia was either color blind or completely clueless about how to dress. She almost asked this Jumping Jack where she got her Marine Corps boots but decided a simple introduction would be best. She elected to learn about Cecilia in small doses. The thought of walking through the train station with her made Sheila anxious to get out of sight and into a car.

"Hi, I'm Sheila," she said with her right hand extended for a shake. "You must be Cecilia! It's great to meet you." She was emphatic and masking her trepidations about being roommates.

"Oh, I am! I am!" Cecilia squealed as she threw her sign over her shoulder and gave Sheila a monster crush of a hug and lifted her off the ground. "So you are Sheila! Sheila, it's so wonderful to finally meet you. I've heard so much about you, about how smart you are and how you'll figure out all of our program bumps and how we'll all make so much money! I'm so happy to have you for a roommate! I can't wait to start helping you with your work! I can't wait to see how you solve these glitches that have put us so far behind our schedule with BASE Amalgamated. Their people are so demanding. Everything is an urgent, drop everything else priority with them. They make endless calls to George and Henry to cover the same things over and over. I'd love to shove their magnetic resonance project right up their New York asses.

"We are so relieved that you are finally here! Oh Sheila, let me stop my bitching and give you another welcome hug!" With that came another monster bone crusher and a look from her eyes like the look from a child's that discovered the Easter Bunny. "If there's anything you want; if there's anything I can do for you, just ask! The men at the shop say you are so brilliant you can figure out how to walk on water! Is that true? Is it? Could I help you with something? Just tell me! May I carry your bags?"

"Well, you can start by putting me down," said an over-whelmed Sheila. Then you could show me to a ladies' room so I can freshen up. You could watch my bags while I'm in there. I'd appreciate that." Sheila tried to reciprocate some modulated enthusiasm from her own voice.

"Okay. I'll go in there with you and I'll keep your bags with me. That way we can keep talking," asserted Cecilia.

"No, Cecilia. Just wait outside for me. That'll be fine," said Sheila drawing a boundary.

"Okay." Cecilia's voice betrayed her dejection when it retreated from full blast enthusiasm to matter of fact dull. They found the ladies' room. Sheila freshened up while Cecilia waited outside. Then they left the train station and made a short trek to Cecilia's vehicle. It was an old Toyota Land Cruiser, complete with a canvas top, rolled open and tied down for summer driving. There was that purple again! The car's purple tie downs held the canvas to the roll bar and perfectly color matched Cecilia's pig tail ribbons. It was the first sign of any color coordination that Sheila observed from this unusual woman.

As they got closer to Cecilia's wheels her friendly personality outwardly displayed itself in the form of bumper stickers. Actually the vehicle was less of a car and more of a billboard disguised as transportation. Its stickers shouted out to fellow motorists and passersby, 'KISS ME; HUG ME; LOVE ME;

LOVE ME, LOVE YOU; LOVE IS WHAT TO DO; LOVE NOT HATE; PEACE NOT WAR; I WILL; JUST ASK; U R OK; LOVE IS BEAUTIFUL; SEX SAVES; SEX SLAVE; LOOK UNDER MY HOOD; TASTE GREATNESS; COME SOAR WITH ME; I'D RATHER BE IN BED; MY OTHER CAR IS MY BED; LOVE ME TRUE; YES YOU CAN; JUST DO IT; HONK IF YOU WANT TO BE FREE; THE WORLD NEEDS MORE LOVE; BUFFALO BILL EATS HERE; GREAT EATS; MAN EATER; BIG STRAWS WANTED.' The stickers were plastered all over the back of her cruiser and along its sides and fenders.

When Sheila saw 'Old Yellow,' the name Cecilia gave her wheels, she almost turned around and walked to the cab stand. But she squelched that thought. She wouldn't know where to go or where to stay. And, it was her new employer that sent Cecilia to retrieve her from the prairie. There had to be something special about her or Bear and Otter wouldn't have hired her. But right then she didn't want to know another thing about Cecilia or anything else. She only wanted to put a bag over her head before getting into the passenger seat. Then she wanted to slink down, curl up on the floor and suck her thumb. 'What would any man think seeing two women riding in a mobile billboard that advertized they were sex crazed,' she wondered. Too Late! Cecilia threw Sheila's bags into the cruiser's back well, then leaped onto the driver's seat and started Old Yellow's engine. As soon as Sheila sat in the passenger's seat Cecilia popped Yellow's clutch. The mechanical beast sounded a backfire blast and lurched, then blasted and lurched again, and then it blasted again but lurched no more. It moved forward belching a trailing cloud of blue white smoke. And they were off!

CHAPTER THREE

WALTER

B ack East in New York City it was 8 am on a Monday in late September. Walter Black was already in his office. Walter was President of the Bank of All USA and Europe Amalgamated, or BASE, as the employees termed the organization. The guards on his secured floor had logged him in an hour before. Walter was an impeccably dressed patrician with a perfectly dimpled maroon silk tie that complemented his five thousand dollar tailored blue silk suit. His guards were bruisers, individually qualified to guard Walter, experts at martial arts and weapons, and physically imposing. Both men were over six feet five inches tall. Both had canoes for shoes and hands that could crush a human skull. Walter himself was far less physical. Walter was a wimp and the guards regarded him as such. At five feet four inches in height he had tiny feet and hands, effeminate wrists and gestures, and a slippery sort of motion to his walk. He inspired veiled contempt from the men who guarded him. Earlier this morning Walter had greeted them in a more clipped tone than usual, as if he was on an important mission.

"Morning men, lovely day!" Walter had chirped to them. After he passed their metal detector the senior guard looked at his partner and rolled his eyes. Then they both sat down at their guard desk. Likely they wouldn't see Walter again until he left for the day. He mostly made his appointments in the bank. He held one on one's in his office. He used one of the conference rooms for groups or department heads and he preferred the officers' dining room for bank relationship selling. For maximum impression, secret dealings, arm twisting and implied threats, he used his private dining room.

Walter sat at his massive black leather paneled desk in his cavernous corner office. He looked out over the Battery and further to the Statue of Liberty. It was a beautiful fall day in Manhattan with a blue sky and a light breeze off the Atlantic to buoy one's spirits. A few puffy cumulus clouds drifted lazily along aloft. Down on the streets summer short sleeves and cotton dresses were giving way to light woolen jackets. Even the occasional coat could be seen.

Walter noted the harbor craft disembarking workers arriving from New Jersey and Staten Island, and tourists from the first launches were already exploring Bedloe's Island. 'God bless the Americans' thought Walter to himself. 'There's always a supply of the fools for everything challenging. Somehow, miraculously, they show up to fight the country's wars and collect its garbage. Predictably, some of them show up daily to make the arduous climb up to Bartholdi's Torch.'

Some helicopters were inbound to the roof tops of nearby skyscrapers where they would disembark their overpriced talent, including some CEO's of his arch nemesis banking competitors. Walter nestled back in his massive leather desk chair and waited for his call. Life was good, as it should be, except for the occasional detail that needed his involvement. He tapped his fingers on his desk, waiting for the call.

Walter was handling this detail personally. He preferred the word detail for this sort of thing. The word operation sounded too clinical or too military and possibly too messy. He couldn't chance having some interloper piece together what the plan was and he couldn't trust the idiots in the bank's operations department to assist in doing it without asking uncomfortable questions or turning him in to the police. No, those geeks were best left to monkeying with their computers, their security protocols, their never ending requests for why they needed to shut down to rewrite software code or scrub files or back something up.

Walter was convinced they were all idiots, but their entire computer geek world was populated with like minded idiots. They all spoke nonsensical gibberish. Walter had long ago given up trying to manage that mess of flashing lights, whirring disks, rubber floors and that dratted incessant hum of little electrons going here and there doing only God knows what. The nerds commanded 144,000 square feet which sprawled over two floors of prime Manhattan headquarters real estate. Walter dreamed of the rents he could rake into the bottom line if he could only move them to someplace where he wouldn't have to deal with them or look at them, like Siberia.

When he first looked at the Bank's budget for them, he used to cry. Now he just called in their head man, a corporate senior V. P. named Sal. They did a familiar routine together, a pantomime of two played without an audience. Walter pretended to know what he was talking about when asking Sal operational questions and Sal pretended to believe that Walter actually did know what Walter was talking about. For these quarterly interludes from other things both men would rather do they parried and sparred, feinted and thrust, until both believed they clocked enough time discussing things they knew they would never resolve. The operations department needed new these's and that's because it simply did. It needed to occupy prime real estate to be close to everything because that's what the demanding electrons preferred.

And, the personnel who worked for Sal couldn't possibly conform to the bank's dress code because they lived in that infernal cave of theirs. And they couldn't possibly relate to others of their kind unless they all dressed like sloppy pigs. Somehow, mysteriously and miraculously, they got things done but only if they looked and smelled like they fell into a mud splattered wallow after wearing the same clothes for the past six months.

After enough time passed in the quarterly meeting, after both men intuitively knew they clocked enough time exhaling hot air toward each other, they arrived at their predictable conclusion. Walter told Sal the budget was outrageous and had to be reduced twenty percent. Amazingly, the super geek always found a way to comply; and, just as amazingly, the bank kept running fairly well. Sal always complied with his President's demand, departed the meeting with a grim face telling Walter it was a tall order from a tough taskmaster, but assuring him that trusty Sal would find a way. Walter always suspected Sal came into these meetings with his budget padded by an extra twenty or thirty percent; but what could he do about it? Likely these geek trolls had secret meetings with others in like positions in other banks and likely they all agreed to pad their budgets twenty or thirty percent.

Every time Sal left Walter's office, Walter stewed for about two full minutes. After Walter was certain Sal left his office spaces, Walter threw a pencil at the door that Sal had recently closed on his way out. It never accomplished anything to do that, but it made Walter feel better. Walter couldn't wait for the merger to take place. The geeks didn't know it, but he was going to smile widely when he told their head idiot, Sal, that he was eliminating his entire department. Mergers have their benefits; and, Walter would get a board approved incentive payment for axing those smelly bastards. He didn't like the clothes they wore to work and he didn't like the smells of their floors. He salivated at the prospects of getting rid of all of them.

Walter's extension rang. He picked it up without saying a word. The voice on the other end was low and raspy. "They're going up now," it said and then hung up.

CHAPTER FOUR

TEN HOURS

Walter was exasperated. He'd lost his aplomb three hours ago. Now he paced the floor of his office. The Colorado call was six hours late. He should have gotten a progress report. It was now 7 PM Eastern Time. Walter worried he might raise suspicions if he stayed longer. He rarely worked past 5 PM and never worked past 6 PM. It was his mantra that one's efficiency declined dramatically after 4 PM and he prided himself on maintaining his aplomb that everything in the bank was totally under control. He left the bank for home, exasperated at not knowing what happened in Colorado. His wife, predictably, would be fuming. They'd be late for a benefit dinner at one of her favorite charities. He looked forward to the refuge of a double martini.

It wasn't until three days later that Walter got a second call from the contact.

"Plan B concluded. Nothing found."

"Wait a minute!" Walter broke his own passive response protocol. He sounded frantic. "Who ever said we went to plan B?"

"I called and told you we needed to go to plan B three days ago when plan A didn't call in."

"I never got that call," declared an anxiety stricken Walter.

"Well, somebody did," said the raspy voice.

Walter began to worry. His contact told him a status call was made but he didn't get it. That meant somebody else got it. Walter called Sal, the operations manager to his office.

"Sal, I want to know who got a call three days ago on the bank's 800 line, can you get that for me?"

"In a word, no. I can only tell you what numbers called the 800, but once the call hits the bank's internal phone system I can't tell which extension the call went to."

"Why not?"

"Well, Walter, that'd be one of those extras you tell me to cut out of my budget, so I don't do extras. Besides, even if we paid for that it would take another week before the phone company ran the tapes back for the week and showed us where the call came from, unless......." Sal's voice trailed off.

"Unless what?" Walter had agitated thoughts. 'Why isn't anything going right lately? The supposedly whizz bang genius consultants from Colorado are way behind on their project. What was I thinking to hire a firm called GRAB? Why did I let Jack talk me into this mess? I'm risking everything for this brass ring idea of Jack's but now the whole project is running into complications and I'm losing control. Are all people from Colorado completely unaccountable? Does everyone smoke dope out there? Now this! I have a total lack of information in my own bank that supposedly has the best information systems in the world.'

"Jesus Christ, Sal, I feel like I'm herding fucking cats here! What kind of ship are you running down there in operations? Spit it out, Sal. Unless what?" Walter lashed out blindly.

Sal saw Walter's vulnerability and frustration and realized he had this socially polished nit wit right where he wanted him.

"Unless you agree to pay for extras!" Sal leaned over Walter's desk and smiled at him. Sal sensed there was an off court game going on and Walter was involved in it. If only he knew how vulnerable.

"Okay, Sal. Go ahead and order that package of extras. I don't want any more information voids. Got it?" Walter snapped his hasty order.

"Got it," smiled a cynical Sal. "Whatever you say, boss." Then Sal turned abruptly and left Walter's office. He lingered for a couple minutes outside the closed door. Sure enough, the dull bump of a pencil hit the door's other side.

Walter began to sweat. Little beads of perspiration formed over his upper lip. The thought of subpoenas and grand juries flashed through his mind. A cold sweat broke out on his forehead and trickled down between his shoulder blades. He didn't dare make a record of an outgoing call to the Alamosa contact to pursue why the first call didn't reach him; but he needed to know who got that call. He called Jack at his father's law firm. It was Jack's idea to use this old buddy of his from Alamosa, Colorado. He needed to find out what happened to the damn call.

"Jack, Walt here. Listen, about your Colorado man. How reliable is he, really?"

"He's reliable, Walt. What's wrong? Why are you asking?"

"I was supposed to get a call from him three days ago, but I didn't got that call; then he called me today and said he called me three days ago. Am I going crazy, Jack?"

"Did he call you on your direct line?"

"No, I told him to use the bank 800 and then my extension."

"Good. Let me think a minute. Hmmm. Walt, what's your extension there?"

"It's 1113"

"Well, Walt, Jim might have thought he talked to you but he might have hit another extension in the bank. I didn't think this was worth mentioning at the time I arranged this for you, but Jim had dyslexia problems when he was a kid. When he gets excited, it can still show up. He might have punched 1311 or 3111 or 1131, something like that. I doubt if he would have dropped off the top row of his phone's punch buttons though. Dyslexia tends to make people misarrange things on the same line. His fingers sometimes get ahead of his mind."

"Jack, you should have told me before I gave the go ahead to use him."

"Well, how many people do you think there are that go in for dark ops, Walt?"

"Never mind." Click. Walter hung up. At least he now knew where to begin. He got the bank's internal extension directory. There was no 3111 or 1131, but there was a 1311. It was to a Sandra Wentz, a secretary in the Investment Research department. He paused to think for a moment, and then decided to call her.

"Ms. Wentz, this is Walter Black, bank president, Could you come to my office, please?

Sandra Wentz was a great worker bee and an extremely conscientious research associate. She was a 120 word a minute error free wizard on the keyboard and a perfectionist at spelling and punctuation. She was fresh, pleasant looking, bright eyed, rosy cheeked, blond hair and blue eyed, neatly dressed at all times, and plain spoken. She took business classes at Cornell, understood financial statements, and was attending night school at Columbia to earn her Masters in Business Administration. She was a young woman from the mid-west who came to the big city with stars in her eyes expecting to find a good husband. She had an openness and innocence about her that contrasted with the coyness and coquettishness of a city born sophisticate.

Somebody should have told Sandra the best prospects for marrying were back where she came from, but here she was at BASE, working her tail off for good money during the day and offering her tail for idle promises at nights in her search for a man to love her and help her raise babies in the suburbs. Her buxom body was feeling nature's call to procreate, but unfortunately her mother never taught her the secrets of getting men to chase her. She chased the men, took them home, fed them, and slept with them. Shortly after her catch figured out her agenda she'd wake up finding a note on her pillow telling her he left her. She had more than her fair share of morning after notes but remained undeterred. She fussed with her hair before she entered Walter's office.

"Yes, Mr. Black? You called for me."

"I did Sandra, may I call you Sandra?"

"Yes sir, of course sir." Sandra puffed out her chest.

"Thank you Sandra. What I called you about is a delicate, confidential matter. I was expecting a phone call three days ago and I didn't get the call. It came through on the 800 line and the fellow who called it in called back just a while ago and swore he talked to me. I've noticed that some people might possibly get your extension confused with mine, and I need to ask you if you were the recipient of a call three days ago."

"Oh, no sir, I didn't receive a call for you."

"Think hard, Sandra. It would have been a very short message. The caller wouldn't have even mentioned me or asked for me by name. Are you sure you didn't get a call for me?" Walter's eyes peered into Sandra's like a snake's focused on a tasty mouse.

"No sir, Mr. Black. I am certain that I received no such call."

"All right, Sandra. Thank you for indulging me. That will be all." Walter slumped back into his chair. Sandra turned and walked out, leaving Walter perplexed. Somebody certainly got the call, but whom?

After about a half hour, Walter called Sandra again. "Sandra, Walter Black here. Can you say with certainty that you were at your desk all morning three days ago?'

"No, sir, I wasn't. I was over on the trust department floor for about an hour."

"Why were you away from your desk, Sandra?"

"Well, every Tuesday I go over to Mr. Weitzman's office, the head of the trust department, and take down his questions for research to answer during our joint department meeting on Friday."

"I see, said Walter. Well, then who would pick up your phone if it rang while you were away?' Walter sensed he was honing in on the mystery call recipient.

"Well, likely that would be Mr. Santifalo, the assistant department head. I work as Mr. Meester's assistant, but he's out this week. If my phone buzzed, I doubt if anyone would have heard it except...."

"Except what, Sandra?"

"Except possibly Mr. Santifalo. He often walks out of his office to the research assistants' area to see what we're doing. If he happened to be near my desk and if it rang in on line four, that's the departmental research line that 800 line callers ring into, sir; then Mr. Santifalo probably would have picked it up since Mr. Meester and I were both away from our desks. My first three lines are for individual direct, interdepartmental, and interbank calls. No one else has that fourth line except Mr. Meester, Mr. Santifalo, and me."

"I see. Thank you, Sandra." As Walter hung up he realized he got more straight answers faster from this research assistant than he ever got from Sal, the head of operations. He needed to talk to the employees more often to learn what was going on in his bank! His search focused on whether or not Mr. Santifalo was in the vicinity of Ms. Wentz's desk when her phone rang. This was now a delicate matter and problematic to verify. He cogitated, but not for long. Ms Wentz called him.

"Oh, Mr. Black, this is Ms. Wentz, again, in research," said a cooing bubbly Sandra. "I think I can be helpful to you. I just spoke with Mr. Santifalo and he said he did pick up on that call you asked about. He said the man hung up after saying something about a plan B. Mr. Santifalo thinks the man was talking about a stock strategy or something and dialed the wrong extension, then the man abruptly hung up."

"I see. Thank you so much, Sandra. Say, tell me as a personal matter, does Mr. Santifalo often think about stocks and stock market strategies?"

"Oh, Mr. Black, that's all he ever thinks about. Speaking as a woman it would be refreshing if he could broaden his horizons just a bit, if you know what I mean?"

"I do know, Sandra. Thank you for your help with this. As for the horizons of Mr. Santifalo, I'm afraid you are on your own." Walter made a mental note to find an excuse to contact Ms. Wentz in the future. A body like hers needed to become acquainted with a man who could appreciate it. Walter assumed the assistant research director was some kind of a dunce.

"Yes sir. Good day, Mr. Black." Sandra's voice had the hint of an invitation in it.

"Yes, and a very good day to you as well, Sandra. I've noticed your enthusiasm, Sandra; and I must say, listening to you was like a breath of fresh air for me, what with all the drudgery I deal with. Perhaps you'd be willing to come to my office unofficially sometime and help better acquaint me with the goings on in the research department?"

"Oh, yes, Mr. Black. I'd certainly like that a great deal. Just tell me when."

"I will, Sandra. I'll be in touch. Good bye and have a wonderful day."

Walter hung up and immediately called Jack. "The man who got the call was our assistant research director in the investment research department, a man named Santifalo."

"Thanks for that, Walt, I'll deal with him."

CHAPTER FIVE

GIRLS' NIGHT OUT

S andra, Patricia, Linda and Connie became close friends and classmates while getting Bachelor's degrees at Cornell. They all sought careers in banking and all four landed jobs at BASE. They continued in close contact during and after their bank indoctrination classes; now, a year later, they networked about the goings on within the bank, and evaluated, sifted, swapped and culled their professional contacts. They also met for a girls' night out dinner on the last Friday of each month at an upscale restaurant to share their personal lives and relationships. Each month the women took turns hosting their ritual meeting. The hostess's duty was to reserve their table at Tee O's, remind the others of their meeting, buy the first round of cocktails, and open the conversation. Tonight, Connie hosted. The ever attentive maitre de knew these four BASE women regulars on a first name basis. As they arrived he proudly mentioned to each of them that the restaurant had recently added a Spanish guitarist to their staff.

He proclaimed as matter of fact that Tee O's was head and shoulders above any other restaurant in the city. Not only did the haute cosine eatery feature the finest Spanish gourmet cooking, it now also employed Sebastian, a handsome guitarist and vocalist. As the women were escorted to their table they passed an alcove where Sebastian was softly strumming

'Romance Anonimo.' His mastery of the guitar and his passion for music resonated through the strings of his instrument. The piece he played relaxed the women and any inhibitions they may have had about discussing the goings on at BASE. Sebastian wore a white silk shirt opened two buttons down to hint at the manly chest it wrapped. His soft warm brown eyes devoured each woman as she passed by him to her table. And as each passing woman caught scent of his sexy cologne she imagined for that instant that she was in bed with him. Their confidence in the restaurant was reconfirmed. Te O's knew how to set a table.

Connie, this night's designee to first divulge her past month's experiences, was from a very wealthy family. She grew up in a massive stone mansion in Greenwich and her parents still lived there when they were in the United States. Her father was overbearing, outspoken, deliberately rude and extraordinarily accomplished in business. He was an international tax consultant to multi-national corporations, a deal maker who took a part of the action for himself, and a ruthless negotiator. Never one to be outsmarted or bested in a deal, Mr. Rockman unfailingly ensured that all back doors were sealed tight, all objections contemplated and anticipated and all skids greased including government Commerce Department and State Department officials, foreign tax authorities, and heads of governments. He controlled three offshore slush funds to facilitate the necessary greasing of his deals. His operation was so sophisticated and organized that he had three separate contact lists. One was for ordinary business, Regular Clients; another was for persons of influence who would accept bribes, the Corruptibles; the third list was for Facilitators. These were people who could contact the right people to facilitate a murder or get a military unit to take action to cover up a messy matter. Mr. Rockman was the proverbial biggest fish in the biggest pond.

Connie's mother was a multimillionaire heiress grand-daughter of a Fortune 500 corporation founder, and Connie, herself, was a multimillionaire trust baby. Her father referred corporate clients to the BASE bank and kept the family trusts there as well. It went without saying that Connie was on the fast track to major career success at BASE. While, technically speaking, she worked for BASE, in actuality much of BASE worked for Connie. Department heads in the trust division handled her with kid gloves, and whatever she wanted, she was given on a silver platter. Employees who got in the way of what she wanted were relocated to other departments or dismissed for one nefarious reason or another. Her indiscretions, of which there were many, were overlooked.

When at a restaurant, her insistence for outstanding service was demonstrable, a trait that she learned from her mother. Inattentive waiters were treated with contemptuous behavior, such as deliberately throwing a full glass of water on the floor; never liquor, only water; but the resultant uptick in attentive-ness was predictable. Tonight, such theatrics' weren't necessary. The service was outstanding, and a tall handsome Latin waiter stood attentive within easy motion reach of the women. After cocktails and ordering it was Connie's turn to open the conversation.

"I've now been rotated to my third departmental apprentice-ship of my middle management fast track program. I've been sent to the investment research department. I hope I'll like it better than the bond department. Those guys were dull beyond dull with their calculators and their sheets of bond holdings. Who spends their life time trying to squeeze a tenth of one percent yield out of a bond trade? They are so obsessive over small gains! They squeeze their nickels until the buffalos poop. I thought I'd die in that place. I'm so glad I'm out of there. I miss my time in the stock trading department. I hated to rotate out of there. I could have stayed there forever. The action is so fast and the traders are all such fun guys. They love to party. The whole world's a big joke to them. Nothing's sacred, nothing's off limits, everything has a price. Their world is trade, drink, blow dope and fuck, fuck and fuck more; then go back the next day and do it all over again. I just loved those guys. They'd walk right up behind me when I'm trading and feel me hard, make me squeak. You can't take it personal with them. They're just animals, and I learned to love all of them. I've fucked all seven of them at their parties except Freddie. He's gay. He was always with some outside guy and acting real secretive."

"I thought you said last time you were doing Mole, the guy who wears the green eye shades? Last time you talked about bonds, you were excited about Mole. What happened there?" Linda cast a curious look at Connie. Her eyes tried to lift facts from the enchanting brown windows into the inner workings of her friend's mind. Just how did Mole stack up in the male rankings at BASE? Linda's eyes asked.

"Oh, yes. Well I needed to end that," Connie responded. She was on sensitive ground because she'd interfered with a marriage. She made a quick mental calculation to put the blame for the entire affair on Mole.

"The whole affair was his insistence from the get go. I went along with it because I felt sorry for him and, well, I needed the good review from him. He had a possessive wife, poor man. Mrs. Mole started asking him too many questions. She was a stay at home type with her little Moles. She made dinner for the Mole family every single night. Can you imagine a woman like that? So, Mole and I rarely went out to dinner. When we did he hardly ate a thing because he had to rush home to Mrs. Mole and pretend he was working late. That whole routine left me feeling hurt and empty. I still don't understand how he could choose to go home to his plane Jane wife instead of spending the evening making love with me. I went along with his behavior, though. I reminded myself that there was a good grade at the end of my internship.

"Our working late routine only worked a few times before his wife got suspicious. After all, why does a bond trader need to work late? So, Mole started sneaking me off to the Sheraton during the day. He'd get us a room then he'd quickie fuck me for a half hour. I never even got any foreplay. He barely even took the time to kiss me. I couldn't even get myself lubricated before he started shoving his cock into me. It was just a bam, bam, and thank you Ma'am thing he did to me. It got to where I didn't even like it. He always needed to get back in such a hurry in case one of his brokerage contacts called with a bid to take some bond the bank was trying to unload. It was very frustrating. He never gave me enough time to have an enjoyable fuck.

"But he did have a terrific cock once we got things going. I'll give him that." Connie finally tossed a tidbit to Linda's prurient interests. "He must have super testosterone. He was always so determined to fuck me. I guess that's what kept me interested. He kept it hard the whole time, but all that rushing around made me feel cheap. Still, I tried to go the extra mile with him.

"He knew I'd do anything to get a great performance review from him. I need those good departmental reviews to get into Columbia's MBA program. Daddy made that abundantly clear. My undergraduate grades were so shitty from all the fucking around I did. That's why I've ended up at this shitty bank in the first place. Daddy was really pissed at me over my grades. They were so bad I couldn't jump right into my MBA from undergraduate school. He forced me into the bank for experience and resume building. Dad has a lot of say over the bank's board because of all the business he pumps into this dump. Dad can be a real son of a bitch if he doesn't get his way.

"Well, anyway, going the extra mile with Mole meant going into the bond department conference room. That was his idea. You know that tiny one that no one ever uses? It's between Research and Privately Held's, the offices where they manage private family assets. It's that creepy hole in the wall that adjoins the private assets file room."

The other women nodded their heads in the affirmative, attentive and sympathetic for their poor rich friend to continue.

"Well, we'd go in there, lock the door, and fuck on that small conference room table. He'd even eat me in there. We tried to be discreet, of course, but it's hard for me to enjoy having my pussy licked and not make any noise, especially when my orgasms come. I'm sure we were heard by some of the looks I got from the secretaries in the research department.

"I just had to put a stop to the whole affair. It was too unnerving and there was always that cold hard table. Yuck! It gave me the chills every time I took my panties off and had to lay my bare ass on that freezing cold wood. I mean, really! What else could I do? I couldn't walk around the trading floor carrying a blanket with me. What would all the traders think of me? 'Have blanket, will fuck?'

"Anyway, Mole gave me all 'A' grades, and as soon as he gave me my "A" review I stopped seeing him. It was just business for both of us. For a while I actually hoped it could be more, but with Mrs. Mole in the picture it just wasn't worth it. I earned that "A" though. Mole used to fuck me sore."

"Have you stopped seeing George, too?" Patty recalled Connie's infatuation with the bank's small capitalization stocks trader. The last time they'd had dinner Connie declared she was totally smitten by him.

"Oh, no, I'm still seeing him. In fact we're having diner tomorrow evening. He likes to go to those rowdy places where the construction workers hang out and watch sports on TV while he drinks beer. He's nothing like Daddy with his dinner jacket and martini routine. George is my dream man. He's all man, all the time."

"So, you two are still fucking?"

"Yes, of course we are. George takes my breath away. When he gives me that certain look and that slow open-mouthed smile of his my spine starts to tingle in the back of my neck. Then the tingle just sort of slinks its way down to my pussy and I feel myself getting wet for him. I look into his eyes and I just want to open all the way for him and take him inside me and hold him there and fuck him until we both get so sticky we're glued together like a couple of sex crazed dogs. Yes I'm still fucking George. Sometimes I don't think I could ever stop fucking George."

"Is this getting serious?"

"Well, I don't know. I wouldn't say that. Not yet. Maybe in the future, but I don't push anything with George. Besides, I don't think I'm ready to get serious. I still have graduate school to think about, and I'm sure I'll meet some men there. I don't yet know what I want in a man, so I'm just taking things as they come. I'm not sure I'd want to settle down with George. He's just a carefree fun loving guy."

"With a great tongue and a hard cock, right," Linda sounded a bit cynical and a tad jealous.

"Yes, of course those male capabilities are my minimal requirements, but I'm much more attracted to intellectual types. I guess I secretly want a man who is more like Daddy. George will always be a trader unless he fucks up something huge and gets himself fired.

"George offers an okay life style, but as I get older I don't want to be going to football and basketball and hockey games with all those people screaming their heads off at players getting knocked around, neon messages flashing on stadium screens and getting shit faced plastered drunk with orgies afterwards. It's just a non stop headache.

"I want opera, symphony, gallery openings and travel. I want to be invited to the crème de la crème society parties and meet the candidates and the new authors. I don't want to have a fat husband drunk on a sofa, belching and farting after drinking a six pack watching some stupid football game. I don't want to have to remind him to cut the grass. I want a lawn service to cut the grass for me. I don't want to go up to Daddy's lake house with him and sit out on a boat the whole time casting for some stupid fish. I want to read novels on the shade porch listening to soft music while sipping a gin and tonic."

Linda and the others nodded their heads. They were feeling sympathy of sorts for the emotional and social needs of their friend with sex addled thinking. They looked at her with that certain understanding that women have for each other's predicaments in a male dominated world. Their empathy encouraged Connie to continue.

"George is okay, and he is by far a much more considerate fuck than Mole. George really works on his fucking. He gets into it like it's the main thing he lives for. He knows how to love a woman; but I can only deal with his Casanova sex appetite in small doses. I have to be in one of those 'I don't give a shit' moods. Then George can just take control of my body, fuck me, run his hands and tongue all over me and play with me all night long."

"Didn't you learn anything from Mole, other than how cold the private asset department's conference room table was against your bare ass?" Linda had heard enough. She was the most business oriented of the foursome. After all, these meetings were ostensibly business related.

"Well, a little, if you could call it learning. Mole showed me how to work the bond computer. You put in things you know, like price, maturity, coupon rate, payment frequency; and it gives you yield to maturity. You can also use it to see total return to a certain point in time in the future, internal rates of return on money streams into and out of the bond. It's all just a lot of data crunching, very boring stuff."

"What did Mole think about the future, especially interest rates?" Linda was on a business track. She was in corporate lending and just wanted a sense of whether Mole agreed with the bank's economists.

"Mole's really smart there. He has to be. His job depends on him being right. He's very short term oriented, extra sharp, nothing like the bank's economists."

"So?"

"Well, just three weeks ago, before he gave me my grades, he told me the entire banking system was on thin ice and ready to blow up any minute. He constantly checks derivative spreads and keeps a special computer program he wrote himself that shows the way the yield curve dances along with what the derivative spreads are doing along the curve for the different bond qualities. He doesn't share it with the bank's economists. He's extremely secretive."

"Yeah, I've heard that about him," said Linda. "Why does he think the system is on thin ice?"

"Well, he looks at those derivative spreads and the maturities on the Fed's balance sheet; and he says he can tell the Fed is under tremendous pressure to maintain demand for collateral paper to back up all the derivative writes. He says even the Fed isn't deep enough to swallow all the crap that's getting issued; and Europe and the underdeveloped nations' liquidity are even worse."

"So, the economists are too complacent?"

"Well, Mole thinks the market is choked on doggy debt and the only thing holding it together is the derivatives. That's why he keeps checking spreads. He keeps spreads in his head. He knows the deltas, thetas, gammas, omegas, alphas, and all the cross duration spreads between spreads. I honestly can't explain all of it to you. I think Mole likes it that way. He's the only one who knows this complicated shit. He says the markets are paper thin on size at the spreads. Dealers will honor their bids for five thousand bonds face amount, but the next fifty thousand face amount is down ten dollars a bond or more.

"Mole says he can't even off load more than a million face amount in any issue less than triple A in this market. Even U S treasuries are thin bids in the out years. So, yes, the economists are complacent. If I were giving you advice, ala Mole's view, Linda, I would get super liquid and build up my capital cushions.

"The next downturn will blow out lots of issuers and defaults will mushroom. The high yield hogs will run for their lives and there won't be any market for all kinds of stuff. People will be losing their pensions and they will be pissed. Mole says the bond and income markets have been like eight lane freeways going in but they'll be goat trails trying to get out."

Linda said, "Mole's probably right. Economists don't trade bonds. All they have to do is forecast and jerk everybody off. Their models don't have Mole's insights. He relates the derivative spreads to the strength of bids on the curve over the qualities. So, maybe he's hen pecked. Maybe he'll never be a considerate lover. But he knows bonds and interest rates." Connie's raised eyebrows and head nod affirmed her agreement with Linda's comments.

After hearing Mole's advice filtered by Connie, Linda believed she learned all she needed for the work she was doing as a loan officer. Her thoughts drifted away from the conversation. She tuned out Connie's pitiful rationalizations for fucking every man she worked with. Her attention settled on the guitarist. His play and her wine were settling her into a light minded romantic mood. She followed his touches on the strings. She noted that he'd moved his fingers closer toward the bridge of his instrument.

Now his slowly plucked tango notes lulled her mind away to a far off place. She slipped into a dreamlike trance. As her head gently swooned, she imagined herself lying naked next to the guitarist. As he plucked each note she felt his fingers touching her side, seductively making their way from her face and lips down the length of her torso onto her leg. She felt his touch through his music. She breathed deeply, wistfully imagining her hand slowly caressing his massive chest. 'The foreplay with this man will be so delightful. I bet he's a real animal in bed. Yes, I want him. I must know if his loving is as wonderful as his music.' She was anxious for the meeting to end.

"Have you sized up the male menu in the research department?" It was Patty again. Her question was aimed at Connie.

"It's a little early. A woman can't rush into these things. All I know, so far, is I'm paired with this guy named Paul. He's supposed to be very smart. He was tops in his class at Wharton. His MBA was in finance. He's very recently been divorced. I know he has a kid but his wife doesn't let him see her. It breaks his heart, or so I'm told by one of the secretaries on the floor pool. I don't know what happened there."

"Is he interested in you?" Patty's curiosity was up.

"I don't think so. He only spends one hour a day with me. I've just had two sessions with him. He isn't much of a teacher. He just shows me what he's doing. He's looking at some mining companies, showing me the balance sheets he's studying, showing me how many tax loss carry forwards they have, how much the mines should make, how much they should cash flow. He talks about which companies should acquire which others. He sees pro forma balance sheets in his head. He's totally smart. He follows politics in foreign countries to avoid investing in companies where governments are getting too greedy. He talks so fast and expects me to follow along, but I can't do that yet. He has a very quick mind and all, but he doesn't take time to explain anything. I'm afraid if he quizzes me, I'll fail."

"It sounds like he's a lot like your dad. Is he good looking?" Patty's lips hinted a smile when she spoke.

"Well, yeah, come to think of it, he does remind me of Dad. He's all business, fast mind and all."

"Well, he couldn't always be all business." Patty liked confrontations, even small ones.

"What do you mean?"

"You said he has a kid, a daughter. He had to love a woman somewhere along the line."

"Oh, right."

"How old is the daughter? How often does he try to see her?"

"Patty, stop. Enough! I just met him. I don't even know him. I don't even know if I'm interested. I don't know if he's interested."

"You're interested all right." It was Patty again.

"Why do you say that?"

"You dodged my only important question: Is he good looking?"

"Yeah, okay, yes, definitely. He's magazine cover gorgeous." Connie blushed.

"I bet by the end of summer you'll be fucking his brains out." Patty just wouldn't let up.

Connie didn't respond directly to Patty's tawdry quip. Instead she lifted her arms into the air, smiled, and pretended she was a conductor conducting an orchestra. Then she sang out a tune for her friends: "Que Sera Sera! Whatever will be, will be; the future's not ours to see, Que Sera Sera." She already imagined Paul's penis in her hands. After licking his balls and the tip of his cock, she was about to guide it into her welcoming pussy.

The waiter and Sebastian looked on, smiling. The singing woman gladdened their eyes. She was a lovely winsome bodied brunette with a perfect oval face, deliciously inviting lips, mischievous dancing brown eyes and seductively charming. Both men were experienced in the ways of women. The two men instinctively recognized a femme whose flower bloomed with a bursting lust for life.

Sebastian caught Linda's eyes looking at his. He detected a pinch of hurt. Linda saw that his eyes lit up as they feasted on the possibilities of making Connie's acquaintance. His heart went out to Linda. She was equally beautiful and more poised. He admired her subtlety. He instinctively recovered from his unspoken slight to her. He inhaled deeply, his eyes framed Linda's face and lingered there, and then ever so slowly and expertly his dreamy warm pools silently undressed her and vicariously kissed her breasts, her stomach and her sex.

Linda was a stunning woman. She had a lovely Anglophile oval face with beautiful blue eyes and full inviting lips. Her posture and figure was one of the finest he'd ever sampled. When his eyes met hers their imaginations followed nature's course. Both became aroused. No one else noticed this flare of first flame. Linda knew Sebastian had singled her out from the others. Her mind drifted away from the conversation. She contemplated introducing herself to Sebastian and wondered how many other women made the same calculation.

"Speaking of research, Sandra, what's going on in your world? You skipped right through the intern gig and settled full time into the BASE research department. So what is Mr. Santifalo up to these days?" Patty had heard enough of Connie's sexual exploits and wanted to move the conversation along.

"Oh, it's mostly just the same ole, same ole for me. I type reports, look at financial summaries and then cross check the analysts' calculations on cash flows. They usually get the financial stuff right but most of them can't spell. I haven't had much to tell Mr. Black lately."

"Mr. Black? Did you say Mr. Black? What's going on between you and him?" Patty's eyebrows shot up. Suddenly six eyeballs riveted on Sandra. It was unheard of for one of the BASE thirty thousand underlings to have direct communications with the bank's chief executive officer.

Sandra blushed. Walter wanted their liaison kept in complete secrecy, but she craved the limelight of their monthly foursome. Listening to Connie boast of her sexual conquests had become tedious. By mentioning Mr. Black's name she appeared to have inadvertently let the proverbial cat out of the bag. After a faux blushing awkward moment she was ready to let them have it.

"Oh, yes. Well, it's our little secret you see. So, I need your pledges of confidences for what I'm about to tell you." After a round of promises from her cohorts and a suitable interlude of silence Sandra divulged her confidence. "Walter and I have been sort of getting it on. It started innocently enough. There was this weird phone call that came to the bank. It was supposed to come to Walter but somehow it ended up in the research department. Walter thought I got the call that was intended for him and that brought us into contact with each other. We got to talking and we discovered that we shared a lot of the same values and thoughts and one thing led to another and before I knew what was happening I was falling for him. We became intimate just a few weeks ago. He's very sweet. He takes me to the nicest places for our secret rendezvous'".

"So, what sort of places? Does he take you out of the city?" Patty, eternal skeptic that she was, needed details.

"Well, no. We stay in the city."

"Wait a minute, Sandra. I can't imagine he'd risk being seen in a public place with a woman other than his wife. It must be some hideaway he has, no?" It was Patty again.

"Well, not exactly. If you must know he takes me to some very nice hotels." Sandra's voice betrayed her nervousness. Patty was about to pierce her illusion.

"Oh, I get it. He sneaks you into some hotel and screws you in a nice hotel room, right? I bet he orders room service. Has he ever taken you to a restaurant, even a hotel restaurant?"

"Well, not yet, but he keeps telling me that pretty soon he and I will get away somewhere." Sandra was regaining the offensive. Her assertiveness and confidence pushed back against Patty's skepticism.

"Who made the misdirected phone call?" Patty super sleuth struck again.

"Oh, well I don't know who made the call. Mr. Santifalo is the one who took it."

"Huh, Santifalo gets a call and you end up sleeping with Walter? It makes no sense."

"No, I didn't make sense of it. It was something about plan B. Who knows and who cares? It brought Walter into my life and now I've finally got a man who is steady and dependable. I know he won't leave me. He's right here in the bank and I can see him almost whenever I need him."

"Okay, I get it. You really think you have a future with him? Are you sure he's not just leading you on? His wife is Mrs. Society in this town. She's richer than God, too. Do you honestly think he'll ditch her for a farm girl from nowhere in Nebraska?" Patty could be blunt and a bit vicious, but her words had the ring of honest questioning. Connie and Linda joined Patty's skeptical look. Sandra felt uncomfortable and squirmed in her seat.

"You're making me feel like I'm some kind of fool." Sandra blurted out her hurt feelings to Patty.

"Hey, this is what friends are for, Sandra. I'm just saying you need to think this through before you get your emotions deeply invested in Walter Black. The word around the people I work with is that he's a no good low level snake that would sell his mother up the river in a hot New York minute." Patty put her hand on Sandra's. "We just want to make sure that you consider the possibility that he's using you for something or other, that's all."

"You mean for sex, and that's all?"

"Well, maybe. But maybe there's even more to this than meets the eye. A guy like Walter, wimpy looking though he is, can get sex pretty much anywhere he wants it. But here you are enjoying something with some permanence about it. Good for you. I'm just trying to tell you to be careful and watch out for the old curve ball. I just don't want to see you get hurt."

After that exchange the ladies made their farewells. Hugs were passed around between them assuring this corporate sisterhood would endure until next month. As they departed Linda approached the guitarist and whispered some enticing words into his ear. She learned his name was Sebastian and complemented him profusely on his vocalizations and guitar music. As she discretely took his card and slipped it into her purse she secretly wished the card carried his scent.

CHAPTER SIX

GIBBY'S MAP

The morning broke cold and dew frosted with no clouds. The first light of early dawn touched the snow capped peaks above and their glistening reflections blinded out the blue sky they poked into. Gibby lived alone up here, high in the San Juan's of Colorado, two thousand feet above Imogene Pass and its thousand foot cliff drop. He didn't need a clock here and there was no need for electricity or the creature comforts of the mountain town, Ouray, lying like a speck below. No comforts, not for him, not anymore. He was done with it, a lifetime done. A mountain ground squirrel chattered out its barks and woke him. It was likely spooked by a Red Tail Hawk. They launched below on the land breezes that raced up these high slopes before the sunrise. The hawk caught an early mountain thermal and was already above twelve thousand feet. Likely it was a female with mouths to feed. He heard the rustlings of a marmot shortly after the squirrel's bark. There were several families of them living here above timberline. Every now and then he killed one and ate on it for several days. The marmot supply was inexhaustible.

He forced himself out of his sleeping bag and sat on the edge of his cot. The entrance to his tunnel was visible now. He liked this arrangement. If anyone came to the tunnel mouth Gibby would see him silhouetted against the sky but the intruder wouldn't be able to dilate his pupils and see Gibby until he came twenty feet into the tunnel. He needed to get ready. They'd be coming up.

He was born in a cabin in nearby Silverton. He'd roamed these peaks as a child and knew the mountain tops like the back of his hand. He'd gone into many of the old mines up here and explored their workings. He chose to live at the Dead Mule Mine. It was close to an overlook that commanded the approach trail to the surrounding peaks.

Walter believed Gibby had the old prospector's map along with his gem stash. Walter didn't care about the gems; but for his purposes the claim map was priceless.

The irony was that Gibby didn't realize the map had any value at all. Tt was just a perplexing oddity he'd acquired. He traded a Tillamook squaw for it when she showed it to him. She told Gibby she got it in Alaska from a Tligit woman, who got it from the squaw of a dead prospector. The prospector mapped the location of his discovery but the map was made by hand and the old prospector, now dead, didn't put any coordinates on the map; so it could be a map of a two hundred fifty mile square area located pretty much anywhere in British Columbia, the Yukon, or far Eastern Alaska.

The old prospector went away for months at a time roaming everywhere studying rocks, outcrops and old mine workings. He dug trenches by hand across gossans and vegetation scrub stunted by acidic near surface bed rock. He noted anticlines and Alpenglow that shined more brightly than others with his hopes of finding gold. He panned and lived off the land while he was gone. The searching was more interesting than the finding to this man who'd made hand drawn maps to help him find his return to the same places he'd been.

The Tillamook told Gibby the Tlingit heard from the prospector's squaw that the last entry in her husband's journal was about a camp he made about sixty miles due north of Atlin

Lake, British Columbia. He kept the rocks in a backpack under the bed in their cabin along with the map to their location. And he guarded these particular rocks with his life. He told his squaw that these rocks were much more valuable than the color. Color was what he called rocks that held gold ore. He kept a journal of his days in the field and his finds. Three journal entries before his last he'd made a notation about strange rocks. He noted that they made a colorful residue on his hands. His entries were made daily, but every three weeks he summarized his thoughts and findings. It took a strong man a full day to walk four miles through the thick brush and downfall in those parts. It was also grizzly bear territory, so people moving in those forests moved slowly and cautiously. By deduction, the location of his discovery was likely somewhere within a sixty mile radius of his last campsite sixty miles north of Atlin Lake, because he never mentioned the rocks in any of his entries while he was at Atlin Lake. According to the Tillamook the map showed the location of very unusual rocks no Indian had ever seen before. Their ancestors never mentioned them. They broke apart easily when struck together or hit by harder objects; and the most curious thing about them was the slight film like residue of rock dust that stubbornly clung to your hands after handling them. The residue wouldn't wash off. It had to be scrubbed off with hot water and grit mud. And the residue gave off sparkling colors.

The prospector took one of his rocks to the British Columbia Geological Survey office where it was tested. It showed dazzling colors when touched by a drop of hydrochloric acid. They changed from greens to blues to reds, alternating these colors were hues of purple and orange. Then, they returned to dull gray black as if they'd always been that way. The prospector never told anyone where he found his magical rocks. The rocks stayed there where he found them except for the samples under his cabin bed. Then, one night, the old man died.

He died while sleeping on his cot over his unusual rocks. The old man's squaw who first sold the map remembered him telling her he thought the rocks might have some value to somebody but he had no idea what use they might be to anybody. He died never knowing what they might be worth. His squaw said a young man from the government came by a year before her husband died. He asked how they liked living in the forest. He said he was studying forest people, but he got around to asking about the rocks and where the prospector found them. The prospector wouldn't say. When the young man left the cabin the old man and his squaw both agreed that the young man knew more about their rocks than he wanted to tell them.

The squaw became needy in her later years. She traded her husband's maps for food. She traded her last map, the one that contained the location of the special rocks, to a Tlingit woman for twenty pounds of smoked salmon. When the young man from the government returned one day to ask her about buying the map he got upset and agitated when she told him she'd traded it. Now Gibby had come into possession of the map. He owned the map for its trading price of four boxes of .30 06 180 grain shells.

The Tlingit told Gibby that an old prospector thought there could be a mine made out of the place where the rocks came from. He never put much stock in her stories but he traded with her often and to keep good will with her he made the trade. Besides, he'd traded his 30.06 rifle and a jewel for his Weatherby .308 Magnum rifle some time ago and he didn't need 30.06 ammo anymore. He liked the .308 better. It had more velocity, more punch and less drop at 500 yards. It was a great rifle with no barrel wear and accurate enough to shoot the eye out of a hawk. Most men couldn't handle a powerful rifle like that his .308 because of its recoil kick, but Gibby handled its shoulder punch easily. He was accustomed to recoil from his days as a Marine Corps sniper. He never flinched and he never jerked a shot.

He was part of an isolated mountain culture that had sworn off all banks and dollar transactions many years earlier. He always paid cash or traded and he liked to keep his dealings untraceable. Not knowing the value of his map, he assumed the men in the jeep were likely coming to kill him for his jewels. He had no idea that some banker named Walter sent these men to get his map.

But Walter knew that Gibby's map showed the location of the rocks. He understood that this map was more valuable than any gold mine or all the jewels in Gibby's leather pouch, or all the jewels in Colorado for that matter. The map was the key to unimaginable power and riches and Walter was willing to murder for it.

CHAPTER SEVEN

IMOGENE OFF RAMP

"I don't see any sign of life up there" said the driver to his rider. The rider didn't reply to the driver. Instead he opened his sky phone and made a call to his contact in Alamosa.

"We're in position. We're going up." The call was made to a hotel lobby desk phone, to a contact these men didn't know. The contact was to relay the report to Walter through the bank's toll free number. Nothing was to be directly traceable to Walter.

Gibby had spotted their Jeep the day before. He caught the glint of movement as the sun reflected off one of its windows. He presumed it was the usual tourists. He thought the Jeep would stop at the snow bank and turn back, but it didn't. Gibby watched through his binoculars as two men got out of the Jeep and shoveled through twenty yards of snow four feet deep. Tourists didn't work that hard. They always turned back at the snow field, so these two men weren't tourists. One of them had a rifle. Most likely they were claim jumpers or thieves. He figured someone told them he was up here with his gold and his jewels and he reckoned they were coming for him. It was late afternoon when they finished digging through the snow drift. They seemed tired and moved slowly. Altitude did that to flat-landers. But they didn't turn back. They went behind their Jeep and disappeared. Gibby didn't see them reappear. He figured they stayed on the mountain because no movement came out of the downhill side of the Jeep. He figured they must be pretty determined to stay on the mountain at eleven thousand feet. The altitude was hard on unseasoned people. Likely they bedded next to the Jeep in sleeping bags and they'd come for him at daybreak. It would take them a good hour of tough jeeping to reach the hairpin. By the time they reached it he'd be ready for them. He was well rested this morning.

As he settled into his spot on the outcrop he heard the faint whirring of their four wheel's low gears. Shortly after hearing them he acquired them in his binoculars. The one with the rifle got out and walked behind the jeep as it traversed Imogene Pass. The driver of the C J 5 hugged the mountain side of the crossing. He drove like he'd crossed the treacherous pass before. Likely he was hired from one of the local guide shops, probably doing this on his own time as some kind of a side deal. No matter, Gibby wasn't going to take any chances. The guy on foot walked cautiously and deliberated every step. He never looked over the drop, not even from a smidgeon of curiosity. He was all business. He looked up a lot scanning the terrain like he had some experience with this sort of thing. He'd have to be taken first.

Walter was sure Gibby was his man. He'd sent a private eye to Ouray and Telluride earlier that summer. The report came back that there was such a man in these parts who fit the description Walter gave him. He was looking for a tall, stringy, rugged appearing fellow with blue eyes. He'd likely be wearing soft tan camouflage that blended with the browns and black shadows of the high mountain tops. He was square jawed, with a quiet fierceness about him. He spoke with clipped speech and economized his words. The report on him said he came to town infrequently for his supplies, packed them in pantaloon bags and duffels, took two horses from a local stable, loaded them, and walked them up high. He walked in front of the horses, leading them with a lead rope. He never rode them.

The information said he lived somewhere near an old mine in a camper shell removed from a truck mounted rig. The place was nigh inaccessible to all but mountaineers, rock hounds or the most intrepid hikers. In the early nineteenth century someone named the place the Dead Mule Mine. It was a good mile on horseback or foot past the end of the High Alpine Ridge Trail, which, according to the locals, was so washed out that it wasn't even a trail anymore. It was more like a treacherous shale or mud slide for any vehicle that tried to traverse it. Some tried anyway, oblivious to the danger. Their vehicles slid for a good hundred yards downhill before they flipped and rolled another half mile down, hit the boulder field and broke apart. There were five shattered vehicles on the boulder field and probably some remnant human bones as well. Locals didn't think anybody had driven the trail in the last ten years or more. The U. S. Geological Service gratuitously posted a sign at the start of the old Alpine Trail that told vehicles to turn around and that it was too dangerous to proceed. But Gibby was up there alone with his truck mounted camper shell, without a truck, horse or mule.

The man they hunted had walked these ten miles uphill then unpacked the horses and sent them back on their own. Tough as nails, he was used to the rigors of his chosen lifestyle according to people who had dealings with him. He was quiet, chewed jerky, traded for things, and used jewels of high quality for trade. He carried diamonds, rubies, sapphires, jade, topaz, and emeralds in a leather pouch slung over his chest. He also wore a .357 magnum long barrel revolver in a hip holster. No one tried to steal from him. Most of his jewels weren't from around here. No one knew how many he had and he never said. When asked where he got a stone, he just stared at the inquirer. Someone said he once told them a single word when asked that question. "Traded." he said. Other than that, the man called Gibby was a mystery.

Many assumed he was hiding from the law. These parts were good for hiding and some did that. Some men talked about going up to his camp to talk to him but then thought better of it. About two months ago he went to the local gun shop and ordered .308 magnum armor piercing. That was off the charts rare. Hunters used soft tipped rounds for big game. It cost him five dollars a round. He said he'd be back in a month for his package, and he did come back exactly thirty days later. He gave the dealer a small diamond for it plus five boxes of .22 caliber long rifle ammo, acceptable for marmots and rabbits. The owner of the gun store figured he kept two rifles for sure, maybe more.

Walter, being resourceful as he was, got the mine maps for the Dead Mule Mine from a local lawyer and real estate broker. The old maps were hand drawn, not to scale; and they showed that there was a main adit that the old timers drove about five hundred feet following a galena vein. About four hundred feet in they crossed a pocket lens of high grade four ounce per ton sulfide gold ore that shot out of a fault through a porphyry which somehow bulged into some hard to cyanide leach telluride ore. The old miners didn't understand the geology. How could they? Even modern geologists get confused about the different intrusions, formations and faults that make up San Juans, but that doesn't stop them from writing books about the area's mines and geology.

The old timers just followed the rocks, the ores or the color as they called it, and their hunches. They tunneled down dip in a sub horizontal layer of gold bearing copper porphyry until they got about twelve hundred feet below the entrance to the adit; but they made at least a dozen drifts off their tunnels looking to find the mother lode of high grade gold. They were constantly teased by Mother Nature's sheer faults and auriferous pyroclastic fluid channel markers that petered out and went nowhere. The rock was brecciate and faulted and generally not competent ground to work in. In the early nineteenth century mules carrying ore filled pantaloons were whipped unmercifully up and down the mines' steep inclines. The footing was treacherous and many a mule fell to its death in the workings. Additional mules died from being worked to death in the effort to bring out the gold, hence the mine's name. Miners also died in rock bursts and cave-ins, and the Dead Mule Mine was eventually abandoned.

"I don't see any signs of life up there," said the driver to his rider.

The rider ignored the driver. Instead the rider opened his sky phone and made a short call to his contact in Alamosa. "We're in position about a mile out. We're going up now." The contact relayed the call using the hotel lobby's desk phone to dial the BASE 800 line. Once the call reached the voice mail system he dialed Walter's number. Not traceable was how Walter said he wanted it done. Not traceable was good.

"What do ya know about this guy?" asked the driver to his rider. The driver's voice held a trace of trepidation. He was second thinking the deal he made.

"Don't care to talk about him." said the rider with the rifle.

"Come on, man. We're going up to some fuckin mountaintop to get a map from some asshole guy. What makes ya think he's even up there? What makes ya think he's gonna give ya that map? What makes ya think he won't jump us? Why are ya willing to pay me $2,000 for this? That's four times my normal rate."

"I said I don't want to talk about this!"

"Well, listen mister, I got a right to know. If this means I could get hurt, I got the right to know. And if ya ain't gonna tell me, I ain't going to go no further."

"You'll do nothing of the sort. We made a deal."

"Yeah, but circumstances is changed, fella. Ya took your rifle out of its case back aways. Ya said ya was going to take it along to maybe poach an elk up here, but we ain't seen no elk. There ain't no fuckin elk gonna be this high above timberline, but you got that rifle at the ready. Ya's not telling me what this is all about. That jist ain't fair."

"Okay, so if I tell you there could be trouble, what difference will it make to you?'

"Well, I hear he's got jewels and gold he trades for things with. If I go on, I want the jewels since you just want the map, okay? You gotta say okay or I'm turning back and you ain't gonna find nobody else to jeep jump these rocks like we's got up here like I can jump them. So you gotta say we's got a deal, okay?"

"Okay, deal."

"Well, tell me about him, then, so I knows what I's up against."

"Okay. Look. The guy's a recluse. He's old, in his late fifties maybe early sixties. He's a little skittish, afraid of being around people. He'll probably run away and leave the map and the jewels. Are you better now?"

"Yeah, better. Thanks. Remember, we's got a deal!" the driver shouted emphatically.

"Yeah," the rider just nodded his head in the positive.

Gibby had paced off the distance to the hairpin below him two years before and wrote it down. It was a three hundred yard horizontal distance and a one hundred yard drop from his post on the outcrop. Now Gibby rested the .308 on his soft target bags, checked the wind marker next to him and the one he planted on the trail by the hairpin years ago. It was a simple rebar rod taken from the mine workings. He drove it into the ground then tied a long piece of twine near the top of it using a simple clove hitch. The twine lifted this morning, indicating a steady ten mile per hour morning breeze moving air and bullets from left to right. He'd aim one deflection click left of his center crosshairs to compensate.

As the two men in the Jeep approached the hairpin the driver saw the wind marker first. "I wonder who put that there?" he asked rhetorically. "Trail cut outs is marked by rock cairns in these mountains, but somebody marked one here with a steel rod and I don't see no trail."

The shooter hadn't yet seen the stake and twine. He'd tuned out the babblings of this fool and his gibberish a mile back. Now he lifted his cowboy hat's brim to see what the driver was talking about. He never saw the twine fluttering from the stake. The last thing his eyes saw was a muzzle flash from Gibby's .308.

When the shot rang out the driver froze in place and let his foot off the gas of the jeep. That stalled the vehicle. He looked to his right, to his shooter, for instructions. It was useless. The man's neck was severed through near the base of his skull. He died instantly. The driver panicked. He put in the clutch instinctively and started drifting backwards, the thought being that he would pop the clutch and restart the jeep and get out of there. It was too late. The next bullet from the .308 came through the windshield, entered the driver's right occipital lobe and exited the back left side of his skull. The left foot of the driver slipped off the clutch. The jeep jumped from the reengaged clutch and stopped in place with the two dead men inside it.

Down below, in Ouray and Telluride, people heard the cracks and dull thud echoing's of the two rifle shots' resounding from the mountaintops, but they could never know where the echoes came from or who was shooting at what. Poaching of big game takes place in Colorado's mountains. The Department of Wildlife tries to stamp it out, with fair success; but it still goes on, even in modern times. People need to eat and elk are the best eating meat. Bears, mountain lions, wolves and coyotes will all attest to that. The locals aren't alarmed or mystified when they hear rifle shots. They just stop and reflect that a beautiful animal was taken; many hope it will be put to good use, not just used for a wall mount, and then people just go about minding their own business.

Gibby watched the jeep with the two dead men in it for a half hour. He wanted to be sure they'd journeyed alone and that they were both dead. He took his time walking down to the jeep. He never acted hastily when he approached a kill. He was careful to not disturb the ground he walked over. He left no scuff marks and didn't slide down over the graveled slope leaving a disturbance. He was nice and easy about killing. When he got down to the jeep he poked each man with his .308 barrel tip. They were dead all right. Not much blood either. 'It's good to have armor piercing when wet work is required,' he thought.

"Good job, sweetheart," Gibby spoke softly to his rifle. The sound of his own voice was the only human voice he heard up here for weeks at a time. He complimented himself on his shooting. He hadn't missed a beat from the old days. He took the men's identifications from their wallets. The one with the rifle was not from Colorado. His driver's license showed he was from Long Island, New York. This was odd, indeed. What was a New Yorker doing up here with a rifle out of elk, moose, or deer season? And why did they come up here, above timberline? They'd worked their jeep around his boulders that blocked the former trail. They'd ignored the USGS (US Geological Survey) closed trail sign, a third closed trail sign from Bureau of Land Management, his own private property signs and his warning signs that trespassers would be shot. They had a rifle uncased at the ready. They were definitely coming for him. There were no big game animals up this high and bighorn sheep didn't graze these slopes; and nobody was crazy enough to use a 7 millimeter magnum rifle with 175 grain soft tipped ammo to hunt rabbits or marmots. Obviously these two men were coming to kill him; but, why?

There was a backpack in the back well of the C. J Jeep. Gibby lifted it out and sat on the ground with it. Going through it item by item he pieced together what this ill fated expedition was about. There was the usual stuff: some sandwiches, chocolate bars, trail mix, apples, extra underwear and socks, a thermos filled with coffee, three bottles of water, toilet paper and an envelope. Gibby opened the envelope expecting to find plane tickets or possibly money; but instead he found a page from a notebook with a description of himself and another page with a description of the old prospector's map. Likely the map would be found in a tight metal cylinder about one inch in diameter. Gibby's head went back. These guys were looking for the map he got from the Tillamook woman! It had to be valuable to somebody, but to whom, and, why?

His own description amused Gibby. His description said he was six foot seven. 'I've grown three inches' he thought. He was sharpshooter and parachute jump qualified. That checked out. He was blue eyed, black haired now, sharp angular featured. That checked out too. He spoke rarely and spit frequently. Very good! 'Somebody did their homework on me,' he mused. He did not smoke and had no woman. That was another fact that sort of checked. He was wily and clever. 'Thanks for that guys.' And he didn't think twice or hesitate to kill. 'Well, bravo on that one kids,' he thought.

"I'm surprised they didn't say I breathed fire from my nose," Gibby commented again to his rifle.

What the page omitted was how Gibby, or Gibson Theodore Ward as he was named at birth, got to be the way he was.

Gibby was one of those Vietnam veterans who volunteered to leave a Pocono Mountain town at the age of seventeen pretending to be eighteen, to go over to the jungles of Southeast Asia to make the world safe for democracy. Somebody in the Marine Corps figured Gibby, who'd been shooting squirrels since he was ten, to be a good shot so he was sent through sniper school, where he excelled. He was assigned to 3/13, a Marine Corps artillery battalion that supported two Marine infantry battalions, 1/13 and 2/13 of the fifth Marine Division. He made two deployments to Nam and he killed thirty seven enemy combatants. Killing affects different men differently. Some are in perpetual shock from it. They lapse into a thousand yard stare for years; even decades after the killing experience and wear the experience in their souls as a sort of eternal shock to their consciousness. Other men cringe at the sound or sight of perceived threat. They jump when a firecracker goes off or a car backfires. They take that latent inner fear with them into their graves. Still others get used to killing and they relish the thought of doing more of it. They seek it out for the adrenalin rush and satisfaction they get from stopping another human heart.

Gibby was different from all of the stereotypes. He went beyond being used to killing people. He became numb to it. Killing other humans was just a normal part of life for Gibby, like shining a pair of shoes or brushing his teeth. It was just something he had to do every once in a while. He learned, as a Marine, to accept killing as a way of life. He viewed himself as just one very well functioning part of the big green killing machine that was the United States Marine Corps. The Corps put that calculating cold numb feeling into him and it was never going to come out. He was a mercenary now, on call for wet work assignments from our government and others; and he'd come to regard human life as a cheap commodity. His military experience encouraged him to get that way.

Years before, at his Marine Corps battalion headquarters he got to know two fellow marines who worked in intelligence. Basically, their role was to take three dinks up in a chopper, push two of them out and then write down everything the third dink told them so he could save his miserable Ho Chi Minh brainwashed communist asshole life. Then, they pushed the third dink out too. The dinks all went splat on the ground whether they cooperated or not, and whether they told the truth or not. The intelligence guys explained to Gibby that their work was all good fun and a welcome break from drinking Heineken beer for a nickel a bottle at the Non Commissioned Officers' club.

All was well and good in Gibby's world until the Marines decided to upgrade him. He was sent stateside to spotter's school between rotations. The Marine Corps plan for Gibby was to get him qualified as a forward observer as well as a sniper. That way Gibby could kill many thousands of dinks, and the Marine Corps would have a guy who could handle himself in the field as well. The Marines are not stupid when it comes to killing people. They constantly think about ways to kill more of their enemies faster and cheaper. They are famous throughout the world at their killing skills and they work diligently at perfecting their skill sets.

Gibby found himself in spotter's school along with a bunch of Navy squids. The Navy and the Marine Corps intersect in the spotter department. Marine artillery battalions have attached to them a company of spotters, typically led by a Navy Lieutenant squid, two or three Lieutenant Junior Grade squids, and typically ten or so enlisted marines under command of the squids who are under the command of the Marine battalion commander, who is under command of the Marine division general, who is under command of Fleet Marine Forces

Pacific, who is under command of Commander Pacific Fleet, who reports to the Navy Admiral and Marine Corps General on the Joint Chiefs of Staff, who report to the Commander in Chief, the President of the United States. From Gibby's perspective, all he needed to know was if it had more bars or stars or chevrons than he had, he needed to say 'yes sir,' and salute it, or as one of his instructors said: "All you need to know about authority, Marine, is that shit rolls downhill."

At spotter school, Gibby was trained to be among the most proficient killers on planet earth. He learned all the different kinds of ordinances that could be carried on all the different kinds of aircraft, from B52 bombers to Navy carrier based fighter and attack aircraft. He became expert at using all the different kinds of ammunition that could be shot out of all kinds of navy guns, from eighteen pound 3 inch 55 rounds to 16 inch two thousand pounders that could level city blocks. He learned all the different kinds of projectiles that could be fired from the standard Marine Corps 105 millimeter howitzer, the 155 millimeter self propelled rifled field gun, and their deadly 80 millimeter mortar. Then, the spotter school instructors taught Gibby the proper command sequence to use to put these deadly instruments upon his chosen targets; how to hit a target with a flat trajectory, or with the drop in methods used when the target is in defilade from the weapon; how to coordinate napalm drops from Air Force F105's, with high explosive fragmentary 87 pound air bursts fired simultaneously from five inch gun mounts on Navy destroyers. His calls for fire resulted in the spraying of thousands of dime sized steel fragments, each with the killing effect of a high powered rifle bullet, thus ensuring the death of every living creature within a hundred yard radius. Gibby excelled at school. When the school instructors were satisfied, they graduated Gibby telling him he was now the deadliest weapon on the face of the earth because he was a Marine who knew how to use all the wonderful killing tools God and the Marine Corps placed at his disposal.

Gibby went back to Vietnam where he applied the skills he learned in the field. And, he got medals for his deeds, one bronze star and one silver star; and he got a purple heart from a dink shot in his leg thigh that sent him to Subic Bay, Philippians, to heal and recover at the Naval Hospital there. That's when Gibby got disillusioned.

In the hospital Gibby found himself lying next to a Navy Lieutenant Junior Grade squid. Marines don't ordinarily lower themselves to speak with lowly squids and Navy officers don't ordinarily condescend to chatting up enlisted men; but, here they were with time on their hands and the two men got to talking. Gibby told the squid how he did his part to keep the dinks from coming down the Ho Chi Minh trail, and how if the war could only continue for another couple years. He remarked that the Tet Offensive resulted in a terrible ass kicking for the Dinks and confidently stated that we'd win the war on the strength of our body count numbers alone. Gibby proudly bragged to the squid we were now killing sixty Dinks for every American killed! That's when the squid doused Gibby's world with cold water.

"Sergeant, let me relate to you an experience I had just a short year ago," began the squid. "I was on a gunboat, a big four thousand ton Hull class with three five inch mounts. Are you familiar with one of those, sergeant? Ever worked one?"

"Yeah," said Gibby, "up near the demilitarized zone. One was working targets in I Corps. I was inland about eight miles up the Qua Viet River from the beach. She was all I had for artillery support. They don't tell you in spot school that all these wonderful weapons platforms aren't available to you when you need them. You take what's available and make do, ammo too. Can't begin to tell you how often I called for fuse quick high explosive and got Willie Peter instead. Instead of blasting a weapons cache I fried fifty people in a village. That's tough shit about war, but we called it up the line as Victor Charlie kills, rang up the body counts. Don't matter much. A Dink's a Dink; but, yeah, those gun boats are damn good shooters. They could get a round on target with three or four spots. They had tight deflection and tight dispersion. They're better shooters than an '05 battery. I got to like working with you squids."

"Let me tell you something from my perspective, sergeant. I don't think this war is about winning anything. It's about something else. I was in the wardroom one day; me, the skipper, ops boss, and the xo. It was a quiet time between shoots. We were off the gun line to meet up with a supple ship. We went through ammo like crazy, shot our barrels down to where the inside sleeves were half gone and deflection was fifty yards at ten miles instead of ten yards. We couldn't get up to Yokosuka for new barrel sleeves, so we just kept shooting rounds into Nam. Lucky we didn't get any Comanche Board errors and kill our own spotters. We were so bad on deflection instead of putting five rounds of fire for effect on target we were putting twenty to make sure something hit it. Anyway, this was a moment when we officers got to talking about what it would take to end this fucking war."

"So, I'll bite," says Gibby. "What did you squids come up with that would end the war?"

"It was my idea. I said to Skipper: 'Look, Captain, every day we see these soviet block freighters and trawlers chugging up the Tonkin Gulf. We steam within a half mile of them. Then they come back down the Gulf riding higher than kites, all freeboard showing. We know they're dropping supplies off at Haiphong. That stuff is going down the Ho Chi Minh Trail to kill our boys over there inland. We could stop it right here. Captain, the commie bastards come out on deck, drop their pants and moon us. They drop trash over their stern when they go by on their runs up. Then they give us the finger. They got no respect, Captain. We need to teach the commies respect.'

"'What's your thought, Lieutenant?' The skipper always called his JG's Lieutenant. It made us aspire to greater importance.

"'Well, skip. I say we just start sinking the fuckers. Just think what a couple of five inch rounds into their waterline would do for the Dink supply chain. We could end the war right here, right now.'

"'Come off it, Lieutenant. You're talking about starting World War Three. Those are East Block flagged carriers. They are aligned with Russia and China. There are treaties where the Chinese and Russians are pledged to protect them. If we start sinking Romanian flagged ships out here, we'll have the entire Pentagon and State Department on our asses.'"

"'Really, skipper. Do you believe those chicken shit Russians and Chinese would do anything? Do you really believe that? My thought is we give them the old put up or shut up test. Look, we could sink a couple of their ships in five minutes. Then we could say we were having a gun fire exercise and our gunners fucked up. Instead of hitting a sleeve tow, they thought the ships were there to get sunk and they sank them. Hell, skip, everybody knows gunners screw up sometimes. What would the Chinese and Russians do about it, scream, and protest? Fuck them I say. Our boys are dying over there and we're not preventing it out here on the ocean where it counts the most, where we have the upper hand. We're letting American kids die with their hands tied behind their backs. Boys eighteen to twenty five are getting ground up like hamburger and we act like nothing is happening out here. It's inhuman, Captain.'"

"'Okay, Lieutenant. That's enough. You've said your peace. We're not sinking any East block commie ships. I'm not risking my career on the hunch that the Pentagon Brass and the State department will have my back; and, I'm certainly not going to try to clear this idea ahead of time. I want to make Admiral and retire much more than I want to go down in the history books as the nut that started World War Three.'"

"So, you never sank any commie ships?" Gibby's eyes widened at the thought that our government would deliberately let its soldiers and marines die without making any effort to stop the enemy's armaments from going up the Tonkin Gulf unimpeded.

It amazed the JG that so few people were aware of this huge disparity in America's war fighting strategy. Instead, the media was complicit in the phony narrative. They dutifully reported on the numbers of air strikes, missions flown, and bombs dropped on the Ho Chi Minh Trail; none of which made a dent in the supplies reaching the regular North Vietnam regiments operating in South Vietnam. It was bull shit reporting to distract from the real problem of how the war was conducted and intended to cover up a shameful disgrace.

"No, sergeant, we never sank a single communist supply vessel. We never even issued a blockade or a hazard warning to them. Lyndon Johnson and Robert McNamara just let those boys fighting the war in Vietnam get slaughtered like they were cattle in a corral standing there to get murdered. I figured it out, sergeant. It was a deliberate plan. It was murder for money. The politicians get big political contributions from the defense contractors, even commissions for setting up Pentagon procurement deals. It's dirty business, but very profitable. So what if a woman loses her husband or boy friend? What are fifty thousand boys in a country that gives birth to one and a half million boys annually? You see, sergeant, war is just business for these perverts. The people are stupid enough to sign on to the war fighting, to vote for it, to send their sons to fight it.

"Just make the money, they figure. Make all you can while it lasts. For every boy that gets killed, say fifty thousand over ten years, there will be fifteen million born to replace them. But, the money for the defense contractors is fabulous! So, give the dead soldier a nice send off! Play taps for him. Put a flag on his coffin. Cry a little. Put a notation of his rank on the headstone. Put flowers on his grave. Go to some concert and hear some pathetic sad songs. Then go home, sit in a chair and stare at your boy's picture on the wall or on the mantle over the living room fireplace. Talk to people about how nice he looked in his uniform.

"Don't let yourself think about how he felt when he took a shot in his guts or how he writhed in pain knowing his life was slipping away while his liver was bleeding out and leaving his blood in the dirt ten thousand miles from home. Don't think about what his final thoughts might have been. Don't ask yourself if he wondered whether his girl back home gave a shit about him or whether she would waste much time before she started fucking some other guy.

"Don't think about those fucking bastards in Washington who murdered your little boy whom you loved so much. Don't think about them making a fortune and going to their cocktail parties and strutting to each other about how important they are and how well connected they are. Just look at his picture and smile at him and remark to your friends how nice he looked in his uniform."

The fervor of the Lieutenant's convictions shook Gibby to his core. Sometimes in a person's mind a light goes on and everything the person believed before is whisked away. The truth does that when it's heard. Gibby didn't go AWOL or get disorderly. He was too smart for that. He went back to Nam that third time and killed some more; but, now he did the killing with a different mind set. Now, it was just business. The passion of the fight was gone. He no longer took crazy chances. He cared more about his own survival.

Some say that's when you let your guard down and become vulnerable. They say you actually lose your survival instinct when you start to think about surviving instead of killing. Gibby survived despite what people said. After his third Nam tour he was offered all the Corps had to offer. He could go to the Naval Academy with time in grade and come out an officer, an Ensign with eight years' pay, money as good as a Lieutenant's with four years' pay; or he could go to flight school and become a helicopter pilot and a warrant officer; or he could turn his back on war and become a recluse. He chose the latter.

Gibby moved west to Colorado. He liked the mountains as a child and he wanted more of them. He didn't care to see another jungle or kill another dink for the rest of his life. He met a woman and lived with her for about six years. He worked the physical labor side of life as an outfitter, wrangler, and rodeo rider. When things were slow he hauled wood from the forest and split logs. He trapped some and poached a little, but only when their money was low and they needed meat. Somewhere along his path of life he did work for an older woman who took a liking to him. She gave him a bag of jewels and some gold before she passed away and told him he needed to learn to be a trader. She told him to never bid or offer first, to always go way outside where the deal would be struck, and to walk away from an impasse, and to stay away once he walked away and never look back. Gibby became a great trader. His stash of jewels and gold grew. Then he became disillusioned with the human species a second time.

He was outfitting an elk hunt for a guide service that ran horses out of Meeker, Colorado. The first season hunt went well and his clients took three bulls. The second hunt was an eye opener. His clients showed up in camp, checked their rifles, and left for the Rifle airport to take a plane to Las Vegas. They were businessmen from Missouri who wanted to go away for a week and cheat on their wives and were willing to pay for a guided hunt to pull off their romp with the whores of Sin City. As things turned out they got back two days early and didn't want to hunt. They were going to tell the wives all sorts of stories about how the big ones ran away, how their guide took the wrong trail, how a horse went lame, and other assorted lies. It made no difference to Gibby. They paid and tipped him well and he left for Ouray two days early. Driving home he couldn't help but wonder about the moral compass of some people, but he was confident that the beautiful love of his life, Jo Anne, would be thrilled to see him when he got to their cabin in Ouray. He imagined making love to her as he drove. The closer he approached Ouray the stiffer his prick became.

When Gibby got home he learned the truth first hand. Jo Anne was on top of a man Gibby recognized immediately. He was the owner of one of the local art galleries that sold Native American jewelry, Indian rugs, clay paintings, silver works, saddles, western clothes and the like. He was a prosperous fellow and his wife worked the store with him. They had two kids and Gibby reckoned him to be in his early thirties. There was Jo Anne bouncing up and down on this dude's cock with her eyes closed in heavenly bliss. Her lovely up tilted white tits and pink nipples were jiggling like bouncing ping pong balls when Gibby opened the door of their one room cabin.

At first, Jo Anne couldn't make up her mind whether to stop fucking or to simply say 'Hello.' Her mind raced. She needed to make a quick decision. 'Here I am, caught red handed, just about to pop,' she thought. If I just grind my clit hard into this rock hard cock a few more quick times I'll get off. I'm so close! Damn it! If I come, Gibby will be grossed out and he'll never forgive me. I love him, but he'd never get over seeing me come with another man. Shit! I'm going to stop. I'll make it up to Gibby later. He'll forget this in time. I know he'll keep me. He won't throw me out.'

She kept on bouncing for a bit while trying to make up her mind, and then realized she had to give it up if she'd have any chance of ever holding onto Gibby. She reluctantly gave up on her budding orgasm and sat hump resting upon her guest's phallic organ like a flat tire straddling a log. Gibby just stood there taking in the poignant scene for a moment before he broke into a wide grin. He laughed out loud. Jo Anne was beautiful to behold with her full red hair, green eyes, pale white freckled skin and full inviting lips. She was an irresistible sex pot of a woman. Watching her in the moment made Gibby want to push her paramour aside and possess her himself, even if she had less loyalty than an ally cat. But his pragmatic self overrode his desire for her. How could any man have a sane life with a woman like this?

"Well, hell, Jo, I thought some day you might try to upgrade your situation, since I never offered to marry you, but this skunk scum bag chiseler and pussy whipped man is about the worst piece of shit cock you could have ever stuffed up your twat."

The man got up and started apologizing, putting his pants on.

Gibby said: "Shut up you yellow dog before I break all your teeth and take your britches to your wife and set them on fire right in front of her. Jo, you pack up your things this minute and get out of my cabin. I don't want you back here again. Anything you forget and leave behind is mine, understand?"

Jo Anne started to speak. "Gibby, I was just in the moment. You're gone away from me for so long I get lonely. He's nothing to me. I love you Gibby. You know I love you. I do love you Gibby! I'll make it up to you. Believe me."

"Times a wasting, Jo, get out." Gibby was not moved by her plea. At the minimum he was intent on teaching her a lesson. No woman of his was going to sleep around, no way.

After the philanderer and Jo left, Gibby went to the local realtor and put the cabin on the market. He packed up his things and left. He bought an old four wheel drive truck with a camper shell mounted on the truck bed and somehow, miraculously, got the rig and his belongings up to the Dead Mule Mine. He unloaded his things and took the shell off the truck. Then he drove the truck back to town. He sold the truck and walked the ten miles back uphill to his new home at the Dead Mule. Gibby wanted to be far away from the human race. He did his best thinking when he had distance between him and people.

Now it was time to finish the job of killing. Gibby decided it was best to make it look like these two adventurers died by accident. That meant he couldn't take any of their belongings, nothing; especially not the rifle and not even the 7 millimeter shells for trading purposes; nor the thermos; but he did take their sandwiches. They were roast beef and too good to waste. Gibby got to work. He placed the body of the driver in the back of the Jeep well, and then drove the Jeep to the upper end of Imogene Pass, just before the cliff drop. Once there, Gibby pointed the Jeep toward the edge of the pass road.

He parked and set the brake. Then he placed the driver back in the driver's seat and made sure both passengers had their seat belts fastened. He took a rock that filled his hand in size and smashed both corpses' skulls front and back to conceal the passage of the .308 round through the driver's head. He shoved the shooter's neck through the gear knob to widen the hole that his .308 round made through his neck. Now it appeared the man somehow jammed his neck through the gearshift during the crash. Gibby next burned the envelope and the page with his description and the page about the map. He let the ashes of the papers blow away in the wind. Up here they'd scatter for hundreds of yards and be unrecognizable. The gas cap would be problematic if this job was not done right.

The jeep needed to burn at the bottom of the cliff, but the gas cap needed to stay on.

Gibby opened the Jeep's hood and broke the fuel line by pounding it with his rock. When he saw gasoline dripping on the road he lit a match to the exposed fuel line and started a gasoline flame. Then he released the brake and gave the Jeep a little push to help it slide off the cliff edge. The jeep tumbled end over end, hood and doors thrashing wildly, until it hit the rocks a thousand feet below and burst into flames. Up above, Gibby scattered the dirt where the gasoline dripped onto the trail. He looked at the creation of his work and saw that it was good. Then he walked back up to the Dead Mule.

It was impossible to tell the crash was staged. The assassin's rifle stock burned with the Jeep but the barrel's presence was evidence there was no theft. The wreckage gave the appearance that these two charred corpses were bad men who had no business being in these mountains. They were likely poachers who deserved no sympathy; the poachers' bullets exploded in the heat and left their shell casings behind. The sheriff noticed the fuel line snapped in the wreck which was understandable. The gas cap was on, as it should be.

The sheriff's report stated that his team examined the wreck site and the bodies. The driver and passenger were beyond saving. There was no evidence of theft, otherwise the rifle, charred wallets and ID's would not be there; there was no evidence of murder either. Both bodies were terribly banged up in the fall and burned beyond recognition. Up above on the pass the sheriff noted there was still wet snow melt. He concluded an Easterner hired an inexperienced driver and probably distracted the driver or persuaded him to drive too close to the edge for sightseeing reasons. The driver likely had a lapse of attention. One of the Jeep's wheels probably slipped and slid over the edge, pulling the rest of the jeep with it. The driver was too stupid or too panicked to properly control the vehicle. Possibly he over steered the Jeep as if it was in a skid not realizing that there was no longer any road on the passenger side. Then gravity undoubtedly took control away from the driver. It was not the first vehicle claimed by this treacherous cliff edge on Imogene Pass.

The sheriff and his rescue team drove back up to the pass for one last look. There he just shook his head while looking down upon the carnage. He scratched his head thoughtfully before he finally addressed his rescue team with his conclusion. "Terrible accident, just damn terrible; poor unfortunate devils! Them fuckers are damn good and dead all right. That fall must have scared the shit out of them. Easterners shouldn't be allowed in these mountains. Let's head back down to town. I'm feeling a little thirsty." Then the sheriff and his investigation team went back to town for lunch.

CHAPTER EIGHT

THE WOMAN CAVE

C ecilia tried not to think about what she knew about men, that they could be disarming and deceptive, that their minds could be muddled about where they were trying to take their lives and hers along with theirs, that they could be incredibly stupid and insensitive about the most important things a woman needs. But, knowing all their foibles and deceits, their incapability to feel her soul or understand her hints and longings, Cecilia was undaunted by men. She loved them, almost all of them. Maybe it was her Iberian Peninsular bloodline, blended over six centuries to create a modern day Casta, a mixed race descendant of the conquistadores.

Her blood was thirty generations removed from that conquering helmeted handsome hero who first rode into Tenochtitlan, the Aztec capital, on that sun drenched day of contact. The people never saw a horse before the hero man came. The people decided that the man and his horse were one unit and it was a god. And the new god took what he pleased. He took gold and jewels. And he murdered what he displeased. The god took for his consort a winsome Aztec woman whose husband he'd just run through with a lance. The people accepted this union of the god with one of their own and felt that the husband honored the new god by giving up his life so that the god would find pleasure with the woman he took.

The god and his woman bore a strong spirited girl, one of the original Mestizo offspring of the new world. Over the generations Mulatto blood of African and Indian mixing procreated with Cecilia's Mestizo blood and made Cecilia taller and stronger than her forbearers. In the last two centuries, her bloodline lived in California, New Mexico, and Colorado. Her ancestral intermarriages with northern European Anglos and Scotts made Cecilia taller still. Over the generations her hair turned from black to brown. It flowed and tumbled from her head like a cascading sparkling waterfall. She bore full crimson lips, a perfect oval face, and a petite Spanish nose. Her eyes flashed a dark brown with minute flecks of green - gold pigmentation. They danced in a man's heart and raised his hopes when she smiled. Possibly an ancestor of the brown eyed girl she was now mated with Irish blood a few generations back.

She was tawny skinned now. It was impossible to pinpoint whether she was Caucasian, Indian, or Negro. She had become all of the above. She was too white to be Negro or Indian, but too tawny skinned to be of pure European descent. Whatever the permutations and distillations of genetics were that took place over the centuries to make Cecilia they succeeded in creating a stunning, beautiful woman. And her blood coursed with near surface passions and emotions. The bloodline of the conquered now conquered its conquerors. And the result of these five centuries of bloodline mixes was a stunningly beautiful woman named Cecilia.

She was a magnificent creature and proud and quick of mind and wit. Confidence carried itself in her posture and strength of will paced her strides. A stereotyped hot blooded Latin she was not. She had bridled her emotions and measured them to mete out her reasoned persuasions. She commanded respect at Bear and Otter Consulting. Her opinions on subjects of conjecture were often decisive. As a natural leader she decided to take in Sheila as her roommate and the company's management voiced no objection.

Cecilia's heart and devoted Catholicism were too big for grudges or hatreds from past disappointments. Setbacks that would make a weaker person crumble gave this unusual personality a steady inner strength usually reserved for men engaged in combat against impossible odds. She was a silent stoic soldier who fought an unsung battle against her past adversities; knowing that she could only look to herself for comprehension of life's meaning. She did not complain about her son's tragic death. She soldiered on without her lost son and without seeking forgiveness from others. But she never forgave herself.

And there were men in her life. They came along after the tragedy but they meant nothing to her. When they parted she never tried to hold on to them because they never understood her in the first place. Her forgiveness quotient seemed inexhaustible. This day, this year will be better, different, she always told herself. She believed in the future and she lived for it like a priest lived the beatitudes of the Christ. Her blood treasured life. It told her the same thing it told her ancestors. Life was good but never satisfied. It was vibrant, alive and wanting something better. So Cecilia looked upon Sheila as a blessing that came into her life, a soul to befriend, enjoy and cherish, for God must certainly have sent this incredibly brilliant genius woman to her for some good reason.

The yellow Jeep pulled into its assigned space in the basement of the building. Sheila and Cecilia gathered Sheila's bags and made their way to the elevator. The building had good security. Garage access required a coded clicker to open the door. Building entrances required a coded fob key to open the access doors. The elevator required a resident key to turn a cylinder lock before it would move to the floor that the pushed button indicated. The building was in downtown Plaintown and only six blocks from the offices of Bear and Otter Consultants. Once in the elevator Cecilia pushed the button for the building's top floor loft, and turned her security key. Fourteen floors higher the elevator opened into Cecilia's pad.

"Well, here we are, home sweet home," bubbled Cecilia. "Your room is the one on the far left. It has a king sized, as does my room, a walk in closet, as does my room, and your own private bath, just like mine." Cecilia nodded toward the left. There were two hardwood doors that opened to the two separate bedroom suites. The two women stood in a cavernous room with hardwood floors and a twelve foot ceiling. Looking further clockwise from the bedroom doors, there was a corner space that served as a kitchen, another distinguishable space separated by about five feet of open floor space that served as a study or family room area, complete with a wide screen television and a work station with a computer console. Looking to the right of the study area there was a large sitting room with huge cushy leather sofas and chairs. All the way over on the right side of the loft there was a third hardwood door. It was bolted and locked. Cecilia had plastered more of her bumper stickers on it. One said KEEP OUT in huge letters. Another said RADIOACTIVE SUBSTANCES INSIDE. STAY OUT! Another was a sticker of a skull and crossbones. Next to the door was a treadmill, a rubber mat pad and a set of free weights.

"Excuse me for asking Cecilia," said Sheila. "Are you expecting me to stay here with you? I'd planned on getting my own place as soon as I learned my way around." Sheila sounded authoritative and in control.

"Nonsense," replied Cecilia. "This *is* your place, Sheila. Consider it *your* home. It's rent free, compliments of Bear and Otter. I'm here to facilitate your needs. If you want something, just ask me and I'll get it for you. You have your own set of security access keys on your dresser in your room."

"But this looks like *your* home, Cecilia. It looks like you've been living here for some time," protested Sheila, although not too strongly. The place was luxurious. She knew she'd be hard pressed to do better.

"Well, yes. It is my home. I got a terrific deal on it when some lawyers were about to file for bankruptcy. Their practice went down in flames, their clients were suing them and they needed cash fast. I stole it! Then, when I heard you were coming and I was to be your office helper I made a deal with Bear and Otter Consulting to pay me half your living allowance. You can keep the other half. It's yours. I'm not greedy. I just wanted to have some company, and I just know we'll be good company for each other Sheila. Please try it. I promise I'll be very quiet so you'll have plenty of privacy and time to think. What do you say? I'll be good for you Sheila. You'll see, I've already made you a good deal!"

"Well, let's just say we'll try it for a while. That's a tentative okay, *okay*? Only, tell me what's in that room to the right? You don't actually keep radioactive isotopes up her do you?"

"No! I'm not completely crazy. That's just to keep guys away from that room when I'm inside working on my project. That's my woman cave."

"What guys? What project?"

"Well, sometimes I drag a man up here to get my complete exercise, if you know what I mean. When I do that, I'll keep him in my room, honest. He won't bother you. If you are bothered in the least I'll use a hotel instead. The building's rooms are solid concrete walled. You shouldn't hear anything. You shouldn't even know if anything's happening in my room. Besides, I'm not a screamer. I'm very quiet."

"*How* often?" Sheila was suspecting her potential roommate could invite danger in for both of them.

"Not often, maybe one night every two or three weeks. And it's only with a couple of guys I know very well. They're both married. It's just a physical thing we have for each other. Their wives don't know and it's all very safe. I've known them both for years, and I only see them one at a time. I'm not in my teens anymore."

"Okay. Well that's your business. I promise I won't interfere. What's the project that needs the radioactive sign warnings?"

"That's a little weirdness I'm working on. It's a personal thing. It's something I'm trying to understand myself. It has to do with this strange deep darkness I think I can see sometimes when it's late at night, when I'm here alone just looking out of the windows that open away from the lights of the town." Her description heightened Sheila's interest and caused her eyebrows to lift.

"What's this darkness like? Why do you say it's strange?"

"Well, it's hard to describe. It's like the darkness has something darker inside of it and somehow this something is alive inside the darkness. It kind of rolls over and over on itself, like something ever darker keeps emerging from the darkening darkness that preceded the darkness it just left. It's like it can turn itself inside out. I don't know if it's my eyes or my imagination or some kind of thing that shouldn't even exist, but it keeps coming back to me like it's somehow trying to communicate with me."

Sheila felt a chill. "You don't say. Tell me, how long have you been seeing this dark thing whatever it is?"

"It started about the same time when I wished I could die and leave planet Earth. It was right after my little boy died. It was a hard time for me. It's still a hard memory. I think it always will be."

"Oh, you had a child. I'm sorry. You were married? Would you care to talk about it?" Sheila's voice expressed sympathy

"Yeah, I'll tell you about it sometime, but not now. Right now you must be tired. You've been traveling for days and you need some good bed rest."

"Okay, you're right. I am tired, but I'd really like to know more about you, Cecilia, when you're ready, of course. I mean if you're sincere about wanting us to be friends."

"Oh, I do Sheila, I do. Yes of course I want us to become friends." Sincerity resounded in Cecilia's deep tone. "I don't have many girl friends. I guess I don't have many friends at all, that's one of my problems. We'll talk more about things, I promise. Meanwhile, please call me CC. Now, my orders are to get you to bed for a good night sleep. Tomorrow I'm taking you with me to Bear and Otter and seeing you as far as the security desk. Then I'll catch up with you at the end of the day, okay?"

"Okay then, CC it is. I'll see you tomorrow morning." With that good night the two women shared a hug. CC's hug was more than a simple ordinary hug. It was a sincerely warm squeeze and hold tight for an extended time hug. Sheila knew from that hug that she and CC would become good friends and she looked forward to the friendship. She needed a friend too, although with her reserved nature she was reluctant to admit it. When CC relaxed her hug Sheila ambled off to her room on the left, opened the solid oak door and collapsed onto her bed.

CHAPTER NINE

CARLOS

Linda arranged her appointments to make sure her Friday workday would end at 11 am. She reserved Fridays for her dunning calls. Delinquent loan accounts got reminder calls on Fridays. Borrowers that made wrinkles in the BASE cash flow models deserved to be annoyed before the weekend. Management's motto was 'Shit on others before they shit on us.' She had just finished ruining a borrower's weekend with threats of a court filing if an overdue payment was not received by the following Thursday.

"No," she'd said, "I don't want to hear any more of your pathetic excuses.

"No, I don't care that your daughter is deathly ill and in a hospital with an incurable disease."

"I really don't care if you need to max out your personal credit cards at 26% interest to make your overdue payment.

"Yes, that's right; I will foreclose and seize your business assets and sell them at auction for ten cents on the dollar. You were told about this two months ago.

"Look, stupids, I don't give a shit that you are calling me ruthless. I am absolutely heartless and ruthless. You're not telling me something I don't already know.

"Yes, you're right. I'd even sell your sickly child if I could get money for her or for some of her body parts.

"Look you assholes, you're the ones who borrowed the money and the bank wants its money back! I don't want to discuss this fucking mess of a loan any further. Our terms are final. Now I need to end this wretched conversation to make another call. And don't call me again unless you have the money. Okay, then fuck off to you, too." Click. Linda slammed down her phone.

She swiveled her chair so she could face the window and enjoy her view of Central Park. There was a touch of fall on the trees. Some tinges of red and orange were beginning to encroach on the verdant green hues of summer. She took her shoes off and propped her feet on the low window sill. She twirled her fingers through her hair and parted her legs. 'How did some people manage to get their lives so fucked up?' she wondered. 'They weren't bad or evil people, just idealistic and stupid like most of the other irresponsible fuck ups. God, I hate it when grown people start crying and begging for mercy and I can't give them mercy. I'm not a fucking priest. I work for a fucking bank! What did they expect?' She needed a few moments to stop hating herself. She thought about her coffee meeting with Sebastian Carlos de Carmella, or Carlos as he preferred to be called by those he invited to become his friend. He told her he was free this weekend. She took a sip of water from her glass and contemplated. She took a few deep breaths to let her emotions unwind from her nasty bitch routine.

She wished she could simply tell that poor couple whose flower shop dream was on the BASE deathwatch list to just forget their stupid loan. She wanted so badly to tell them that charging off their miniscule loan through forgiveness would cost BASE less than one thousandth of one percent against BASE's next quarter's earnings. She wanted to tell them that BASE was going to give them two hundred thousand dollars as a gift and as gratitude for their fifteen years of customer loyalty. She wanted to tell them that she felt terribly sorry for them and that she loved them and their child whom she had met the year before; but she couldn't do any of those things and keep her job.

She had to be a bitch, not just an ordinary bitch like a woman who was having a bad day. No, she had to be that heartless, mean, destructive, ruinous, impossible BASE bitch that would make them go home tonight and cry and fight and threaten each other with divorce. She had to be so ruthless that they would feel like their lives were hopelessly ruined forever and that they would seriously consider committing joint suicide. But by maxing out their credit card debt they could stave off the plague on their lives for another couple months even though their financial hole was going to become so deep that it would surely swallow them.

'A woman has to do what she must,' thought Linda. 'After all it's a dog eat dog world. Everybody knows that.' She'd made the call she had to make in order to keep her job at BASE. If she hadn't made the call someone else would have. Now it was time to take off her nasty mask and become normal Linda again. She wanted to forget that horrible painful call. She wanted to let it fall away from her mind and allow thoughts of Carlos to enter.

He was a standout charmer. From the moment she saw him that first night at Tee O's he melted her heart like it was a slab of butter on a hot skillet. Her butter was sizzling now. She wanted him and she wanted him to know it. That massive chest, broad shoulders, and sinewy arms ignited her feminine flame. This man with his broad smile and perfect white teeth, this man with curly brown Spaniard hair, sexy deep brown irises, and beautiful long fingered hands would be in her bed tonight. Oh yes, that's exactly what she wanted. She felt this man was going to be a major part of her future as she made the call from her personal cell phone.

"Carlos. Hi, it's Linda. I'm calling about this weekend." Pause. "Yes, of course I intended to call you. Do you really think I could ever forget?" Pause. "Well, I'm not like those other girls, Carlos. When I said I'd call you, it's because I'd call you." Pause. "Yes, I had a lovely time too. Of course I still want to see you." Pause. "Okay, let's spend the weekend together like we discussed. I'd like to start by making dinner for the two of us. Come to my place this evening at 6 pm, dress casual and bring an overnight bag. I have a spare bedroom; all you'll need is your essentials." Pause. "Yes, I'm sure." Pause. "No, I'm not worried about having you in my house. I told one of my friends you were coming over and she knows where you work. So, if you don't make a pass at me, she'll report you to Tee O's as an unsatisfactory employee."

A brief moment of Linda's seductive giggles accompanied the next pause. "No, honestly, I have an excellent wine selection. Just bring yourself. If you must bring something besides your handsome self I'd love to hear more of your guitar playing. Please bring it along." Pause. "Yes, I'm totally serious. Please bring it. Yes, that would be a lot of fun. I can't wait to hear you compose a song. Okay. You have the address. See you at 6." As she disconnected the call Linda noticed she had gotten moist. 'This will be one glorious night,' she thought as her gaze lifted from the park to the early autumn sky.

CHAPTER TEN

UNBUTTONED

S heila stood before her bedroom mirror thinking 'Why are you letting yourself think about Johnny? You know you need to stay focused. Today you meet the project director, the man who pays you and decides if you'll get hired on after the project. Try to think about what sorts of timelines he's likely to throw at you and how you'll respond. Try to imagine that you'll be introduced to several assistants they've selected for your project team. Maybe you'll meet a very handsome intelligent man who wants to be faithful to you. Or, maybe not. But, damn it girl, stop thinking about shithead Johnny! Stop second guessing yourself. When he called you begging for a second chance you told him to go to hell. You slammed that door; now stop wondering if you should have changed your mind. He was a shithead! What sort of creep fucks his girlfriend's roommate? Come on, stop thinking about him. Just stop! Why did you let him out of your mental mouse jar this morning? This morning of all mornings!

'Today is business, all business. You don't want Bear and Otter to send you packing and cancelling your contract because you can't focus, do you? You can't let them think for a moment that despite your brains, degrees and academic papers that you're just some airhead female on a man hunt. No, you can't let them think that. But, you are, aren't you? Be honest. Get it out of your system right now. You are terrified that there is something very wrong about you, that there's a reason you are a twenty-four year old virgin. You are secretly worried that men somehow detect you are not normal. That's why they tend to shy away from you. Maybe it's your smarts. Maybe all men are afraid of smart woman. Maybe there *is* something wrong with you. Even when eligible men do make passes you just blow them off, don't you? Yes, you've done that. You told yourself you were saving yourself for Johnny; but maybe what's really going on with your mind is you are just plain terrified of being fucked.'

Her page boy hair cut was neatly brushed. She wore it longer now that she was out of college. It only needed to grow another inch until her ends would lie on her shoulders. Her lipstick was a conservative peachy rose color and her eyelashes were lightly touched with black mascara. She chose pearl earrings for an elegant understated look. No makeup, no blush, no lip gloss, nothing. That would be fake, not her. She took one last look, inhaled a deep breath and exhaled. It was show time.

The autumn sun was already up and casting long west reaching shadows from the buildings onto the streets below and onto the buildings on the other sides of the streets. The lingering moisture of the high plains had lifted away ten days before. The plants were already beginning to wonder if they would be lucky enough to catch an afternoon thundershower. They came in these early fall weeks, arising from the colliding wind patterns over the high snow fields on the east facing slopes of the Rockies. Below the high bright blue skies city folk were out bustling from parking garage buildings to office tower buildings. There was a brisk wind blowing out of the southwest today. Officially it was a Santa Anna wind, blowing heat from the parched deserts of Arizona. That happens when a high pressure ridge swings far enough south and directs its clockwise flow to heat and dry out the state. The down slope effect of the wind rushing off the mountains agitates the air molecules and makes the desert air even warmer than it was when it crossed into Colorado.

Cecilia set a brisk pace. She usually covered the six blocks from her pad to their work in six minutes. Today she walked slower to let Sheila get a feel for their surroundings. As the women walked across a street, a light gust lifted Sheila's skirt. She wasn't expecting it.

"Ooh. What was that?" She started.

"That's a little wind gust from the Santa Anna effect. It's just desert air passing by. You'll get used to them." After two blocks the women noticed two men lying on the street. They were young men with a grocery cart next to them filled with what appeared to be all their possessions. The women detected the odor of stale urine.

"Do you have a lot of those?" asked Sheila, nodding in the direction of the two men.

"Unfortunately, yes we do. Plaintown is a magnet for druggies. They come here because the State made Marijuana legal. Our politicians are idiots. So the dopers come here and end up staying. A lot of them are stuck here and that's not all their fault. They came with the notion that there was opportunity here, but then the terrible conditions that have gripped the rest of the country arrived here too. Now they are trapped and hopeless. Every month it gets worse. At first it was kind of sweet. There are so many promising young men among them. I used to think they'd make it here; but now I just feel sorry for them and I'm even becoming afraid of them. You hear more and more about violence. They are getting desperate and they will steal. So watch out for getting mugged and possibly even raped."

'Oh, great,' thought Sheila. 'I've saved myself all these years for Mr. Right and now I find out I have a good chance of becoming a rape victim.'

Sheila's eyes turned skyward as they entered the broad granite plaza from which a gigantic monolithic obelisk rose like a phallic symbol. The towering glass building seemed to announce that it was superior to all the lesser buildings in Plaintown; and it implied by its presence that all who leased offices in it were a cut above those who leased at its surrounding inferiors. She noticed that all the floors were transparent glass except the very top floor which was cloaked in opaque dark black glass.

The duo navigated one of the building's twelve massive revolving glass doors which opened into a breathtaking lobby. White marble laced with veins of gold was everywhere. The gold testified to the mineral riches of the state. It was on the floor under their feet and on the cavernous walls. It was even on the lobby ceiling.

At the far end of the lobby was a hallway that held the building's bank of elevators. But before people could enter the elevator hallway they had to pass a huge concierge desk. Behind this massive black desk was seated an official looking bald headed man in a dark blue silk suit. But that wasn't the end of the officiousness of the lobby. Flanking the concierge desk were two muscular early thirtyish men. Sheila gauged they were both about six feet four inches tall. They were strikingly handsome. They sported crew cuts and clean shaven faces and both wore blue silk suits that perfectly matched the concierge's suit. Blue silk was apparently the dress code for the lobby desk. Sheila thought about the possibilities of saying hello to these two; but then she noticed both men had their jackets unbuttoned. One of them pointed off to his right as he gave directions to a bicycle helmeted message carrier. His open jacket revealed he was carrying a holstered pistol. Sheila recaptured her thought as her goose bumps raised a chill on her back. She nodded politely in their direction. She confirmed in her own mind that her first would have to be more of the intellectual type. Yes, it was important to get laid, but it still had to be Mr. Right. She couldn't and wouldn't simply ditch her sense of self worth to get banged by a guard dog. She and Cecilia walked briskly to the elevators.

"I'll go up the elevator with you and take you to the door where Mr. Palmer and Mr. Kelly office," said Cecilia. "I don't go in there unless I'm called. I go to my cubicle in the assistant pool. And, don't be afraid of the two marines. That's defense department stuff. They want those guys there because the missile project we're working on is extra top secret. No one can get past those guys unless they first pass through the security door. There's a green light and a buzzer that lets them know you are cleared. You have all your papers and your security stuff in your briefcase, don't you?"

"Yes. I have everything." Sheila sounded a nervous reply. The building was like something out of the far away future. Everything was officious and intimidating.

"There. Cecilia pointed to a solitary door that accessed a smaller elevator car. Its capacity was for four people, unlike the lobby elevators that each carried twelve people. They walked past the lobby elevator bank to the small elevator. "We use this one," she said. When she pushed the call button the soft clicks of a high resolution security camera were unmistakable. Sheila looked up. Just under the small overhang of the single elevator door was a small glass orb. They'd been filmed by a device that provided a much sharper image than a grainy video camera's feed. Her chill which had subsided reawakened.

Cecilia used a key card to open a panel that revealed the elevator's two floor choices, the thirty-ninth and the fortieth. Cecilia used a manual key to turn the floor button on the thirty-ninth floor to the on position. Then she pushed the button. As the elevator car began to ascend Sheila asked "who goes to the fortieth floor?"

"I don't know. I don't believe any of us knows."

"Oh." The two women were silent as the car whooshed upward and finally slowed and stopped.

"See you later, roommate," said Cecilia as she turned away and walked down a long corridor to their right.

"Okay, CC, and thanks for getting me here." Sheila looked straight ahead at a large wooden desk trimmed in brass. 'What is it about desks in this place,' she thought. 'This is so much like the lobby set up it's uncanny.' Here on the thirty-ninth floor was another desk manned by a middle aged bald man and flanked by two large handsome men. These two were uniformed marines armed with automatic rifles with ammunition clips inserted. They stood at attention and stared straight ahead, all four eyes fixated on whoever disembarked from the elevator.

She sensed they had orders to kill certain unwelcome people. She had no doubt that these two men wouldn't hesitate or shrink from doing whatever it was they were ordered to do. Again her chills made their presence felt. The hair on the back of her neck rose. She began to wonder if she shouldn't have taken a corporate job or looked for something in academia. But, she was warned that Bear and Otter would look like this, and it did. She lifted her shoulders and walked confidently to the front of the desk.

The marines continued to stare at the elevator even as it closed. Neither spoke a word. They ignored her. Apparently a closed elevator door was more attractive to them than she was. But she intuited that somehow their silence was a good thing. These were men that would obey their orders even in the face of certain death. The bald man was face down reading something. He seemed intense. "Ahem. I'm Sheila Carson. I'm here for my appointment with Mr. Palmer," she announced her presence exactly as she was instructed. The bald head did not flinch or look up. There was no sign of acknowledgement whatsoever, not even a repugnant male grunt. The head continued reading. After making her suffer his silence for a disrespectful minute a voice sounded from the downward looking head. It discourteously refused to show her the face it was attached to.

"Escort Ms. Carson to Mr. Palmer's office," was the only utterance from the mouth of the bald head which still faced down on the desk and still did not look up or give her so much as a welcome hello. At that moment the marine on her right placed a firm hand on her upper arm. Again the chills made their presence felt.

"Come with me, Ms. Carson," he commanded in a no nonsense voice that she wouldn't dare say no to; and he began moving while gripping her firmly by her arm toward a large wooden door with massive brass handles.

"How does he even know it's really me? He never looked up to see who I was," said Sheila as she was being man towed toward the door.

"He did see you Ms. Carson. He knows it's really you. You were confirmed," said the marine with that tone of unshakable confidence. Then Sheila remembered the camera click at the lobby floor.

"Yes, of course, facial recognition, thank you," was all she could say. Again that chill rose on her back. 'What have I gotten myself into?' she wondered. But the marine's presence made her feel safe somehow and the chill immediately started to subside. 'What is it about a marine taking me in tow that makes me first feel terrified and now safe?' She couldn't frame the silent words to answer her own question.

The brass handles were untouched by the smudge mars of human hands. They shined a bright reflective polished real brass gleam, not the almost fresh gleam of polished brass buried beneath a coat of protective lacquer. The polished oak doors with polished handles swung open in response to the marine's push of a button on the wall to their right. Before her, flanked by two more marines standing beside his rather smallish inlaid oak desk, was Mr. George Palmer III. He was standing, waiting for her to cross the room to him.

George Palmer was the opposite of what she was expecting to see. After the recurrences of bald men she was pleasantly surprised to come face to face with a man who had a full head of hair. 'Hmmm, maybe Mr. Palmer will be my first. He'll certainly do for looks. I like the full head of wavy brown hair. He's got a slender build, but looks muscular beneath that blue silk suit. My God, there must be a thing about blue silk suits for the men around here. His face is very attractive and his eyes are bonny blue, like out of the *Blue Boy* portrait; and his face is a bit ruddy roseate. Very masculine, this one. Oops, he's stepping out from behind the desk and, darn it. There's a wedding ring on his left hand. I need to keep my head on business all the way with this guy. He's extending his right hand. Better get on your A game, girl.'

"Greetings Ms. Carson, we're very glad to see you made it here safely. Welcome to Bear and Otter Consulting, LLC. Let's step over here to these chairs where we can get acquainted." George motioned to two tapestry covered classic Italian sitting chairs. Sheila noted they were very well stuffed and comfortable when she seated herself. "Would you join me in an iced tea, Ms. Carson?"

"I'm very pleased to meet you, Mr. Palmer, and yes, I'd love an iced tea." 'Careful, girl, the word love was inappropriate. He's got the ring on, don't forget. Do not throw out any suggestive words you'll regret later. But, he is a keeper. Obviously someone else already figured that out.'

After a man in a white coat brought them two iced teas on a silver platter and they'd each had a sip, George Palmer opened the conversation. "I'm curious, Ms. Palmer, why did you come by train instead of by plane?"

"Please call me Sheila. I'd like that if it's permissible here."

"Of course, as you wish. Call me George when we're in working mode and with peers, but when we are presenting or with instructions to the associates, you and I will be Mr. Palmer and Ms. Carson. I hope that's all right by you."

"Of course, I understand perfectly. And whom do we present to?"

"Well, let's not race ahead of ourselves, Sheila. Allow me to ask the questions. After that I'll break down the basics of what we're trying to accomplish with your two projects and then——"

"Two projects? I thought I was contracted to debug and simplify intercept targeting telemetry issues applying my knowledge of feedback corrective loops and dynamic sampling technique using magnetic field variation mapping methods as I demonstrated in my theoretical physics papers. What two projects?"

"Relax Ms. Carson. Let me ask the questions please, or we'll never get off first base. I promise I'll explain everything."

"Okay." 'Whatever heat I was feeling for him is sort of switching on and off and back on again. He's a little slippery. No, I'm the one that's feeling slippery. Just cool it and answer questions. He seems like a man who can think logically, unlike most of them. He wants to stay on his track and he's signing the paychecks, so cool it and be polite.'

"Well, not to belabor it, but I'm curious why you chose to make the trip by train. Three days instead of three hours. Can you tell me why you made that choice?"

"I wanted to see the country."

"That's it? You wanted to see the country? If you drive one hour east from here you'll see the prairie. If you drive further east for another three days you'll see more of the same. Is seeing the country the only reason, Sheila?"

Sheila felt the gotcha moment in the tone of George's question. Of course she didn't just want to see the country. "Well, to tell you the truth, the other reason was I'm not all that trusting of the safety of air travel anymore."

"Okay, good, why not?"

"It's the terrorists, George. They are getting more and more creative with their methods. They can make devices that will destroy an aircraft in flight and we haven't come up with a fool proof way to prevent it. I want to live, George, and if that means not taking unnecessary risks, even though the risk of one event is small, I'd rather not take it. You won't hold that against me will you? You wouldn't want to have to search for a new project leader if I got unlucky would you?"

"Not to bicker, Sheila, but have you considered they can also target trains and they have already done so?"

"Yes, but the payoff for them is lower and the evidence is more easily traced to the source and train wrecks don't horrify the public like a plane disaster does."

"So, you're saying that they like a big payoff, lots of sensationalism, right?"

"Yes and that's——"

"Very good, Sheila, you are starting to touch on why we have two projects for you instead of just one. As you said, the bad guys are getting more creative. They are so creative that we didn't want to risk telling you exactly why you were being hired. You have an experimental project top secret clearance. Now we've confirmed you are the person we sought out and hired. Now, here in person with you I can speak frankly.

"We need to stay one step ahead of these demented bastards and we need your expertise in math and electro particle physics to beat their next tactic before they deploy it.

"Our intelligence people have infiltrated their strategic planners. They're not all that interested in airplanes anymore. They've discovered the capabilities of drones. We're getting intelligence that they plan to do sensational attacks with drones that they can buy off the shelf at toy stores. We don't know what their plans are, but our people at CIA have developed some scenarios and they are chilling. Just a few theoretical examples of what they might try using drones for are to attack a large event like an NFL football stadium with a drone swarm using nerve gas or radioactive waste and exploding the drones or sprinkling the radioactive waste onto the crowds of people. We need to stop that before it happens. They could also use drones to disable an aircraft on take off or landing by getting a drone swarm in front of the flight path and destroying the plane's engines. We're looking at possibly dozens of ways they can use these drones to bring civilization to a halt. We're concerned that our entire military industrial complex is all geared up for yesterday's wars and the enemy is gearing up for low cost asymmetric warfare. And the truth is, Sheila, we don't know how to harden the nation and our allies against drones and drone swarms."

"How serious do your intelligence people believe this threat is?"

"Well, that's the devil of it. We can't put a probability on it. You see, we conquered their countries. We went into their places like a swarm of locusts. Do you know anything about locusts, Sheila?"

"That's more in the discipline of etymology, pretty far from math and physics."

"Yes, yes of course. Well here's the thing about them. They eat everything in their path. But after they swarm they lay their eggs and die and the eggs can lie dormant for years. Well, like I said, we went into their countries destroying things like a swarm of locusts. We destroyed everything in our path. Then we went dormant. But now our eggs of destruction have hatched. We've seeded our own problems. The people of the places we conquered have long memories. They remember we killed their family members when we were the locusts. In North Africa locust swarms move towards the Atlantic on desert winds, but then the winds die out at sea and the ocean swallows up the locusts. The Americans are spared the plague of these locust swarms by Mother Nature, you see.

"Okay, I get it. Locusts can't swim thousands of miles."

"Oh, but this new variety *can* cross the Atlantic, Sheila. This is a locust of the human kind, and it has a long memory. This locust even remembers that there were battles of faith that took place fourteen hundred years ago and the locust of today will still fight to avenge a defeat from that long ago. And the modern locust has upgraded his capabilities. He now crosses the Atlantic on airplanes. He sings his song of hunger to other would be locusts and he resonates with them. They excite and come alive and they want to eat everything we have and they live right here among us. And this modern locust flies into our border countries then slips into our country through our borders, just like real locusts will creep into houses through loose floorboards. Once inside a house locusts will eat everything. They are here by the thousands now, in our house called America, and their ranks are growing. They are eating away at the fabric of our free society. We are way behind in our efforts to counter this hoard."

"So you're telling me you have no idea how many of them are already here. Let me guess. You also have no idea how many or what sorts of drones they have amassed or where they might be, am I getting this?"

"Yes, but despite the lack of good intelligence we figure we can blunt the locusts and make them die off. Like a desert wind that blows itself out and drops its locusts into the Atlantic, so to speak. If we can prevent them from using drones to do their terror that will take some of their wind away. We believe that eventually many of them will eventually assimilate, or at least many of their children will. Assimilation will be the death of their radical thinking."

"Oh my, I see what you are saying, but what makes you think I'm the person to figure out a solution to this? I mean any nut can go buy a drone and who knows what their beef is, where they'll use it or what they'll put onto it?" Sheila was intentionally being the devil's advocate. She hoped to glean more insights into George's thinking.

"Yes, yes, we understand those things, but look at what we do know. You're the smartest brain we've got, Sheila. Look, every drone needs to be controlled and sent to its target. That means it has some sort of navigation system. If we could——"

It was Sheila's turn to interrupt. She knew every drone needed to be controlled. This wasn't helping.

"George. I don't want you to tell me what we could do. Just stop there. That's premature in the problem solving space. Before I even start to tackle this, I want your assistant pool to come up with every known drone model, its electrical components and software if you can get that. Also, get me the capabilities of each drone, like its lift payload, ceiling of operation, speeds, radio frequency ranges of operation, manufactures' production models, obsolete models, turning radius of drones in flight, acceleration rates, deceleration rates, fuel types and capacity, battery types and capacities, materials used in the construction of each drone, the type of landing gear on each drone type.

"Then I'll want the capabilities of the various lethal agents they could get their hands on, even the ones you think are inconceivable to acquire. I'm looking for Sarin gas, anthrax, radioactive isotopes, the old World Wars I and II gasses, and let's not forget the bang stuff like dynamite, C4, PBX, white phosphorous, and nitro glycerin; and I'll come up with more stuff as I think more about this."

"That's a tall order to get all this data before you've even begun to think about how you'll attack the problem."

"George. I need to know all I can about these things before I can begin to model a solution. You're telling me it's an asymmetric weapon with a variable ordinance carrying platform. Any nut can get them. Just how do you think we can thwart an attack that will leave fifty thousand dead if we don't start learning commonalities of these things other than the fact that we know they can fly around? I don't have answers for you. I don't even know where we need to start to find answers; but this much I do know. When we look at data, I mean critically look at and analyze data; the answers about where we need to start asking questions begin to show themselves.

"Every problem that exists is only a solution in disguise, George. One thing I do best is think about how to solve a problem, and I do my best thinking when I can wrap my mind around a lot of data. And that's another thing George. I do my best thinking when I'm alone and in surroundings that help me think. I don't expect your people to understand this, but I can not solve this sitting in an office. I'll need to go for walks, sit under trees, lie in fields looking up at clouds, and just generally be free of structure."

"But, your security, what will I tell my superiors in the pentagon?"

"Tell them if they don't want a drone swarm to unload on them and kill all of them they need to let me do this my way. Got it George?"

"Okay, Ms. Carson, as you wish. I'll get a team on it right away."

That was more like it. A warm feeling surged over Sheila when her eyes joined with George's. She detected a slight wry smile on his lovely face. She could tell he was willing to trust her. "And George, I'm Sheila. Sheeeila, remember."

"Sheila, yes of course, Sheila." What was it about this woman that left him curious to know more about her, George wondered as he escorted her out of his office to show her to her new office.

As she settled into her officially designated location space Sheila unbuttoned her blouse two buttons to allow some body heat to escape. 'The task ahead is going to be a mathematical and operations research gaming challenge, I can see that. It's also going to take some experimenting with principles used only in theoretical physics so far, and it will require using artificial intelligence against some assholes with cockamamie schemes grounded in asymmetric warfare, but I'll be dammed if some brain warped nut jobs are going to outsmart me. I just can't let a stadium full of clueless innocent people die. I'll outwork the nut jobs all right. I know I will. But, working with George is going to be even more challenging than outsmarting the nut jobs on several levels. I felt myself wanting to hold his gorgeous off limits head in my hands and kiss him smack on his lips like a smitten school girl. I'm afraid I might like him too much. I can't give myself to a married man for my first time. I just can't do that. It would be so wrong on so many levels.'

Sheila looked out her window to the mountains beyond. There were glistening white snow fields high on the east peaks and cumulous puffs were forming above the peaks for a move eastward. A possible afternoon thundershower was birthing in those lovely white puffs.. It was all so dreamy and lovely to stare at those peaks. In the privacy of her office Sheila casually opened a third button on her blouse.

CHAPTER ELEVEN

EASIER

'A perfect evening begins with preparation' was the thought that guided Linda's afternoon. Her perfect night was planned backwards from the last event first. She fitted her king sized bed with freshly washed densely threaded cotton sheets. Her menu was fitting for a man who would need plenty of strength. She purchased her meats from an exclusive butcher shop. Tonight's fare featured a pound of tenderloin filet, cut nine ounces for him, four for her, and three to spare in case he had a ravenous appetite. Her appetizer was freshly shucked blue points. September was here, the "r" was in the month and the Chesapeake Bay was shipping the world's tastiest oysters overnight to her neighborhood butcher. 'The hell with costs,' she thought. 'This man will need his protein.'

Her wine choice was an Argentine Malbec. She thought Carlos would appreciate a familiar touch. Music was a problematic choice. While she loved guitar she hesitated to put a CD of another guitarist on. Possibly Carlos would feel insulted to think she preferred another's music to his own. She selected an opera instead. La Boehm would likely be familiar to him and certainly it would signal that she was in the mood for romance. Lastly, she decided she would dress plainly. There was no need to put on airs with him. From their coffee date she knew he was an uncomplicated sort of man. He'd seen many women, including her, at Tee O's. He'd seen her that first night in a perfectly lovely dress with an accessory handbag, shoes, jewels and pearls. He also had to know she was a woman of means to be one of the BASE girls in their management program. It was important to dress casual tonight and not frighten him away. She wanted him to know she was completely accessible. She chose a simple blue cotton skirt, a peach colored cotton blouse, no bra and no panties, and blue flats for shoes.

Everything Carlos told her at the coffee shop checked out. After talking with him for two hours she was initially skeptical. She couldn't be that lucky to have discovered such a handsome man with such varied accomplishments and talent; or could she? He told her that his family was from Venezuela. His father, a Spaniard, met Carlos's mother to be in Italy. They moved to Venezuela for the opportunity to build a business. The father started a metal fabrication and plastics extrusion firm. Over twenty years the family became wealthy and his parents raised three successful children, Carlos and his two older sisters. Carlos was educated at the Sorbonne in Paris. One sister earned a degree at Harvard, went on to Bucknell and became a pediatric doctor. She was not married. The youngest sister went to the University of Alabama where she became a cheerleader, graduated and married a football player. They recently had their first child, a boy who was fated to become a linebacker.

Carlos had the most unusual background of the three siblings. After undergraduate study he went to the University of Pennsylvania's law school and became a lawyer. He returned to Venezuela, set up a practice in Caracas, and took on all the administrative and legal work for his father's business. Carlos prospered for a few years, but then Venezuela was turned on its head. The leftists took power. Suddenly the country was run by a former army sergeant and a bus driver, neither of whom had any inkling of what it took to run a business or a government.

At first, the government sent a bureaucrat to his father's company to have meetings with his father and Carlos. These meetings were necessary, they were told, to ensure the workers were adequately protected and safety standards were being met. In truth, the government didn't give a rat's ass about worker safety, worker health, worker pay, or worker anything. The real purpose of these meetings was to learn how much the government could squeeze the business.

The concept that a business needs profits or there's no point in being in business seemed alien to the bureaucrat. Carlos and his father repeatedly told this simpleton that without profit they would need to shut down. Then there would be no jobs for the workers. Then the government would need to take care of the laid off workers, which would mean the government would need to squeeze more businesses harder than they squeezed them now. Eventually this demolition of profit would ruin the country, the people would revolt and the army sergeant and the bus driver would be run out of power and hanged.

None of the protestations of Carlos and his father were heeded. Each month a new decree was issued. More workers needed to be hired. Prices paid for raw materials needed to be increased. Prices received for finished goods needed to be reduced. Workers couldn't work eight hour days. Six hour days were better. Workers needed more paid vacation days. Month by month the profits disappeared until there were none. Carlo's father closed the plant and returned with his wife to Spain. Carlos stayed in Venezuela for another six months but then left for America. He decided he would watch the collapse of his native country from afar with the idea that he might possibly return if the sergeant and the bus driver were routed from power.

America was reported to be a paradise for lawyers. Carlos spoke excellent English, had no trouble passing the New York bar, and had no trouble getting a job with a prestigious New York law firm. But, increasingly Carlos saw America's paradise for lawyers becoming a paradise lost. He noticed the intrusive tentacles of socialism slowly strangling the American economy and the early parallels to the Venezuelan calamity disillusioned him. What gave Carlos the greatest difficulty was witnessing the rationalization away of ethics. Carlos was ethical. He didn't like to double bill his hours. He didn't like misrepresenting and telling half truths or concealing facts he had a duty to disclose, nor did he like to represent certain clients who were using unethical means to undermine or smear another party.

He felt the attraction of music in his heart and yearned for the tug of a guitar's strings against his fingers. Since his earliest childhood Carlos cultivated a natural love of music. As he matured he developed a passion for it. He'd made good money in Venezuela and as a New York lawyer, but he walked away from all of it. He didn't mind living a simple life as long as he could play his music and enjoy each day of life as it came to him. Being descended from a substantial European family he was by no means poor; but when he realized his choice was music combined with poverty, if it came to that, or corporate and civil law without his music, Carlos chose music. He became an accomplished guitarist. He grew a pony tail and played in bands. He swung his hair wildly when he played his electric Fender Telecaster guitar in a heavy metal band. He made virtual love to his Telecaster when he jammed on stage with his rock band, and he crooned soft melodies and strummed his acoustic guitar to patrons of fine restaurants. Carlos and his guitars were in constant demand by the time he reached thirty. Linda was not the first woman who sought to bridle this stallion of a man.

Carlos arrived wearing a white linen shirt opened three buttons down. His pants were casual blue slacks, tied in front like sweat pants are tied. No buttons and no zipper. And he brought a bouquet of long stem red roses. "Good move, Carlos," said Linda with a cherry wide mouthed smile. "Roses signal to a woman that a man is interested in more than filling his stomach. Is that a good assumption, Carlos?" Linda's eyes finished their appetizer of roses shortly after they saw them. Now they slipped away to feast upon Carlos' massive chest.

"You are a very perceptive woman, Miss Linda," said Carlos flashing a mischievous smile. "My hunger is in my heart not in my stomach. And I believe you are the only woman in this world who can satisfy it." As he spoke those flattering words he pulled her to him with his free arm lifting her bosom slightly while pressing it against him.

"Oh, Carlos, you are quite the charmer, aren't you? I'll bet you say that to all the girls," Linda teased. His words had made her blush. She loved his hint of impending intimacy. She loved feeling her chest squeezed against his. He was melting her heart. Her urges were already firing. She couldn't wait to put her hands on the baritone chest that was pressed against her. She could spend hours rubbing that chest and playing her hands all over it. Just seeing it bursting out of his shirt for the first time stimulated her. She thought about touching it right then and there before leading him in from her doorway. She knew once she touched it there could be no stopping.

She imagined her hands fixed upon it until she was ready to lower them to his manliness. She remembered what she told herself earlier about preparation. This was a man a woman should try to keep and not rush him into the sack like all she cared for was his marvelous body. But from her first sight of his championship chest her thoughts fixated on his body and her body, naked together; her hands on his chest and then on all of him. 'My hands, you are in for a wonderful treat. Yes, dear hands, I will let you run wild over him. Yes, you will first fondle that beautiful chest and then his cock. You will help me discover if it's as magnificent as I imagine it to be. Yes, these are delicious thoughts I am having, but I must let him approach sex first. He may not react well to a woman who is aggressive. But, maybe he already made his first move with that squeeze? No, he was just being grateful for the invitation to spend the weekend. Keep your mind on dinner. Keep your hands to yourself for now.'

She compartmentalized her feelings. 'He will be here for the whole weekend,' she told herself. 'He must not get the impression that I'm an easy slut. I'm sure he's known plenty of those. Best you feed him first and have some conversation, then see where that leads. And you, Miss Passion, I feel you rising in my chest. I know you are there. Just wait. Be patient. We'll have time.' She gathered herself together.

"You're right on time Carlos, I like that. Welcome to my home." she said as she lightly pressed her body against his, returning his welcoming hug with one of her own. She made sure her neck brushed against his. She had strategically dabbed a midnight gardenia perfume on her neck. Her scent would stay with him all through dinner and play on his mind until they lay naked in her bed. "Come and sit a while. I have a dinner prepared. All I need to do is place the tenderloins under the broiler for a few minutes and then everything will be ready."

She showed Carlos to a huge manly leather chair. It was a deep luxurious piece fit for a king. It swallowed everyone who sat in it and totally relaxed their bodies. Carlos accepted the comfort of the chair, let his head fall back upon its upper back support and closed his eyes in comfort. He observed that Linda was a woman who knew how to appreciate a man. He loved her artwork choices. There were some original oils selected from promising new artists. And there were museum prints of Van Gogh, Monet and Michelangelo. He recognized the prints. They were relaxing country scenes that he first saw as a young boy when his mother took him to the Prado in Madrid. They fired his imagination then about all things that were possible in life and they fired his imagination now, but now they fired his thoughts in a more comforting and appreciating way than they did when he was a boy.

Her music selection softly played the Si mi Chiamano aria to Rodolpho from Puccini's La Boheme. 'This magnificent beautiful woman has excellent tastes,' thought Carlos. 'She is introducing herself to me without words because words can never convey feeling as well as music and art. She is using music and art to give her feelings to me and she is doing it softly and subtlety. I like her. I want to make love with her and I want to love her like she's never known love making before. She will appreciate beautiful love making. She will appreciate love making with feeling and passion being exchanged.

'We will make beautiful love together. But I must not rush her. *Festina Lente*, Carlos, *Festina Lente.* You are a guest in her home and tonight you will also be a guest in her womanhood's place. Be patient and treat her gently. Be deliberate. She wants to make love. That message is written in her eyes. Be responsive and quick to appreciate what she is offering, but be slowly deliberate. Take your time with her. Make her believe that this is her greatest love, her only love. Remove her inhibitions. Release them tenderly one at a time. And love her. And love her long. Above all else fall in love with her. That way you will both enjoy it more and everything will be easier.'

CHAPTER TWELVE

BALD EAGLE

It was two in the morning. The tourists had packed it in, but the Bald Eagle Bar was still open. It was usually the last place in Ouray to close and a few of the die hard local drinkers were still there, barely sitting on their stools, sipping lightly on their whiskey, and getting totally hammered. Tonight one stool was occupied by one of the waitresses who had checked out an hour ago. She stayed and just stared at her reflection in the huge silver flecked mirror behind the bar. She slowly sipped a light beer.

Fat Sam, the bartender, had an eye for her. She became a local three years ago and she was a beauty. There wasn't a man in the town who didn't want her in his bed. Her natural red hair and light freckles gave her an easy welcoming look. And that figure of hers! What man wouldn't die for the chance to hold her naked body next to him? She exuded femininity, a true femme ala femme, a die for babe who made a man's tongue drop to the floor when he looked at her.

Sam couldn't figure why she settled down with Gibby over a year before. The guy was distant and unsociable. His personality was worse than a pissed off mule. He chewed the vilest of tobaccos and spit it everywhere including onto the floor of the Bald Eagle. Sam thought better of taking a swing at Gibby. He knew Gibby would get the best of it even if Sam landed the first punch. Most locals considered Gibby a downright nasty mean hearted son of a bitch ass hard bastard who'd just as soon spit on you or shoot you as say hello to you. But here was JoAnne, the most beautiful female within at least a hundred miles, sitting and sipping. This was getting to be her regular routine and that bothered Sam. By his logic, no piece of prime female ass should waste itself sitting and mooning over any guy. And for her to be mooning over Gibby was downright sinful and wasteful. He just couldn't stand it.

"Jo, look what you're doing to yourself, and for what? I see you in here every night now and you keep saying you're trying to get over him. Well, it's time you did something about it. You're too much of a woman to waste yourself pining away over him." He appealed to her sense of pride.

"We've been through this before Sam. I told you to mind your own business," she snapped. She didn't want male logic to interfere with the way she was feeling. It was a process she needed to work through on her own.

"Yeah, I heard you the first ten times, but look at yourself. Just take a good look. You're getting bags under your eyes. Your eyes are all red. You're crying yourself to sleep nights, ain't you?" A tone of empathetic pity was in his voice.

"Well, what if I am. It's my business Sam," shot back Jo Anne.

"Well, I'm making it my business too Jo. I write the paychecks around here. This is my place and I need my help looking happy and smiling. I can't have customers thinking I'm abusing you back in the kitchen or out in the barn in back."

"I know you wish you could. Just don't even think it, Sam," she warned.

"What the hell is so special about him Jo? He's always abused you one way or another. He threw you out. He told you he never wanted to see you again. What more do you need to know, Jo? The guy is an asshole. He's always been an asshole and he'll always be an asshole." Sam reached over the bar and put a big right hand on her shoulder as if that might snap her out of her funk.

"Don't Sam. I just need time to figure this out," she pleaded.

Sam could tell nothing was going to work unless Jo figured things out for herself, and the thought came to him that maybe Gibby wanted her to do just that. He decided to plow new ground about the subject of Jo's love life. "Tell old Sammy, Jo. What made you want to get involved with that shithead pussy whipped huckster in the first place?"

"I was never involved with him. It was just that one time and Gibby just happened to walk in on us. Never involved, Sam. I just got lonely with Gibby gone so much. I couldn't stand it. Sometimes a girl gets the itch, just like a man does. I needed a scratch on my itch is all it was. I picked him because he's safe, being married with kids and all. I knew he'd never be able to come after me afterwards is all. Sam, I just needed to be fucked is all and he was convenient is all. There ain't nothing more to it. Nothing!"

"Okay. I get it. But what made you fall so hard for Gibby in the first place?"

"Oh Sam, don't get me going." She shook her head as a trance formed in her eyes. She was thinking of her times with Gibby. She held up a straight arm to Sam trying to make him stop asking questions.

"Jo, it'd be good for you if you could talk about it. Otherwise your soul is going to ache and that's not healthy. Come on, talk. I'll listen and whatever you tell me stays right here with old Sam."

Jo took another sip and stared at her reflection in the mirror. Sam was right. She looked like shit. She realized Sam was trying to help her. It was time to open up to him.

"Okay Sam, here's how it is," Jo said haltingly as she fought back her tears. "I'm a girl like a wild mare, see. I'm like one of those wild ones that must be chased down by a stallion and bitten on my neck until I bleed a little. I need a man who puts me in my place and dominates me and hurts me just a little, like Gibby does to me. That way, I know he wants me, Sam; because he's showing me that he wants to keep me in line. That's the understanding he and I had, see. We'd agreed we'd be faithful to each other as long as we lived together. There'd be nobody else for either of us. We agreed to that. But that was before I realized he'd go away for as long as he did and as often as he did.

"I just got to where I resented him being gone. And, damn it, Sam, I just needed to be fucked, is all. It's like how a wild mare needs it when she has the itch. I'm an animal too, you know. I'm young and I like it with a stick in me. What else can I say about it? When you cut to the chase of it I have needs too, Sam. I need to feel it inside me every once in a while. But now I'm confused. I broke my promise to him. I cheated. I never complained to him about being away. I just cheated is what I did." Jo's eyes teared and the tears began running down her cheeks.

"There, there, pretty girl." Sam handed her a huge man sized handkerchief. She accepted it without hesitation and began wiping her eyes and blowing her nose. Then she broke out into an uninhibited bawl.

Bawling like a school girl who just skinned her knees on the playground, Jo blurted out in halting words between her sobs, "What can I say, Sam. I love him. I love him with my whole heart. He's my man, he's the only man for me, and I fucked it all up because I'm just a dumb fucked up cunt. I didn't know how much I loved him until now that he's gone."

Sam had seen this sort of thing before. It was a lovers' spat blown way out of all proportion because egos got bruised and pride got stepped on. It was time for his forty five years of accumulated wisdom to assert itself. "Jo, you listen to old Sam now, and dry up those pretty green peepers. Your make up is running all over the place. Soon you'll have a black mascara puddle on my wood floor and I don't want that." Jo obediently wiped her eyes and performed a hearty nose blow before her eyes met Sam's. "Now, based on what I know about men folk and based on what I know about that asshole Gibby fellow, all of this is just his way of telling you he loves you."

"But he left me," Jo screamed and pounded her fist on the bar. "He fucking left me, Sam," she screamed. "He was never supposed to do that!"

"Well, now, just hold your horses, Jo. Did he really leave you like he went away out of town to parts unknown, huh?"

"He might as well have done that."

"Now just wait a minute, girl. Everybody in town that knows what's the goings on around her knows he's camped out up at the old Dead Mule Mine. Now if he really wanted to get away from you don't you think he'd have gone off and moved to Aspen or over to Utah or New Mexico, huh? And don't you think he'd have taken up with another woman if he really wanted to leave you, huh?" Sam's eyebrows rose. His question was a good one.

"Well, maybe he's got another woman by now." Jo was breathing with halting sniffles now as if she was starting to hope against hope that Gibby still held a flame for her.

"Oh, come on girl, be serious. What woman in her right mind is going to go risk her life hiking way up to over twelve thousand feet with loose shale rock and cougars up there to be with an asshole like Gibby? There's no other woman up there with him. I guarantee it. What woman would even think of going up there?" Sam shook his head to dispel the possibility of another woman living at the Dead Mule.

Jo was starting to get Sam's point. "No woman would go up there unless she really loved that no good asshole son of a bitch, would she, Sam?"

"Nope, she'd have to really love that asshole to do that. That's the only kind of woman that would do that. She'd have to be the only woman in the world who could possibly be stupid and ornery enough to love that one particular no-good asshole son of a bitch out of all the no-good son of a bitch men in the entire world. She'd have to be a woman who knew she was a one man only woman. She'd have to be that kind of woman wouldn't she?"

Jo got Sam's reasoning. "Sam, do you really believe that if I went up there to that mountain top to the old Dead Mule Mine, that Gibby would take me back, that he'd forgive me? Is that what you are trying to tell me?"

"That I can not guarantee, Jo, he's the crustiest, nastiest, meanest son of a bitch I ever knew. But I can tell you this much. That time when he threw you out and sold the cabin and took his things up to the Dead Mule he came back here to sell his truck. But after he sold his truck he stopped in here for a shot of whiskey. Now he knew you worked here, didn't he?" He nodded his massive head in his wise knowing bartender kind of way.

"Yeah, he knew that. He knows everything about me. He knows me inside and out."

Jo wiped away a tear. Sam could see by the way she wiggled her ass back and forth on the bar stool and by the glimmer of a twinkle in her eye that her spirits were starting to lift. The Jo he knew, the perky red head that turned men's heads, was coming back to her senses.

"Well, he could have gone to any one of a half dozen other watering holes, couldn't he?" Sam pursed his lips as he nodded his head, as if he was a detective having an 'ah ha!' moment.

"Yeah, I guess so," she sniffled.

"But he came here, to the Bald Eagle. Now, old Sam noticed him looking around real good when he was here, but you weren't here then. Gibby then shot back a whiskey and slapped his glass down on the bar, but before he left he said something to me." Sam's eyes twinkled.

"What did he say, Sam?" Jo's eyes lifted, displaying a flicker of hope.

"He said, 'Sam, you'll need to look after Jo and make sure nobody gets it in his head to hurt her. You do that, Sam." Those were his exact words, Jo. Now, no man who doesn't give a shit about a woman tells another man to look after her, now does he?" Sam shrugged his shoulders.

No, I guess he doesn't. He really cared about me, didn't he Sam? Do you think he still cares about me?"

"Well, Jo. I was in the service just like Gibby was in the service and we took oaths. And oaths mean something to guys like that no good asshole son of a bitch Gibby and myself." For the first time Jo's ears smarted when she heard Sam calling Gibby names. Suddenly she felt like she had a duty to protect Gibby's honor, but Sam continued. He had one more point to make.

"So, just because you broke your oath to him that does not mean that he would ever break his oath to you, Jo. Think about it Jo. What you did tore the guts right out of him." Sam's eyes pierced into hers to drive home his point. Suddenly it struck Jo that loyalty and fidelity meant everything to a man like Gibby.

"He still loves me, doesn't he Sam?" For the first time in a long time Jo's eyes were hopeful. She was letting her true heart show itself. She was a one man woman.

"Woman!" Sam's voice bellowed throughout the bar room. The few late night drunks slowly lifted their heads to see what the ruckus was about. "There's only one way to know if that man still loves you."

Jo got it. She slipped off her bar stool, shoved her half empty glass toward Sam as she straightened herself upright. Suddenly she was a woman on a mission. "Sam, I'm going to be gone for a while. I just want you to know where I'm at. I'm going to hike up to the Dead Mule Mine to get my man back." Then she started crying all over again. As she walked out the bar she started babbling, "I'm coming for you Gibby. I'm coming for you. I've been a real asshole and I'm sorry. I'll be a good woman for you, you nasty son of a bitch; and you'd better never throw me out again!"

CHAPTER FOURTEEN

RAINED OUT

The deluge came during the first inning. It was getting late and cold. The second game of the late night double header was on rain delay. There was no telling when the game might resume. George and Connie got soaked because George forgot to bring raingear or umbrellas. George was just being George. He never took precautions about anything. He lived recklessly like the way he traded stocks. He quaffed six beers during the first game and was too impaired to drive, but he drove anyway. George was the best drunk driver in the city. Connie tolerated it and rode with him on those times. She even helped him steer the car. All she drank when she was out with George was diet sodas. Tonight George annoyed her more than he did most other nights. He slurred his words and screamed profanities at the umpires when close calls went against his home team. Connie didn't care who won a baseball game. She'd have been just as happy in a dentist's chair.

She'd finally had enough. Her own car was in the garage beneath the bank. She told George that she wanted to get her car and go to her own place tonight and sleep in her own bed. After his drinking binge she knew George wouldn't be able to get it up anyway, so what was the point of staying in the same bed with him? Sleeping alone was a better option than smelling

George's body odors and farts all night. She wanted to dry off and change into dry clothes before driving home.

After George dropped her off at the bank's garage entrance she took the elevator to the trust investment floor. She kept an extra skirt, blouse and bag of undergarments hanging in the woman's clothes closet. She was always prepared for those just in case times. When she got off the elevator she noticed light steaming into the hallway from the research department. 'Likely the night cleaning people forgot to turn out the lights,' she reasoned. As she gathered her emergency clothing stash from the closet she was struck by a voyeuristic thought. 'I'll go in there and change right out in the open, in the middle of the research floor. I'll feel naughty. I'll pretend every man in research is staring at my naked body.'

When she walked into research she was stunned. Paul was sitting there working at 8:30pm. He had not gone home. There were companies' quarterly financial reports spread all over his desk. He was diligently recording financial statement data with a pencil onto a huge elongated spread sheet he'd taped together. It was eight feet long and it spilled onto the floor. He was working intensely, completely oblivious to her presence. Suddenly the difference between George and Paul struck Connie like a lightning bolt. Paul was an intellectual and a workaholic. He possessed a rabid curiosity for detail and facts. He was diligent, meticulous, and relentless. He was not a blowhard flying by the seat of his pants jerk like George. He was a lot like her father.

The comparison between George and Paul this night was glaringly obvious. George was a drunken lush who was never going to amount to anything. Eventually the bank would replace George and he'd end up being a bar tender or a cab driver or retail clerk. 'E gads, what have I been doing wasting my time with George?' was the first thought that flashed through her mind. Then her thoughts quickly shifted to Paul.

'What I want in a man is sitting right here in front of me! I'm standing right across the room from him. He's perfect, he's just like Daddy! No, better! He's better looking than Daddy! He'd make the perfect husband for me. Could I get him interested? He probably knows my slutty reputation. Does he even want a woman? Just keep your cool. Everything is perfect. It's only the two of us. Don't startle him. Be warm and caring toward him and start talking to him.' Connie softly cleared her throat to let Paul know someone was in the same room with him.

Paul looked slightly up and from side to side before he visually acquired her. Then his eyes squinted as they changed focus from his spread sheet to the unexpected woman in the room. He realized she was dripping wet but couldn't make out who she was at first. Paul was nearsighted and he worked with his glasses off. He'd never seen Connie in soaking wet clothes before.

She wore no bra and her pink button nipples showed through her wet white blouse. George told Connie that he wanted her to stay braless no matter where they went. Braless female chests expedited George's tit squeezing. Months before George had told her that bras were unnecessary obstacles to foreplay. She had since complied. She did anything and everything to keep George happy. She needed those high marks on her performance review to get into her MBA program. But now standing across the room from Paul with her nipples showing beneath a clinging white blouse she suddenly felt embarrassed by her chosen path to advancement. She decided she'd better take control of the situation by speaking first.

"Paul, what are you doing here so late at night?" Connie's challenge had the desired effect. Paul's eyes had momentarily gazed upon her nipples, but now they lifted to her eyes. He looked like a child caught with his hand in a cookie jar. His eyes showed he felt guilt by being discovered working late hours by the bank's number one party girl.

"Well, I'm obviously working," Paul replied with a budding easy smile. He realized it was Connie when he heard her voice "The bigger question, I would ask, is what are *you* doing here? You look a little wet."

"I was just going to change my clothes," she blurted out haltingly. 'Rats,' she thought. 'He's taken my lame initiative away from me, and he did it just like that. Damn it! He's exactly like Daddy.'

"In *here?*" Paul was quick witted. He knew he stole the march on her. Her position was ridiculous and they both knew it. He pressed his advantage and wasn't about to let go. "You came in *here* to change your clothes?"

'Oh, he's just like Daddy,' she thought. 'I'm screwed. There's no use pretending. I might as well get it over with.'

"Well, yes, in here. You see I wanted to have a little freedom to move around and I wanted to feel uninhibited and free as a bird for a few moments. It's this thing I have about myself. I'm sorry to bother you. I'll go to the ladies' room and change."

'Shit,' she thought. 'Now I'm sure he believes I'm a total airhead.'

"No need," Paul chuckled. "Don't let me stop you from doing whatever it is that you feel the need to do. I'll just keep my head down in these numbers. I promise not to look."

'Double shit,' Connie's thoughts sank. 'Why couldn't he ask if he could watch me? He's too much like Daddy! Well, if he's that much like Daddy then I'd better work him like I've seen Mommy work Daddy. I know more about his personality than he could imagine!' She approached Paul's desk and stood in front of him. She was still dripping water on the floor. He couldn't help but notice her move. He looked up at her again. This time his look had more of a personal interest about it. Paul's matter of fact dismissive facial expression had disappeared. His new look emboldened her.

"Do you mind if I walk around behind you and change behind your back?' she teased as she canted her hips slightly. She noticed his glance at her hips.

"No, go ahead." Paul's tone was dismissive, but his authoritativeness was gone.

Connie went behind Paul's desk and changed her clothes. When she finished she took a few quiet steps closer to the back of Paul's chair. She wore her hair straight and below shoulder length. It still held a lot of moisture. She leaned her head back then tossed it violently forward. Her move had the desired effect. Her hair flew forward. A few droplets of water sprinkled over Paul and onto his work papers. He reacted, as she had hoped, but ever so slowly. His head lifted mechanically from his work. He did not turn around. There was a moment of silence. His reaction, his demeanor, his deliberate style were all exactly like her father's. It was uncanny.

"Are you finished back there?" Paul inquired nonchalantly. There was a bit of tease in his voice this time.

"Yes. Thank you for your tolerance of my silly moment. I'll be leaving now."

Connie's reply sounded hopeful. She detected his teasing tone. She hoped Paul would ask her to stay.

"Goodnight," This time Paul's clipped reply betrayed no emotion whatsoever.

She couldn't stand it. Paul was quietly controlling her the same way her father did. The only way she could make her feelings known to her father was to come right out and tell him. But Paul was not her father so she couldn't be direct. She remembered how her mother opened conversations with her father. 'It must have been hard for mother,' she reflected. 'Daddy was such a business nerd and mother was like a carefree butterfly. Now, how did Mother get Daddy to pull his head out of his work,' she asked herself. She kept her parents' interactions in mind as she walked past Paul's desk to leave the research room. Suddenly she whirled around and faced Paul. Her movement brought his head up. He was looking at her again. She caught his eyes studying her windswept wet hair in her face. She looked like a magazine cover model when she flipped her wet hair forward like that. Her gambit worked. Silently she thanked her mother for her education in women's ways. It was an education a girl didn't get in school.

"Paul. What's the matter with you?" Her direct assault was right out of Mother's playbook and it worked brilliantly.

"What do you mean?" Paul was shocked. Here was his new understudy intimating there was something wrong with him. He was a man of cold stone and numbers, but now he felt like putty in her hands. He gave her the frightful look of a boy about to be punished because he forgot to take out the trash.

'God bless you, Mother!' Connie thought. 'We women have our ways with these dull beasts, don't we?' Connie was very pleased with herself and the methods she learned by watching Mother's moves on Father. Mother could make Daddy do anything. Mother held Daddy in the palm of her hand and he never even suspected it. Her dad could wheel and deal with the best wheeler dealers from all over the world, but he more than met his match with Mother.

Connie moved in for the kill. She walked back to Paul's desk and put her hands on it. Then she leaned forward. She invaded his personal space by placing her gorgeous face not more than two feet away from his startled eyebrows. Drops from her still wet hair fell on his precious papers. She had him reeling. If he'd been standing he would have been back on his heels.

"What I mean is you're always working. You never take any time away from the office to enjoy yourself. You're missing out on life, Paul." A woman couldn't be more direct than that. Most men would jump at her initiation. She was not expecting to hear what she heard next.

"I don't expect you to understand this, Connie, but I was married before. I have a daughter. I've been through a very difficult divorce and my ex does her very best to keep me from seeing our daughter. I'm not interested in getting involved with anyone because I don't want anything or anyone to come between me and my daughter." His eyes warned her to back off.

"What makes you think a woman would want to come between you and your daughter," her eyes shot back a questioning look. What if there's a woman who would love to include your daughter in her relationship with you? Wouldn't you want to explore that possibility? What I mean is you might be doing your daughter a favor if you allowed her to be exposed to another woman besides her mother. Have you ever looked at things that way?" Her eyes searched his to see if he would consider what she asked.

"Look, it's not that easy. You don't understand my ex. If she doesn't approve of what I do with my little girl she won't even let me see her again."

"But the courts don't allow that kind of stuff anymore. It's really child abuse." Connie was taken aback. Paul's situation with his ex presented a real impasse.

"Like I said, you don't understand my ex. She doesn't give a hoot what the courts say. If her back gets up she'd take a contempt citation before she'd let me see my kid. Then she'd leave the state and run and hide."

"Sounds like she's just nuts," Connie chided in mock disbelief.

"Ah, now you're getting it," Paul exhaled.

"Yes she is nuts. And I think she's so nuts that she might even harm my daughter if she felt I was giving my daughter an unhealthy environment. My ex believes she's the only judge that matters here. It's kind of like the way female bears get with their cubs. Reason doesn't matter. Now can you understand how things are?" The forward shrug of his shoulders telegraphed he wanted her to back off.

"Yes. I get it," she answered. But she wasn't about to give up.

"I've heard of those situations where a woman uses her child to indirectly control her ex husband. Those women like to have their cake and eat it too. My own theory on them is they never wanted to get divorced in the first place. They just use divorce court to throw temper tantrums. But there are ways to deal with them. I'd like to help you if you'll let me. Would you be willing to listen to some suggestions?"

"Yeah, sure, I'd be willing to try anything." His shoulders relaxed when he realized Connie was one determined woman. "Not so much for myself, understand, but for little Margaret. I agree the way my ex keeps her cloistered isn't healthy for her. And what's happening to her perception of me is terrible. I can tell she only thinks of me as a cash machine that takes her to fast food joints and amusement parks. That's no way for a little girl to think about her father. It's horrible. It's going to give her a warped view of men and life in general."

"Tell you what, Paul. My parents have a lake house in the Adirondacks. Why don't we plan a long weekend up there with your daughter? I'll invite some other couples that have kids and we'll let her gain some new friends. How does that sound? I'll arrange the whole thing."

"It sounds very generous, Connie; but on those rare chances when I do get to see Margaret I don't want to be committed to someone else. And I don't want to have to tell a woman that I can't be with her because I might miss a chance to see my daughter."

"That's okay Paul. You won't feel any pressure from me, I promise. I'd just like to offer this as a friend. I understand you are in a holding pattern. When we do the weekend you bring Margaret in your car and if you need to leave with her, you'll just take her home. We shouldn't expect much from this at first. Let's just view it as an experiment."

"I don't know how I can thank you, Connie." Now Paul's whole demeanor changed. He looked at Connie as if he was seeing a saint.

"Well, maybe when we're up at the lake you can explain what it is that has you sitting here glued to your desk at nights? It must be fascinating." Connie had more in mind than financial statements, but she held her tongue. Paul was like her dad. She'd need to lead him where she wanted him to go, much like Mother led Father.

"Okay. Yes, I'm seeing some fascinating stuff. After I do more research I'll know if I can share it."

"Secret kind of stuff?"

"Maybe, I have a ways to go before I can be sure."

"But you'll tell me?"

"I don't know yet. It's sensitive."

"But would you tell me if you saw something that affected my money?"

"I'll do my best for you. That's all I can say."

"Okay, deal." Connie held her hand out for a handshake and Paul accepted. In her imaginative mind a deal was made, and a plan was laid.

CHAPTER FIFTEEN

THE SILHOUETTE

Sheila and CC were alone in their apartment loft. It was early summer. The two women sat looking out their west window at the sunset over the Rockies. The sun's bright yellow fire ball was slowly sinking behind the peaks. Gradually the sky turned from high azure blue to paler blue. And the stratus clouds that laced the sky were starting to show belly blush colors of crimson and orange. Off below the distant horizon a solitary hawk winged northward, casting its silent silhouette shadow along the hogback formations along the foothills. It was looking to put down for the night as many raptors did on that flyway. In the morning it would catch a mountain thermal and soar up to twenty thousand feet; then it would tuck its wings and drift glide all the way to Wyoming. The two women were silent, each watching the majestic bird of prey, each respecting the others' solitude.

Sheila had accomplished a great deal in her first three weeks at Bear and Otter.

The ballistic missile intercept program was an easy task for her. She first studied every conceivable input variable. She deconstructed the equations for every threat rocket's performance, and then she applied all the telemetry programming for latitude, longitude, magnetic field variance, Coriolis Effect, Earth's precession, atmospheric data, and hundreds of additional variables into a matrix that could be quickly solved by a super fast calculation supercomputer. Then she did something out of the box and wrote the equations for her concept. She then programmed her solution and ran thousands of beta tests on it. The results were astounding. She successfully increased the probability of interception of the threat rocket before it reached its apogee from 88 percent to 99.975 percent. She still wasn't satisfied with her result. She was shooting for 99.999 percent success.

"Why do you drive yourself so hard?" CC was the first to break the silence.

"It's part perfection and part economics," explained Sheila. Perfection means we've identified all the unknowns and modeled them. That's advancing physics. If we get to ninety nine and three nines it means an enemy needs to put up one hundred thousand rockets to have a one hundred per cent likelihood of getting one through. No nation can afford to build that many rockets."

"And the economics?"

"That's more subjective. Assume that one rocket hits New York and kills off ten million people, but that ten million people represent five trillion dollars of annual economic loss. If that happens it would take ten years for the economy to fully recover to where it was before the hit. That's roughly twenty five trillion dollars of economic loss. That one hit alone would have untold ripple effects and the indirect losses would be two to five times greater than the direct loss. So an enemy could figure that shooting off a hundred million dollar rocket to get potentially fifty trillion dollars of economic loss is a great trade off."

"But the enemy would need to build out a rocket program."

"They've already done that," Sheila shot a 'where have you been' look to CC.

"Yeah, right," CC caught the look and her response sounded dejected.

"But, that's where math comes into it. You see, it's the likelihood of success that an enemy must calculate and that has to be weighed against the likelihood of failure, because this country will definitely retaliate after a strike and we have the most firepower. So, it's no longer a question of building up more rockets, but it's about knocking them down before they reach apogee, or if they do reach apogee, we knock them down before they get over the country to burst out of flight and reenter. Now, if I can get the intercept probability near 100 percent, then we're not going to have a nuclear threat. Get it?"

"Yeah, I think so. What drives you like this, Sheila?"

"Oh, I guess it's because life is more important to me than money or anything else. I'd hate to think some little boy would get burned to a crisp and never know what it feels like to play pitch and catch with his dad, or for a young girl to never grow up or know what it feels like to get laid."

"And you see our country as freedom and liberty's best chance, right?"

"Well yes, of course. And we're lucky to still be having that chance. There's been a systematic effort to secretly install a global communist government controlled by the world's central bankers ever since Woodrow Wilson. I believe that's what the two world wars were all about. They both made the country more indebted to the bankers. The wars since then have just made the indebtedness worse. The more debts we have, the fewer freedoms we have, the less individual property rights we have. Whenever a genuine freedom loving leader stood up against the march of world communism he was pushed aside, like General Macarthur; or he was murdered, like President Kennedy."

"I didn't know you admired Macarthur."

"He understood the issue. If left to lead he would have conquered China and they would now be just another vassal state instead of a world rival. But the bankers, through Truman, didn't want a strong controlling nation. They wanted a muddle mess with encroaching communism. We live with that muddle mess today in the Progressive Socialist movement. It's just a nice sounding mush word for creeping communism."

"And this sort of thinking is why you took on this project?"

"You bet it is. Without freedom there is slavery. The bankers and their communist facilitators want the whole world enslaved. I don't. I can't imagine a dull anathema of a world like that. It makes me want to puke. I took this job in a heartbeat."

"That's sweet, Sheila. I'm glad you're on our side. How did you manage to get your probability to jump up to 99.975 percent? And how did you do it so quickly?"

"Are you cleared for this CC?"

"I think we can speak in generalities and hypothetical. If you showed me your equations I'd just glaze over. I'd never understand that stuff in a million years; I can't even balance a checkbook."

"Okay then, in general this is how I did it. I began by thinking outside the box. Let's say I have a huge array with five thousand variables. Now, if I recomputed each variable before I gave a command to the rocket's targeting gyros that would take lots of computer memory and lots of time. Remember, these rockets are going fast. Combined velocity gets upwards of fifty thousand miles per hour at altitude. So, to speed up the calculations I created some sampling equations to do dynamic sampling of the variables while the rockets are in flight. The program that runs the equations I call my loop sling. It will randomly sample the variables continuously and run a feedback loop to the main flight equations without causing self cancelling instructions to the thrusters and the gyros. It makes the rocket fly smoother and it cuts each cycle's computation time by eighty three percent."

"What does that mean?"

"Well, for a rocket aloft it means the mid course corrections come every seventeen microseconds instead of every hundred microseconds."

"What's the significance of that?"

"Well, at the speed of these birds aloft it means a smoother correction takes place every half mile of flight instead of a jerky one every three miles of flight. It means the difference between a hit and a miss."

"Because?"

"Once you miss by three miles, you can't make it up. The speeds are too great, but a half mile is more doable. If the rocket is ahead of track it slows a little. If it's behind track the thrusters pour on more juice. Once I get our bird within the intercept envelope its high frequency radar locks onto the target missile. Then we get a kill."

"Oh, okay, but what about your sampling? Won't you miss something and won't that let your rocket get way off course?'

"Possibly, but that's extremely unlikely. I put in another program for that. I call it my wave whip. If any variable randomly sample tests greater than one percent out of its expected tracking value, I whip it. That means I go back and retest it constantly and its retested value is continuously reinserted into the flight equations until it returns to normal. It gets whipped back into line so to speak."

"Wow Sheila. You think of everything, don't you?"

"No, not even, CC. It's a scary world out there. A bad actor could bring in a big one on a slow surface boat or low level missile. My program can't do anything about that threat. Also, there's always the possibility that there's an *unknown* unknown. Something out of the blue that no one has ever thought about could affect my equations and I wouldn't know about it until after we saw the effect in real time. And, don't forget, unless we can solve a beta test to 100 percent, there's still a flaw in the work that we are using. It could be in the equations or the programming or the transmission of the instruction to the intercept rockets, or even in the computer memory. There's no such thing as perfection when we have these sorts of speeds and this many variables."

"Sheila, are we going to die? CC chided."

"Yes for sure, but probably not tonight."

"How are you doing with your other project?" CC's question seemed innocuous enough.

Sheila's guard went up. She didn't think CC was supposed to know anything about the drone project, but she thought it best to play along and not let CC know she was told that CC wasn't supposed to know.

"Oh, that's going kind of slow CC."

"What's that even about?"

"It's about designing a system to defeat asymmetric warfare where the enemy uses drones."

"Like what?"

"Like killing everyone who is attending an NFL game by dropping nerve gas or anthrax from a drone, or anything like that. Just use your imagination what could happen using those things."

"Well, how would you stop it?"

"Working on it CC. It's a problem in search of a solution. I have some ideas but they are just ideas right now. I need time to think."

"Okay, rocket girl. I'm going to bed. I'll let you do the deep thinking. Good night."

"Good night, CC." With that Sheila turned again from talking to CC to look at the darkening sky. She wondered about CC. Just what did CC know about her work and why was she asking about the drone program when George Palmer told her that CC wasn't supposed to know anything about it?

Venus, the evening star was brightly shining in the western sky and the first stars were peeking out when Sheila got up from her chair and went to her bedroom. Along the foothills a large female Cooper's hawk glided onto the uppermost branch of a lone cottonwood tree. She would rest there until the morning when the thermal updrafts would waken her. She would again spread her majestic wings and ride the warm rising air until she was high above the earth; then she would tuck her wings and resume gliding the sky on her journey northward.

CHAPTER SIXTEEN

SPANISH GUITAR

"Have you ever considered resuming your law practice in this country, Carlos?" Linda's offhand question revealed her hopes for this budding relationship. She wanted to be able to say to her friends that she was married to a lawyer. She imagined telling them that she married an expatriate guitar player would be a little cumbersome.

"Yes, yes of course I have. In fact I continue to maintain my license with a view to opening my own practice. I expect I'll do that within the next year. I have had my days in the sun with my guitar. I am thinking seriously about settling down with the right woman and beginning a family." Carlos nodded his head. As he gave a reassuring smile to Linda he widely opened his eyes expecting she would swoon into their deep caramel colored pools.

The oven's scent of broiled tenderloin lingered in the dining room and summoned Linda's desires to feast on the Adonis before her. Her sex moistened as she studied Carlos closely. She loved the way he unhurriedly chewed his tenderloin. He occasionally licked his lips to savor the juices of the rarely cooked meat; and his tongue's licking motions were very sensual. She imagined where the two of them would be in a short while and what else his sensuous tongue might care to savor.

"Would you like to take your desert now, Carlos? I've prepared a lemon meringue pie for us." Linda asked. Her voice tone intimated hope that Carlos might suggest a different desert choice.

"Perhaps we could enjoy your pie later, Miss Linda?" Perhaps it is time that we need to first explore our feelings?" Carlos was attuned to her hopeful tone. "Please allow me to get to know you better. You are my first desert choice." A sincere loving continence appeared on Carlos' face. He sensuously rubbed his lips together.

"You shall have your first choice, my dear sweet Carlos," Linda said as she arose from her chair. She crossed the distance from her end of the table to his. Then she held his head in her hands and kissed his lips. "I've waited and dreamed of this moment. Come with me." Linda took Carlos's hand and led him to her bedroom.

"Allow me to untie you," Linda requested. Slowly and with gentle hands she removed Carlos's shirt. Her hands were reluctant to leave his massive chest. She felt it breathing, first with a powerful inhale then a slow exhale. She pressed one hand hard into its center and held her head against him next to her hand. Linda liked to take her time with intimacy. "I feel your heartbeat. It pounds hard against my hand. I excite you, don't I?"

"Excite me? Woman, I am like a caged lion and you are like catnip pressed against me. You excite me beyond my mind's ability to control my body. I want you. Oh Jesus in heaven, I can't find words to tell you how much I want you." Carlos held her close with one of his massive arms.

"Let's see if you can even want me more than that," said Linda as she untied his sailor pants. She guided him to sit by the side of her bed and removed his pants. Without another word she placed her hands on his scrotum and placed his penis into her mouth.

Carlos moaned. "You are doing it. I want you more than I can express. Please, come into bed with me."

Linda slipped out of her clothes and lay down beside Carlos. She again rubbed her hands over his chest. Her hand slipped down to his penis. He was fully aroused and ready, but Linda wanted this first time to be memorable. To her way of thinking intercourse was something that should never be rushed. It was more like a loan application where all the disclosures needed to be made and where all the disclosures needed to be verified. She rolled onto her back and placed his hand upon her breast. "Do you like my body, Carlos?"

"Oh yes, oh, Mother of God, yes. I adore your body, Linda. I yearn to savor it, to love it always."

"It pleases you, then? My body is pleasing to you? I can please you as a woman pleases a man?"

"Oh my God, yes Linda. I would love your body all the days of my life if I had the chance. I would be your lover until the day I died."

"Carlos, I am falling in love with you. I believe that some-how I am fated to love you. Tell me, Carlos, how can we know if what we are feeling in this moment is real?"

"The time for words is passing, Linda. This is the time for making love." Carlos stopped talking. He put a finger over Linda's lips to silence her questioning. Then he began to kiss her, and he kissed her everywhere.

'Oh,' she thought, 'he's nibbling my breasts like an elk nibbles the high grasses at the mountain tree line in the warm summer. He is gentle and slow. He doesn't rush foreplay. His lips lift my nipples like the elk tugs at the sweet succulent grass blade before he clips it from its root. Oh, I am feeling a tingle through my entire body from this. My sex is getting wet now.' "Oh, Carlos, that's very good, very sweet," she said as she rubbed her fingers through his curly locks.

"Shhh, enjoy my darling. Allow me to give you pleasure," were Carlos' only words. He enjoyed giving pleasure to a woman.

'Oh, now he's rubbing my tummy and my sides with his massive hands. I feel like a little toy in his hands. I'm feeling pleasure shivers all up and down my spine and all through my skin. I feel my legs trembling. I am warm clay in his hands. He is shaping me, making me ready for his fire. Oh, I love this feeling of anticipation. My brain is turning over and over with warmth I've never known before. I am loved by this man. I feel it. I know now what it means when people say that love is something you feel. I am so wet and slippery. I want him inside me. I want like a shameless animal. I think of nothing else.

'Oh, now he's moving his lips lower. Like an elk he is going into the tree line to taste the long sweet blades that lie by the bases of the trees. Yes, he tastes me there, wrapping his tongue around my grass blade, feeling it. My blade is swelling up now and I feel my earth around my blade swelling up. Something wonderful is happening. I feel his arms over my chest and his fingers upon my nipples, pinching them. His head, his arms and fingers are like cool butter on my body of warm toast. He is melting into me. We are one together; a warm and tasty oneness unites us now. Oh, I am swelling very fast now.' "Carlos, come into me. Come into me now." she urged.

Carlos complied. After a few moments of his rapid thrusts Linda exploded in a torrent of orgasmic juices. She showered his penis in her soaking release and Carlos responded by shooting a torrent of pent up semen into her vulva's uppermost reaches. Neither took precautions for this eventuality, but they didn't care. Both of them knew deep inside their consciousness that their relationship would be a permanent one. They could never explain that sense to any inquisitor or interloper, but they knew it, and they were the only two that mattered. They had each other and they were bonded in love.

After they came together Carlos lay on his side and cradled Linda in one of his massive arms. Then he began to touch her arm and her haunch with his finger tips.

"What are you doing, my love? What sort of game are you playing?" Linda asked.

"I am thinking of you as I compose a little melody in my mind. Your body is like my guitar to my fingers. They are stroking the notes of my mind and tightening and loosening the strings to get the perfect resonance." Carlos continued his after play with his fingers. He seemed deep in thought.

"And, do I play well for you? Is my body adequate for your talents?" Linda asked while kneading his testicles. She liked after play as well.

"You are more than adequate," Carlos assured her. "Your body is like a fine violin. I, a simple guitarist, feel humbled to play it." Carlos kissed her lips. Her response told him there was more fire within her. He hardened and soon entered her again. They made love three times that first evening; and when they awoke they made love again. They realized they had become inseparable.

Linda's father was a manufacturing executive with a Pennsylvania based tool company. Since childhood she heard business talk at the dinner table. She remembered how her mother often looked helplessly across the table at her father. Business has vicious cycles in the capital goods segment of the economy. Orders into her father's company overwhelmed his small operation when times were booming. Then he complained that his margins would be much better if only he had more tool and die men and more equipment. In boom times he needed to pay double overtime to meet orders and his profit margins stayed pretty flat. But he had no choice. If he didn't meet orders his customers would go elsewhere.

In the down cycle times he couldn't get enough orders to keep his bankers happy. They were constantly calling him, dunning him for late payments on his business credit lines. Linda watched her mother's eyes during those times when her father told her they needed to pull money from their savings; even from the money they saved to put Linda through college. Linda remembered one of those times very well. She listened at her parents' bedroom door that night after Mother stoically put up the dishes. Father was trying to find words that would sooth Mother.

"The up cycle will come back. It always does," he said.

But her mother wouldn't be comforted. Mother cried uncontrollably. Linda remembered her mother's only spoken words that night, blurted out between her sobs.

"John, what about our children? It's getting so bad I don't know how I'm going to feed the family. What will happen to our children?"

Linda remembered a special quality about her mother from that recession. Her mother got a grip on her crying time, sucked it up and got a job. The extra money Mother brought in fended off the bankers until the economy picked up and the business recovered. Her father had always loved and adored her mother, but from those days onward he worshipped her. Linda never forgot her mother's example of standing by her man.

Now, once again seated across the long table from Carlos after a month of dating and lovemaking, Linda wondered if she was hearing the real reason why he didn't go back to practicing law. Linda believed there was a latent potential in Carlos that he had kept hidden, even from her. It was time to probe her man and find out from what sort of cloth he was cut.

"Carlos, have you ever considered going back to Venezuela and reopening your family's plastic extrusion plants?" The right side of her mouth twitched a little. It did that when she asked a serious question. It was one of those little tells she had.

Some people noticed it but Linda was unaware that her mouth did that.

Carlos noticed it. He wasn't sure of its significance but he ventured an honest response to her opening bid. "Well, yes of course. I'd love to restore the business. It would uphold my family's honor and put many good people back to work. Venezuela desperately needs to get people working again. The misery there is palatable. And, when it's operating at only half capacity the business makes a great deal of money as well. But, as long as the country's goon squad government holds power there is no possibility for my family's business. Their policies of theft and confiscation make profit impossible."

"But, would you go back, would you reopen the plants and put people back to work if the government was changed?" Linda posed a hypothetical. How much of himself would Carlos reveal?

"Oh, yes of course. In a heartbeat I would go back." Carlos' smile was open, innocent.

"You must realize that the government's hold on power is tenuous." Linda hinted that she knew about conditions in Carlos' country.

"Yes. I watch it with great interest." His eyes shined with a glimmer of hope, signaling that he hoped the government would fall.

"Are you in touch with others who also watch?" Linda scratched through the surface of Carlos' misfortunes. She was approaching the subject of revolution.

"Yes. There are others who have felt the boot of the idiot goons on their necks. We stay loosely in touch, of course."

"So, what prevents you and the others from changing that government?" Linda cut to the chase.

"Well, we have considerable sympathy among the armed forces there. There are also militant opposition factions in the civilian population. We cast about for the key elements we need."

"Which are?" Linda cocked her head as if listening for a signal.

"WE need leadership and money, Miss Linda. Both are needed to effect change," his outstretched hands opened their palms as he barred his soul to her.

"Would you be willing to provide that leadership, Carlos?"

"Yes, of course." Carlos' eyes flamed matching the assertiveness of his answer. The fire of a revolution was in his belly. His spontaneous answer revealed eagerness to fight the tyranny that strangled his country. "I have the right contacts in the country and in Spain. With financial help we could form a government. We could get recognized by the United States, England, and Spain. Then, all of Latin America would follow, then the whole world. The country would arise from its death bed. Oil and prosperity would flow again."

Carlos' reply was music to her bank lender's ears. He hit all the right notes. Linda heard in his reply the concepts of family and business honor, empathy for his fellow man, and profit, glorious profit. Profit was what made bank loan repayments possible. Profit makes employment possible. It makes the world go around. Profit was not some dirty word to Linda. It was an aphrodisiac. Carlos was a dream that comes true so rarely in a woman's life. She realized she could, through her position at BASE, facilitate his dreams and join them to her own. Echoes of her mother's loyalty to her father reverberated through her thoughts. Her mother's help had saved a business. Linda saw the possibility that, with her help, a whole nation might be rescued from ruin.

"If you had the money, Carlos, and if you were able to succeed, what sort of government would you install after you replaced the existing one?"

"Well, I have given this great thought. It must be formed upon the identical principles that the United States was founded upon. It must have honest money and three co-equal branches of government so that a tyrant can not take absolute power ever again." Carlos again hit all the right notes.

"Carlos, suppose I could be instrumental in getting you the money you needed to support your revolution. What role would you be willing to offer me in your new government?"

"Why, Miss Linda, you would be my finance minister or treasury secretary. You would hold the government purse strings." Carlos did not hold back any reservations. He rolled out the red carpet for his potential ally.

"Is that the only role you believe I could play?" Linda teased while pressing her bargaining advantage. Her tongue slid slowly over her upper lip.

"Oh no, my dear sweet Miss Linda, you would also hold another equally important role, should you desire it, of course."

"Which would be what, Carlos?" Linda shifted her hips in her chair. His answer to this question would be the most important of all.

"You would be First Lady of the nation, of course. You would be the Angel of the Nation and you would be my wife. The position would be yours if you wished to have it." Carlos' eyes invited Linda to join him in his cause and his life.

"Yes, Carlos. I do believe I would like to have both of those positions. In fact, I insist that I would have them both. As far as the First Lady position, Carlos, I would also insist that there would be no second lady or any liaisons of an adulterous nature." It was the banker in Linda that sought to nail down all the loan requirements.

"Yes, of course that is understood. But when a man suffers a temporary weakness, surely that would be understandable?"

"I suppose, as long as the weakness is temporary and easily disposed of; and as long as my husband can understand that his woman might also suffer a *temporary* weakness." Linda's eyes flared a cautionary hot blooded tone. It was a look that a man dared not challenge. 'Men must understand their boundaries,' she thought. 'We need this understanding from the outset.

It's all so ridiculously unnecessary anyway. The poor man doesn't yet know the full extent of my passions. He will be so exhausted from the favors of my bed he will never have time or energy for another woman.'

"Linda, you can do this? It is not a small sum we need." Carlos took the discussion from the hypothetical to the real. Having an open credit line with one of the world's largest banks was more than he dared to dream about.

"Yes, Carlos. I can give you your revolution." Her sex moistened as she studied Carlos closely. She dwelled again for a moment on the way he chewed tonight's tenderloin, unhurriedly. He occasionally licked his lips to savor the juices of the rarely cooked meat; and his tongue's licking motions were consistently sensual. She adored the way he performed in bed. She imagined where the two of them would be in a short while and what he would be savoring next. 'Oh, yes, Carlos, yes,' she thought. 'You shall have your revolution and you will savor all of me, always.'

Linda was already mentally on her way to a new life. She had long detested the unpleasant aspects of her role as loan officer. There was nothing she hated more than making threatening calls to poor unfortunate borrowers who, through no fault of their own, had fallen behind on their terms.

She relished the thought of trooping through the jungles of South America next to Carlos, her man, her revolutionary hero. She would spill blood for the cause. She would much prefer toting an AK47 for a just cause to flaunting a Gucci handbag at a store clerk. She even visualized her future titles when introduced in polite circles. She would be known as Mrs. El Presidente, Mrs. Sebastian Carlos de Carmella, and Angel of the Revolution. She would be proud again. She would set an oppressed people free.

She made a mental note to make copies of two documents from files in the bank's cashier's office during her next day at work.

Chapter Seventeen

Out of control

Walter took the general's call on his direct line, the one he should have had his contact use in the first place. By telling a dyslexic mission coordinator to use the bank's toll free line he mistakenly created two possible circumstantial witnesses that could expose his involvement in the conspiracy. He was working on that problem on his own. He didn't dare tell his associates in crime how he planned to handle it. It was bad enough that they would be angry over not getting the map.

This phone call was not going to be pleasant. For the first time since he joined the conspiracy Walter worried. He was risking life without parole if discovered. His associates in this venture all had plausible deniability. He didn't. He felt vulnerable and desperate now. He swallowed hard before he took the call.

"Yes General. I've been expecting your call." He tried to sound upbeat.

"Are you alone?" the general spoke in a matter of fact voice tone.

"Yes." Walter's voice betrayed some trepidation.

"Walter, the one thing I hate in my line of work is a fuck up." Now the General's voice boomed into Walter's ear. "You're a God damned fuck up, Walter. I lost a good man killed on that mountain. I also sent a chopper with five marines up there to look for some God damn fucking map that you say you *think* holds the key to control of our entire government. They were my best men, Walter. They found nothing, Water, *N O T H I NG;* the General first spelled the word and then screamed *"NOTHING!"*

"You fucking dumb son of a bitch. Is your bank as fucked up as this operation was?" The general didn't wait for an answer. His voice seethed with anger. "I don't believe you even know what you're talking about. How much bull shit do you think you can shove up my ass? I can't send career sergeants off on some cock a mammy lark mission again. No way. They'll ask questions. I'm not sticking my sweet neck out for you any more, asshole." The General didn't mince words. His raised voice reflected his elevated blood pressure.

"We've been over this, General. There's only one reason why BASE wants to acquire that little advisory firm. We need to get to that property first, find out what's on it and remove it before BASE gets it." Walter sounded officious and a bit desultory.

"I don't like it when unexpected changes fuck up my mission plans, Walter." The general brushed Walter's redundant explanation aside. "That always tells me somebody held back an important plan input. I *hate* surprises Walter. It's *not good* when I start to feel hate, Walter." the general's voice carried a veiled threat.

"But, you said you were getting the best sniper around. You said he was a guaranteed kill shot. You said———— "Walter's back peddling was cut short. The General was screaming now.

"Don't you give me any shit, you pipsqueek asshole son of a bitch. That was a damn good man. Who knows if he told anybody why he was out there in Colorado? Who the fuck knows? This blown mission is all your fault, asshole. You told me our target was a recluse. You never said he was a crack

Marine Corps sharpshooter. Didn't it occur to you that a guy like that might be tough to kill?" the general's voice tone was that of an angry man with a choke hold on Walter's neck.

"I didn't—"Just as Walter tried to speak the General cut him off.

"Shut up and listen dick wad. We're not going to fuck up any more. I got it figured this asshole we're after now knows about the map. I figure he's got the map on his person and he is on the move. I'm now guessing, Walter. I'm guessing he's going to go back tracking. He's going to try to find the person he got it from. That, or else he's going to try to identify what area of the world that map is a picture of and he's probably going to go there.

"Now you think *real hard* with that prissy socialite asshole brain of yours, Walter. Think hard because your miserable life may depend on this. What more do you know about this guy and about that map that you are not telling me? No more games, pretty boy. I'm not going to take the fall for your fuck up. I'm not going to have another man killed by this hermit fellow either. Listen good, dumb fuck. If there's any more trouble or bad information I will kill you and put an end to this scheme. You are fucking with the wrong soldier and I will not think twice about killing you. I'm right into your ass now and I want straight answers. I want everything you know about this guy." The sadistic tone in the general's voice was unmistakable. It dawned on Walter that the general enjoyed killing people more than making money.

"Let me think, just calm down." Walter played for some time.

"Don't you ever tell me to calm down!" the general's snarl was more threatening than a Doberman's. "Don't you *ever* give an order to me, you worthless asshole. I want *answers!* I want answers *NOW! RIGHT NOW!*" The General was screaming again. His sadism had yielded to rage.

"Okay, okay." Walter was rattled. He spoke quickly now, reeling off all the facts he could remember. "He has or did have a girl friend who worked in a bar in Ouray. She was a red head, a real looker. He got the map through a trade with some Indian woman at one of those local flea markets or a garage sale sort of thing. He trades for things. He doesn't have a checking account or any kind of bank connection." Walter's hurried voice was interrupted again.

"I imagine the bank info is about the only thing you are sure about, or can you give me something that verifies what you are telling me." The General finally sounded more like a businessman. Walter's excited heartbeat slowed a bit.

"Yes. You could have someone ask around in that town of Ouray. They'll remember him. He's always chewing a plug of the most awful tobacco. Someone will verify what I'm telling you. Also, he carries a pouch with him at all times."

"You mean like one of them faggot sissy pouches that them girly men carry?" The General sounded skeptical.

"Yes. Like one of those. But he carries jewels and gold in it, not girly stuff."

"Okay." the General was calmer now. "What else?"

"He spent some time in a naval hospital. I think it was Bethesda. He got shot in Iraq in his leg. I don't know which leg."

"Does he limp?"

"I don't know. I don't think so. I never heard that he limps."

"What else?"

"That's about it. Oh, wait. There's one more thing. I did hear that he's known to and accepted by the Indians. They think of him as one of them. He gets along very well with Indians."

"What else?" the general squeezed Walter for more information. Walter was getting crushed for information like an orange for its juice.

"The one other thing I got was that he has no feelings. He has no loyalties to anyone, no weaknesses that way. He'd just as soon kill somebody as shake hands with them. I think that includes that girl too. He's a mean son of a bitch. He has a natural kind of meanness about him. He's been know to just punch people in the mouth without warning if they insult him or act rude to him. My guy out there said meanness was in his bones." Walter's tone sounded exhausted from the squeezing his mind had suffered.

"Sounds like the kind of guy I'd like to have on my side in a fight. Sounds just like me. That's it, that's all you got?"

"Yes, sir, General, if I think of anything else I'll call you on your secure line."

"That's better, Walter. You're doing better now; and I *like* being called sir, Walter. You *remember* that." the General's elongated way of saying the word remember and his tone left a lingering undefined threat in the air.

"Yes *SIR*, General." After his emphatic acknowledgement Walter gently cradled his phone receiver.

"I hope Gibby kills you first, you miserable son of a bitch, but do find that map before he kills you," Walter spoke angrily to his hung up phone. For a few seconds Walter wished he'd never been tipped by his contact in the State Department that British Columbia's Geological Services Department estimated their prospector's sample rocks were unique and of inestimable value, with properties capable of changing the world's balance of power. The materials the rocks were made of were from fifth generation stars. They made possible advances in science that were simply unattainable from Earth's elements. Awareness was dawning on Walter that he might be involved in something that was mushrooming out of his control. He had a nagging feeling that he was mixed up with ruthless power players that operated on a level that was over his head. He wanted to go home to his wife and have a martini.

CHAPTER EIGHTEEN

BOATHOUSE

Paul's daughter was miserable on her first visit to the Rockman's lake house. The little girl had been closely guarded by her mother and cloistered from other children all her life. Connie sought to introduce Margaret to other children to help her develop her playing skills. She had included three other couples on this first trip, each with small children Margaret's age. But things did not start off smoothly. While the other children swam and played little Margaret just sat in the gazebo and cried for her mother. Each adult, in turn, went to the gazebo and offered encouragement and comfort to little Margaret, but the child would have none of it.

Paul and Connie tried to humor her with hand puppets and dolls. They took turns sitting next to her and reading to her from children's books. Margaret rebuffed all their approaches. She turned her head away from the hand puppets and pushed the books away from her. The harder everyone tried, the louder the child wailed: "I want my Mommy! I want to go home! Please Daddy, take me home to Mommy! I don't want to be here! I miss my Mommy!" It was plain to all that little Margaret was distraught. She clung to her blanket and her teddy bear while crying herself hoarse.

George and Patty came along for that first visit to the lake. When Margaret lost her composure the two of them quickly gave up trying to comfort the child. George just sat on a folding lawn chair out on the dock with a fishing pole and a cooler of beers. Patty went inside, made herself a gin fizz, and read romance novels. The other children tried to tease Margaret into playing with them. They ran about the gazebo playing bean bag tag, then hide and go seek; but soon they too gave up on Margaret. They went into the house. They changed into their swim suits and gathered up a beach ball and some rubber dinosaurs.

They weren't about to let one spoil sport ruin their fun. They took their water toys to the shallow waters near the house and went splashing. Margaret noticed they were having fun without her, and for a few moments it looked like she might break free of the misery that clung to her; but the poor child couldn't let go of where her thoughts were. It was obvious to the adults that there was no cheering Margaret's spirits.

She was terrified at being separated from her mother and feared she might never see her again. One by one the adults walked out to the gazebo to check on her. Then they walked the twenty yard distance across the grass back to the lake house. There they sat in the white wicker rocking chairs on the expansive porch deck and made small talk while sipping their old fashions and gin and tonics. There was nothing more anyone could do for Margaret or for Paul.

"I need to take her back to her mother," he said to Connie. "She just won't stop the crying. There's no reasoning with her. I've tried everything I know to snap her out of it. I brought her toys and games. You brought these other kids. I can't thank you enough, but I need to leave." Paul was exasperated. He looked in the direction of his daughter and shrugged his shoulders.

"It's okay, Paul" said Connie. "I expected it would go something like this. Her mind is in the process of forming. She can't reason like an adult. She's a little bundle of emotions and uncertainties. It's okay. It's really okay. She just needs to learn that she's safe with us, Paul. Once she understands she can go back to her mother her confidence will build. It may take some time, but it's okay. I want to help. We'll just keep trying. She'll eventually come around when she feels the love that we have for her. Children can feel love." Connie looked at the pathetic forlorn child.

Margaret had soft golden hair and soft blue eyes to match her heart shaped mouth and small pointed nose. The child clung to her teddy bear and blanket. They were her anchors to permanence. Connie felt her heart going out to Margaret. She wanted to sweep little Margaret into her arms and hold her tight and speak soothing words to her; but she thought better of it. The last thing Paul needed was to have his ex accusing the two of them with absconding with Margaret to the lake to use the little girl for their perverse pleasures. And, from what little Connie heard about Paul's ex it seemed smart to be extra cautious.

"I think I heard you say you feel love for my daughter," Paul's look at Connie was questioning, intended to draw her out.

"Oh Paul, yes of course I do. How could I help but love her? She's a darling, adorable little girl. I'd love to be like a second mother to her and make her a big part of my life. Look at her. I could just take her up in my arms and hug her and stroke her hair and comfort her. That's my heart speaking my feelings for her. Please, let's keep trying to be with her, so she'll get used to the three of us being together. We'll work through this. I'll be good to her and to you Paul. I'll be good for both of you, I promise."

"Well, I don't know what to say. You're very kind. I'd like that very much. I honestly don't know what to say. I feel kind of tongue tied." Paul looked first to Connie, then to his daughter.

"Paul, she's going through a lot for a kid. Right now she's trying to get attention from you. She needs to know that you'll put her needs first. You need to comfort her fears. You go on ahead and take her back. I understand. It's okay. We need to have an understanding that whenever there's any doubt, we need to put Margaret's needs first. Once she knows she can go home whenever she wants to, she won't want to go. Trust me on this. Let's try it again next time."

Connie was patient. She eyed little Margaret and gave the child a warm loving smile. The hugs she physically withheld she gave in abundance through her eyes. Margaret eyed Connie back. It was a little girl's uncertain sort of look. Margaret pursed her lips and frowned, but her eyes betrayed her attempt at pouting. She tried to say with her eyes that she knew something was brewing between Connie and her dad, but that the adults needed to be placed on a probationary timetable; and that her approval of whatever was going on between Connie and her dad would have to be earned. The child's look made it clear that she held first claim on her daddy. After his daughter finished her sizing up look, Paul and Connie shared a loving chuckle. Then Paul gathered his daughter's things, strapped her into her car seat and drove her back to her mother's. Paul had to relent. The weekend was not expected to be a smashing initial success, but it barely met even his lowest expectations.

After two weeks passed Paul again took little Margaret to the lake house. This time Connie arranged for two other couples to be there with their kids. Margaret seemed more sure of herself on the second trip.. She didn't cry. She held back for a while, but then joined in with the other kids. Soon she was splashing in the lake, even laughing a little. That night she was quiet while Paul read bed time stories to her. But, in the middle of the night Margaret woke up screaming "I want my mommy!" The screaming continued for a good half hour until Connie made her a hot chocolate and Paul read a bedtime story to her. Connie next tried a method she learned from watching her mother comfort her little brother.

"Now Margaret, the little birdies have all gone to sleep. The little bunnies have all gone to sleep, and the little sheep have all gone to sleep; and we must go to sleep too. We must sleep so the birdies and the bunnies and the sheep can sleep. All the little animals are waiting for you to go to sleep. Shall we sing to them so they can go to sleep?"

Little Margaret nodded her head and Connie began to sing little children's lullabies. Soon Margaret's eyelids fell closed and the child was sound asleep.

"I've never understood why birdies, bunnies and sheep need to have little kids go to sleep so they could go to sleep," Paul said.

"That's simple," said Connie. "The children relate better to baby animals than they do to adults. Baby animals are safer. If the animals think it's a good idea to sleep it must be a good thing to do."

"Oh," said Paul. Connie suddenly seemed like a savior for the needs of his child. "What is it about you women that can comprehend things a man doesn't understand?"

"It's about that we're women, Paul. A little girl needs a woman around. It's a female thing."

Two weeks later Paul again picked up Margaret from his ex. Soon after they were on the road Paul knew something wasn't right. Margaret had a chest wheeze, her eyes were droopy and she whimpered that her tummy and her legs hurt. He pulled the car over. Margaret was strapped into her car seat on the car's back seat. She had a fever and mucus was streaming from her nose.

"How long have you been feeling sick, Margaret?" Paul asked. When Margaret didn't respond he asked her if she'd been feeling badly for a long time. She nodded her head. Then he asked her if her mommy had taken her to a doctor. This time Margaret shook her head in the negative. Paul gave her some water, wrapped her in an extra sweater he carried in the trunk, and drove to the lake house.

When Connie saw Margaret's condition she immediately took charge of the child. In less than ten minutes Margaret was tucked in bed. Connie made chicken noodle soup and fed a bowl of it to Margaret, spoon by spoon. Then she gave her a baby aspirin and rubbed her chest with a camphor vapor rub. She wrapped her tightly in a warm blanket.

Paul watched as Connie went to work fighting the common cold or flu that sidelined his daughter. Connie noticed his anxiety. "I'll call the village doctor over here in the morning, and I'll stay in her room tonight," she said. "I'll stay up with her through the night. She needs rest. She'll be all right, Paul. Try not to worry."

The next morning a doctor came to the house. He examined Margaret and decided that what the child needed was an over the counter decongestant. Paul went to the village drug store while Connie sat with Margaret. All that day Connie followed her same ritual for fighting off colds. She made the chicken noodle soup, rubbed Margaret down and kept her tucked in a warm bed. On the morning of the third day Margaret's cold broke. She expiated great streams of mucus and her fever broke. Paul went to his daughter's room after hearing the coughing and nose blowing sounds of the cold breaking up. When he looked into the room there was Connie sitting on the side of his daughter's bed. Margaret was sitting up, clinging to Connie. Her little arms were wrapped around Connie's neck, squeezing her close. Paul watched and felt good for all three of them.

"Is there a hug in there for Daddy too?' he asked.

Margaret shook her head. She continued clinging to Connie.

"Am I in the way of something with you two?" he asked with a smile.

"No, you're not in the way, Daddy. We're just having a girl moment, aren't we Margaret?" Connie said, smiling at Paul. Margaret nodded her head and continued to cling to Connie.

"Oh, okay." replied Paul. He watched them for a moment, then left. Whatever magic they had developed seemed to exclude him and he felt there was something right about it.

After Margaret's recuperation visit their times at the lake were wonderful. On weekends when he had Margaret Paul always took her to the lake house. It became his daughter's home away from home. She had her own room and her own stuffed animals, toys and puzzles. Connie even bought her a child's music player with her own compact discs of children's songs. Soon, little Margaret was excited to go to the lake house. Her inhibitions fell away. Now when she arrived she ran to her room, changed into her swim suit and quickly jumped into the lake.

"She thinks of you as Mom away from Mom," Paul commented. They sat on the dock watching the children splashing in the lake. Something they knew all along would happen between them was happening.

"I could be good for you and Margaret, Paul, and I want to be." Connie reached out her hand and took Paul's. Connie Rockman was honest about her affections.

"I see it," said Paul. He understood Connie better now that he'd spent time with her. She was a very good hearted person. Her father had placed her in an impossible trap at his heavily influenced BASE bank. She needed to please men who would determine her performance reviews. She needed the reviews to be good or she risked not getting into an Ivy League MBA program. Her father could be tyrannical to his own daughter without knowing the effect his edicts were having on her character. Father and Daughter seldom spoke. Connie was floundering for a steady male presence in her life. Paul could see that now. Obviously she had her sights set on him.

"Do you, do you really see it Paul? I see so much in you that I see in my father but with one important difference. I can talk with you. You are patient with me. You understand my feelings." Connie looked wistfully into Paul's eyes. She was as forthright as she could be. Her eyes said she wanted to devour Paul.

"Yes, but what about George? I noticed he's not been here the last three times. Does that mean you two have broken it off? I mean, are you and George, or rather, were you and George——"

"No, Paul," Connie interrupted. "George is in my past. It was never anything more than a good times kind of thing. I was never serious about him. I've never been serious about any man before you, Paul. Paul, I don't know how else to say this. I love you Paul. I know I love you. We've never even kissed but I see the kind of man you are, your kindness and how you are with Margaret. You're everything I want, Paul. I felt it since I first started training with you. Now, after these times at the lake, I'm sure of it. I can't understand why your ex treated you so poorly. She must be crazy." Connie's look was pleading, searching. She wanted Paul and Margaret in her life. She was offering him her soul on a silver platter.

"Connie, there's so much you don't know about me," Paul shook his head revealing doubt. "I can be a terrible workaholic. I can become immersed in work so intensely that I push people away. That's what happened in my marriage. My ex couldn't take it. A lot of what happened was my fault. It was not another woman. My work came between us. She wasn't from a family that understood a man like me. I wouldn't make time for her friends, her parents, her parties, or her babblings about things I couldn't relate to. I should have seen that before I married her. I should have spared her the pain of a marriage. I might not be a good match for any woman." Paul was honest.

"I am undeterred, Mr. Wheeler," Connie's smile said she was not about to be put off. "You are so like Daddy it's uncanny. I've seen how Mother makes her marriage work with Father. I can't imagine any other kind of marriage. I'm not at all like your ex, Paul. I've traveled, I'm well read. I respect what you do and I know how important good analysis can be. I wouldn't expect you to be a nine to five, home on weekends, kind of guy. I'm willing to accept a twenty-four seven, business first guy. Father is like that. When he gets something correct he makes millions. Then he and Mother will take off to someplace on another continent and stay away for three or four weeks at a time. I get it Paul. I really do get it."

"And Margaret, are you sure you can deal with her? Not just on weekends, but for those everyday times." Paul was warming to the idea of Connie as a permanent part of his life.

"Relax Paul. That little girl and I will become best buds. We will have a ball. I will spoil her and I will help her all through life. I'm already madly in love crazy about her. She's part of you, Paul. Of course I'll get along with her." Connie was genuine. It showed whenever she and Margaret were together. She genuinely cared about his daughter.

"Connie, there's something else. It has to do with those spread sheets you saw that night you came in from the wet," Paul's forward lean said this was a serious subject.

"You mean when I looked like a drowned ally cat that wanted to undress on the research floor?" Connie reached for some hope of levity.

"Yeah, except you never looked like an ally cat. You were beautiful," his look said that he adored her.

"Thank you Mr. Wheeler. I feel like purring inside." Connie placed her arms businesslike around Paul's neck. She cocked her head from side to side while smiling mischievously.

But Paul had something on his mind and he wanted her to hear it. "Connie, this is important. You know there's a troubled world out there."

"Yes, I listen to the news," she dropped her hands to her sides. It settled in her mind that getting involved with Paul really was going to be like making a business deal. The sport of love was off the table for the moment. "The North Koreans want to kill us. The Muslims want to kill us. We're being invaded from Mexico. Russia wants to destroy our democracy. China wants to repopulate America with Chinese. The democrats and the republicans are at each others' throats, and the economy is being artificially propped up by the Fed. So why should we be worried? Why can't we just live?" She gave a cynical shrug of her shoulders.

"Come on, I'm serious," Paul's eyes implored her to pay attention. "I told you I might be able to share some of my work with you. I want you to understand my thinking before you decide you want to get involved with me."

"Okay Mr. Analyst," Connie tucked her chin, folded her arms in front of her and looked as serious as an army general.. "Should I go hide in a bomb shelter somewhere in the northern woods?"

"No, just *listen* for a minute. I'm having problems with some numbers I'm seeing. The executives of BASE, Walter and all the others say one thing but the numbers say something different. I trust numbers."

"You think BASE is in trouble?"

"I didn't say that, at least not yet. But things aren't fitting like they should. There are things going on in trading and lending. When I go year by year through the balance sheet footnotes I'm getting a different picture from what the financial statements show. And that's just the beginning. I've got commodity trading and delivery records in gold and silver from all the public data that's out there. I've compared that data with bank trading and lending data. I keep going over my work. I believe it's correct. It's giving me chills."

"This is about BASE, right?" Connie's eyebrows were up. Finally she showed some concern.

"Yes, but no," Paul first nodded, paused, then shook his head. "It's about the twenty biggest banks in the world."

"All of them?"

Paul only nodded his head.

"Paul, tell me. Is my family's money safe?" Connie's voice betrayed a sense of alarm.

"I don't know. I think so for now, but I must do more digging. I need to study more numbers."

"Like what?" Now Connie sounded miffed. She didn't like uncertainty.

"Like liquidity numbers and the availability of gold and silver. Look, this is tricky stuff because I can only make an educated guess about the central banks. They are private companies and they don't report what I need in a way that makes it simple to put together. What I'm working on isn't like corporate earnings forecasts. I can't default to the assumption that our fiat banking system will survive indefinitely."

"So, what *are* you trying to forecast?"

"Whether we'll even have a banking system; and, if we won't, how much longer it will last."

"Paul, what are you talking about?" The anxious child in her voice appeared.

"I need to make an informed estimate of how much liquidity the centrals will provide before——"

Paul's answer was coming too slowly. Connie interrupted him. "Before what, Paul, before what?" now she sounded like a child demanding a lollypop. The suspense was killing her.

"Well, before the centrals can make more money by pulling the plug on the entire unsustainable financial system rather than staying with it as it is."

"What! You think things are that bad?" Her look was skeptical, as in he'd better be sure of what he was saying. Her tone demanded reassurance if there was any to give.

"Look. I just don't know yet," Paul's eyes said worlds about the enormity of getting his forecast correct. "Even when I do have the liquidity data put together with all the other data, it's still only going to be an educated guess. I could be missing something."

"All right, but you think my family's money is safe for now, do you or don't you?" Her eyes looked deep into Paul's.

"Yes, I think for now you'll be safe; but I don't know how long I can say that." Paul tried his best to reassure her, but the cautionary tone in his reply was not lost on her.

"Will you explain more of this to me after I put Margaret to bed? I want to know, Paul. I need to know what I should do. I need to understand." Maybe it was her word 'understand,' maybe it was him realizing that he'd come to trust her with his daughter or that she believed in him; but whatever it was, he felt a quiet warmth surge over him.

Paul looked at her standing there beside him on the dock. In the fading light she was the same Connie that he'd seen for months at the bank. She was the same curious woman he was tasked to train in the methods of financial statement analysis. But she was somehow different now, changed in some underlying way. There was something about her mannerisms, her voice, even the way her eyes regarded him that told him something was happening to her.

His gaze dropped from her face to her frame. She appeared ethereal in the early twilight. Something was happening to him as well. He liked being near her. There was naturalness about this new feeling. He again looked into her eyes. They silently welcomed him home. He felt a swelling sensation where his heart should be and a lump arose in his throat. He cleared his throat before he replied.

"Okay. I'll share what I'm seeing with you, but until my work is finished please swear you'll not utter a word of this, not even to your mother or father. I need time to be surer of what I'm seeing."

"Oh, Paul, you can trust me. I swear it."

"We shouldn't be overheard by your other guests either."

"No, we should be smart about this," she slapped her arm. "Ouch, the mosquitoes are starting to bite," she killed the thirsty female intruder before she sank her proboscis. "I got it! We should get inside. I need to get Margaret tucked in. She played very hard today. Tell you what, while I put Margaret to bed you could make us a couple of gins; then go to the boat house. There's a pile of kapok life jackets in there. They're on top of Father's old day bed. Make yourself comfortable and wait for me. I shouldn't be too long."

The sun had set a half hour before and the low cumulous clouds melted their whiteness into the darkening sky. By the dimming light Connie took Paul's hand and walked with him to the house. Fireflies were all around them lifting from the lawn grass and flashing brightly their advertisements for mates. The crickets were a half inch longer than they were just a month ago. The males' leg chirps were deeper and more inviting now. Their chirps stimulated the females' front leg feelers and they rushed to the males to engulf their sperm packets. A slight touch of cool fall air laced the evening. It signaled to every frog around the lake that it was urgent to procreate. The initial croaking by a few frogs' moments earlier was joined by legions of others in a riveting chorus. Here and there frogs were on the move hopping about looking to mate. Connie and Paul now looked at each other in a different way. They knew it was time to discover their own intimacy, but a human duty needed attention first. It was time to put a tired little girl to bed.

CHAPTER NINETEEN

ACROSS THE WAY

G ibby stayed inside the adit tunnel during the daylight hours. He always liked to figure things out before he acted. Now it was more important than ever that he got things right. His life depended on it. He was dealing with an unknown enemy who had considerable means at his disposal. He figured that whoever sent the sniper to kill him for his map was the same person or persons who sent a Huey helicopter with five men dressed in Marine Corps camouflage to ransack his camp at the Dead Mule Mine. Likely they were looking for the map which he now kept on his person at all times.

He reckoned that whoever had enough pull to send armed men to a Colorado mountain top on a scavenger hunt might have enough pull to order a satellite to sit stationary above his camp too. He decided he couldn't risk being spotted. He only moved about by night. He reasoned that a satellite with infrared might spot him, but there would likely be animals about at night too. The satellite wouldn't know for sure if his signature was a person, a mountain lion, a bear, or a lynx if he moved stealthily hunched over, and somewhat erratically like an animal on four paws.

When the chopper left it only took four men out. One man remained to sit guard post at his camp. Gibby crawled to the near entrance of the adit and watched the man with his binoculars. Every three hours the man made a call on a sky phone. The calls lasted only fifteen to twenty seconds. The man was making check in calls. Gibby figured the man was ordered to call in if he spotted him. The calls in also would confirm that the man was safe. Gibby took two days to think. He tried to focus on the man left sitting guard, the significance of the helicopter insertion, the sniper that he killed days before, and the map. They were all related somehow. They were pieces of a puzzle that was valuable to someone, but to whom?

Trying to think through what, if anything, he should do next was especially difficult because he ached inside from hurt feelings. He missed Jo Ann. He'd yearned to be with her before the sniper came hunting for him, but now he was nearly crazy out of his mind with love and passion for her. He dreamed about her and he daydreamed about her. He tried not to think about her. He tried to tell himself that he could get over her, that she was something he'd learn to live without, that she was just a useless slut and there were millions of women that he could substitute for her when he was out of this mess. But his efforts to push her out of his mind didn't work. He thought of the times he held her naked body tightly to his own and all the ways they made love. He remembered every minute detail about her, her smile, how she licked her lips, the way she brushed her hair from her face with her hand, and how she softly blinked her eyes.

He thought back to those moments when he laid on his back with his hands behind his head watching her suck him. She was beautiful beyond any words he could attach to those memories. She loved sucking him, mouthing his balls and playing her tongue along his shaft and around its tip. When she swallowed his semen her face took on a divinely inspired look. And when his semen was exploding into her pussy he saw that same look on her face. She liked to straddle him and push her clit hard against his member, partnering the two organs together as if they were custom fitted for life. And the way she screamed when she came made him love her more than anything or anyone he'd ever known before. Most of his memory visions of her didn't even have anything to do with sex. His mind drifted to thinking about kissing her bare shoulders and nuzzling her neck.

As he sat in his cold dark tunnel his regrets mounted. How could he turn her out like he did? Why couldn't he sit and talk things out with her again or walk through town with her? Being with her made him proud. She was fixated in his brain. He knew he'd never stop thinking about her. He'd pressed his hands to his temples to try to drive thoughts of her away, but that didn't work. It only made him want her more. Squeezed his head only made him realize that somehow, some way he'd have to swallow his pride, find her and tell her he wanted to try again. 'Woman, I need you and I want you so badly. If you only knew how badly I want you.' the same thought reverberated endlessly through his mind.

The second day passed with the guard man still standing watch at his camp. He fell asleep thinking *Jo Anne, Jo Anne, how I miss you.*

When he awoke the third day the man was still there. Then his reasoning kicked in. 'If the man disappeared, would the chopper return? If it did, would they have a better chance of finding him than they did the first time? Who knew these mountains better than he? Would he have warning they were coming? Yes. he would hear the rotors from five miles away.' Gibby's combat instincts revived. He decided to one up this new enemy's game.

In the gathering dusk of the third occupation day Gibby watched the man finish his call. Gibby knew he had three hours. He was in the shadow of the mountain. The man would not see him. He slowly crawled on his belly out of the adit and upward until he was just below the crest of the ridge that rose up to his mountain's peak. He watched the man intently. The man turned his gaze away from Gibby's mountain. He looked to his right to check the long trail that led up to the Dead Mule. That's when Gibby slipped over the top of his ridge and dropped below the man's line of sight. Then he moved cautiously along the other side of the ridge until he reached the same side of the valley as the man. He reappeared about one hundred yards from the man and upslope from him. He still had an hour. He rested ten minutes to catch his breath and relax his heartbeat.

When Gibby lied down in the prone position the man still had no inkling of danger. A few long minutes passed. The man moved out a few steps from the Dead Mule to take a last look across the shadowy valley. It was a classic mistake. The guard silhouetted himself perfectly against an afterglow sky. He was looking over the valley toward the adit Gibby had just left when Gibby settled the cross hairs on his head. The man never heard the shot. Gibby's trusty .308 echoed through the hills. The guard's head blew apart like a watermelon slammed by a sledgehammer. His mouth was trying to form a word while his brains splattered over ten yards of mountainside. Down in Ouray one old man was walking down the main street when the rifle's report sounded. He stopped and muttered to himself, 'Fucking poachers. Where are the fucking game wardens? Somebody needs to put a stop to this shit.' Then he sauntered into the Bald Eagle Bar. No one else seemed to notice or care that another elk was taken. Likely somebody needed meat.

After he killed the guard, Gibby sat next to the dead body. The three hour time came and went. Another ten minutes passed. Gibby's hunch was right. If the guard didn't call in, somebody would call the guard. The sky phone rang.

"Yeah," Gibby answered.

"Hey Bravo, how come you didn't call in?"

"I was pissing," Gibby mumbled.

"You all right, you don't sound all right"

"Tired, nothing going on, need sleep," Gibby yawned as he uttered his mumblings.

"Okay. Give it a rest. Don't forget to call in again though or I'll have to report you to General Porter."

"Yeah, night," Gibby did his best groggy tired soldier imitation and hung up. As soon as the call ended he took the dead man's rifle and pistol. The stiff was carrying a Vietnam era M1 rifle modified for sniper shooting. It had a side mounted scope as well as elevation sights. His ammo was not regulation issue either. It was from a reloading press. The bullets weighed about 100 to 110 grains, he reckoned. They were much lighter than the normal 150 to 180 grain 30.06 commercial rounds or the 175 grain 7 millimeter commercial round. He pulled one from its cartridge and cut into it with his knife. It was cast of lead with a copper jacket, a two step process. Obviously it was poured by a professional shooter with reloading equipment and metallurgical know how. The bullets were aerodynamically designed. They had the appearance of miniature cigars with tapering on both ends and a fat middle. Whoever made them knew the right thickness to catch the rifling groves of a medium caliber rifle, like a 30.06 or a standard military issue M1 rifle; but the genius of the rounds was their tapered tips and tailings. The tip had a small groove cut into the copper jacket into which a tiny drop of soft lead was poured. These rounds were ideal for a long distance kill shot at a human being. They would travel flat for a far distance and they would mushroom on impact. Likely they would go into a body or head with the diameter of a sharpened pencil tip and they would make a hole the size of a dime's or nickel's diameter when they exited.

But what opened Gibby's eyes were the home made cartridges. They were necked down to fit the smaller bullets and carry about twenty percent more gunpowder than regular issue. Gibby held the rifle in the dimmed moonlight and examined it closely. The elevation sights were set for five hundred yards, the distance from his adit across the valley to the Dead Mule.

He felt a flood of thoughts. The dead man's rifle and ammo told him his enemies were not active duty marines. They were private contractors under control of a general named Porter. And they were expert shooters. Regular troops didn't use home reloading equipment to create bullets that could travel an extra hundred yards before they began to drop. The rifle's elevated sight setting meant the dead man could put his cross hairs on a target and hit it from five hundred yards away. The man he killed obviously had some inkling that Gibby could be holed up in one of several adits across the valley from the Dead Mule. His neck felt a chill. He realized if he had showed himself this man he just killed would likely have killed him first. His enemies were hired killer marksmen like himself.

There was nothing special about the dead man's side arm. It was a standard Navy .45 caliber. The man had a clip inserted and a round chambered. Evidently he was concerned that Gibby might sneak up on him. Gibby set his rifle, the stiff's rifle, the pistol, the man's ammo and his phone aside while he undressed the body. He checked the sky. Monsoon clouds from the Gulf of California were building.

Thundershowers threatened. When the sky was sufficiently dark Gibby dragged the naked body to the tree line five hundred yards below. He continued into the pines until he came to a clearing. Then he covered the body with dead branches and pine needles from the forest floor. He walked away from the body a few yards and broke off a pine branch. Then he returned to the body and walked back over the same steps he took to enter the forest. He swept the ground behind him all the way back to the Dead Mule, removing all traces of his track.

When he reached the Dead Mule he rolled out a bed roll on the ground and wrapped the dead man's clothes around some rags and empty plastic containers. He set an empty milk jug on a pillow and placed the man's wide brimmed recon hat over the jug. He made it appear from a distance that the man was lying on the ground sleeping. He made sure his contrivance was visible from his adit across the valley. When his work was finished he gathered up the rifles, pistol and ammo and returned to his adit across the valley.

He was proud of himself. His kill reaffirmed that he still had his edge. He sat about ten yards inside his adit where he felt safe. Then he resumed thinking. His latest kill gave him a lot of information. The five men the chopper inserted might be the extent of their forces. General Porter was using a military chopper for private purposes. Likely he was dirty and on the take. The five men either were marines doing undisclosed side work or private contractors dressed as marines. Likely their chopper needed to refuel at least once and they needed to appear to be real marines on a real mission. That was significant.

These guys were sloppy. He didn't need to call out his identity to the voice on the other end of the call. The voice's idle threat to report the guard's neglect to General Porter told him their chain of command was poor. A real chain of command would have simply reported it; unless the voice suspected something and didn't want to give his suspicion away to Gibby. That seemed unlikely. There was no hesitation in the voice on the other end. A suspicious voice would have revealed itself. These men were likely hired mercenaries getting day pay.

Gibby smiled at himself. He hummed a simple tune in his head, '*I'm getting to know you, and I'm getting to know all about you.*' He felt better than he had in days. His enemy had revealed another part of himself. For the first time since this weirdness started he turned his thoughts to offensive actions, his preferred mode. 'You and I will have our person to person moment, General Porter. You're one no good son of a bitch.

And when I get through with you, you're going to learn what a real son of a bitch is like.' he said aloud. As he nodded off into sleep his thoughts again gravitated to Jo Ann. He wondered if she was all right. He knew he'd dream about her again. His heart ached for her. He missed her terribly.

CHAPTER TWENTY

LIGHTNING STRIKES

Jo Ann got off to an early start. She put her most important things in her back pack, strapped it to an aluminum frame along with her bed roll, and started up the mountain toward the Dead Mule Mine. She hoped she'd find Gibby at the mine, but if she didn't she was prepared to search for him. She'd hiked these mountains a few times before. She had some survival experience from an Outward Bound trip, and she'd been in the hills with Gibby a couple of times. She told herself she could find him if she went from one high valley to another calling his name. Surely he'd hear her and at least come and talk with her, she reasoned. One way or another she had to find out if Sam was right.

'Does he still love me,' she asked herself as she started out. 'I'm not crazy. A girl has to know for sure. Before I go and take up with another fellow, I need to know if the fellow I love loves me back or if he doesn't.

'How can I ever fall in love with another fellow when I love Gibby? That wouldn't be right. It wouldn't be smart even. Maybe I'd be giving up on Gibby when he still loves me. A girl has to know if her man loves her or not. I've got a right to know, and I've got a right to hear the truth when nobody's being emotional. But I can't get myself to be not emotional about love. I don't know if Gibby can not be emotional about it.

All the time I knew Gibby our love was the only thing he ever got emotional over.

'Maybe if I gave up on Gibby I'd be putting a good man in the trash bin for some other girl to pick out and take for her treasure. But, I didn't put him into the trash bin. He put me in the trash bin. But Sam says he didn't put me in the trash bin. He was just pissed at me was all. Gibby gets real mean when he's pissed at someone. He gets plum nasty. I'm glad I'm a girl, 'cause when he was pissed that day if I was a man he'd of killed me for sure.' With these deep thoughts in her mind and tears in her eyes Jo Ann kept putting one foot in front of the other.

Every fifty yards or so she muttered to herself what words she'd say if she met up with him. 'Gibby. I'm so sorry. I love you Gibby. I'll go anywhere with you. I'll do anything for you. Please give me one more chance, Gibby. I won't never be no whore no more. I'll be a good woman for you. I promise.'

Then she'd get down on her hands and knees and beg. She'd put her arms around his legs and lock her hands so he couldn't shake her off and get away. She'd have no pride at all, none. All she could offer was her complete unashamed love. He'd have to kick her away to get rid of her.

By mid afternoon she had climbed to eleven thousand feet. The Dead Mule was another fifteen hundred feet higher, and she knew it would be the hardest part of her trek. Rest felt like a good idea. She took off her back frame and sat with her back against it. Her eyes took in her surroundings. The aspen were turning already. Little tinges of yellow gold were on the leaf tips. Gibby always said that trees knew when the sun turned south. He said that the sun's decline from its highest latitude was what told the trees to turn and that it had nothing to do with the temperature like most people thought.

Gibby told her that trees were smarter than people. That's another thing she liked about Gibby, she thought quietly to herself. He was smart. He usually knew what to do about things, all sorts of things. She knew she wasn't very smart. She was below average in her school classes. But in those school years she never gave much thought to getting smart. She was into boys then. They were after her all the time to kiss her or feel her up. She believed then that as long as boys were interested she could rely on her looks to get by in life. That seemed like a good idea when she was a kid. Now she was almost twenty six and she was starting to worry more about her future.

Was she going to have a life with Gibby or would she end up waitressing all her life? The more she thought about it the more she worried. Getting a good man who loved her wasn't going to be easy if she didn't have Gibby. And, how would she know if another man really loved her? Most men are liars. She knew that from waitressing. They'd say anything to try to get into her panties.

But Gibby was not like those men. He was honest. He meant what he said and he was strong. Plus he was a great shot. He told her they would never starve because he'd always be able to kill an elk or a deer. They'd always have meat. That reassured her that she was right to go looking for Gibby. He was a man who could put meat on the table. But the part about Gibby meaning what he said bothered her. She kept going over the logic in her mind. When Gibby told her to get out that made her think they were through. And then Sam said that Gibby's behavior only made sense because he still loved her. She hoped with all her heart that Sam was right.

She looked up into the sky to wonder about these questions that vexed her. Men, especially Gibby, were hard to understand. She noticed a turkey vulture was circling high above and about a half mile distant to the north of her. She wondered if Gibby had killed something up here or if it was the remains of a dead elk from a kill by a bear or cougar. There was only one vulture so whatever it was it was likely killed fresh not too long ago.

She noted its approximate location in her mind in case she ran out of food up here. She had sandwiches and protein bars but no meat. Gibby always said you could tell by the vultures where the meat was, and you could eat on dead meat for a while before it got rancid, unless it showed signs of rabies or other disease. Once again she reminded herself that Gibby was very smart. She resolved that if she found him and if he took her back she'd do whatever he said.

Thunderheads were building. She knew that could be trouble. She figured she'd better get moving and push herself to reach the Dead Mule before dark. If Gibby was up there he might not throw her out again, especially if it was raining. He could be nasty but she never knew him to be cruel. Anyway, she felt she had no choice but to push on. If she stayed put in the open she'd get soaked for sure. So, despite the high risk of mountain lightning strikes during thunder storms, she slipped into her aluminum framed back pack and resumed climbing.

Gibby had been looking out of his adit tunnel that afternoon when two bull elk trotted across the valley. They were four pointers (four antler points on each side), junior fare by big game hunting standards but excellent eating. He was tempted to shoot one for meat, but thought better of it. If his enemies returned they'd know it was him. He wouldn't have time to gut and quarter it either, and no matter how fast he worked he'd leave a blood trail. He checked his impulses and watched them run past. Then he got to thinking. Those elk were moving at a good clip. They should be lower down and grazing to build their antlers for the fall rut in case they got lucky. The careless way they moved told him they were spooked. Someone or something was down below and coming up the trail. He thought it could be his enemies. They knew he wasn't at the Dead Mule any longer so they might risk coming up the trail for him, just like the sniper and his driver. Would he do that if he were them? He reasoned that he might.

They didn't know where he was, but they did know where he wasn't, or at least they thought they knew where he wasn't. He decided to use his physical advantage. He had mountain lungs and mountain blood with more red corpuscles than flatlanders. He moved with ease up here. They got winded after walking twenty yards. He listened for the sound of a chopper and he heard nothing. He had time. He took his .308 and a box of ammo with him and ran back across the valley to the Dead Mule.

Lightning flashed and thunder cracked. Gibby sat at his outpost position glassing the approach trail to the mine. It was hard to make out anything through the rain. He put his mind into his enemy's. A downpour would provide perfect cover for men who wanted to search the high valley adits. They could come up the trail undetected, and then fan out to search the Dead Mule and the adits in the mountain on the opposite side of the valley. He knew he was risking being killed by lightning. By sitting in the open exposed like he was he traded one risk for another. But the payoff could be huge if his hunch was right. He could possibly kill one or two more men from the original five, giving him better odds of survival. The lightning strikes were getting closer. He flattened his body as close to the ground as he could; knowing lightning usually strikes high points.

"Gibby, Gibby," he thought he heard his name being called from a distance. He strained his eyes looking down the approach from where he thought the sound came from, but he saw nothing. He thought he could be hearing things. Maybe his mind was playing tricks on him because it sounded like Jo Ann calling for him. Could his enemies have a woman with them? They might be working some kind of trick. He decided he couldn't rule out anything with these bastards. Another half hour passed. The lightning cracks were almost on top of him now. The thunder was deafening. A major storm cell was releasing its hostilities directly over him. He couldn't see anything through his binoculars. He heard the voice call his name again. It sounded like a tired voice and closer than before.

Jo Ann passed the tree line to open tundra. As hard as her ascent was to this point it was nothing compared to the difficulty she had now. Her hiking boots were caked with mud and no longer gave her any traction. The downpour had reduced the trail to gooey slippery mud. For every step she took forward she slid one backward. She looked down at the trail and then at her feet, both mired in deep brown mud. She wasn't getting anywhere. A feeling of helplessness swept over her and she began crying.

All around her lightning cracked like deafening rifle shots. The thunder booms reverberated through her body. They terrified her. "Please God, let this end. Make it go way. I promise to be a good girl if you'll just make this storm go way. Please." But God only sent her more lightning and thunder. She dropped to all fours. Crawling through the mud was faster than walking. As she inched forward she kept calling out for Gibby, but her strength was failing her and her voice was weak. The rain was coming down in sheets. The lightning cracks were hitting very close by and hail stones began pounding her head and back.

A huge storm cell was unloading a downpour on her and it was just starting. Small hail pellets hurt when they hit her now. She feared larger hail stones would soon fall and possibly kill her. Her quest to find Gibby had turned life threatening. She knew enough about hail storms to realize she was in mortal danger. If the stones got to golf ball or baseball size they would surely kill her. Even if she survived the storm she was soaked through and through and risked hypothermia. She knew mountain temperatures fell sharply after cold fronts passed and if the hailstones didn't kill her she knew the hypothermia would. She began to shiver, the first sign of hypothermia.

She needed to get under cover and out of danger. It was now vital that she reached the Dead Mule.

Suddenly something knocked her flat to the ground and took her wind away. She feared it was a bear or cougar. When she wiped the mud off her face and regained her focus she saw Gibby. He'd knocked her down and now he was lying on top of her. She believed God had answered her prayers! She thought Gibby was heaven sent to save her.

"Gibby, Gibby, I love you. I've missed you. I'll be good, Gibby. I'll——," she was silenced. Gibby had his hand over her mouth.

"We need this back pack off you right now!" he shouted above the thunder. He pulled her pack straps away from her arms, setting her free of the frame. As soon as he did that he picked up the pack frame with one hand and with his mighty arm flung it as far away as possible. Then he laid himself down on top of her to shelter her from the hailstones.

"Gibby, all my things are in my back pack. Everything I have in the world is in that back——," again she was interrupted. This time it was by a close lightning strike. She felt the ground current pass under her. She was safe. Gibby was safe. She looked to where Gibby had thrown her pack. The frame, her bed roll and everything else she had was incinerated by the lightning. The only thing she had left in this world was now lying on top of her. Gibby stayed with her like that, lying on top of her until the dark cell passed.

"Get up, Jo. We've got to move fast," he said as he lifted her off the ground with one hand. "Come on, hold my hand. We must run. You keep up," Gibby was his old self, barking orders as if nothing ever happened between them. Together they ran up to the Dead Mule. There Gibby allowed Jo Ann to catch her breath. But as soon as she did he made her run again. He picked up his rifle and handed her his ammo box. "Come on," he said. "We've got to get across the valley pronto." Jo Ann ran as hard as her tired legs would carry her. Gibby practically dragged her with him.

Back inside his adit, Gibby explained what had transpired in the last few days. He told her about the sniper in the jeep, the chopper insertion, the guard at the mine, and the set up he left at the Dead Mule.

"You've killed three men, Gibby? Is that all right? Will the police be after you?" She expressed her naïveté about a combat situation. She was not yet in Gibby's war world. She was still thinking like a civilian.

"Look, Jo, these are bad people. They are up to something very bad. They want to kill me because I have something they want. They are at war with me, Jo. And, now that you are with me they will be at war with you too if they discover you." Gibby didn't tell her about the map in case she was captured or separated from him somehow. He thought it best to keep that information close.

"Is it okay to be at war with people right here in America, Gibby? We won't get anybody mad at us if we're at war with these people, will we?" Jo was swimming in her wet clothes and her confusion.

"Yes, it's perfectly okay Jo. We are not going to be in trouble for being at war with these people. You trust me, don't you?" Gibby studied her face to see if there were any doubts.

"Yes. I trust you Gibby. I'll be good to you. I'll be a good woman for you, I promise. I came here to tell you something, Gibby." her face was the most serous he'd ever seen it.

"What," he felt some anxiety. Might she know something about his enemy?

"I came here to tell you I love you, Gibby," she blurted her words out like she was a school child admitting to a crush on her teacher. "I ain't never gonna whore no more, Gibby, honest I ain't. I cut way back on my whoring from when I worked at Shanty's strip club."

"Jo, I don't need to hear this crap right now."

"But I got to say it to you Gibby, Sam said so. I should tell you the whole truth and not hold nothin back. Sam says that I should tell you all of it so if you take me back it'll be unconditional that you love me like I love you too, so I'm tellin you Gibby.

"When I was at Shanty's it was because I needed money bad an Ole Shanty tells me I can make extra by fucking customers so I got into doing that. I discovered I loved fuckin but didn't like the men I was fuckin. Many was old and fat men or men that was ugly looking or stinky, and some was pervert men that stuck stuff in my pussy like carrots or cucumbers and then they'd eat off them. Some liked fuckin me in my ass and I did that too, but I didn't like it. But then I got to working at Sam's Bald Eagle. Sam let me waitress and fuck his customers too. And Sam was good to me, Gibby; he never took a cut of my fuckin money like they did at Shanty's. Sam just paid me my waitress money is all. I and Sam are good honest friends. But it was the same thing with the men. The old fat ones and the perverts got me so upset that I didn't want to do whoring any more. I decided no matter what I was going to settle myself on one good man and give up the whoring. That's when you started coming to Sam's, Gibby.

"I seen you and my heart went pitter patter flippity flop. 'Oh Lordy,' I said to myself. 'This is my man. He's the one for me.' You walked into Sam's so tall and handsome with your square jaw and that tough look about you. I knewed you was a real man's man. I knewed you was gonna be my man. I knewed it, Gibby. An I knewed I loved you when I seen you that first time. I wanted to fuck you right then and there. I resisted the urge to go right up to you and ask you up to my apartment so I could fuck you that first time I seen you. But I needed to mind myself hoping you'd ask me out. Do you remember that first time you asked me out, Gibby?"

"Yeah, Jo, you were wearing your white halter top and red hot pants. I remember."

"And do you remember how I asked you up to my apartment and how we kissed that first time?"

"Yeah, Jo, it was a beautiful kiss. I'll never forget it."

"An do you remember how I pulled down my top an asked you to kiss my nipple and how you liked that and you said I had beautiful button nipples? And I told you my tits were 34B?"

"Sure I remember, Jo. It was a beautiful moment."

"Then you remember how I took my shorts off and sat on the edge of the bed an told you I'd love it if you'd lick my pussy? And how you came to me on your knees and pulled off my silk panties and spread my legs way out and licked my pussy that first time? Do you still remember, Gibby? Do you remember how clean my pussy was that first time?"

"I'll never forget it Jo. It was beautiful."

"Okay. Now do you remember when I said to you that I loved having a cock inside my pussy and how I loved the feeling of a cock shootin cum into me? And how I loved the sensation of a cock pulsing inside my pussy when it's shootin cum into me, an how I loved the feeling of cum sliding out my pussy and down my leg? And how that cum slipping out of me made me feel like a real woman? Do you still remember, Gibby?"

"Yes, Jo. I remember all of it. And I remember how you held me close and whispered all of it in my ear. It was incredibly sexy. I felt your body against mine and wanted you forever then."

"Well, Sam says to be honest with my feelings to you, Gibby. So I'm being honest. I still have those same feelings about you, only now more so than I did back then. See, back then I thought being in love was a game to play, but now I know it's special and doesn't come to a person maybe more than once in a life. And now I'm sure of it Gibby. I'm sure you are the only man for me forever. I want us to be like that first night all over again, Gibby. And I want you kissin my nipples and my pussy and fucking your cock in me and pulsing out big gobs of cum into me every day and night, Gibby. I want to fuck you like you ain't ever been fucked before, Gibby. And I swear I'll be true to you forever if you'll have me back. I'll cook and clean house for you too, Gibby. I want to be with you no matter what. I want to give my life to you, Gibby. I just wanted to be totally honest and tell all my feelings like Sam said to. I love you, Gibby."

"I love you too, Jo," he responded to her confession with a huge hug. He felt better than he'd felt in many years. "Now, go back in the tunnel a ways. Dry yourself off. You'll find some towels and a pile of dry clothes back there. Get out of that wet stuff before you get sick."

"You're so sweet to me Gibby. You knew I was coming didn't ya?" Jo smiled the look of a woman who learned for the first time she was appreciated and thought about.

"Yeah, darling, I knew," he responded with a white lie. There was no point in making her feel less important now than she was. He'd planned to go back into town for her after she learned her lesson, but he decided not to tell her that. This way was better. He knew he loved her and he knew she loved him. That was all that mattered.

When she dried off he held her close and kissed her face while she fell into a sound sleep. 'Poor thing, I shouldn't have put her through this much. I almost got her killed. From now on I've got to remember to treat her more like a woman,' he thought as he caressed her hair and watched her beautiful face. She was the picture of happy innocence, lying on his lap sleeping. He slept sitting up with her head in his lap that night.

The sound of rotor blades roused them out of their sleep. His enemies were coming again just like Gibby figured they would. It was early the next morning. The skies were brilliant blue, clear of all clouds. Now there were five turkey vultures circling his kill. That would tell his enemies something if they were smart. Jo Ann's fried back pack might be another clue for them, but there was nothing he could do about it now. He was not about to risk exposure by going out in the open. This time there were only three armed men plus a pilot and the chopper they came in was a civilian job. That told him someone had shortened the general's leash. The chopper could have carried five men. That told him they were a close knit group and likely a limited number of people. He reasoned that very few people, himself included, understood the importance of his map. But he didn't yet know why it was important. Maybe General Porter did.

He and Jo Ann got themselves ready. He had both rifles sighted in on the Dead Mule. He waited until the three men walked from the chopper to his decoy. The pilot left the chopper to stretch his legs. Patience was the key to Gibby's plan. Jo Ann watched the pilot and told Gibby when his head was turned away. Gibby didn't want the pilot to identify where his shots were coming from. At the precise moment when the pilot got curious and looked off in the opposite direction, the three armed men got caught being stupid. Gibby fired off two shots from his .308 before they had time to react. Both shots killed. One armed man remained. Terrified, he ran for the chopper hoping to get away. Neither the man nor the pilot saw where Gibby's shots had come from.

The pilot had already raced back to his helicopter and started the engine. The third man grabbed the landing runner and lifted himself up to board the chopper, but it was too late. As he opened his side door to climb into the craft, Gibby shot him clean through his neck. The pilot started lifting off with the passenger door open and the dead man sliding from his landing runner. Jo Ann handed Gibby the M1 just as he'd instructed her to do. He wanted to change rifles to get more range. He flipped the scope up and sighted the M1 on the chopper's rotor assembly. He had time for only one shot. It was a beauty. The high velocity customized M1 round tore into the rear rotor assembly right where it attached to the tail of the craft. The helicopter lifted up for a brief while before it began spinning out of control. Then it plunged back toward earth. The pilot's face showed terror as the helicopter's main rotor blades dug into the ground. An explosion and ball of flames followed. Gibby had killed them all.

Jo Ann had a ring side seat. She was awed by Gibby's shooting and stunned by what happened to the helicopter. "Gee, war sure is fun, ain't it, Gibby. You're a real good shot, ain't you Gibby?" she remarked wide eyed. She was more confident that Gibby could do anything than she had ever been. He was one man in a million and he was going to be hers forever. Seeing her man kill those other men made her pussy gush inside. A rush coursed through her blood and an intense feeling of love and devotion welled up inside her. A wild primordial sensation swept over her skin and flushed blood into her face. Her breast swelled with a deep pride that would remain in her bosom long after Gibby killed his foes. She was a huntress now. She helped take blood with her partner hunter. Enthralled with her newfound sense of invincibility, she felt her sex become juicy slippery wet.

She threw her arms around his neck, pressed her body close to his and began kissing him wildly. "I liked watching you kill those men, Gibby. It felt real good seeing them die when you shot them. I'm so excited, Gibby. Do you think we will kill again?"

"Maybe, if they throw more trouble our way, then yes, we'll kill again."

"Oh Gibby, I love you so much. I loved how you killed them. I really loved it! I have to make love with you right now. I just have to." Her lips quivered with overwhelming desires to unite with him. She quickly undid his pants and pulled on his cock until it was proud, hard and anxious. Then she led him to the ground and fucked him until she collapsed exhausted. All the sensations she had missed for weeks were returned to her and multiplied. She felt his massive organ pulse and shoot great wads of cum into her eager pussy. She had her Gibby back with her forever.

Gibby didn't resist her. He never did. He couldn't. He knew what wonderments followed soon after her kisses. He had so often dreamed of making love with her while sitting up here on the mountain that he'd nearly gone insane. Now she was finally here in his arms. He loved her and everything about her. He adored her honest simplicity and open heart. They had an unshakable chemistry that made them inseparable. He loved her kisses and the way she got goose bumps when he nuzzled her hair and kissed her neck. He adored every inch of her body. And he always loved making love with her, every thrust into her, and every lifting up of her wild fuck crazed ass by his big hands that pulled it up hard and firmly planted against his cock. And he loved feeling his hot pulsing releases into her welcoming pleasure palace. He loved every second of it.

CHAPTER TWENTY-ONE

VISITORS AT THE TROUT POOL

There's a special tranquil place where Rosemary, the story teller woman, goes when she needs solitude. It's a good four hour walk from her cabin into the deepest part of the forest. It's a spot next to a fresh water stream that widens out into a deep green pool below a cascade of small waterfalls. Tourists don't come this way. A large granite rock juts out over the pool. She can crawl onto the far edge of the slab, lie belly down and look at the trout school holding in the pool below. They lie mostly stationary, their heads into the current and their bodies only a few inches above the bottom. Their backs are dark green like the bottom. The slow sinuous motion of their bodies and tails sets them apart from the sticks and rocks. These native brook and cutthroats evolved their green-black backs and transparent fins over millions of years so hawks and eagles can't spot them from above. A speckled side or belly flashes dazzling colors when one shoots up from a deep hole or darts from behind a bottom rock to nab a drifting morsel. The flash disappears as suddenly as it appeared when the trout dashes back to its holding place.

The Great Spirit of all Living Things first revealed herself to Rosemary there at the Trout Pool. She appeared as a wispy angelic human like form as if she walked out from and upon the air. She came to see Rosemary. Something was on her mind. Startled, Rosemary challenged her, asked her who she was. She needed to know she wasn't dreaming. Was the apparition the Goddess of Eternity that she said she was or was this an imaginary happening? Suddenly, yet ever so gently, the Eternal Goddess placed her arm under Rosemary's middle and effortlessly lifted her up beside her. The goddess and the mortal floated together, suspended in mid-air over the trout pool.

"Would you like to see trout dance on their bellies?" asked the goddess.

"Yes," said Rosemary. She was afraid that she might be dropped into the pool, but that didn't happen.

The Spirit gracefully held out her unoccupied arm and rhythmically motioned it above the water. About fifty trout magically rose up to the water's surface. They simultaneously rolled over on their backs and swam in a sinuous circular movement around the pool.

"Now dance for us," she said while waving her free hand up and down. Every single trout thrust itself upward out of the water. The fish then held themselves suspended upright above the water's surface by thrashing their tails rapidly under the water's surface. Then they twirled about for a full minute, revealing their beautiful white bellies and colorful red, blue, black and orange speckled sides before returning to the water's depths.

"I'm convinced. Please forgive me for doubting you." Rosemary spoke to her as if she'd found a long lost friend. The goddess returned Rosemary to her granite rock slab and sat down beside her. Ever since that first time when Rosemary met her spirit friend, she's been able to come to this secret place, close her eyes and allow her thoughts to drift dreamily along like the waters flowing by below. That's when her stories come. They are not Rosemary's stories. They are stories from the goddess. For some reason she chose Rosemary to put her stories into written words. Rosemary takes her stories and returns to her cabin. At home with Bud, her cat, sitting on her lap, her writing table or lying on her feet, she writes the stories told to her by The Goddess of all Living Things.

The last time they were at the pool Rosemary asked the Spirit why she chose the story of Marty and David in *The Secret and the Butterfly* to be her first.

"Your readers needed to understand that there is real evil in the world. Most importantly, I wanted them to have an example of the tempting forms evil may take. I wanted them to see how evil walks among you."

"But, Marty wasn't really all that evil, was she?" Rosemary asked. "I mean, she was abandoned during childhood by her greedy mother. Don't you think she was as much a victim as an evil doer? Why did you have to choose her? I actually began to empathize with her. Sex is pretty glorious after all, isn't it? And all her partners were willing participants weren't they? I can think of many women in history who were far more evil than our Marty character from *The Secret and the Butterfly*. Take Queen Isabella who championed the Spanish Inquisition or how Cleopatra had Caesar murder her sister and brothers, for example."

"Actually, Marty was to you an imaginary person but to me she was a real person from one of my other planets that I decided to tell you about. Marty is a real woman, Rosemary. And the essence of Marty lives hidden in every woman in the universe on every planet. Every woman feels her urges and wants. We spirits want it that way. Evils, including coveting and lusts are vital to move civilization forward. A universe without Marty's in it would be static and uncreative, boring beyond words. I spared you the darkest side of Marty. Marty reveled in evil."

"Why did you spare me?"

"Well, it's very dark, almost too dark for someone with your sensitivities. Besides, Rosemary, you weren't curious enough to ask."

"I did prostitution in my former life, before I took up writing. I believe I can handle anything. What did I fail to ask about Marty?"

"Think back to when you were dreaming about David's murders. Victims from his drug operations showed up at the barnyard already dead. Now, wouldn't that be incredibly messy? How many murders would go unsolved if victims were getting shot? How would David's henchmen avoid leaving a trace of what was going on? There'd be blood, bullets, murder scenes for crime labs to profile, all sorts of additional clues would lead to David getting caught."

"But he didn't get caught."

"Exactly my point. Not for those murders. Not until our second book, *When the Butterflies Come,* when Marilyn blind sided him."

"So, please tell me, Spirit. How did David's drug murders go down?"

"Your Marty, your sweet corrupted innocent little girl, played a willing part in all of them. She worked the murders with David. That's how he roped her into the Firm so tightly. He filmed all the murders. He kept the films to prove to his drug dealer clients that he actually did the murders and he kept the films to blackmail Marty so she'd never stop working for him until he was ready to get rid of her."

"So, how did the murders take place? What was Marty's role in all this?"

"Well, there was one thing consistent about David's murders. He got rid of all the evidence of each murder. When he finally murdered Marty, he even got rid of every trace of her. Getting completely rid of the bodies was the key to the operation. But to get rid of the bodies and leave no clues behind all the victims were murdered on site."

"So, they were murdered in the barnyard, like Marty was murdered?"

"No, silly, these were tough men. They were career criminals. They were, in many cases, murderers themselves. David used an ingenious plan to lure each of them to his farm. He relied on the old Aesop fable where the fox looks up to the tree branch and tells the crow how beautiful it is. The crow is holding a piece of meat in its beak, but can't resist crowing its approval of the fox's praises. It caws, thus dropping its guard and its meat. The fox gets the meal that the crow loses. It's a technique David perfected."

"So, he flattered them somehow. Tell me, please."

"Okay. When David got the word from the drug kingpin that a guy needed to be murdered, that guy would get a call from David. David would tell the guy that his outstanding accomplishments were getting noticed in high circles. He told the victim that the top gangster wanted him treated to the finest piece of ass anywhere in the country; and all expenses for her were prepaid."

"That piece of ass would be Marty, right?"

"Right, David would invite the guy to an orgy at his farm where Marty would be the star attraction. Once the victim arrived David would take him into a secret room."

"To the green room where David kept all the insects?"

"No silly, this was a separate room. It was also on the lower basement level of David's house, but it had its own hidden door that opened from the left side of the bookcase. Opened, the door revealed a tunneled passage covered with alluring mauve colored flock wallpaper that led the victim far away from the insect room. Marty escorted the victim through a long tunnel that opened into a huge cavernous underground room. It had a massive domed ceiling with recessed lighting. The lighting had a blinding effect if you looked up at the ceiling, but down on the floor of the room the lighting had a soft seductive warm glow about it."

"And David was there waiting for the victim?"

"Yes. He hid in the dark behind the entrance door. Marty went to the far end of the room and disappeared into her dressing room. Then she reappeared under a soft blue spotlight dressed in seven sheer colored silks. There were two other men there, hidden from sight of the victim. They were there to assist in the murders as accomplices after the fact and to help Marty complete her ritual.

"Then what?"

"Well, then Marty danced a very seductive dance to soft music, a sort of belly dance called 'The Dance of the Seven Veils'. Marty did a perfect imitation of Salome, the temptress who seduced King Herod and demanded the head of John the Baptist as her reward. Marty worked herself into a seductive trance at these affairs. She loved her role."

"So, she danced for the guy?"

"Yes. She put on a very seductive performance. She made writhing movements with her torso, performed rhythmic undulations with her shimmering oiled and perfumed belly. She moved her hips to simulate fornication, then canted her pelvis and sensuously rubbed her opened pussy before her victim's face. She walked over to a raised leather bed. It had a head rest at one end of it that was supported independently upon steel rods rising from the floor. The bed, except the leather padded headrest, was covered with a soft red satin sheet. It was a very sexy scene.

"Just imagine yourself in the mind of the male victim. He sees Marty lying there on the red bed sheet, opening her legs to receive him. His thoughts are racing wildly. 'This woman is fantastic. She's the sexiest, most beautiful woman I've ever seen.

My heart is pounding, my mouth is salivating. I want her. I must have her. I must make love to her.'

"He's thinking great thoughts now. After stripping layer by layer, Marty is completely naked. She casually lies down upon her raised bed and begins sucking the two other men. She opens her legs widespread revealing her butterfly tattoo. She invitingly writhed and lifted her pelvis, flaunting and fingering her pussy while sucking the cock of her victim standing next to the bed. After watching this exhibition for a short while the victim became obsessed with thoughts of making love to Marty. By now he was out of his mind with desire. Here's where Marty played her critical role in the murders.

"'You have such a handsome face' she would say. 'Before you put your beautiful cock into me would you, could you, please, please put your handsome face in my pussy and lick her? She wants you to kiss her so much. She'd love it if you'd please kiss her. She'd love it if you would give her an orgasm.'

"The victims all agreed to comply with Marty's request. What man wouldn't? She then explained her most satisfying orgasms happen while she's standing upright. She instructs the man to take her place on the bed and place his head upon the headrest while she stands over him with her legs straddling his head. The bed level was designed so that when Marty stood over the man's head her pussy was resting softly upon his mouth. All he needed to do is thrust his tongue upward and stroke her clitoris. She caressed her victims' heads while they licked her.

"'Oh, yes. Yes. That feels so wonderful,' she began talking in her soft seductive voice. 'You are soooo good. I love feeling your tongue inside me,' she whispered softly.

'Oh, keep going. Kiss my pussy. That's it. Lick my clit, you big handsome man. Yes, yes, keep going. I'm almost there.' Marty continued talking excitedly to her victim, all the while tenderly caressing his head, while he brings her to orgasm.

At the moment of her coitus Marty let out a scream. 'Oh, wow, I'm coming!' she screamed. 'I love you! This is the moment I've waited for!' At that exact instant Marty arched her head and torso backward and grabbed the victim's head by his ears, pulled his mouth and head upward and held it tightly against her pussy thus stretching his neck, while releasing her orgasmic fluids into his mouth. Marty then screamed 'I'm coming! I'm coming *now, NOW!*'

That was David's signal to flip the switch.

"From the ceiling high above a massive guillotine blade was released. It fell from its position exactly above the edge of the bed where the bed separates from the independently supported headrest. The razor sharp blade falls cleanly through the victim's neck and decapitates him while his tongue is still deep inside Marty's pussy being drenched in her juices. Marty's part in the execution was finished, but then she did much more than what David asked of her.

"She lifted the severed head to her mouth and kissed the victim's lips. While the victim's blood and Marty's orgasmic juices mingle and dribble from the severed throat she maintained her kiss, pressing her own head hard against her victim's. She stared lovingly into her victim's eyes while they blink in the combined wonderment of her eroticism with their horrible reality of traumatic death. Her debauched deed of simultaneous coitus while committing murder stimulated Marty into a trance-like ethereal state. She appeared beholden to the murdered head, as if she had performed a holy deed. She was spellbound by the head. She imagined she could travel with it as it transits from the earthly world into the spirit realms.

"'You have a great tongue,' she'd tell the still conscious head. Marty always complemented her victims' dying heads. She understood that a dying head experiences a transitory time while it still has all its sensory functions in tact. She wanted to impress her unbridled passionate love upon it so that it would carry that love with it into eternity. In her uninhibited passionate way Marty wanted each of these severed heads to know she truly loved them. She loved all her lovers intensely like that. Carl, Donny, Darren, the four J's, her teacher, her orgy partners and Bob all felt her same intensity. It bonded her lovers to her, even the lovers that moved on to other women. That was her obsessive nature. She had a possessive fetish about every man she ever made love with. It's the nature of a nymphomaniac.

Marty could not stand the thought that any man who once knew her love could ever love any woman other than her. She studied each of the dead men's heads while its expressions changed in its final seconds. She liked to frame a memory of each dead head and burnish the memory of each decapitated lover into her mind. That's a woman in desperate need of love, Rosemary. Marty's quest for love drove her to extremes of madness.

"Some severed heads would express grief, some wonderment, some puzzlement. She smiled joyfully like a happy child at each dying head as its brain went through its final convulsive horrors. She knew she had sole possession of the head's final thoughts and impressions. She lovingly rubbed the head's nose in her scented pussy one final time. She used her special funerary fragrance of White Star Lily blended with white gardenia and white rose. That's how she communicated her condolences to her victims. They were not genuine condolences in a mortal sense. In her mind and in her spirit sense she believed that through her condolence ritual she took possession of the head's spirit and introduced it to her own, its perpetual lover in its spirit life. You could say she was a sensuous, sympathetic spiritual murderess. Senses of scent and sound cling to life for some time after the vision sense dies. She lavished her sensory finale upon the dying head's spirit when she rubbed its nose in her spiritual holy place, her sex. In her mind she was giving her eternal self essence and love to those heads.

"By the time she finished, each head would have heard her pleasured mirthful laugh, lusty sensuous voice; tasted her pussy, seen her face and welcoming loving smile close up, heard her congratulate it for the joys its tongue gave her, felt her gentle caressing touches and her forehead pressed against its own; and inhaled her pussy's perfumed erotic essence. When the head's brain was no longer capable of exhibiting signs of life through eye blinks or facial contortions she gave it to David. The victim's role in the ritual was finished. The decapitated body was rolled onto a cart. David took it and its severed head away for rendering and insect processing. Marty then made love with her male assistants in a craven orgy on the blood soaked table next to the still dripping bloody guillotine blade. This pagan deification ritual sanctified her pussy and released Marty from any misgivings she may have had about committing murder. She believed she was a goddess who performed holy acts of ritual murder, thus saving these men from the travails of their lives of crime and their eventual imprisonment.

"These murders stirred a euphoric primal urge within Marty. Murder returned her spirit soul back to ancient times. It elicited her pagan carnal urges. In her mind she was a pagan priestess from another time and place, presiding over the decapitations and eviscerations of her tribal foes. Her emotive release was venerated by her victorious warriors. She became deified through her blood lust and orgies. She felt a glorious triumphant release coursing through her blood when she murdered and when she romantically engaged those dying heads. She exulted in her insane wickedness by consorting with her helpers. The murders also moved Marty's spirit forward into eternal time where it could recombine with its many lovers.

"David gave Marty special compensation payments to reward her for her role in these murders; but these payments were only incidental to the thrills the murders gave her. She relished her role of seductive unrepentant murderess. Mortal earthlings may view Marty as a she devil, a man eater, the female anti-Christ, but we spirits only see an abused mortal soul imprisoned by her emotions. Her soul cried out for love, begged to know love, but she couldn't have it. Murder freed her soul of that terrible burden. No one should have to go through life without knowing love."

"Was David just another mortal soul?" The differences between mortal and immortal souls had never occurred to Rosemary.

"Yes, just another mortal soul. Every mortal soul has good and bad within it. The mortal soul expresses its emotions and lives them. The immortal soul is contained within creation space itself. Its purpose is to be and to be again and again, to come into mortality and return to immortality. It's a going in and a coming out over and over, forever.

"In this fashion the mortal souls of Marty and David murdered and disposed of some twenty men and five women who caused problems for David's crime syndicate. Each execution took place over a spongy floor mat that caught the spilled blood. The mats were burned. The bodies were methodically dispersed to the pigs, the goats, the wood chipper, the insects and the guinea fowl."

"Spirit, how can you justify allowing a mortal soul, like Marty, to behave in such immoral ways? How can you permit such cruelty to be visited upon one mortal being by another?"

"As a Spirit, Rosemary, spirits like Marty's can't distinguish between good and evil."

"I don't understand."

"It's a process, love. You see, I only create the spirit in a mortal soul and attach their soul spirit to their unborn DNA.

Once they are born and develop I only play a partial role in the human's life. I can implant a thought here and there. I can set up a circumstance and whisper some guidance but it is up to the individual human soul to decide which of my whispers to listen to or which of my circumstances to pursue. Each mortal soul follows its own self determined path. That's apart from the person's immortal soul. It's a separate spirit dimension."

"I'm more confused than before. Can you explain what you mean by using Marty as an example?"

"Yes. Try to see Marty as unformed clay. Her immortal spirit enters her at the same time her DNA tells the clay it is to become Marty instead of a giraffe or a whale. What I'm saying is the eternal spirit is bound to her DNA. The eternal spirit fixes to her clay, her mind and body."

"Where did this eternal spirit come from?"

"It came from everywhere. It exists and pulsates in the spirit world. It appears and reappears in human clay, in human bodies throughout the multitudes of universes and planets. It is affixed to what you humans call dark matter. It does not actually travel. It simply makes its appearance and reappearance. It's before, after and with the concept you refer to as time. It's omnipresent and all knowing with eternal cognoscenti. It doesn't need to travel from one universe or one galaxy or one planet to another. It doesn't need to move faster than the speed of light to appear in one human somewhere or another human somewhere else. It's much faster than light speed. It is instantaneous. Light speed to us spirits moves like molasses in January to you humans. Light speed is infinitely slow. Spirit incarnation is instantaneous."

"But, Marty was so evil. How can you allow people like her to even exist? What's the purpose of even having them?"

"I can't reveal a purpose to you as if there is some end goal to life. Life's purpose is to experience its emotions. It is not to go to another planet through space travel or to go to some other star system and meet people like yourselves and conquer them or play football with them. Human life is without purpose except to experience the emotions that well up within the human spirit and the human soul. There's no need to do space travel as humans. Your spirits already exist throughout space. Humans just like you already exist on other planets in other worlds. You are already in untold trillions of places."

"Really, that seems incredulous," said a skeptical Rosemary.

"Why? You are taught in religions that God made man in his own image and he was happy with his work, right?"

"Yes, I remember that."

"Well, if he was happy with the humans he created on Earth it stands to reason that he created humans everywhere in the universe, too. You are right now being born again somewhere and a mortal soul is being attached to your exact DNA. When your mortal body expires you will instantly have a new life somewhere, a reemergence from your immortal soul. You do not need to ride a rocket ship and do space travel to get to where you already are and where you will be."

"So, could you please explain Marty's evil persona to me in a way that I can understand her."

"Okay. Marty needed to be a bad girl because that behavior was what released her spirit from its anguish. The anguish was the feeling of abandonment when she was a child, when Marilyn left her at the boarding school. That experience scarred Marty's mortal soul and she spent her whole life trying to remove the scar. Similarly, Barbara spent her whole life trying to make her father, Big Chief, proud of her. Bob spent his whole life trying to redeem himself from his guilt. He believed it was his fault that his father died and left him orphaned with a manic mother. He tried to overachieve and be good to everybody."

"But, Marty murdered. How does her spirit justify murder?"

"Marty's spirit is a lot like a Pawnee warrior's spirit. When a Pawnee takes a scalp he believes it gives him spiritual power over his enemy and he believes that the Great Spirit will find him worthy as a warrior. That's an emotion that makes him feel good when he scalps. That emotion wells up in his mortal soul.

"When Marty participated in decapitations and when she romanced her victims' dying heads, her mortal spirit hoped to ensure that the Great Universal Spirit would shower her with many loving lives freed from her nagging abandonment feeling. Her spirit knew that each dying head had a brief life of perhaps a minute or so before the human brain died from lack of oxygen. Then the spirit of the head would return to the dark matter and bind with it until released in another life. During that brief interlude between mortal life and death Marty's mortal spirit tried to communicate in every sensory way to the mortal spirit of the dying head. She touched it lovingly. She kissed it lovingly. She spoke lovingly to it. She lovingly imparted her scent to it. She stared lovingly into its dying eyes. She actually loved the dying head with her whole heart and soul. Within her spirit Marty was finding peace that somehow in other lives her immortal spirit would reunite with the immortal spirits of those dead heads and those spirits would combine and reappear in mortal happiness together. Marty's behavior which you term evil was to Marty's spirit a very loving behavior. She gave the fullest measures of her love to those dying heads. Her human emotions found peace with that. Each murder was a good and wonderful experience for her."

"So you spirits are okay with her evil? You, the Great Spirit of all living things are okay with her evil?"

"Impertinence and labels will never help you understand the forces that drive emotions nor will they help you grasp the profound beauty of the spirit. Life does not actually track like some formulaic romance novel, Rosemary. Spirituality is so much deeper, so much more beautiful and so much more dimensionally diverse."

"Even the spirit that shows itself as evil to us humans?"

"Yes. What one person would see as evil another may see as beautiful. Perspective is an individual thing. The mortal world defines right and wrong, but the spiritual world simply accepts behaviors as the natural outgrowth of emotions. We spirits simply observe. That is our role. It is not to judge or to proscribe behaviors or to make laws. That is the role of you mortals."

"But, at the moment of her death, didn't Marty repent?"

"Well, yes, she did."

"And, aren't you going to allow her another chance in another life? Isn't that what the little Pieridae butterfly told her? Aren't you going to keep your word?"

"Here, Rosemary, hold me close." With that, the Great Spirit of all Living Things pulled Rosemary to her bosom. Then she kissed her on her mouth as if they were soul sisters. "If it helps you feel at peace, then yes, Marty will have another life, and it will be a good one."

"How can you do that? I do not doubt your powers. I'd just like to know, that's all."

"Well, as I said there are many worlds like your Earth and many soul spirits to inhabit them. It's really quite simple for me to make it happen."

"But, how?"

"There are trillions upon trillions of planets like Earth throughout this universe; and there are trillions upon trillions of universes. And, believe it or not there are trillions upon trillions of human inhabitants on trillions of these planets; and, that's just a smidgeon of the different life forms and different planets available to welcome souls in need of a fresh start."

"But, I always thought all the different planets would have different life forms. Isn't that true?"

"No, that's not true at all, Rosemary. You've been seeing too many crazy Hollywood movies. There are no creatures from other worlds with weird wrinkles on their heads, there are no furry faced men that look like teddy bears that talk, there are no raging monsters that arise from the oceans and eat entire cities, and there are no huge blobs of gunk that slime all over people and devour them. That's all just nutty Hollywood stuff to sell movies. Long ago we spirits did some experiments with different life forms all over the universes. That's why you see the Egyptian tombs with men that have bird heads and why you see a man's torso on a horse; but we gave up on those ideas eons ago."

"Well, why did you give up on your experiments?"

"We found that the human DNA was the most adaptable, best suited life form for all mortal living evolution. It can change over time, it can learn abstract concepts, and it is incredibly sensitive and emotive. We love humans, so we populated the entire universe with humans, along with accompanying assorted other lesser animals, of course. Some of my spirit friends, especially my male spirit friends, even appear in earthly flesh to copulate with you humans. That satisfies our urge to procreate throughout the universe. Your biblical stories accurately reflect some of those happenings."

"So, there really are people like us all throughout the universe?"

"Yes, exactly like you humans here on Earth."

"Exactly?"

"Exactly, down to the numbers of hairs on their heads. See those aspens higher up on the forest hillside? Each one is like a person, a human person. But each one is part of just one plant that has an underground life. You would call that a root system. I call it a soul presence. When an aspen dies, its root doesn't die. Well, when Marty died, her immortal soul didn't die. That soul can't die. It just pops up again on another earth or even here on your earth, manifest within a newborn child. It will grow to become an adult human woman. It will have identical feelings and emotions in every respect."

"But will her soul be good or evil?"

"I will ward off the dark forces from it. Her next soul will be good. She'll be so good her nickname will be Goody Two Shoes. She may even have a hard time losing her virginity. You may even get to meet her new soul. That's something I'll need to think about."

"Why didn't you ward off the dark forces from the Marty that was here on Earth? Why did you let these awful things happen to her? Why did you let her become so evil?"

"I allowed it so that her eternal soul would appreciate and cherish goodness when it reawakens. Bob was just her taste of the bountiful goodness that will come to Marty's new soul. Her mortal soul first needed release from the horror of her abandonment by her mother. Her life took a twisted path, but ultimately her soul found its release. That's what's most important."

"Then, what about Barbara and Bob? Was Bob evil to go with Marty? Wasn't there anything evil about Barbara? And, why did you make me wait until my second book, *When the Butterflies Come,* before you finally allowed Barbara to make love with Bob? And why did you come up with such a suggestive cover for my second book?"

"Bob was an innocent soul who was twice romanced by evil. He was romanced by both Marty and David. But evil could not have Bob. I wanted him to discover the love that Barbara had for him. I wanted him to come to the understanding that all women are not alike. There's a huge difference between a hot pussy and true love. He needed to figure that out for himself. He needed to learn that waiting for a good woman is worth it. Men can be pretty dense, you know.

"Barbara's beautiful face makes a wonderful cover for your second book. The face of a woman is the very definition of beauty. There is nothing more beautiful than a woman's face. She is pursing her lips to mouth the word 'when' because that's her signal to Bob that she wants to make love. That's when her butterflies come. That's when Barbara had her first orgasm. Those little Pieridaes helped her lift her spirits to where she experienced nirvana.

"Barbara was a good woman throughout her entire life. Her father taught her about good and evil. I mix characters' natures because we spirits need to amuse ourselves by watching you humans fumble around with your life choices. No two people are identical in thought and behavior. You are like individual snowflakes. Of the trillions of planets that I watch over, Earth is my most interesting. You Earth humans take yourselves way too seriously. You are lovably ridiculous sometimes, but you are, each and every one of you, fascinating creatures. Earth's humans are great entertainment for us. We spirits can't just pop into a movie theater like you do, you know.

"It's getting late for you. Run along home now and feed Bud. He needs you. Get some sleep then wake up in the middle of the night. A new story will come to you."

"It will?"

"I promise."

"You can promise that?"

"Shhh," she put her finger to her lips. "Of course I can. I'll reveal my secret code to you."

"What code?"

"The Tesla Code, it's about freedom. It harnesses the power of the deepest darkness within dark matter. It frees and combines separated souls. It masters wave whips and loop slings."

"Wave whips? Loop slings?"

"Tomorrow, Rosemary, go home and sleep now. I am sending some people to see you. They are in desperate trouble. They must escape planet Earth. They'll explain their plight when they meet you. They are being pursued by the greatest of evils, the evil of darkest darkness. Give them comfort. Show them how to release themselves from earthly cares and trust the spirits of the butterflies. One woman among them is part Indian, part White and part Hispanic. Her name is CC. She is a strong character. Help CC feel the freedom that the Mariposa, the butterfly, feels when it emerges from chrysalis. Now scoot, Rosemary. It's late. You've got to get on home. There are wolves prowling the forest at night. I need you safe to give voice to the people I am sending you."

With that the Spirit kissed Rosemary's forehead, walked into the air and disappeared. A single white Pieridae fluttered into the space where she vanished. Rosemary knew wonderment.

CHAPTER TWENTY-TWO

ADMISSION

S heila's mind turned with thoughts. She categorized what things she could define and solve. The missile defense of the United States was simple. The math equations were finished and turned over to the implementation programmers. But the aerial drone problem was more daunting. There were variables she couldn't define and factors she couldn't quantify. Her goal of creating solvable polynomial equations of variables and coefficients with predictable outcomes was getting nowhere. Asymmetric warfare seemed impossible to quantify. It did not matter that the country had a trillion dollar defense capability. It was more of a battle for the minds of potential terrorists. How could she quantify what was happening inside the thoughts of a teen or young adult somewhere in the world? How could she quantify what would turn that brain toward destruction and carnage? It was mind boggling to contemplate the probability chains.

She tried to analogize her problem but the best she could do was to visualize a man with a sledgehammer, the defense department, trying to smash a million mosquitoes, the terrorists, inside a vast convention hall. Sure, we could kill some of them, maybe with a lot of work we could even kill most of them; but we could not kill all of them before one of them drew blood from someone in the convention hall. It was a given that she did not have the license to exterminate all flying insects, or whole populations, only mosquitoes, or terrorists. She realized she could never know the exact number of mosquitoes or control their behavior, or propensity to draw blood. So her mind turned toward ways to control the way the mosquitoes flew and the way they delivered their deadly payloads.

How could anyone know how many terrorists had drones? How many terrorists had access to multiple drones? How could their access to radioactive wastes, nerve gases, anthrax, biological diseases, or even high explosives be defined? That also seemed impossible. Our intelligence didn't reach deep enough into every adversarial nation's capabilities to know with certainty whether or not they would supply deadly agents to terrorists. So, the access to drones, the delivery platforms, and the payloads, the deadly agents, could not be the main weakness of the terrorists. It had to be in their ability to control drones in flight. How does one control a mosquitoes' flight path? What were the chances and methods of accomplishing that? But those possibilities, too, were difficult to quantify and defeat.

She wracked her brain but kept hitting the wall of no. No, she couldn't block enemy access to drones. That was a non starter. Producers of the things were ubiquitous. People could resell them and controls on purchasers were practically non existent. They could be bought and dismantled in other countries, shipped here and reassembled. And no, she couldn't control what foreign entities might be sympathizers with the terrorists and sell them lethal payloads; and she couldn't rule out domestic sympathizers either. A source control nightmare that was impossible to model was all she could envision.

That left flight interruption or disablement. But how to discern which drones were enemy drones? She was stumped. Unless every single drone had to be government inspected, a chip installed that responded to a nationwide sensor grid, like aircraft that squawk friendly, she was left with venue by venue protection schemes. Bulky, human dependent, costly analog systems that aimed lasers at suspected hostiles were certain to be ineffective. The enemy could beat those pedestrian methods by sheer numbers. She was back at the sledgehammer and mosquitoes dilemma. Only one drone in ten needed to get through a human defense team at a football stadium. That would be enough to kill everyone at the venue. She decided that, for now, she needed to give her mind a rest and let the problem percolate in her subconscious in the hope that something reasonably reliable and cost effective would emerge like magic out of somewhere.

But there was another problem that vexed her thoughts. It played against the drone problem in a nutty sort of way that she didn't understand. It bedeviled her because it was a human behavioral problem. She knew she was not good at understanding human behavior. Johnny proved that. This drone problem was like her boyfriend Johnny problem. It was shadowy, elusive, evasive, and deceptive. It had to do with why she was even here in the first place. Why was she chosen for this contract? Surely there were legions of operations research types in the armed forces departments that worked on the drone problem. Surely they had better intelligence at their disposal than she did. It seemed like it was more of a search problem or a linear programming problem to optimize the odds of the least lethality being inflicted on the population. That was pretty pedestrian mathematics, so why ask her to jump into this?

And why was she paired with CC? And why was the top floor of her office building darkened? And why had she never been introduced to Henry Kelly, the co-chief executive of Bear and Otter? And why did a marine need to accompany her everywhere she went unless she was accompanied by CC? And why did CC have those sex advertisements plastered all over her jeep? She'd never actually seen CC with a man. She'd never detected any sign that a male had been in their apartment or their jeep. All women know that men are messy by nature. They leave their marks on things. There were no dirty dishes in the sink, no forgotten umbrellas, papers, books. There were no signs of a man spilling something around the table, no crumbs on the floor, and no signs of raids on the lunchmeat in the fridge. There were no dirty hand prints on any of the doors or window glass. There were no sounds of a male either. No grunts when they came with a semen shot, no loud farts, no calls of 'Hey Babes' sounded from CC's bedroom on the nights she entertained. And there were no man smells. Nothing. No raunchy male body odor on the furniture, no lingering smells in the air after they left.

But there was something else. Some nights when CC entertained she heard soft moans emanate from CC's bedroom. Then recently somebody got careless. Last night she couldn't sleep thinking about the terrorist drone problem. She woke up at 3AM and went to the kitchen for a glass of milk. Earlier that night she'd heard the moans from CC's room. The revelation came in the still of the night. She was barefoot, like she always was when she went to the kitchen at night; and she kept the lights off. She always kept the lights off so her eyes wouldn't think it was daytime. She needed them to stay within their circadian rhythm to put her back to sleep.

Then it happened. Her foot stepped on something round and made of cloth. It was a G string. But CC wore panties, not G strings. She suspended her repulsive instincts and picked up the G string and smelled it. It had the distinct smell of Channel # 5 perfume. She held it up to the dim light that came through the loft windows. It had a blond pubic hair stuck to it. She'd seen CC naked many times. CC's body hair was all black. Revelation spoke its silent truth. CC was not what she pretended to be. She was a lesbian. Her jeep billboard display was a classic deflection tactic. The real CC screamed out to those astute enough to catch it. She used purple tie downs for her Jeep's canvas top. And, she used purple ribbons in her hair. Those were not coincidental mishaps of someone who couldn't dress herself. They were subtle signals telling others of like persuasion which sex CC preferred in her bed.

Sheila and CC had a morning routine. CC rose first and made breakfast. Sheila showered, ate breakfast with CC then cleaned the dishes. This was the morning after Sheila's discovery. Scrambled eggs were the morning fare. The two women sat opposite at their small kitchen table. Neither woman spoke except to say 'Good Morning.' Sheila waited. When the coffee pot percolated and summoned CC to take it off the stove Sheila struck. CC's back was turned when Sheila placed the errant G string on top of CC's eggs. When CC returned to the table she saw the evidence of her nighttime adventure lying there on her plate. Her eyes showed alarm when they looked into Sheila's.

"You eat more than eggs, don't you CC?" Sheila's face was somber. Since finding the G string she had time to think. If CC lied to her about her sex preferences, then what else was CC lying about? It was time to discover the truth.

"That's personal. You have no business prying into my private life." CC picked up the garment and stuck it into a pocket in her bathrobe.

"Oh, but I do, CC," Sheila leveled a grave stare that bored through CC's eyes. "You are now a security risk to the projects I am working on. I'm sure George Palmer will understand when I tell him that you are the reason I must resign from my contract. I can not risk being part of some nefarious scheme of yours.

"You lied to me about who you are. Old Yellow's hetero-sexual posters are phony misdirects, just like you. You're no friend, CC," Sheila shook her head in slow deliberation.

"You're a traitor to our country. This may lead to an investigation. Oh, no, not may. This *will* lead to an investigation. I promise you. You may even spend hard time in Leavenworth for compromising my top secret projects," Sheila nodded while maintaining her hard stare.

"We're through, CC. I'm not your friend. I don't believe your story about your son or why you joined the Corps. I don't know you. I don't trust you," Sheila bared her teeth in a snarl as she spoke.

"I'm not your source of information for the spy you had in your room last night. You better lawyer up right away. You know what, CC? I've never called anybody this in my life but I'm calling you this now. You are an asshole, CC. And, speaking as one woman to another, CC, you disgust me." Sheila pursed her lips and shook her head to demonstrate total contempt for the vile lesbian traitor.

CC's world shattered. She couldn't deal with Sheila's accusations. The woman who left that G string was just her friend. Nothing sinister was going on. CC just loved women. She was soft hearted and loving. She'd never hurt a fly let alone betray her country. She broke into sobs believing Sheila was going to destroy her life.

"Sheila, it's not like that. Honest it isn't," she whimpered through her sobs.

"I'm not a traitor. I'm a good American. I'm a good person. Please don't say anything. Please Sheila," she pleaded.

"Please don't tell," she begged. "It's not what you think. I love you Sheila. I'd never hurt your projects. Never!

"Please let me explain," she blabbered. She put her hands palms down on the table and bowed her shaking head as she spoke. "That woman doesn't know anything about what we do at Bear and Otter.

"She's just an old friend," she said, now lifting her head and staring into Sheila's eyes as streams of tears ran down her cheeks.

"I've known her since before I was married," she continued with halting sobs. There was shame in her voice, and honesty too. She was letting the truth about herself come out. Her defenses dropped away, revealing her honest self to Sheila.

"We go way back, Sheila. We love each other. That's all it is. She's never asked anything about our projects and I've never told her anything. You need to believe me, Sheila. Please believe me." CC was reduced to a blubbering pile of Jell-O. She was totally at Sheila's mercy. Her potential loss of career and possible prison shook her to her core.

"Why should I believe you," Sheila's head canted and her eyes squinted, peering deeply into CC's soul. "What else are you not telling me? I have questions I want answered or I'm going straight to Mr. Palmer about you. And you'd better be completely truthful, CC," Sheila's tone carried an ominous warning.

"I'll tell you everything, Sheila," CC's chest heaved while she sobbed. "Just please don't tell on me."

"We'll see," Sheila's voice tone carried a hint of possible redemption. She wanted to hear a complete confession. "Let's start with how you ended up in the Marine Corps. Were married once or weren't you? And did you have a child or didn't you? And who was in your room last night?"

"Okay. Yes. I was married. His name was Mick. We had a child. He was a boy named Frank. My lesbian girl friend's name is Carol. I knew Carol before I met Mick."

"So, you are bi sexual?" Sheila raised her eyebrows. She was curious about CC's bizarre sex life.

"Yes. I love the feeling of a penis inside me, but I must admit I don't have that experience too often anymore. Carol is bi-sexual too. She has a husband."

"First things first, tell me what happened to you and your husband?"

"It's a long story."

"That's okay. I'm calling in sick today and you're staying home to watch me and run for things I might need. We've got all day." Sheila's tone softened. She could tell CC had a deep need to unburden herself. She was sympathetic to women who'd been knocked around in a man's world.

"Well, it starts with my blood."

"Your blood, what's your blood got to do with it?" Sheila's jaw went slack.

"Yes. My blood is a weird fucked up blood type. My chromosomes cause hemophilia in a male child. Mick and I were married in Mexico and we didn't do a blood test before we got married."

"So, when you had baby Frank he was a hemophiliac and Mick divorced you because of that?"

"Well, not exactly. Mick was good for a while. But one day while I was watching Frank everything changed. Frank was three years old. I kept him in a big playpen in our front yard. He was safe. I kept him out there so I could watch him from my kitchen window. But one day an asshole who ran some big mutual fund company came driving down our street in an old Cadillac sedan with flags hanging out the side. He was screaming on a bull horn something about there was going to be a nuclear bomb attack and everybody needed to get off the streets. He was a fucking nut."

"It sounds like he was crazy."

"He was crazy, a total nut job. But when he came barreling down our street he saw kids playing in the street so he swerved right up onto our front lawn to avoid the kids in the street. His car hit the corner of Frankie's playpen and tipped it over. Well, little Frankie got frightened. He ran toward the side of the house. Then he fell on a rake that I had left on the side of the house and the rake cut his leg.

"Frank started bleeding pretty badly. That panicked him. He ran toward the back yard looking for me. This is painful to tell." CC wiped her tears.

"Go on, CC. I'm listening." Sheila's voice sounded sympathetic.

"Okay," CC sniffled. She began talking haltingly as she relived her painful experience. "Right at the corner of the back yard on the side of our house I had this little rose garden. Frankie stumbled into the roses and cut himself more. Then he panicked terribly and ran from rose bush to rose bush. He cut himself everywhere. It was so horrible, Sheila" CC sobbed and her breast heaved in grief.

"Go on, CC. It's all right." Sheila could feel CC's pain.

"Finally poor little Frankie made it to the back steps of the house. He was weakened from blood loss and terrified. He fell onto the back steps head first. My poor little boy bled to death because of that crazy son of a bitch who drove like a mad man. Oh, my poor, poor little boy. He was so beautiful, Sheila. He was such a good little boy. I loved him so much." CC sobbed and cried streams of tears. Her grief was unbearable. What happened to her son brought back memories of unbearable pain.

Sheila watched CC relive her sorrow and waited a respectful interlude for her crying to subside. "Tell me what happened next, CC," she said softly.

"Sure," sniffled CC. "Later we found out that the reckless driver was just annoyed because the regular street had a parade on it, so he did this terrible thoughtless thing. But the cops only gave him a warning. Can you believe that? He murdered my son and he only got a traffic warning! The law isn't fair. Little people get stepped on like ants. Oh, Mick and I tried to sue that son of a bitch, but he had these high priced lawyers.

They claimed it wasn't his fault that the rake was there or that we kept Frankie in the front yard. Can you believe that? It wasn't his fault that he drove like a fucking nut. They blamed Frankie's death on me. It was my fault for keeping my hemophiliac son where I could keep an eye on him. It was my fault for having a rake propped against the house. It was my fault for having a rose garden. I love roses. What's so wrong about a woman loving roses? Those fucking lawyers! I wanted to kill them, but that wouldn't bring little Frankie back. I've let it all go, Sheila. Well, I try to let it all go, but it's so hard. It's very, very hard."

"I'm terribly sorry, CC' Sheila's voice was fully sympathetic now. No woman could fake CC's flood of emotions. The woman's life had been totally destroyed by forces beyond her control. "And then Mick divorced you?"

"Not right away," CC shook her head. Her tears were subsiding and being replaced with anger.

"He beat me quite a few times telling me I was careless and stupid. Finally I hit him back real hard on his mouth and then he divorced me soon after that. I just was not going to take it anymore. My blood type isn't my fault. What happened to Frankie was a series of accidents set in motion by the reckless driver. Frankie's death wasn't my fault either. I didn't care if I lived or died after I lost my child.

"And I couldn't take getting hit by Mick anymore. He became a drunken son of a bitch and he'd just hit me all the time. We couldn't have another son because my blood wasn't right for having sons. They'd all get hemophilia. So, we stopped having sex. Then Mick kept hitting me and hitting me until I wished I was dead. That's when I punched him right in his face, really hard. I was not going to take his shit one more day.

"Then he divorced me. I had no way to support myself. My parents were dead. So, I joined the Marines. They love me and I love them. So, please, Sheila. I need to stay a marine.

The United States Marine Corps is everything to me. I have nothing else. Please understand." CC was sobbing.

Sheila offered a handkerchief to her. It was time to make amends. "CC, if you want to stay in the Marines you need to trust me now," said Sheila, holding CC by the hand. "It's important. I want you to forget what you've been told about this contract I'm working on and what they told you about me. You need to believe that I am a good American and I am putting the country's interests ahead of all other interests.

"Listen to me. CC. There are things going on at Bear and Otter that make no sense, and I am concerned that there is more to my contract than I've been told. Do you know what I'm trying to say?" Sheila peered into CC's eyes.

"No, I don't. Honest I don't, Sheila," CC shook her head. She was clueless about Sheila's suspicions. "I don't know what you're getting at."

"That's okay. I shouldn't expect you to do anything more than what they tell you to do. But you need to help me, CC. It's very important."

"What's important?" CC lifted her head to look at Sheila. She was willing to be needed by her friend and hopeful that she could be of help to her.

"I don't know yet, but that's why I need your help. Listen, CC does it make sense to you that the government would have me working on this drone project when there are all sorts of people and resources available for that already in place?"

"I don't know. I guess not," CC realized Sheila was parting a fog about Bear and Otter. CC admitted to herself that she had no idea why the firm did the work it did.

"And does it make sense to you why we must use a private elevator and go to a floor beneath a floor that is always dark?"

"No, it doesn't." CC wondered why she hadn't asked herself these questions.

"And why haven't I ever met Henry Kelly? Can you explain that? Have you ever met him?"

"Yes. I've met him. I see him every week."

"Why, CC? Why do you see him?"

"I don't know why I must see him. I take coffee to him. He always asks about you, if you've made any calls, met any people outside the firm, or copied your hard drives onto thumb drives. He asks me all sorts of stuff about you."

"I see. And the top floor, have you ever been up there?"

"Yes. That's where I go to take his coffee to him."

"Describe the floor to me, CC."

"Well, there's a stairway to the roof so when the people in the helicopters land on the roof they can walk down to the top floor and leave from the top floor without letting anyone see them."

"Have you ever seen any of them, CC?"

"Yes, several times, I did. They were all older men and they wore expensive suits and carried leather briefcases. They go to a conference room on the top floor with Mr. Kelly. One of them was an Army general. He wore his uniform one day. I saw his stars. He was a four star."

"Could you see their faces?"

"Yes."

"If I got pictures of them could you describe them to me?"

"Well, yes," CC nodded her head with enthusiasm. "I could point out which pictures went with each man I saw." CC was feeling better now and she was willing to throw in with Sheila, wherever the journey would take her. She could tell Sheila was getting wise to something that was no good about Bear and Otter.

"Good, CC. Very good. Now tell me what's on the top floor." For the first time in their conversation this morning Sheila smiled at her friend.

"Well, not much. It's basically an empty floor with a single conference room and Mr. Kelly's office, except there's some kind of huge apparatus that moves around on tracks with rubber wheels. It's got big rubber wheels that ride along over rubber tracks. It's real quiet. It has a huge dish-like plate that points down at the floor. It moves around real slow, then it stops, then moves around some more, then stops again. I watched it one time for about a minute and then Mr. Kelly came and took my arm and said I should get back downstairs, so I left."

"Where was it on the floor when you saw it, CC?"

"It was always on one the side of the floor, around where your office is on the floor below."

A chill swept through Sheila's body. She had long suspected she was being spied upon. This was the first tangible evidence that she wasn't paranoid. She was actually being spied upon, but why?

Spying is a murky business. They don't teach it in colleges. You won't find manuals on how to spy on the internet or in public libraries, at least none that can explain the latest methods used. Of all dismal sciences, spying is the most dismal. Economics is a dismal science, but so are automobile repairs to a lay person who doesn't know a fan belt from a garter belt. The thing about spying that gives it that thriller zing is that people get killed doing spying. Some economists should be killed, no doubt, for all the misery they inflict with erroneous forecasting; but we don't kill our economists. We pay them to give speeches and give them awards for forecasting when they occasionally get something correct. Not so with spies.

We don't know who is a spy or why they spy, or who they spy for or if they are a double agent super spy. We can usually guess about what kind of money an economist makes, unless he or she works for the Fed or a government agency and has some sweetheart side deal that you'll never know about. But spies?

Try finding out what a spy gets paid. Look in the job pages and see what they'll offer to pay you to spy. You will find nothing because spying and espionage are fields where the players write their own tickets. They charge what the market will bear and never divulge all they know.

Some spies have national loyalty, but how can anyone know for sure at what price a spy will trade loyalty for a big payday? No, spying is the murkiest of all the dismal sciences. It's creepy dirty bloody stuff. People get rich doing it and people get killed doing it. That makes spying a zero sum game. Winners get a fat bank accounts and villas in the Italian Alps. Losers get death.

The revelation that CC made about the spying from the floor above cracked open the door to discovery for Sheila. Sheila was not Langley Central Intelligence Agency spy trained. She'd never worked in the field nor knew anyone who did, that is before now. But Sheila had a brain. She trusted her own reasoning abilities. Now her brain was telling her to get more data. Obviously CC was a low level spy in some sort of scheme that was intent on knowing what Sheila could tell them about drones used in asymmetric warfare. Sheila decided she needed to work CC for all she could learn from her.

"Thanks for being honest with me CC. Now that you've told me about the top floor, you have to tell me everything and hold nothing back. I'm sure Mr. Palmer doesn't want me to know about the top floor. And I'm sure you don't want him finding out about your friend Carol either. So CC you only have one choice now. You must have total loyalty to me, not to Bear and Otter; and not even to the Marine Corps. I will, with your help, get to the bottom of this and I promise you it will result in you getting treated very well by the Marine Corps. But first you must tell me more. I want all my questions answered. Understood?"

"Yes." CC nodded her head as she dried her eyes. She was in Sheila's hands now and would do her bidding.

"Okay. Let's start with your radioactive room. I want to go in there with you and see what's so secret about it."

"It's nothing, really. Okay. Come on, I'll show it to you." CC and Sheila crossed the open space to CC's woman cave. CC unlocked the door. In the middle of the bare wood-floored room there was a chair and a tripod that held an artist's palate of colors. In front of the chair were three easels. Each one held a white canvas and each canvas had a similar painting on it. Sheila stood gawking at the paintings her roommate guarded so zealously. They were all full sized drawings of a woman's vagina. There was a curious black blob on the upper right of each vagina. Each blob was irregularly different from the others in shape and each blob looked as if something was inside it trying to push out of it. It appeared that the blobs were somehow being tortured from inside themselves.

"What are these paintings about, CC?" Sheila was in a state of shock. The blobs were exactly like the deep darkness she'd experienced on the train.

"I can't explain it to you. The vaginas are there because I think about sex a lot. The blobs are there because I thought if I could draw them I could understand them better."

"Draw them?" Sheila asked. "Does that mean you have seen them somewhere?"

"Yes. I see them. They appear to me some nights when I'm alone in my room. I try to touch them but they move away very fast. They appear out of nothing, from the dark, only they are darker than the dark. I'm afraid I might be going crazy, so I paint what I remember seeing. Please don't say anything to Mr. Palmer about this. I'm supposed to be watching you at all times except when you're sleeping. If he knew about this I'd possibly get replaced."

"CC. You aren't crazy. I've seen the exact same thing. It's some kind of phenomenon I can not explain. For some reason we have some commonality that causes us to see this thing whatever it is. I saw it outside my train window when we were about a half hour into Colorado."

"Why do you think it showed itself to us?"

"Not sure. We have the project in common. Other than that———." Sheila stopped talking. Her jaw dropped. "Wait a minute, CC. didn't you say earlier that you loved me?"

"Yes, I did say that." CC looked intently into Sheila's eyes. Plainly she wanted to say more.

"How do you mean that CC?" Sheila looked just as intently into CC's eyes. She knew something she'd never felt before was happening.

"I mean I love you, Sheila. Like I love you, like I feel I'm in love with you." CC started to cry again.

"Do you mean love like you love Carol, CC?" Sheila's eyebrows went way up on her forehead. She never would have thought that she could become involved with another woman. But suddenly there it was. CC wanted her as a woman to love sexually.

"Yes Sheila. Please don't be angry with me. I can't help it. I see you every day. I walk to work and back with you. I think about you all the time. I just want to be with you all the time Sheila. I don't ever want to be away from you. I never see you with a man and I wonder if you feel about men like I do. I don't feel safe with a man anymore, not after the way Mick treated me. He was so abusive, so terrible. Men can be so cruel and mean. They don't care about our feelings. They're nasty and selfish and they do not understand love. I just hoped that maybe you felt the same way about men and that maybe you and I could find love between us. I'm sorry Sheila. I'm being honest."

Hearing the lamentations of CC gave Sheila flashbacks to her father and mother and their vain attempts to dissuade the men from the government condemnation board. They screwed the very life from her parents. They were mean spirited arbitrary bastards and had no compassion, no feelings for her poor parents. She was listening at the top of the stairs when her mother and father tried to reason with them at their kitchen table. Her poor mother cried. Her father kept pounding the table screaming their price was not fair, but the government people were like impassionate stone walls. They gave her family only one third of what their farm was worth. When they said their price was final and there was no appeal she heard her mother's anguished screams. Her mother would never be the same after that. She continued her screams years after she was put into the asylum. Those men tore her life right out of her. Her mother's long wailing screams haunted Sheila ever since.

Then there was Johnny. She swore she'd never think about him again, but CC's admissions brought that experience back. Johnny promised he'd save himself for marriage just like she did. But he never intended to keep his promise. She wasted eleven years of her life on that creep. He didn't have any honor. He didn't care about her feelings. He was just a base animal. He broke her young woman's heart and thought it was all a big joke. Humiliation and hurt sent her reeling.

She wondered what love was, or if there even was such a thing. She took her promise to Johnny seriously. She had honored her word. She wondered if all men were so vile. When she found out her roommate was just one of Johnny's many dalliances she felt like the biggest fool in Boston. She couldn't hold her head up on campus for months. She heard the snickering behind her back. Everyone knew she was a virgin saving herself for Johnny. Damn men! She hated herself for being played for the fool.

Hearing CC and watching her cry while she recanted her abuses melted Sheila's heart. This was a good hearted human being who needed to be loved. Her senses suddenly sharpened. Her blood warmed. Suddenly she didn't care that CC was another woman. She felt herself falling in love with her. She turned to CC and hugged her, but she didn't break from the hug. She held it and squeezed CC closer to her. CC responded. Then CC held her face and kissed her on the mouth. The feeling was electric. Suddenly sex with CC seemed natural and wonderful. Sheila decided to be perfectly honest from the start of this, whatever it was and wherever it would go.

"CC, what about Carol? How will she feel about this?"

"Carol is an army wife. I'll probably never see her again. Today she and her husband are leaving for Ramstein, Germany."

"I'm sorry."

"It's okay. Women like us understand these things. We just accept them."

"I need to tell you something. I'm a virgin. I still have my hymen." Sheila held CC by her shoulders and looked into her face.

"You mean you haven't even———." CC's jaw dropped.

"No. Not with a man or a woman, nobody, nothing."

"Oh wow. Girl, you have missed a lot. You've never even been kissed down there?"

"No, like I said. There's been nothing. Please try to understand. I had a promise I made and I wanted to keep it. That's how my family was. Our word was everything."

"Whoa. I really want to make love with you, but I'm afraid if you———."

"Stop CC. You said you love me. I just realized something. I love you too. Yes I do. I feel love for you and I want to make love with you. But I want to be honest. I want to have a man some day, if I ever find a good one that I could love too. I want him to have my hymen. Can you understand that?"

"Yes, love, I can understand. That's fine with me. We can make love and I will not puncture your hymen, I promise. It will be beautiful. You'll see. I'll be very gentle with you. You'll love what I do with you, and then you can do it with me. You'll orgasm and you'll love it. I promise. It's beautiful. Once you do it you'll want to do it more. It's very natural. Look. Let's be happy together and we'll take what comes.

"Maybe we'll find a really good understanding man who isn't an asshole and he'll fall in love with both of us. I love men too, you know. Maybe there's one open minded man on this planet and we'll run into him. He could give me a little girl child, something Mick wouldn't even try to do. I can get myself tested for a little girl. If he gives me boys I'll just get their fetuses aborted and try again until I can have a healthy girl. That way I won't have the hemophilia nightmare again. And our dream man will break your hymen. You'll have a kid too. We'll live together, the three of us and our beautiful children. We can have it all. We'll just have to find an understanding guy who really loves to fuck. He'll have to be a stud horse of a guy to keep us happy, okay?"

CC made a lesbian relationship sound so simple even though such a fantasy arrangement seemed whimsical and crazy. But, 'why not,' reasoned Sheila. Surely there was some good man somewhere who would love to have two attractive women willing to share him. But that was in the future. Sheila held CC's face in her hands and kissed her on the mouth. "Okay, teach me something about love, CC. I am ready to be your lover."

"Well, we should go to my bedroom," said CC.

"Let's go then," replied Sheila. The two new lovers went into CC's bedroom and closed the door.

CHAPTER TWENTY-THREE

CRIMSON AND PINK

Sheila awoke in wonderment. Was last night even possible, she mused? But it was all real and wonderful beyond her imaginings. She lay on her side. Her loving eyes rested upon the still sleeping face of her lover. 'CC, did you feel one tenth the pleasure that your crimson lips gave to me,' she asked herself. 'How can I hold myself back until you awaken? I want to kiss your velvet gateways to my soul. How can I wait so long until we love again? Might I dare to touch your thick auburn brown black curls that lie casually against your beautiful face, or must my hands wait patiently before they touch you there and everywhere that you are a she? And your delicious crimson nipples that now rest beneath the barrier of a white silk sheet, what of them? When I suckled them and you squealed with pleasures and sighed with your warm inviting moans were you feeling enough pleasure? Or is there some way I could give you more? Will you allow my eager lips to suckle your nipples again and again; because I now so desperately want to? May I dare intrude upon your beautiful sleep to touch them with my anxious lips or my impatient fingers? Can you suspect, sleeping there, how I curse the thin transparent silk barrier veil that covers you?

'How can I wait until you awaken when I so badly yearn to cup your sex in my mouth again? Oh CC, I love you for releasing me from my self inflicted bondage. Awaken soon, my love, so I can express myself! I am maddened with my desires to touch and kiss every inch of you. My loins ache to receive your mouth again. May last night be the beginning of thousands of nights for us. I want to come again.

'Oh, dearest CC, I lie here impatiently looking upon your lovely face and those almond eyes that caressed my face with unbridled desire. Please wake up. Let me touch you again. My eager hands and lusting lips long to touch you. Can you read my mind while you sleep?

'Were my tiny cherry blossoms a joy for you? Did your thoughts take you to the same places that mine took me when I kissed and played my tongue on your crimson wonders? Did you pray as I did when I kissed you, that your lips were pleasing to me? Did my kisses on your wonder stem bond your spirit and soul to mine as my spirit and soul has bonded to you? Did your passions flare as mine did?

'I await your arrival into near sleep when perhaps you will ever so slightly part your crimson lips to moisten them with your glorious tongue. Will it be that same tongue that danced a tango with mine and that kissed my sex where I was never kissed before? Will it crave my juices as my tongue craves yours? I am frozen here in my wonder stare and deep in thoughts of passion.

'And will your fingers be those same delicate butterflies that danced upon my body, tickling and kissing me? Will you touch me like that again? When your fingers ran through my hair did they feel a wonder of beauty as mine did when I ran my fingers through your soft locks? Do you think I am beautiful?

'Oh CC, if my tongue could be a pen it would write possession notices upon your crimson buttons a hundred times each day. It would tap them gently to deliver their notice of capture; and then it would retreat in deference to my lips.

They would suckle your crimson wonders and lavish their yearning upon them.

'How can you lie there sleeping, my angelic goddess, when I lie here wondering how I could ever hear the *Ave Maria* again without imagining my head upon your breast? How will I ever hear the *Our Father* prayer without remembering my tongue caressing your heavenly clitoris?

'I am changed forever. You are my goddess now. My heart can know no greater love. What happened to me? Last night was my awakening, but I am not afraid. I am compelled to study you as you lie there. I must understand this love you have shaken from slumber. I have this need to obsess over you and then obsess even more.

'Can you possibly know how badly I want to kiss your warm exotic belly that once bore you a son? Can you know how much I pray for you that your belly will bear another child and more? Do you know that I would like a child as well? Could we raise our children together as one family?

'Do you believe as I do that we will find our accepting wonder man? I want you to be there with me when his beautiful member overcomes my resistance. Will you feel my joy when he releases me from my self imposed exile! Will you tremble and quiver with ecstasy and share my nirvana with me? Can we love him without reservation? Please say we can.

'What do my thoughts make me, CC? Am I now a whore, a lesbian, a mind damaged cunt, a shameless slut? If that's what unashamed love is labeled I will hold your hand and kiss your lips before the world and wear those tiny minded labels with pride. When you awake please say that you felt the same flowing heat of heavenly wonder that I felt last night. I must know whether I pleased you enough. I would rather die than know you were unhappy with me. If only you knew the intensity of my desire for you this very moment, sweet CC.

It's hard for me to not roll onto you and press my mouth against yours and kiss you everywhere.

'I yearn to join my soul to yours by holding my body tightly embraced to yours. And I want so badly to touch your shoulders and your back. I want to grasp your heavenly ass cheeks with my hands and crush your sex into my anxious mouth.

'Oh, CC, how can you just lie there sleeping? Don't you know that you have the face of Eros? The ancients erred when they thought a man wore that face, for no one in all of history could have ever worn it as erotically as you do now. Your sleeping smile of contentment silently shouts that you revel in lovemaking. You must be the reincarnation of Aphrodite, the temptress and ruination of the moral soul! Did you know your face is more beautiful than Helen's of Troy, and that you have already launched the thousand ships of my endearing love? I am fated to never retrieve them. You have stolen my heart, my passions, my love, and all of my soul.

'Do you know, sleeping there, how much my spirit loves you? You have freed it from its cage. It soars on wings of joy and passion.

'Awake when you will and I will be here next to you, anxious for you and wanting more and more of you. I want to touch you everywhere, my beautiful wonderful love, and I want us to love again before we allow another daylight moment to intrude upon our pleasures. I am smitten by you and I love you, my darling precious CC.'

'I know I will soon need to ask you to help me unravel the mysteries of the top floor. I will ask you to place your very life in danger as I know I will be placing my own; for we are involved against our understanding and consent in a great nefarious evil plot. It scares the hell out of me, CC; but I know I am compelled to get to the bottom of it and defeat it if I can, or I fear the forces of evil will destroy us both. Our time to act will come and I pray you will not waiver from my side. But for now in this precious time we have, I want to only think of you and the wonders of your body and your love.'

Sheila inhaled deeply. Her lungs savored CC's essence. The wafting smells of her partner's lotion and perfumes aroused her to near madness. She ran her fingers through her own hair as if that would placate her desires until CC awoke. She never had any sort of sexual experience before last night. The part of her mind that lay dormant for so many years now cried out to her. It wanted more. It couldn't imagine ever being able to have enough of CC.

While she contemplated holding CC's sleeping head in her hands and softly kissing her alluring almond eyes, those same dreamy eyes slowly opened. They were the deep delicious color of a full dark wine. They studied Sheila's searching look and smiled their soft welcoming smile to her. CC pulled away the gossamer barrier of silk that covered her, revealing her luscious tawny golden body. As she lifted her arms above her head and stretched, her nipples lifted upon her chest.

"Good Morning, love, did you have a pleasant sleep?" whispered CC as if speaking aloud might void the sanctity of the night before. Sheila was one with her now. They'd shared each other's chamber of passion. CC wanted to hold onto her feeling.

"Oh, I did, my love. I slept better than I have in years. My mind forgot all its problems and cares about anything except our wonderful love. It is refreshed and alive like never before. What we did last night was so good, so wonderful. I've been lying here watching you sleep, hoping you'd wake up. I've been hoping we could make love again before we go to work. I love you, CC. I know I've told you that, but I love telling you that. I so much love being your lover."

"Is there some urgency about you getting over to the office today?" CC's smile had a hint of disbelief.

"No, but Mr. Palmer might suspect something if we're late."

"Relax, love. Give me a moment to freshen up. We'll have our time together. Trust CC on this one." With that assertion, CC took control of the day's agenda. She told Sheila to shower and freshen up for the day while she did the same. After what seemed like a prolonged time in her bathroom, CC emerged in a sheer nightgown. Her hair was freshly brushed, her skin was obviously freshly oiled, and her crimson lipstick was lightly applied. She was positively lustrous. Her special fragrance warmed the air. And Sheila's appetite for more intimacy skyrocketed, if that was even possible.

Sheila was in awe of her partner. Suddenly CC was the most beautiful, most inviting creature she'd ever beheld with her love starved eyes. She watched CC's every move, her eyes adoring every movement as CC walked across the open floor to the sitting table that held the phone.

CC touched the digits and rang the office. When the marine on duty picked up the phone she explained her dilemma in a calm authoritative voice. "Jimmy, I see you have the duty desk this morning. Yes, it's CC. Look Jimmy. I called to leave a message for Mr. Palmer. Tell him I called in and tell him that Sheila will not be in today. Yes, that's right. She'll be out all day and I'll be with her. No, she doesn't need a doctor. It's not a medical thing. It's a woman thing Jimmy. If you must tell Mr. Palmer anything, just tell him she's having an unusually heavy flow this month, an irregular one. Yes, it happens sometimes to every woman. No, there's nothing you need to do for us.

"Tell Mr. Palmer I need to stay home with her, just to keep her company, comfort her, and fix food and soups for her. Yes, that helps it a lot. I don't know yet. It just started. We'll see how it goes. Hopefully we'll be in tomorrow, but maybe not, either. Sometimes these things can go on for several days.

Pause. Yes, that's why I need to stay with her. These things can make a woman terribly weak. I need to take care of her and make sure she keeps up her strength. Pause. Yes, Mr. Palmer is married, Jimmy. He'll understand. You won't need to explain it to him. If he needs an explanation, tell him I said he should ask his wife. She'll explain it to him. Okay, Jimmy. Pause. No, you don't need to bring us anything. If we need something I'll call you. If she needs more time I'll call you tomorrow morning. Yes, I'll keep you posted. Yes, do that. Thank you, Jimmy. Assure Mr. Palmer that she is going to be all right and that I'll check in tomorrow morning. Okay, Jimmy. Yes, we'll take good care. Good bye now." Click.

As soon as CC hung up she dropped her nightgown to the floor and bounded naked across the room with open arms to an amazed Sheila. She wrapped her arms around Sheila and held her close to her naked body. Then she kissed Sheila fully on the mouth.

"You see, my love. A good rule to know about men is that they are incredibly ignorant about the workings of a woman's body. They'd rather watch football or change the oil in a car than even think about our bodily functions. That's why we can tell them anything and they'll believe us. So, you see, my love, we've just bought ourselves two whole days of delicious love making. Are you good with that?"

"Oh, CC, I love you, love you, love you," squealed Sheila. Her eyebrows were raised in disbelief at her good fortune. She kissed CC wildly on her lips and pushed her tongue far into CC's mouth. "Thank you for making that call. I wouldn't have had the courage to do that. You are wonderful, CC. I love you. We're being naughty girls now, aren't we? We're being a couple of lesbo sluts, aren't we? I'm actually playing hooky from work! I love it. Let's not waste a single second of our happy time. Let's get back into bed. We can have breakfast later. I want to devour you and then I want to make breakfast for you."

"As you wish, love," CC led Sheila back to her bedroom. There she removed Sheila's robe while she kissed her whole body from her face down to her sex. CC's soft fingers explored every inch of Sheila.

"CC, I want you now, My skin is so alive and my sex is on fire. I want you so much." whispered an anxious Sheila, "let's kiss again like we did last night. Please. It was so wonderful. I can't get enough of you, CC."

After their renewed expressions of love, the perspired women laid side by side on CC's pillows. Sheila spoke first. "Do you have the same feelings I feel when you come into my mouth? I mean, do you feel this internal closeness the same way I feel it with you? I mean, do you feel like you are one complete being with me like I do with you and do you pray that I'm feeling joyfulness like I pray you are feeling when I am kissing you and you are gushing wildly into my mouth?" Sheila's fingers played upon CC's chest, lightly stroking the valley of her cleavage. Her fingers occasionally pinched and tugged CC's nipples while she lovingly kissed her eyes and lips.

"Yes, of course I do. I want your happiness always, and when you burst with orgasms into my mouth I feel completeness with you. It's unlike any feeling I've ever had." CC's right hand caressed Sheila's face, lightly touching her eyelids, lips and cheeks. Her other hand rested on the crown of Sheila's pussy while her fingers lovingly continued stimulating her clitoris and the apex of her outer lips. The afterglow of sexual satisfaction and total acceptance of CC's love was on Sheila's face. CC beheld her new lover and was pleased. Sheila had lily white skin, dazzling starry blue eyes and a rosy hue of eagerness on her lips. The two women kissed again and again, smiling deep pleasures into each others' eyes.

"CC, please tell me about Carol. Will you miss her? Will I be enough for you?"

"Oh, sure I'll miss her. We go back quite a ways. But yes love; you are more than enough for me. I totally love you. You are all I need. I am very happy. I'm not interested in looking, if that's what you are asking."

"Can you tell me how you met Carol and how you became lovers? I'd like to know CC. I want to know all about you. I care about you. Please," Sheila's eyes implored CC to reveal everything. Their trust in each other and their vows of love had grown a quantum leap from the accusations of yesterday. As CC's affirmed partner, Sheila felt entitled to know everything.

"Sure, I'll tell you. It's a little crazy. If you want me to stop just say so. I promise you everything with Carol is in the past and there is no one else. You are my only love, honest."

"Okay, at least until we find that wonder man. Then we'll be three of us in love, right?"

"Yes, crazy girl. And when we do find him, you must promise me here and now that you will love him equally as you love me; and I make that same promise to you. And we will continue the strong love we have found in each other always. We'll tell him that and he will have to accept us as we are. Agreed?"

"Yes, completely agreed. Now, please tell me about Carol. I want to know so I can understand you better. I want to feel your heart closer to mine by knowing all about you."

"Sure. Carol was divorced for a while with no kids and little money. You know my situation and how Mick beat me. Carol lived in an apartment on our block during those times and I kept seeing her in the local coffee shop. One day she came over to me and we started talking. We became friends. Now Carol is not an average looker, not even a way above average looker. She has drop dead gorgeous looks. She's a one of a kind sexpot femme. She'd gotten a gig as a magazine centerfold. She was outfitted as a man killer, a naked woman holding a pistol, ribbing it on her pussy, kissing it. That's not Carol at all. She's not violent. She just loves sex. Anyway her gig sold lots of magazines and that got her this call. She told me it was for the Ruby and Pearls Gentlemen's Dinner Club. She took their job offer. After a couple weeks she wanted to know if I'd join her working there. She explained the job requirements and the money. I wondered about it, but I decided I could always quit if I didn't like it, so I went with her.

"This was not your ordinary club. It was a private sex club for wealthy men. There was an initiation payment of fifty thousand dollars and a monthly dues payment of a thousand dollars. It was like a country club for rich men who wanted sex with beautiful women. Carol made thousands every night for her performance. She would first do this sensual striptease. She slowly revealed each layer until all she wore were her pearls and a gold chain around her waist. Suspended on the gold chain was an oval white platinum heart, and mounted on that heart was huge ruby studded with diamonds. That heart with its ruby and diamonds covered her pussy, and let the men know she was expensive goods.

All the men got for their membership and dues were tickets to watch her striptease show. But that just got them stimulated. They lusted after the pussy behind the ruby. When she undulated suggestively and did her soft twerks, the effect of that heart bumping against her pussy drove the men crazy.

Besides money for stage acts the club let the girls make extras. The club took fifty percent of the extras. Carol's first extra was to sit on the edge of the stage, spread her legs, and let a man come to her and lick her pussy for a short minute. The idea was to get him excited and wanting more. The club charged a hundred dollars for that. I couldn't believe men were so nuts about sex until I saw that.

"Then she went to her pole. She did an upright leg split. She had a strap loop attached high on her pole. She'd put her right foot in the strap. Another girl supported her torso so she wouldn't get tired. The club charged a thousand dollars each to five men who wanted go onstage and fuck her. I couldn't imagine what I was seeing that first time. Each man came on stage and fucked her, one at a time.

She played her role well. She moaned and whispered seductive words into a microphone that the club had suspended above her head. She has a deep sexy voice. She'd whisper 'Oh, yes, fuck me, fuck me more and fuck me harder. Oh, I love your big cock inside me. You fuck so wonderfully. You have such a beautiful cock. I love you when you're fucking me. Please could somebody put another hard cock inside me? I want a man with a strong hard cock. Can't you see my pussy wants another hard cock inside her? Won't you please come and make love to my pussy? Oh please. I need to fuck some more.' She said those sorts of things while cum oozed down her leg. She drove the men in the club crazy.

The club was always innovating for their kinky members. They wanted an act with another woman up there with Carol, but suspended from the ceiling with her legs spread. That second woman was me. My so called job was to let Carol lick my pussy while she was being fucked by the club members. Carol and I each got a thousand a night extra for that trick. I felt disgusted about it at first, but that's how I discovered how much I loved oral sex with Carol. I mean at first I was really embarrassed, but after that I figured if those men were crazy enough to pay me to feel wonderful like while I moaned and screamed to Carol to keep going, what the hell. I was going to do it. I know that show was totally debasing towards women, but it paid extremely well.

"After our stage act Carol and I went to the club's bidets and freshen ourselves; then we'd apply lubricating ointments to our pussies with a hint of perfume. I liked gardenia. Carol used Channel #5. When we were all fresh and tasty we'd go out onto the dining floor and sit naked on these tables. The tables had

Lazy Susan's so we could be rotated around. So, there we were, our pussies fully exposed, getting rotated around on these two dining tables.

"These men were both kinky and rich. They'd put hundred dollar bills in our nylon tops just to kiss our pussies for a few seconds. It was unbelievable the way they threw money at us. Then, if a man wanted us, he would make a private offer, usually for five hundred or a thousand dollars. Then we'd take him to one of the private club rooms where we'd suck him off or fuck him. I was making two thousand to five thousand dollars a night. I never thought I'd like getting paid for letting a throbbing cock pump cum into me, but I really enjoyed it. Carol easily made five thousand per night. Some men paid her two thousand dollars just to fuck her for a half hour. Some men paid for both of us at once. It was incredible money.

"Now, there was this woman named Rosemary something or other. You should know about her. She was part Indian and she was writing a fictional book about corporate ethics. Somehow she knew one of the owners of the club and got him to allow her to watch Carol's act. She wrote this book called "*The Secret and the Butterfly.*" It had a fictional character named Marty who had Carol's same insatiable sex appetite. It was a number one red hot best seller fiction novel for over a year and hundreds of millions of people read it. People all over the world were reading the book's sex scenes and making love while reading them. They still do.

"Her book was recommended by sex therapists all over the world to help people understand their sexuality. People who read it testified that it vastly improved their sex lives. Some women swore that reading it gave them orgasms. Corporate human resources departments gave away free copies to employees who were having marital difficulties, and to their supervisors so they would understand how not to supervise people. Psychologists gave away free copies to patients who felt unloved by their parents and to others to help them recognize sociopathic predators and narcissists. Grocery store chains ordered thousands of paperback copies of the book each week. It flew off the shelves so fast it was hard to keep it in stock. Independent book retailers consistently under ordered it, too. Sales grew by word of mouth until they hit the stratosphere. The book became a world wide craze, a phenomenon.

"Women copied Marty's tactics to seduce men. They swore her methods worked perfectly. Women read Rosemary's love scenes to their husbands, and their men went wild with desire for their wives. That book swept the entire world. There was a movie based on the book and it grossed over two billion dollars. Critics panned it. They said it appealed to peoples' basest instincts. But others said it made all that money because the plot was so intriguing. The public just went nuts over that movie. The actress who played Marty is deluged with fan mail and offers to marry her. Paparazzi hound her constantly. She instantaneously became the national sex symbol. There's another movie planned based on Rosemary's sequel book, *When the Butterflies Come*. It also sold over two hundred million copies. It's an in depth exploration of corporate abuse and the devious behaviors of an insane chief executive. Women with inhibitions and pent up frustrations, go crazy over the Barbara character. They can relate to her because of her patience and unwavering love for her man, Big Horse.

"Rosemary became world famous despite her mysterious secretiveness. Well, the mayor's wife imagined that the Marty character in the book was actually Carol. She insisted that the mayor shut the club down and threatened to expose all its members if he didn't. He got it shut down, but Carol and I kept a lot of money. Rosemary made a fortune selling her books and then she moved to Canada. She said she needed to get away from something. The last thing Carol heard from her was she'd bought a one room log cabin somewhere near Banff National

Park in Canada and she lives alone with some cat. She's crazy about this cat named Bud. She talks to it and pampers the hell out of it. Other than that she basically keeps to herself. That's all anybody knows about her. She tries hard to remain a recluse. Even before she moved to Canada several TV talk shows tried to get her to come on for an interview but she always declined."

"Did you ever talk to Rosemary?"

"Yes, a couple times. I got to know her because she was very interested in how women feel when they have orgasms and why women feel powerful and controlling when a cock pulses cum into them. She was keenly interested in the eroticism of women and their feelings during feminine only sex and the deep feelings of suppressed feminine anger. She asked Carol and me hundreds of questions and took down many pages of notes. She used us as research for her books. She wanted to capture our feelings in her characters."

"Did she ever say what the something was that she wanted to get away from?"

"As a matter of fact she did. She told us about it. She was seeing figures of deep darkness struggling within a lighter darkness. She wanted to get away from them. They frightened her. At first I thought she'd gone nuts. But then I started seeing them too."

"CC. Do you realize what this means? It means that this Rosemary and you and I all have some sort of connection with each other. I need to find out what it is. I have a feeling the struggle in the darkness is the key to controlling the terrorists' drones."

"Really, how Sheila?" CC couldn't imagine how the shapes could relate to the conspiracy plotters.

"Because they are the product of a force that's stronger than gravity. I've thought about the one I saw ever since that night on the train. It was getting its energy from electromagnetism. Somehow it drew on a force that gave it the power to levitate and move freely. Gravity had no effect on it. I must know more about it. Do you per chance know how we could get in touch with Rosemary?"

"Well, like I said, she is a recluse. She doesn't have a phone. But she gave us the address of an old country store near where she lives. She told Carol and me she'd love to see us if we were ever up around Banff Park. She said she'd like to make a coffee for us and talk about old times. Sheila, do you think she's a closet lesbian?"

"No I don't, CC. I think she may be a person with very unusual powers, possibly she's not even from our planet Earth. But, she's the key to an important understanding. I just know it. We've got to go see her."

"Okay, but I tell you, she is one weird lady. She claims she can talk with spirits from the universe, and they tell her things that the rest of us would never believe. She said she fully understands the electromagnetic forces that allow spirits to navigate the universe. She says she's afraid for the human race and what will happen to us."

"Oh, wow. I *knew it, I knew it!* She *is* the key to controlling the drones. I'm sure of it! I've intuited for a while now that there was no natural force on Earth that would fit a solution to my problem. I've intuited that the answer would somehow come from the paranormal and that it had to do with disrupting the drones' control signals. We've got to figure out a way to get away from Plaintown and go see her. Can you arrange that?"

"Sure. Just leave it to sweet CC, and don't ask me any questions about my methods. I'm your girl Friday, remember?"

"Okay, girl Friday, I just thought of something that could help us when we meet Rosemary."

"What? Doesn't your brain ever stop, Sheila?"

"It interrupts sometimes. I can't help it. It's always been that way. Damn brain."

"Well, what is it?"

"I need you to take a big risk, CC. I need you to figure out a way to get into the top floor conference room. Have you ever been inside it?"

"Yes, three times, to get myself some coffee when I was waiting to talk with Mr. Kelly."

Okay, well, does it have a conference table?"

"Yes, a huge one with dark oak wood and there are twelve large orange leather chairs."

"Great. I need you to get inside that conference room again and plant a listening device. I'll give you the device. It's a special kind that's miniaturized. It will secretly transmit everything that is said in that room. Can you plant something like that?'

"I'll probably be killed if I'm caught, but if you say it's important, I'll do it."

"CC, if they're up to what I think they are up to, they'll kill both of us if you're caught, so don't get caught. Be smart about it. I'm convinced these people are not who they say they are and I'm convinced they are up to no good."

"So, what we're doing is good for America, isn't it Sheila?" CC was her sweet innocent child asking what was right. She really did have the face of a goddess.

"Yes my beautiful innocent love. Absolutely we are being the good Americans. We are the indispensable force for good, kind of like the U S Navy and all their warships that patrol the world's oceans." Sheila assured CC's innocent questioning face.

"Okay. Then I'll do it. Don't ask about my methods. CC has her ways. Trust me on this. Just tell me Sheila, will you still love me after all this is over?" CC's question revealed her abiding need for Sheila's love.

"Yes, of course I will. My love for you is forever and unconditional. And now my sweet lover, CC, let's not talk shop for the rest of the day. Let's talk about you. Can you tell me what happened to you and Carol after the club shut down?"

"Sure, after the club shut down Carol got married again. We kept seeing each other and became steady lovers. Her husband never knew anything about our relationship; and now, as of yesterday, they are in Germany and I'll never see her again. Honestly Sheila, if she walked in our door right now I'd tell her that it's over with her and me. I can only love one woman. I'm not all over the place. I'm not like that. And I love you, Sheila. I totally love you and I'm solid with that. When Carol got married I thought I'd give up being a lesbian, so I joined the Marines.

"But Carol found me and we stayed in touch. It's funny how we both ended up in Plaintown. Her guy is a Marine Corps recruiter. He traveled quite a bit so Carol and I had lots of sex time. She and I experimented with lots of things. As you and I get more into our sex, I'll teach you everything I know. And I promise I'll save your hymen for our wonder man. I totally respect that need. It's wonderful with a real man's prick, Sheila. You should have that precious experience with a man. I only wish and hope I can be there with you to share it with the two of you; but that will be up to the two of you. I understand."

"Oh, CC. Of course you'll be there!" Sheila held CC's hands and looked into her eyes. "I want to be kissing your pussy while his cock plunges into me that first time. I want my tongue on your clit and I want you gushing all over my face when he shatters my barrier to completeness. It will be our wonder moment. The three of us will consummate and commit to each other all at once, kind of like getting married. I can't wait! We'll both love him, CC; and we'll always be very good to him. He'll be the happiest and most thoroughly fucked man in the world!" Sheila giggled a mischievous giggle.

"Now, all we need to do is find him. Where are you hiding, Mr. Wonder Man?" Sheila held her hands up and swayed back and forth making antics like a circus clown. "Meanwhile, are you ready to go again? I sure am. I want to make love again. I don't care about eating. Your description of you and Carol at that club has made me all wet inside. I've become a sex maniac! Let's skip breakfast and go again. Can we please?"

"Of course we can, my sweet love." And CC began the rest of their two days of love making by first kissing Sheila on her mouth, then her stomach; and then with the utmost sensitive and patient loving passion, her sex. Never had either woman known a greater joy.

CHAPTER TWENTY-FOUR

TRANSMITTING SECRETS

Sheila heard the steady chop of helicopter blades as the third chopper landed on the building's helicopter pad. That was the same pattern she'd noticed before. After the first two choppers disgorged their passengers there was an interval of about fifteen minutes before the third chopper arrived. She guessed the third member, or members, of the secretive group was the most important. It was time to listen in. She went into her office, closed her door and put her ear phones on. The device CC planted in the ceiling above the middle of the conference table was undetectable and silent when it transmitted. It used less than a tenth of a watt of battery power, even less than a remote for a garage door opener. She made it herself from components she picked up at an electronics shop. Her MIT electronics lab class was paying a practical dividend. The weak signal came into her smart phone and into her head phones. She also had a spliced line into one of her headphones that sent the signal to a hand held recorder in her desk. After some rustling of papers she heard a deep male voice call the meeting to order.

"Any old business we need to discuss? Walter, I believe you had a loose end that you were to take care of?"

"Yes, it's been taken care of, Mr. Kelly. The Assistant Research Director at BASE, Mr. Santifalo, had an unfortunate break in at his home one night last week. The thieves stole some jewelry and some cash and gold coins, and they murdered both Mr. and Mrs. Santifalo. My contact at the police department tells me the thieves left no fingerprints or anything they could take DNA from. There were no witnesses to the crime. It was a clean job by professionals and the police believe they were either from out of town or they had a personal issue with either Mr. or Mrs. Santifalo. They have one rookie detective assigned to the case and no leads."

"What would you estimate an out of town hit team would cost, Walter; or did your police contact mention that?"

"Gentlemen, do we really need to be so obtuse? We're all friends here. I'd guess the cost was somewhere around fifty thousand to get real pros, plus they could keep whatever they could scavenge from the Santifalo's and their home."

"And, what about getting rid of Sandra, the research assistant, Walter? We agreed that even though she was only an indirect link we wanted her silenced. Have you taken care of that too?"

"Not yet. I can't use the same method. It can't be a murder. That would raise suspicions because of the linkage. She worked for Santifalo. It has to be staged to look like an accident."

"What about suicide? Might she not want to commit suicide?"

"No, it's out of the question. I've been porking her. There's always the possibility that she's told someone even though she swears to me that she hasn't said a word. I can't trust the women that work in my bank to keep their mouths shut."

"So, what are you saying, Walter? Are we to simply ignore this indirect link, or do you have a plan and a timetable?"

"I have no plan as of now. I'm still thinking. I see no urgency. The NFL season is a six month season. I believe it's better to put some time between the two events in any case.

And, I'm convinced she's pretty stupid. I'm not thinking it's very smart to kill her."

Another deep voice boomed into the conversation. "You're still thinking all right. You're thinking with your dick, you fucking dick brain. You're a God damned stupid fucked up son of a bitch Walter. Gentlemen, there's a major problem with this whole plan. Our problem is Walter.

"Walter, you told me the man we're after was a recluse. That was only half true. You never told me he was a Marine Corps sharpshooter. You told me the man coordinating this operation had experience in wet work and that he was solid. That was only half true, Walter. He's a fucking dyslexic! The problem with you, Walter, is you think two half truths make a whole truth. They don't. Two half truths make two lies, you stupid son of a bitch. You never would have made it at West Point, you asshole," the general's voice rose into angry snarl. "We learned you don't tell half truths, you don't tell lies. And why don't we tell lies, Walter? Why don't we? Because men die when we tell lies, Walter, that's why!

"I sent five outstanding men into harm's way on this asshole's say so. His intelligence was terrible. His coordination was lackadaisical. His communication was irregular. The men he hired were fucking dyslexics! I got my best sniper killed; then I got three more class A marksmen snipers killed and I lost a chopper and a fucking good pilot too. All because this fucking asshole incompetent never told me the guy we were hunting was a Marine Corps expert marksman.

"How can we proceed with our plan now? I've got this asshole feeding me bad intelligence; I've got some former Seal trained Marine sniper mountain man armed to the teeth on the loose with that fucking map. I now suspect he has an accomplice, some cocktail waitress fuck bunny and arms bearer. Maybe he has other accomplices by now. I can only guess at what I'm dealing with now because of fuck brains Walter here."

Another, milder and more controlled voice spoke. "General Porter, there's no need to get emotional or use profanity. We're all about business here. We all know business has risks and ups and downs. We have unlimited resources at our disposal."

"You fucking bankers have no idea what you are dealing with. This isn't some tidily winks parlor game or some demand for a loan payment. This isn't even about fucking over some piss assed little puke country and ripping out their resources. This is war I tell you. We are at war right now with this mountain goat freak. If we don't get a handle on this immediately he could bring us all down. Mark my words!" General Porter would not be silenced. "The day is fast approaching, gentlemen, when we who understand command will no longer permit bankers to run this country. This country will need military rule to unfuck it from the mess you bankers have made of it.

"I request that you lay your enmity towards Mr. Black aside, General. I'm sure, once our coup has restored order and once we return the former President to power as nation's first dictator you will have all the order you crave to have, General. You must stop bickering with Walter, General. Meanwhile we must move to the next item on the agenda," retorted Mr. Rothstein in an irritated tone. "Now then, let us turn the meeting back to our chair, Mr. Kelly. Henry, can you update us on our drone project, please?"

"Certainly, Mr. Rothstein, allow me go to my slide presentation and use my pointer." Sheila's headphones delivered the shuffling sounds of chairs and papers. "First, you see on the huge national map a red circle around all the NFL stadiums. Then, in smaller green circles near each stadium, you see the locations from which the drones will be launched. As you can see my logistics team has arranged for no less than twenty drones at each location. Each stadium has already been scouted and at least three independent drone launching platform locations have been procured within three miles of each stadium. So, gentlemen, we have thirty two stadiums, three launch locations each, and twenty drones at each location ready for launching. That totals 1932 delivery platforms available on D day. Reminder, gentlemen, we still need to determine D day because only thirteen football stadiums are used each Sunday. We'll need to know the NFL schedule. We won't be targeting the stadiums used for Sunday night, Monday Night Football or Thursday Night Football. We will only actually be attacking thirteen stadiums on D Day Sunday. At an estimated fifty percent kill ratio and an estimated eighty thousand average attendance we should be able to kill about five hundred twenty thousand Americans, minimum. With light winds or no winds we may be successful in killing over a million people. That should be sufficient to allow General Porter here to declare a national emergency and take control of all the TV, radio and print media outlets."

"And how are we doing with those payloads, Mr. Rawbone? The mild voice of Mr. Rothstein asked.

"We're doing well. We have a variety of payloads designated for each stadium. Our payload mix will be one third nerve gas, one third radioactive waste, and one third bubonic plague bacteria. Each provider is on schedule to make final delivery over the next two months." The responding voice sounded officious, possibly a bookkeeper type.

"Very well Mr. Rawbone. Thank you for that update," said Mr. Rothstein. Sheila made a note of another name associated with the nefarious murder plot.

"And, what about the drone control project? Let us hear from Mr. Palmer."

"Thank you, Mr. Chairman. I am happy to report that my team is thoroughly stumped. There has been no progress to report."

"She is getting no movement toward a solution, is that what we are to believe? Mr. Rothstein seemed skeptical.

"I assure you, Mr. Chairman. She is the best and brightest in the country. She has full rein of our resources to explore whatever she wishes. I have heard her anguish over the impossibility of controlling the numbers of drones, the numbers of payloads, and the inability to affect the drones' controls without itemizing and controlling every drone in the world; and she is stumped. She says it's impossible, as we thought she would."

"Very good, well, keep her on payroll for another two months until we can set a D Day. After D Day I suppose you can simply release her back to academia or the civilian world, wherever she wants to go."

"You don't want her liquidated?"

"No. There's no reason for that. She knows nothing and can't find a solution that would thwart our plan, so just let her go."

"Okay, will do."

"And now we'll hear from our last to arrive today, our esteemed Chinese colleague, Mr. Won Hung Low. Mr. Low, will you please update the preparations at the Chinese Central Bank?"

"Ah so, most certainly, I am happy to report that our central bank has made all preparations to effect the new world gold backed Yuan currency. We have finalized all our trading and vaulting facilities. We have amassed ten times more gold than all the Western countries combined. We have established the coinage and minting facilities for gold and silver coinage in metric denominations. We have manufactured all the necessary new ATM machines to issue the new notes and coinage.

"And we have in place all the necessary currency swap lines with the U S Central bank, the European Central Bank, the Japanese Central Bank, the Bank of England, and the next fifty central banks in order of lending importance. The World Settlement Bank is pleased with our progress, gentlemen. They continue to keep their unlimited credit lines open through BASE bank to fund our operation with no accountability whatsoever. We are all deeply appreciative to Walter Black here for facilitating this smooth arrangement. There are no questions asked about any of our expenditures and they insist that we maintain no records. Their thinking is that once our plan goes operational the dollar will rapidly become worthless anyway.

"One last detail——once Operation PBFBW, Pay Back for Bretton Woods, is initiated we will send the documents necessary to the remaining minor banks to effect their conversions as well. Some of these countries, like Venezuela, Cuba, and many other Latin and African countries will quickly become failed states because their U S treasury, dollar and euro reserve asset holdings will rapidly become worthless. They will not have any foreign exchange to purchase food and necessities. Our Chinese partners have been given the option of continuing to sustain them on financial life support; but those with attractive resources may simply be occupied by the Chinese Peoples' Army, then colonized by Han Chinese and their surplus populations exterminated.

"Just what makes you bankers so sure that Pay Back for Breton Woods will go off without a hitch? Where's your military back up? Why aren't we setting contingency plans for resistance? There's five million National Rifle Association members out there don't forget. A lot of them will be willing to fight. It's their second amendment thing, remember?" General Porter ignored Mr. Rothstein's earlier admonition.

"General Porter. I assure you that once the drones attack all Americans will give unprecedented powers to the government. Terrorists will be blamed. All NRA members will be located by Homeland Security and immediately sent to detention camps. A new currency order will be declared necessary to blunt the terrorist's access to cash. We've done study after study, ad nausea, that Americans will believe everything their media outlets tell them. They have been proven over and over that Americans are brain dead and addicted to their sit com television shows. As long as they are assured that their favorite shows and the NFL will soon resume, they will be docile and compliant. They will welcome back their former president into power thinking he will deliver them.

"I'm doubtful about him. You say he's the image of legitimacy and order. I saw he's the image of an asshole that walks like a turkey with hemorrhoids." General Porter was plainly having misgivings about every aspect of the planned coup.

"I assure you, General, our polling never fails. It tells us the people want him back. They will accept him."

"You better pray you are right. Your polling never forecast that Orangejob would win. Don't forget that. I'd like you to search for a more acceptable less divisive person. And remember this, when we strike at this President, *we must kill him*. He's not stupid. He will root out all of us if we don't get him at the get go. Do we all understand me? We must kill with our first strike. We will not succeed if we only wound. Our execution must be flawless. We can show no mercy, give no quarter. We must kill all resisters. No prisoners, understood?

"Yes, General, we understand and we have all heard and rejected your calls for setting off nuclear Electro Magnetic Pulse bursts over Middle America. You were voted down on that. This council and the directorate do not believe it is necessary to kill the entire population of Mid Continent America at this time, General. We determined that they are more valuable as living slaves than dead corpses. Now, please, give it a rest, General." Mr. Rothstein sounded irritated. "Understand, General, we don't need to kill everyone in the entire world. Okay, General?" Mr. Rothstein heaved a deep sigh to end this impossible discussion with the general. "Do you have anything you would like to add, Mr. Low?

"May we all live in interesting times," chimed in the Chinese co conspirator.

"All right," boomed General Porter. "You fucking bankers can have it your way for now; but remember that I have the sixth branch of the military solid and loyal; and with me in control. They are the elite from all the armed forces and our chain of command is rock solid, not like you squishy mother fucking assholes. If you assholes fuck this up my command will be on you like white on rice, get it?

"And when I take over military command there won't be any more niceties. Every pompous ass dirt bag commie in this country is going to die. Every lying, thieving, sniveling Saul Alinski radical and every half truth lying shit bag media reporter is going to disappear, got it? And if any of you assholes stand with them, you'll disappear too, got it? And you, Walter, you slimy dirt bag cunt of a male want to be, I'll be smiling when I put a bullet through that oatmeal brain of yours. On second thought, that would be too good for you. I'll let you watch while I tear out your liver with my bare hands and feed it to my dogs." Sheila and CC could feel the heat from the general's seething voice burning her ears. They could imagine his snarl and the deliberate grinding of his teeth as he glared at Walter like he was about to bite his throat. The man brimmed with hate.

"General, relax!" Mr. Rothstein slapped his hand on the table. "None of that will be necessary. And, lest you forget we have agreements with the Chinese and Russian governments that they will support our coup. Their armed ground forces and missile forces should give you pause. You simply must stop being emotional about this, General. I assure you we will orchestrate an orderly coup. When we have control you will be in charge of the entire military force. And you *will* be civilized toward Walter, General. No more threats. We need Walter and his bank to make the flow of commerce orderly. Am I understood, General?

"Understood, I and my team will do our part. We'll closely monitor everything. And I will be especially deferential to my dear friend Walter here." The General's voice carried the tone of contempt. Obviously he was chaffing at the bit to kill Walter.

"We will soon control the monetary policies of the world and we have decided it is time to replace the dollar with a gold backed currency," said Mr. Rothstein wrapping things up. "The U S has had the exorbitant privilege of reserve currency status for far too long. The largess America enjoyed from Breton Woods will soon end. You need to focus on your task at hand, General. Neutralize that mountain man. Find and retrieve that map that tells us where the extraterrestrial material can be found that can thwart our drone control commands. Now, we'll do our functions and you will do yours. Understood?"

"Yes, understood for now; but in the future, Mr. Rothstein, when you address me you *will* call me Sir. Understood?" The general's voice tone carried a distinctive snarl. It sent a chill down Sheila's spine. The general seemed to be chomping at the bit for an excuse to kill Mr. Rothstein, too. She wondered how a group such as this could possibly hold its loyalties together.

A prolonged silence followed that last exchange. Apparently Mr. Rothstein refused to acknowledge the general's demand for respect. Sheila imagined two power crazed men glaring at each other like two dogs squared off over a bone. Some additional things were said about the timing of the next meeting one month from today. Calendars were checked and more papers were rustled. Then the distant chop of helicopter blades could be heard approaching the building to pick up the distinguished coup plotters.

CHAPTER TWENTY-FIVE

CRIMSON MARIPOSA

Sheila and Cecilia were in shock. They played and replayed their secret recording of the conspirators' meeting. It was hard to get their minds past their disbelief. The people they trusted and worked beside were secretly plotting the overthrow of the government. The recording revealed a treasure trove of dark secrets. A world wide banking conspiracy existed. Its interests were directly opposite to the interests of the American people and, by extension, to all the people of the world. Mr. Rothstein seemed to be the key liaison banker between the international banking syndicate backing this plot, the Chinese who would benefit from a new international gold backed currency structure, and Walter Black's BASE Bank.

There was a General Porter involved. He expressed open enmity toward Walter Black and bankers in general. He was power hungry and willing to kill his opponents without reservation. But he had two problems. One was a woman in his bank named Sandra, a research assistant. Another problem was some mountain man who had a certain map. This mountain man had a possible female accomplice. The plotters desperately wanted this map. It showed where the rocks were that could foil their drones' controls.

The plotters had advanced a drone project which would provide an excuse to declare martial law in the U S. They would use this false flag as a pretext to dismantle the government and establish a new government with a new gold backed Chinese reserve currency. They were calloused ruthless men. They had plans to eliminate any dissenters who wanted a free constitutional republic, especially National Rifle Association members.

One of the plotters, the Chinese member, boasted that the group had access to unlimited funds to be spent in any manner they wished without any paper trail or accountability. Upon hearing that tidbit Sheila and Cecilia stared at each other's faces with their jaws agape. Since falling in love the two women slept together in Cecilia's bed. This night they lied side by side, silently pondering the revelations they heard before they eventually fell into a restless sleep.

In the middle of the night Cecilia awakened. Sheila was weeping. Cecilia listened to her soft sniffles and sobs before she let Sheila know she had also woken up. Cecelia and Sheila were closely tied emotionally now. Neither one could stand idle if someone hurt the other. Cecilia broke the silence of the night.

"I hear you crying, Sheila. Can I get you something to settle you?"

"No, thanks CC, but I don't want to be settled. I just want to think." Sheila just wanted to bury her head deep into her pillow in hopes that what she heard on the tape would go away.

"You can talk to me. Maybe that will help." Cecilia rolled onto her side and put her arm over Sheila.

"Okay. I'm sorry to keep you awake." Sheila said the only nice thing she could say. In truth, she was glad her precious CC had awakened. She needed to talk out her feelings. "I'm having terrible thoughts, CC. I'm thinking all men are bad people. Those plotters are all men. Women would never think about killing a million Americans like that, would they?" Sheila propped herself upright on the bed with her back and neck braced by pillows against the wall. The California King bed didn't have a headboard.

"No, I guess not. I've never heard of women plotting mass murders like that. It's unthinkable. I mean for me it's impossible for me to think the way those men think. I remember how precious my little Frank was. Being a woman I can't imagine plotting to kill like that. In those football stadiums there are certain to be women who have little children somewhere. That's what stops me from even starting to think like those men think. Some little children are going to be with a sitter while their mommy goes to a football game and gets killed by these madmen. I just couldn't do that to those little kids."

"Yeah, I don't have a kid yet, but I can't think like that either. There must be something in the male mind that sort of switches off when it comes to thinking about the consequences of their decisions. They must have an off switch that says after the killing everything will be just fine, with no hurts to care about. Maybe their minds just can't consider that people will be hurt because of them; or maybe their minds know the hurts will come and they don't care; or worse, maybe they like to see people hurt. Maybe they like knowing people will have pain. Maybe they like seeing kids cry. Do you think that's it, CC?

"I don't know what it is. I've always known they were different from us because of their testosterone, adrenalin, macho bull shit and all that; but after what I went through with Mick, the way he beat me because little Frankie died and when I couldn't have another son for him, I started to study men differently. Now I basically hate them. I saw how they cheated on their wives with me and Carol at their kinky sex club. I notice how they order us around, to get them coffee or file things. Now I see them as a bunch of disgusting sloppy ignorant power crazy nasty pigs. I wish we didn't need them to have children. The world would be better off without men in it." CC stroked Sheila's hair and hugged her close to comfort her.

"Does this mean you want to give up trying to find the perfect Mr. Right?"

"Oh, no baby, I just wanted to let my feelings go for a fly. I still want to find him. I still want to be there when he fucks you that first time. I want all of it, and I want to fuck him too. We should always believe. In that pile of male manure, there's got to be a wonderful stud horse somewhere, right?"

"Right, that's my CC. You know, I keep going over that tape in my mind. That's why I couldn't sleep. Remember that Chinese man, how pompous he sounded? Remember how cock sure he was that they'd defeat the United States and how they had unlimited credit lines available to carry out their plot? Remember?"

"Yeah, I remember. And they had no accountability to anybody. There must be some high up power behind these bankers. They can just issue unlimited money without accountability to anybody so they can throw their weight around and even destroy the United States."

"It makes me want to puke, CC. Once when I was in undergrad school I read a book by this ancient Chinese general named Sun Tzu. He talked about using the enemy's strengths against him. I've been lying here trying to think how we could use the strength of these plotters against them, but nothing is coming to me, and I can't sleep. I'm just happy that tomorrow is Saturday and we have the weekend. Maybe something will come to me out of the blue. And we have two whole months before the plot gets executed, so maybe we'll think of something."

"Maybe, baby, maybe we will. I'm glad we talked. Now let's kiss good night and go back to sleep." The two women rolled over, and back to back they slept a restless sleep. But, unbeknownst to the restless duo, their discussion set a chain of events into motion.

The next morning over a late Saturday breakfast Cecilia tipped Sheila that an idea occurred to her. It came to her in her sleep, Like a lowly thistle seed bumped by a passerby or lifted into flight by a wind gust, it floated about and drifted in the unconsciousness of her slumber's ether; and then it germinated in her fertile mind and sprouted into maturity when she awoke.

"You know, Sheila, I went to sleep thinking about what you said last night, about how horrible men are. I got to thinking about Mr. Palmer, our boss. I started working with him about a year before you arrived. At first I really liked him. He was professional and polite and all. But, then I noticed sometimes he'd ask me to get him a coffee or some supplies, or he'd call me into his office and ask me what I thought about something, like I was one of the higher ups on the payroll that got paid to think. I thought it was just him getting used to me working with him, but after a while I didn't think that was it.

"On his credenza behind his desk there's this huge picture of his wife and three kids. They're all smiling real pretty and happy. So, naturally, when I go into his office I see that picture every time. It's like a billboard that says he's private property to all other women and we should keep our hands off him. Now, mind you, I never thought about putting my hands on him anyway. He's too coiffed and formal for me. I've heard other women say they think he's very handsome, but that's because he doesn't always wear his glasses. When he wears the glasses He's kind of geeky looking and I feel like laughing at him." Sometimes Cecilia had a long drawn out way of coming to a point. This was one of those times because she knew that Sheila might not like to hear what she was thinking so she approached the subject matter very carefully.

"So, what's this got to do with how horrible men are?" Sheila asked.

Cecilia knew instinctively that if she trailed the bait out there long enough and far enough Sheila would hit it like a bass nailing a frog on the surface of a lake. Sure enough her plan was working. "Well, do you know what I noticed one day?"

"No, what, tell me," Sheila was chomping on the frog now.

"Well, that polite professional married man was talking to me after I brought him his coffee and his eyes kept dropping down to my breasts. I'm not making this up. The first time I noticed it I just figured he had a weak moment or something, you know, kind of a natural mental slip or something." Cecilia cocked her head and raised her eyebrows to look up from her pancakes into Sheila's face.

"Was that the only time he ogled your tits?" Sheila was chewing hard on the frog now. She was salivating to swallow the hook.

"No, since then he's been staring at them every time he sees me. And, just a couple weeks ago when I was leaving his office I did a quick whirl around move to act like I forgot to tell him something, and do you know what?"

"No, what," Sheila's question ended in an up inflection. She was starting to swallow the frog.

"Well, frankly my dear," Cecilia's voice gave a perfect imitation of Rhett Butler's in the 'I don't give a damn scene from *Gone with the Wind*.' "I caught him in a riveting stare at my ass. It was one of those 'I want to fuck that woman' kinds of stares."

"You're kidding, the innocent model husband, Mr. Palmer? The Mr. Palmer who is so good looking that I actually wondered if he was secretly gay; that Mr. Palmer with the picture book perfect wife and kids? Are we talking about that same Mr. Palmer?" Sheila put her fork down. Her mouth opened but there was no food in it. She realized that she understood absolutely nothing about human nature.

"Yes, love, that Mr. Palmer. I'm telling you what this girl can see and feel. Our Mr. Innocent with the beautiful wife and kids and the polite dweeb mannerisms is a red blooded male who wants to screw my brains out. I'm sure of it." Cecilia let her shoulders drop. She knew her brewing plot would need Sheila's acquiescence if the two of them were to remain lovers and if she were going to be able to go forward with her notion at all. Even so, the notion was, at this point, only half baked.

Sheila let out a long exhale. She sensed where this was leading. Her lover was about to ask her for permission to have an out of relationship liaison with their boss, but why, for what possible gain? "So, partner, lover, what are you saying and what are you thinking?" Here was the moment of truth, that true test of love. Sheila contemplated spitting out the hook?

"Let me finish my thought" Cecilia half pleaded and half commanded. "Remember how we heard the Chinese guy say they had unlimited unaccountable money?"

"Sure, but what's that got to do with you fuck————"
Sheila suddenly stopped talking mid sentence. The same seed that rooted in Cecelia's thoughts had a companion seed that now found root in Sheila's mind too. "Oh, I get it, CC! Sheila squealed. " CC, you are brilliant. You want to get him into a compromised position and then ask him for money, right?"

"Well, yeah, girl, and more. You want to go to Banff to meet this Rosemary woman, right?"

"Right."

"If CC plays her cards well enough we're going to get time off to go to Banff, and maybe you can solve this riddle. Maybe if you meet Rosemary she'll know about the darkness's and the map. Maybe this is the key to finding Mr. Wonderful too, who knows? But I feel it Sheila. I feel like something took root my mind, kind of like you planted a seed there when you were talked about how that Chinese general used his enemies' strengths against them. I just fell asleep with those thoughts and my mind woke up with this idea. They have money and no accountability. We'll use that against them. If it's okay with you, I'll see if I can find a weakness in Mr. Palmer. Will you trust me, my sweetheart? I promise I'm not going to fall in love with him. I'm just going to fuck him until he's near death from exhaustion, okay?"

A wry smile broke onto Sheila's face. She recognized the sincerity and latent genius of her thistle brained partner and willingly signed on to the plot. "Okay." Then the two women returned to their bedroom and sealed their plot. A session of tender late morning love making followed.

Cecilia waited until Tuesday because Mondays were usually all business at Bear and Otter and she didn't want anything to disrupt her intentions towards Mr. Palmer. When Tuesday morning arrived, Cecilia strode confidently into Mr. Palmer's office bearing a small skim milk latte, his usual. But this morning Cecilia wore a dress instead of a pants suit or a skirt and blouse. But this was by no means an ordinary dress. She chose it especially for its neckline plunge and loose fit about her breasts; and she chose to go braless that day. This day she walked around to the side of his desk instead of standing before him. As she placed Mr. Palmer's latte upon his desk she purposely bent down low as if to stretch herself outward to place the coffee on his side opposite her. Clearly, even a total dolt could see that Cecilia was not shoving a latte across his desk to him; rather, she was shoving her torso across his desk for his inspection and approval. The move revealed the beautiful crimson nipples of her breasts.

"Good morning, Mr. Porter. I'd like to know if you'd like to enjoy a little cinnamon with your latte this morning." Her boldness startled him, but she quickly put him at ease by taking his hand from his coffee cup and placing it upon her breast. "I see you every day, Mr. Palmer, and every day leaves me wondering if I please you. I mean, every day I wonder what it would be like if we could be closer Mr. Palmer. Could you please let me know if you feel anything for me, Mr. Palmer? A girl just needs to know these things so she doesn't just dream about them. Do you feel anything for Me, Mr. Palmer?" By now, George Palmer was gently fondling her breast.

"Yes, Cecilia. You have no idea how much I think of you. I'd do anything to be closer to you." He had a dreamy look in his eyes.

" I was hoping you'd say that. May I call you George?" She touched his face with her hand, caressing his cheek.

"Yes, I'd like that, but when others are around us you must call me Mr. Palmer. I hope that's okay."

"Of course, George, I'll never cause you any problems, I promise. I just want you, George. And, George, did you notice that I locked your door when I came into your office this morning? We are all alone, George. Why don't you call Jimmy, the marine guard, and tell him you are working on something extremely important and that no one is to disturb you under any circumstances, okay?" Cecilia placed a soft kiss on George's lips. He offered no resistance to Cecilia's advance and made the call to Jimmy and instructed him to give him absolute privacy until he was told otherwise.

"There's just one small thing I'd like you to do for me, George, before we go any further. Would you mind if I turned the picture of your family around so I'm not reminded of them. I just want to be thinking of you, George."

"How about this, Cecilia, I'll do better than that. I'll put that picture in a drawer so it won't even appear in our presence. Would you like that?"

"Yes, George. That would please me very much," Cecilia beamed her approval.

After he placed the family portrait into a lower desk drawer, Cecilia removed her dress and stood before him. He was awestruck. Everything he imagined for months was suddenly there, attainable. He never thought once about the why of this happening. Men in heat simply don't think. He was consumed with lust for her. Conveniently, there was a large leather sofa in his office. She took him by the hand and led him to it. Then she lay down upon it and stretched her hands far above her head revealing her stunning breasts and voluptuous body.

"George," she said.

"Yes, Cecilia," he replied.

"I'd like you to remove your clothes now and make love to me. I'd like you to kiss my tits and squeeze them very hard, just like you imagined you were doing so many times before today. And I'd like it very much if you would kiss my pussy and then fuck me, George. I'd like you to fuck me harder than you've ever fucked any woman before in your entire life. And, George—" She deliberately let her voice trail off in a wispy wanton sort of way.

"Yes, Cecilia," he was mesmerized now and he hung on every word of the beautiful nymph stretched out upon his sofa.

"And while you are fucking me I don't want you to have any guilty feelings about not being faithful to your wife or your children. That's very important to me, George. I only want you to be thinking of us, George. I want you to only think about how glorious it is that we are making love and how wonderful you feel when you are fucking me. And, George——," her voice trailed off again.

"Yes, what is it, Cecilia?" He was so eager that he was ready to do anything she asked of him.

"George, when your climax comes I don't want you to pull out of me. That would make me feel dirty. And I don't want to feel dirty, George. I want to feel beautiful about this, because what we are about to do will really be wonderful and beautiful. And I want to know that you feel our love making is beautiful too. So, George, I want you to come inside me and I want you to shoot your cum into me until you are completely exhausted.

I want every last drop of your cum inside me, George. Don't worry about me getting pregnant, I'm on the pill. Your cum inside me means everything to me. Will you please do that for me George? It will make me feel that you care about me and that's important to me, George. I need to feel completely loved by you, George, even if it's just an office thing, okay?'

"Okay, yes Cecilia, whatever you ask."

"Okay, then let's make love, George. Let's make love. Let's touch all over, and then let's fuck ourselves crazy."

And, they did.

• • •

Wednesday morning at breakfast Cecilia handed Sheila an envelope.

"What's this," Sheila's furrowed brow showed her puzzlement.

"Open it. Just open it." Cecelia was authoritative in her tone. Sheila did as commanded. Then she looked at Cecilia in disbelief.

"It's a first class round trip airplane ticket to Calgary, Canada, a rental car, a hotel reservation for two weeks at the Fairmont at Lake Louise, and traveler's checks for fifty thousand dollars. What's going on? How did this happen?" Sheila was stunned.

"I convinced Mr. Palmer that you needed a break to solve the problem of the possible drone attack. I told him you were stressed and you needed a lot of time away, maybe a whole six or seven weeks, because your brain works best after it's relaxed. Remember how they were planning to attack in about two months or so? Well, what could be better for them than to have you off the problem for the best part of the next two months? I told him I needed to go with you to make sure you were always guarded and safe, and in case you got sick again, to care for you. I told him we needed getting away money for massages and relaxing fine dining. So, I got us six or seven weeks away and fifty thousand in travel money, each. You know, those guys really do have unlimited unaccountable spending authority. I almost asked for a hundred thousand each, but I thought they might ask how two women could spend that much money. As it is, we have six thousand a week each for spending, and our travel, the rental car, and the hotels will all be paid by the company."

"You amaze me, CC. How did you get him to agree to this?" Sheila had that dumb struck look on her face again.

"It wasn't that hard."

"But, just like that? He gave you this trip for the two of us and all this money? What magic did you use?"

"Not magic, love, it's just a matter of following the basic rules of being a whore. First, you must be bold. Second, you must mean what you say. Third, you must love sex and all its various forms. Fourth, and this is very important, you must never ever sell yourself cheap. The more you cost your mark the more he will think he has something of great value. Fifth, you must always be discreet and tell no one about your business dealings with your mark."

"But, please tell me. Was he rough with you?"

"Okay, since we're in this together to save the world, I'll tell you. No, not rough at all, actually very sweet."

"Please, I'd like to know everything. I'll be okay knowing. I promise not to feel jealous."

"There's nothing for you to be jealous about. It was strictly business."

"Well, then tell me everything. Don't make me beg you, CC."

"Okay. I told him if he'd grant me some reasonable favors, I'd permit him to kiss my Mariposa."

"Your what?"

"My mariposa, it's Spanish for butterfly. I told him he could kiss my pussy. I told him I loved to have my pussy kissed, which is true. I told him I call it my mariposa. I also told him how much I loved to have my tits kissed which is also true. It was the soft pleading way I told him what I needed for my pleasures that made him feel honored to give me pleasure. He kissed my tits and my pussy for the longest time. I even fired off an orgasm in his mouth. He loved it. He told me over and over how much he loved kissing my crimson tits and my pussy. Now he calls me his Crimson Mariposa, his butterfly pussy with the crimson tits."

"Jesus, that's pretty——," Sheila's voice trailed in wonder. She felt a pang of jealousy and uncertainty about her position as CC's love interest. Her expression showed her feelings of dismay and concern.

"Shhh, no jealousy, remember. I promise you it was all business."

"What's he going to expect when you get back?"

"Well. I suppose he'll *want* to fuck me every day, but that's not going to happen."

"How will you avoid him?"

"I won't. He'll want to avoid me. As soon as we're back I'll tell him I have a funny discharge with something that looks like puss in it. I'll ask him if he's been messing around or if his wife's been doing anything. Then I'll tell him I need to get some lab work done to make sure I don't have gonorrhea or syphilis. I'll tell him he should be okay, but he should get checked just to be sure. That will scare the shit out of him."

"You think?"

"I don't think, I know. I'll tell him the clincher. I'll tell him I can't just love only one man that I'm the kind of girl that needs to fuck a lot. That will work to shake him off. It works on every guy I ever wanted to get rid of. They are all terrified of getting clap or syph."

"But, how will you get him to do what you want if he can't fuck you?"

"Simple. I can hint to him that I can play dirty. I have his DNA all over my panties, remember. After he fucked me I just put them back on and left his office. I let his cum ooze out of me. It squished and soaked all through them. I even let his cum run down my legs into my nylons. I didn't wipe up. I saved the evidence. I've saved both my panties and the nylons in my safe deposit box. If we want to play hard ball with George, we can own him based on a sexual harassment charge. I'm sure just the hint of that would scare the crap out of him. He'd never want his co conspirators to learn about that.

"You are amazing, CC," Sheila suddenly felt reassured of CC's love for her. Her partner's actions really were, as she said, just business. Intimacy as a business weapon was a new concept for Sheila and it amazed her how effective it was.

"When do we go to Canada?" Sheila's voice barely contained her giggles. Her facial expression glowed with refreshed esteem for her wily diabolical partner.

"Tonight, get packed my love. Our flight leaves in five hours."

Shortly thereafter Sheila and Cecilia were off!

CHAPTER TWENTY-SIX

AT THE BRASSERIE

The hotel was beyond fabulous. If there was such a thing as a ten star hotel anywhere in the world the Banff Fairmont would be it. Sheila and Cecilia pampered themselves with massages and mud baths. They rolled their bodies in luxury. They ate very well and slept better that first night than they'd slept in years. They drank in the stunning view of Lake Louise from their room. It was such a breathtaking awe inspiring scene that it made the two lovers feel that they were babes blessed in God's perfect cradle. They made love unlike ever before. It was slow and easy, filled with pleasurable experimentations, and thrice repeated. It didn't actually stop. They fell asleep wrapped in each others' arms.

Everything was perfect. Sheila was amazed by the cleverness of her partner in pulling off their naughty girls' scamper. Cecilia was a meticulous administrator. She anticipated every conceivable glitch that might arise to thwart their plan. She booked two rooms, paid for them on her company credit card, and then made a side deal with the concierge to sell one room back to him for the two weeks for a cash discount. She had all calls to her assigned room phone rung through to Sheila's room on a separate line. This was a sensible precaution in case Mr. Palmer called for her. A woman can never be too careful or too circumspect about how she handles a love sick male.

During the second night they were too exhausted from their first night and their hike around and about the lake the next morning to do anything but sleep. In the predawn, after the deep rapid eye movement time, Sheila had a dream, or maybe it was a revelation. She heard her father singing. 'Take a ride on the Reading Railroad, Pennsylvania, Short Line, B and O. If you don't care where you're going, doesn't matter where you go. Come rain or shine or snow, those trains are gonna go! Toot toot! Toot, toot!'

• • •

Then she saw in her dream state her father and mother leap up from the family's dining room table. Her father began chasing her mother around the table. She and Donny, her older brother, giggled and watched them. Her parents were happy people. She and her brother were happy watching them. They behaved like rabbits or squirrels when mating. Round and round the table they ran. Then her mother bolted for the living room. Her father continued his home made ditty song and pretended he was going to catch his wife. Then her mother kicked her legs out as she ran, kind of like she was leading a train of followers in a Congo line; but her only follower was Sheila's dad. Dad eventually caught her, or rather Mom allowed herself to get caught. Dad smothered Mom in his arms, swayed her body back and forth, and began kissing her on the back of her neck. Then her mother squeaked out a high pitched Toot, toot! Toot, toot! That was their secret signal.

While she and Donny were still eating dinner, mother made a mad run for the stairs. She scurried up the flight of stairs to the top and scampered into the right side hall door to her bedroom. Her parents' bedroom had a big window picture window that overlooked the farm's lower pastures and Pohopoco Creek. They found tranquility there watching the forest animals cross their land and different bird species partaking of the bounty of their fields. Then came the happy sounds of her parents. Mother laughed crazily in response to Father's tickles. Then she'd say "Why Bob Carson, just what are you going to do with that big thing you have?"

And Father would say "Why Heidi Carson, I thought we might try to make another Carson."

"Why Mr. Carson, I think you have a great idea there. Did I ever tell you how much I love you, Mr. Carson?" Mother teased.

And her father would say "Yes, Mrs. Carson, but I'd love to hear you say it again and again and again."

And then her mother would say "I love you, Bob. I love you Bob, I love you, Bob."

Sheila watched Donny, her older brother, snicker. She didn't fully understand nature at her tender age. She'd seen the horses and the cows doing strange stuff though and she wondered about it.

"They're just acting frisky," her father would say when she asked about the animals. But that didn't help her understand sex, especially when it came to two legged humans. Her young girl's mind had not yet transitioned from believing the stories of the stork bringing babies to understanding the insemination work being done by their stallion and their bull. Months later when her mother began to show it suddenly dawned on her. That chase evening was when her parents conceived Adam..

Sheila, as a young girl with a sixteen year old brother, knew her mother was a very happy woman and madly in love with her father. She now, years later, felt that message of love a woman has for a man coming through her dream like it was an egg suddenly impregnated and brought to life. But, by what, her drowsy mind wondered. Then she awoke.

It was one of those awakes that's only a half awake because the dream continues in the part of the mind that still is dreaming and that dream part isn't ready to wake up with the rest of the brain. Sheila lay there in her stupor. Her mother deeply loved her father. She knew that special happiness once, before her older brother got killed in Iraq and before the tragedy that befell her younger brother. Her awakening mind turned over a page to return it to her memories of that tragedy. She desperately needed to understand it from an emotional perspective. All her life she tried to make sense of it but could not. Now, possibly this morning, lying here, she could get her mind over that hurdle she always blocked out before.

She remembered all the times her father plowed and how he'd jump down from the tractor, the Big Green Plowing Machine, he'd nick named it. He called it that as kind of a Post Traumatic Stress Disordered response from his service in Vietnam. He had three tours with the Marine Corps up in I corps, near the DMZ, what was laughingly referred to as the Demilitarized Zone; but it was a killing hell known as the Dead Marine Zone, that was anything but demilitarized.

Vietnam played on her dad's mind ever since he'd gone there that first time. Back then he and his Marine buddies referred to the Corps' First Marine Division as the Big Green Killing Machine. They even had this quirky song that said 'If some fuckin Dink has got the best of you, when things ain't going right, and you knows you gotta fight; you best not waste your time; you'd better spend your dime. You need to make that call. It's time to have a ball. It's time to have some fun. It's time to call Big One. You gotta hurry up and order One. We're the great Big Green Killing Machine. You need to hurry up and order One. It's time to call and get your business done! Just make that call today. We'll send your cares away! Go ahead, just call us. We're the great Big Green Killing Machine——' It was an obsessive mind numbing jingle he sang repetitively while he plowed the earth. It made him feel happy and in control to rip through the soils, busting up the sod.

She remembered how Dad ran his big hands through the earth after he plowed a field. He'd pick out an earthworm, throw it into a coffee can and tell it that it was going to become a trout that they would eat that night after he dangled it in the Pohopoco. How happy he was! He had it all. He had a woman who loved him, his farm, his boys and me, Sheila, his geeky daughter who always got straight A's in school.

But then his tragedies came. He was cursed, it seemed. Like Ulysses he was consigned by the gods to an unrelenting onslaught of bad breaks. First the news came that her older brother Donny died face down in the dirt, clutching his blown out guts in a far away place called Fallujah, Iraq. Then there was Adam's tragedy. The horror she blocked out all these years rushed back to her with all its pain.

They'd had Bess, a big Belgian Gray horse, for plowing the high sloped field where Dad didn't trust plowing with the tractor. All three siblings loved to ride the big Gray. Sheila guessed that was really why he kept the horse, for the kids to have fun riding her. Dad told Adam, her younger brother, to hitch Bess to the hand plow that day. He told Adam how to make some cuts along the upper meadow where it bordered Henry Getz's farm. It was a good thing for a boy to do at his age. He was fourteen now and he needed to be helping with the manly things around the farm, not just feeding chickens and gathering eggs. Then Dad left in the pick up truck to get timothy hay for Bess at the feed store.

Dad couldn't know that Bess picked up a stone in her right rear hoof and was lame. Adam didn't have the strength or the know how to get Bess to lift her hoof to pry that stone out. So, instead of waiting for Dad to return, he decided to take the Big Green Plowing Machine to the upper fence line where the tractor tilted at a high angle while it plowed. That was the tragedy. The horse couldn't help what happened. Father couldn't know about the horse or what Adam might do when left alone. Adam was often told to never drive the tractor without Dad being with him, but for some reason, on that day he didn't mind Dad.

The tractor hadn't plowed more than twenty yards before its front wheel was jostled uphill by a rock. That flipped the tractor. As it started to roll over, Adam leaped off. But when he landed on the ground he twisted his ankle and laid there a second too long. The tractor's weight landed squarely on his chest and crushed the life right out of him. Mom heard something. She ran out of the house and up the hill like a crazy person. She was just in time to hold her youngest son in her arms and watch the blood oozing from his mouth. She heard his moans as his life left him. The last thing her son said to her was 'I ain't going to make it Mom.'

Mother sat there in that field holding her Adam in her arms like he was still her little baby and cried and screamed until Dad came home and took her back inside the house. Dad didn't cry or show any emotions at all. He'd seen so much death in Vietnam his mind and body were numb to death. But he held Mom close to his chest and gave her all the love he could.

Mother was never the same after that. She didn't go to church any more. When the church bells pealed on Sundays, she just stared out the living room window and cried. Sheila recalled that her mom had one of those old antique Victrola record players and lots of old black hard pressed clay records. Some had church songs on them. Her mom would sit for hours and play 'Rock of Ages' on that Victrola. She'd hum the words 'Rock of ages, clef for me. Let me hide myself in thee. Let the waters and the blood from thy riven side that flowed. Be of sin thy gentle cure. Let me hide myself in thee.' And then Mother would cry. She cried softly then. Her screams were now just muted sobs. Religious music helped her some, but only temporarily. Her life had suffered an inconsolable wound.

Her heart ached now in a way that was somehow a hundred times worse than when Donny's body came home in its flag draped coffin.

Maybe it was in a part of her heart that only a mother knows, that Donny went looking to fight and to kill, so that was something she could accept; but Adam, her sweet little boy, didn't go looking for death, but death found him anyway.

Sheila was waking up now and wondering if she understood life any better now than she did before she went to sleep. Sometimes you go looking for something and it finds you. Other times you're not looking for something and it finds you anyway. Maybe her dream helped her reaffirm her belief that all men were not bad. Her father was not bad. He was good. But many men were bad.

It wasn't too long after Adam died that the bad men from the government took their farm. Before he blew his brains out her father told her "Government is not for the good people who work hard for a living. Government is for the people who are good for nothing shitheads. It works for the shitheads because shitheads get to vote too and there are more shitheads than good people. And shitheads vote for folks that are like they are, shitheads. The whole democracy concept is doomed to fail because it's a system that got altered by traitors to the constitution for the benefit of worthless shithead voters. Once the constitution was changed so that shitheads who didn't own property got to vote, America died. America was once a beautiful concept, but it ain't no more, just ain't. It's gonna end in destruction because it's nothin but a pack of greedy worthless shitheads now, and they all deserve to die. They just suck off the entire world with their phony dollar and pretend to be something big and mighty which they ain't. They got no morals anymore, no heart, no soul, no kindness and no goodness in them. They're just a nation of greedy pigs and thieves and shitheads. Americans are just shit now."

It wasn't even a month after their father daughter talk that Dad blew his head off. Likely he succumbed to the culmination of things, the endless killing in Vietnam, the loss of his two sons, and now his land and his wife's sanity, his very life. He never complained or showed any bitterness about his life before that day. He was a quiet man who kept all his pain inside him somewhere. When the sheriff told Heidi about the tragedy, she first went into shock. Dad was her rock and now he was gone. Then she screamed again, but this time she never stopped screaming. That's when Sheila and the County sheriff took her to the asylum and left her there.

Her father had been good to her mother. They knew beautiful good happy years. Happiness was there with the two of them. They were happier than any two people she'd ever known. They loved openly and trusted each other completely. They never had a hidden agenda or a ruse to hide or a secret to conceal from one another. They were good people of the earth. But life crushed them. The final straw was when the government broke her father's back. And there was nothing more anyone could do. The last time Sheila visited Mother she no longer recognized her daughter. Her mind was gone from this world now, encased and forever locked away in some impenetrable barrier of anguish. Everything Mother loved was gone except Sheila, but somehow her daughter wasn't enough to break her out of her shell. Mother sat in her wheelchair looking out of a window hoping to see something, but no one knew what. Sheila held her close and kissed her gray head, then kissed her hand and said good bye to her for that last time. Parting was terribly painful. It was hard to close the formative chapters of her life

When a thistle seed senses the time is right it just goes off into the air and lets fate take it where it will. Perhaps it's the lull of the breeze or the full bursting ripeness of the crown head pushing upward away from its root anchor; or maybe it's the tempting warm smells of the welcoming earth, if thistle seeds can somehow smell those smells. But, whatever it is that makes that tiny seed desire to go, it answers nature's dictate and goes off into the wind. That morning after Sheila had thrashed out her past emotional pains something awoke within her. Perhaps it was a premonition or maybe even a spiritual awakening or the nudge of a silent spirit, but whatever it was it inspired Sheila to rub the sleepers from her eyes and get out of bed.

• • •

Then, something called her from within and moved her to freshen up, put on make up, dress and leave her room. Something from deep within her called strongly that morning. A tiny embryo of a thought or a hope had seeded itself in her mind overnight and begun to gestate. It took over her volitions and moved her onward as if she was lifted upward like a thistle seed for her release into destiny. She felt an urge to leave their room, but if asked, she would not have been able to give voice to this feeling for she didn't understand it.

The concept of a woman coming into heat like a bitch dog does is ridiculous, yet Sheila did feel a certain unexplainable urge. It pulled her along faster and faster and got her to making her movements so fast she almost, but not quite, got sloppy smeary with her lipstick. But she didn't get sloppy smeary. She got herself perky and inviting because her feminine mind somehow intuited that looking good this morning was important.

Sheila left a note for still sleeping CC that she was going down to the Brasserie Cafe for breakfast. Then she tip toed out of their room and softly closed the door behind her. At the cafe the maitre de handed her a newspaper and seated her. She laid her paper on the table and picked up her menu.

That's when she saw him. Looking beyond her menu to the table next to hers she noticed a very handsome man. He was lanky tall and rugged looking; square jawed with steely gray eyes and flaxen blond hair. His chin sported a slight dimple and he wore a jacket with no tie and a blue tattersall shirt. He was eye candy for females. He would not look up from the book he was reading. Her eyes acquired his every feature like lasers scanning their target. He was reading with the sort of intensity she noted in her colleagues at MIT or the technical men at Bear and Otter. But he was reading some sort of book with drawings in it, not just text. He toyed absent mindedly with his oatmeal as if it was a bother to him to have anything interfere with his reading. After she ordered a whole wheat waffle with berries she occasionally stole glances at him. Then he finally lifted the book from the table to hold it upright and let book's spine rest on his table. She read its cover. It was a compilation of the theories of Nickolas Tesla! Her heart raced. She almost choked on her waffle.

She thought it had to be fate. She realized her perfect man was sitting across from her at the next table. He wore no wedding ring. His table setting was for one. That meant she could presume he was unclaimed! There he was, a big handsome dog with no collar or leash! She felt a panic flutter. She feared she'd probably be inadequate for him in some way, possibly in every way. He'd probably had dozens of women, maybe even a girl he intended to marry or something. And yet here she was, within spitting distance of him.

But how could she tell him she had a lesbian girl friend up in their room? How could she broach the subject of why she was there, that she needed to find some weirdo fiction writer who claimed to talk to the spirits? How could she tell him she was exploring the possibilities of electromagnetic force fields and their interactions with the supernatural? And, surely he'd think she was a wacko bird if she told him that she was privy to some secret conspiracy that intended to kill a million Americans.

She felt a sudden rush of butterflies in her stomach. She absolutely had to say something to him, to strike up a conversation, but she just couldn't do it. She just looked at him and felt so inadequate. Much like a thistle's bud cup gripped by a sudden chill, her seeds of fate and imagination were swallowed and closed by her fears. But, fate was not to be denied this day. Like a dog brushing against a thistle's cup will shake loose some thistle seeds onto its fur, humans can also have their hopes fatefully carried along by chance.

Just as Sheila's eyes teared up with frustration at her incredulous situation a waitress passed a bus boy next to her table. Fortunately for Sheila and unfortunately for the bus boy the waitress bent toward her to ask if there was anything more she could bring to her table. At that very instant the bus boy, carrying a tray of china and flatware, bumped the derriere of the waitress and spilled his tray, partially onto Sheila's table. A terrible distracting clatter resulted and the object of Sheila's intents looked up in a start.

Then the flood gates of Sheila's helplessness opened. She wailed. It wasn't a restrained cry. No, it was a wailing anguished yelp of a frustrated animal that just caught its foot in a trap. She shrieked in reaction to liquids on her skirt. She felt unable to cope with anything and the thought flashed through her mind that she would now likely never meet this handsome stranger. But she was very wrong.

The stranger immediately leaped to his feet and moved to her table with napkin in hand to begin mopping up the spilled coffee and juices that landed on her table cloth. Then he looked intently into her face.

"Why Miss, you're crying. There, there, it's nothing to be upset about. Here, please take this for your tears." With that gentlemanly gesture he placed an oversized white cotton handkerchief into her hand. It was unused, freshly pressed and it bore the monogrammed initials E. B. His eyes quickly scoured her table for any wayward fluid spills. They were immediately drawn to her MIT rat ring and they quickly gathered in the fact that she wore no other rings. He stared into her eyes with a penetrating direct and hopeful look.

"Please, Miss, come join me at my table. I assure you the service is excellent and the table top is dry." He immediately took charge of the confused situation and ordered the waitress to set another place at his table and to bring a complimentary reorder of Sheila's menu.

"Good morning. This must be my lucky day. It's a pleasure to meet you, Miss. I'm Ehud Burke, or E.B., or, as my friends and family call me, Hud. I'm the Hud of Hud Explorations. We're explorers for mineral deposits and we do a lot of work in the British Columbia Golden Triangle, right next door, actually about two to four hundred miles west of here. I just love to stop here at the Fairmont on my trips back and forth from our mining camp to Plaintown. It's a grand place, isn't it? How about you, Miss? Are you here for very long? Do you come here often? And, by what stroke of great fortune are we finding ourselves here at the same table?" Hud had a charm about him and a smile that melted hearts.

Out of the corner of her eye Sheila saw CC standing at the maitre de podium. She knew this was not a good time to make an introduction. She'd just met Hud and didn't want to frighten him away with the revelation that she was traveling with her lesbian girl friend. "Excuse me, Hud. I'm terribly sorry, but I must excuse myself for a moment. I'll be back shortly." With that she left the table. Being the perfect gentleman, Hud rose when she did and assured her he'd wait anxiously for her return. He sat back down but his eyes never left Sheila. When Sheila reached the restaurant entrance she took CC's arm and pulled her aside. "It's him! I know it's him. I've found Mr. Perfect and I'm sitting at his table. I just met him and I need to be alone with him for a while. I'll catch up with you later. Why don't you go and get room service?"

"Okay, see you later and good luck," smiled CC. She accepted her waive off graciously and departed to return to their room; but as she stood waiting for the elevator she felt a small tinge of jealousy toward the man Sheila claimed was their Mr. Perfect. When she opened the door to their room she wondered if Sheila would close the door on their love.

Sheila returned to the table.

"I see you have a friend with you," said Hud when she returned.

"Oh, yes. She's a great friend. We're traveling together to see the Park. Neither of us has been here before and we're very excited about It." she thought that was a sufficiently fluffy ambiguous answer.

"Why didn't you invite her to join us?' He revealed an eagerness to be friendly to both women.

"Oh, well, Hud, we just met and it is your table. I wouldn't presume to be so bold as to encumber you with two women you've never met before."

"Nonsense, but I see she's gone now. I could tell she's almost as beautiful as you, Miss, and I certainly wouldn't feel put upon in the least. What is your name, anyway?"

"Sheila Carson. I'm a physicist and mathematician. By coincidence, I'm also from Plaintown. I couldn't help but notice that you are reading Tesla. He's one of my all time favorite science heroes. I could talk about his work for hours. I'm very curious about why you have an interest in him. Is your interest related to geology in some way?"

"Yes, it is related to geology; but tell me, Sheila, what makes Nickolas Tesla one of your all time favorites?' Hud was understandably cautious. After all there was serious interest in his mineral claim group but he didn't understand why or who was behind the interest.

"I believe he unlocked the mathematics that makes it possible to travel faster than light." Sheila dropped her bombshell.

"You're joking of course."

"No, I am not joking. I am convinced his top secret papers that were purloined by the government when he died hold those secrets. They raided his home and took the papers that hold the keys to universal travel at speeds vastly faster than the speed of light. I believe our top government scientists have been working on the physics for the application of his math proofs for decades but that they have come up short."

"Why are they coming up short?"

"Because our planet lacks a key element that facilitates harmonic resonance between and among the heavenly bodies, like our sun and our earth."

"You sound like you've done work on this. Have you?"

"Yes and no. I've done the math. I know my equations are solid. I believe I came up with the same proofs and solves that Tesla did; but I can't come up with any way to get or make the missing element I'd need to capture the resonance, amplify it and convert it into a directed energy vector; and I certainly don't have access to the kind of money the government has to get the infrastructure needed to build the crafts that could withstand the forces involved."

"Could such crafts be built, I mean theoretically, of course?"

"Maybe, it all depends upon manufacturing with a new undiscovered or uncreated element. To create it on Earth we'd need to commit all the resources of the entire world's economy and even that might not be enough."

"Okay, why not?"

"Because the kind of element or elements needed would have to come from a fifth or sixth generation star burst. When stars are formed from the dusts of previous stars they make heavier elements than the ones that existed in their prior solar systems. By my equations we'd need to have another five billion years of universal evolution to have enough novas and supernovas to have those newly created elements deposited on planets inside a solar system where they could be mined. I think that's why Tesla kept his work so secret. I believe he was trying to figure out how to short cut one or two more generations of star formation before he was going to reveal his math and his theoretical physics."

"Sheila, you are way out there with this stuff."

"Maybe," Sheila's face expressed her curiosity. "Sometimes I think I'm crazy, but a weird phenomenon appears to me and it's appeared to my traveling companion also. It appears to be an other-worldly darkness and it seems to be trying to tell us something; but we don't know what. I'm entertaining the belief that there are such things as supernatural forces from or of an extra planetary nature that know how we here on Earth can short cut the process of star generation somehow to create the element or elements necessary to achieve Tesla's theoretical speeds."

"How fast does your math say we could go?"

"Well, it may sound crazy to you if you haven't derived the equations; but I have derived them and I've triple checked everything, so I believe my work. It's possible to travel the universe at instantaneous speeds, in other words we could simply designate a coordinate in universal space, touch a button and be there, just like that."

"So, I could go to the nearest Earth like planet if I wanted to?"

"You could, and you'd be there faster than the time it would take the second hand on your watch to move one tick."

"You've got to be kidding!"

"I'm dead serious. Math doesn't lie."

"This sounds too fantastical to be true. Why does a woman with a brain like yours go playing around Banff Park for a couple of weeks when you have such a great ability to solve problems? Surely this place must bore you compared to your equations?" Hud's tone held an element of skeptical disbelief that he wasn't hearing the whole story from this fascinating woman. But, there was something about her. Was this the 'good woman' that the visiting spirits said would find him?[1] He wondered. She was engaging and vastly more interesting than any woman he'd known previously, except possibly his mother, Little Sparrow.

"Your turn, Hud, I like your name. Please tell me about you. Why is a geologist sitting in a coffee shop in a national park which is off limits to mineral exploration?"

"Oh, well, it's getting on towards autumn and most of my work is at high elevations. Our camp is getting snow now so I let the crew go. We're not going to drill again until next June. I stop here on the way coming to and going from camp. It keeps me in touch with civilization."

"But, there are direct flights from Vancouver to Plaintown. Why do you come here? It's out of the way isn't it?"

"I fly my own plane. I like flying through the mountains and coming here. It makes me feel closer to the spirits, or God, if you prefer. I like to be good to myself every once in a while. What we do up in the Kamloops and the Kootenay's is dangerous. We fly choppers above the snow line. We drill rock up there. We take grab and trench samples where we see coloration and then we get down to Stewart and try to make sense out of it. Like I said, it's dangerous work. We lost a chopper and a crew up there last year. Three men were killed

---

[1] In *When the butterflies Come* Hud was visited by the spirits of Big Chief, Big Horse, Little Sparrow and Nickolas Tesla. They told him a good woman would find him.

on a cliff face. One of them was my partner. The winds changed on them and went from calm to gale force in minutes. Coming here is a return to tranquility for me."

Then a primal feeling overcame Hud. It started in his stomach then caused a tickling rush of blood into his cheeks. It came to him from across millenniums of human evolution, rushed itself right into him from the boundary times between the Paleolithic and Neolithic periods, when mankind took that first peek into civilization. He felt a primitive urge to conk Sheila over her head with his club, drag her into his cave and ravage her body until he spent himself making love to her; but then a more subtle refined feeling displaced it. Twenty thousand years of civilizing behaviors interceded to harness his animal spirits.

She was woman. He was man. She required his attentions. She was a special creature sent to him by his ancestral spirits. He must guide, protect and nourish her; and possibly husband her children or lay down his life for her. In that defining moment he became bound by the male's chivalrous pact with fealty. It happens to a man when he recognizes he's been chosen to commit to the well being of a particular woman. It becomes a matter of honor for the man, even if the woman he regards as his woman doesn't even recognize it at that time it first cements his life to hers.

Maybe what set off Hud's wonderment was the slow unthinking way that Sheila moistened her lips while he talked, or maybe it was the way she absent mindedly twirled a strand of her hair while she fixated her eyes into his, like she was traveling into his mind with the intention of staying there. Then, as he shifted his weight in his chair, not from discomfort but from a sense of shared curiosity, his controlled impulse broke containment. The Sicilians call it the 'thunderbolt' moment. It happened when he allowed his eyes to fixate on her face. He saw her empathetic expression when he told her about the loss of his partner. Whatever this feeling was has been written about and talked about for centuries, and there it was. He wanted her. The feeling was strong and undeniable. He forgot to eat the rest of his oatmeal. Sheila noticed.

Suddenly for Hud, everything about Sheila was wondrous, perfect, beautiful beyond description, more exciting than a drill core with visible gold and vastly more appealing than any whore he'd ever drilled. She was a beautiful, brilliant, confident, sexy, friendly, plain spoken, magnificent woman. Then his second revelation came. It hit his consciousness hard, like a sobriety jolt of black coffee hits a man when he's had too many drinks.

She was *that* one! She was the woman the spirits said would find him! That was the way with women, they had said. '*The right woman will find you*,' was what his grandfather's spirit, Big Chief, told him that night in his tent at his drop camp. It was the night when his mother, Little Sparrow Barbara, and his father, Big Horse Bob, and also the other one came. Who was that one? Yes, now he remembered! His family's spirits were joined by the spirit of Nickolas Tesla! He remembered it all like it happened last night.

That night flooded back to him. He was exhausted from rock chipping, trenching, pulling drill core, drinking and whoring. Then they appeared. His grandfather disapproved of his lifestyle and told him so. He said he would send him a good woman. This woman must have been sent to him by his grandfather's spirit.

Suddenly he was overcome with thought, 'I need to cherish her; become her partner in life and her friend. It is ordained by my ancestors. It is fated. Am I living a historic moment? Am I and this woman to do something that will change the destiny of mankind and the world?'

His heart stepped up its pace. But, then he thought longer. 'What was it about what the spirits said? Yes, she did find him.

The way it happened was awkward and a bit messy, but come into his life she did. Maybe the spirits caused the bus boy to bump the waitress and spill the coffee and juice onto her table.'

"Thank you spirits," he said silently to himself. He was certain the spirit of his wise loving grandfather instigated this meeting with Sheila. The old man loved him and had always looked out for him.

His thoughts wondered about her companion. 'What is she all about? I had a joyful feeling about her like a little boy feels when he gets a new bicycle for Christmas. I only had one glimpse of her, but it was enough to observe that she was voluptuous and very beautiful. She looks like what Cleopatra, the Queen of Egypt must have looked like, that curious mixture of Ptolemy blood with Arab and Nubian to create a gorgeous sensuous goddess. Her face burned its image into my mind. She has the sort of face I could hold and kiss for hours. She is the essence of ravenous temptations, casually dressed, and she carried herself as if every fiber of her body knew how appealing she was. Somehow from somewhere in her past there must be goddess blood in her. I want to know her name but it might be impolite to ask. The spirits never mentioned anything about two women. Maybe grandfather overdid it? No, that can not be. He would never send me more than I could handle.'

He was on his own on this one and more than a little baffled about how to deal with both of them. His mind went through its check list, much like it did when he started his airplane. He realized there was only one way to proceed or this venture would never start, let alone lift off. He would be a perfect gentleman toward both of them. He would offer to include both of them in everything he suggested they do. Everything they did they would do as a threesome. He dared not risk alienating Sheila by giving her any false perception that he was trying to separate her from her friend; and he likewise did not want to alienate her beautiful companion by giving her the false impression that her company was unwanted.

He wanted to know both of them. It would be awkward and gauche to slight either of them. He concluded he would embrace them both as if they had all been friends for a thousand lifetimes. And, if they wished it, if they indicated they were uninhibited women who desired a polygamous relationship, then he would also whole heartedly love them both. That thought surprised him and caused his male appendage to harden. He wondered if Sheila noticed.

"I have a thought for you and your friend. How about if the three of us take a tour this afternoon? I'll take you up in my plane and show you an aerial view of the park. We'll have a ball. You'll love it, I promise." Hud was more anxious to please Sheila than a new puppy trying to wriggle his way onto her lap to lick her face. Shortly after Hud's invitation Sheila gathered CC from their room. Then the three of them piled into Hud's Land Rover and they were off!

CHAPTER TWENTY-SEVEN

DEFIANCE

Three hours later Hud, Sheila and Cecilia were seated in Hud's Beech Baron at Calgary airport. Sheila sat next to Hud in the cockpit and Cecilia sat behind her. The women felt adventurous. The sky was clear and blue; a hint of fall was in the air, and everything about pilot Hud exuded confidence. When he fired up the turbocharged twin Continental 520 Lycoming engines his plane vibrated with anxiety. It was a powerful beast. Hud pushed down on the brakes to control its thrust before it leaped into the sky. Sheila watched Hud push the throttles forward. 'Does that inert throttle bar feel the same sensations a man's penis feels when it's inside a woman having an orgasm?' She smiled at her own silent question. 'How does CC feel about going on today's adventure?' she wondered. She was the logical choice to sit in the second row because she was two inches shorter than Sheila, and the overhead of the cabin sloped downward as it went back, but did CC feel slighted somehow?

CC dispelled all doubt about her frame of mind. "Oh Hud, I am so glad to have met you and that you invited both of us to fly with you," she cheerfully burbled. "All my life I've wanted to go flying in a private plane. I can't wait to take off. Promise you'll tell us what we're seeing on the ground, won't you Hud?"

"Sure thing, CC, right after we take off you just loosen your seat belt a few inches and lean your head forward right between Sheila and me. That way you'll see everything in front and out the side cockpit windows just as we see things. When I bank the plane, don't fight it. Just let your cheeks rub up against mine or Sheila's. We're all friends here, okay?"

"Sounds wonderful to me," CC's reply brimmed with enthusiasm.

"Now, I'm going to do some pilot to tower talking, so just relax. Soon we'll begin a little jog to the take off runway. Then I'll feed these monster engines their juice. We'll accelerate pretty fast. We'll take off into a fifteen knot headwind and be off the ground in less than a half mile of runway. We'll climb much more steeply than you would in a commercial airliner. Don't let that frighten you. This little race horse can almost fly straight up, but we won't do anything too crazy on your first ride with me."

Both women caught that subtle nuance. Obviously Hud wanted to see more of them than just today's sight seeing trip. CC's thoughts turned to how quickly he would find his way to their bedroom and what fun they would have there. Sheila thought hopeful thoughts. She imagined Hud as the father of her children and wondered if he was as good a man as her father. She wished he was. He seemed much like her father.

The big Lycoming engines roared and the Baron trembled, anxious to fly. Sheila felt close to Hud and safe with her life in his hands. With his quietly voiced 'Here we go!' Hud throttled maximum fuel to the Baron's engines. It leaped alive with excitement and the rush of raw power. Hud released its brakes. Like a hard spurred mighty steed the craft hurtled down the runway. The women saw the ground slide by at a rapidly accelerating rate. Their heads pushed back into their head rests and they clinched their lips in anticipation of going airborne. The ground became a fast moving blur. And then they were off!

Fifteen minutes after take off they were criss-crossing the continental divide, sliding down from altitude and skimming along a thousand feet above the treetops. They shot through the Vermillion and Kicking Horse Passes and slowed their airspeed as they overflew a herd of elk. Hud tipped the Baron's wing. The elk stopped their grazing. The cows of the herd began to run down slope to get away from the plane. Hud turned and followed them so they could watch their buffed white rumps bounding gracefully across the high meadow and melting into the high forest. About thirty cow elk preceded a magnificent herd bull. 'He's an eight pointer!' Hud shouted out his admiration of the majestic antlered monarch. The bull turned his massive head skyward in defiance of the plane. He stood ready to fight and protect his precious cows from this skyborn threat. Sheila and Cecilia realized they were glimpsing the noble behavior of a champion. They were seeing one of nature's valiant moments.

"Why are their rumps lighter than their hides in the front of them? asked an excited Sheila.

"The hunters say it's to confuse predators, distract their vision from seeing which animal is the slowest or the weakest," answered Hud.

"Do you agree with that? asked CC.

"Well, I'm not sure. You see I've never talked to an elk," chuckled Hud, "My own theory is that it helps them know which end of the cow is which. That helps them get their mating done quicker."

Both women laughed at Hud's sense of humor. They liked it that he could relate sex considerations to the elks' anatomy.

The plane flew onward. Hud pointed out the different mountain peaks; and then flew through Bow Pass and changed course to Mount Willington. Hud decided to show off a little. He banked the Barron hard onto its wingtip so that he was flying perpendicular to the ground. Sheila and CC were pulled by gravity so that CC's head was pressed against his cheek and Sheila's body was leaned hard against his. Onward they flew staring straight out the cockpit window at the mountain's peak as the plane pirouetted around the mountain on its port side wingtip. Flying this way they completely circled the mountain's top.

The experience was an exhilarating display of man's technical excellence. The craft could do what only a bird could do and the pilot could do what only a man of conscious competence could do. The maneuver bonded the threesome in a shared breathtakingly beautiful experience. When Hud shot out of his hard bank he soared to altitude. Then at eighteen thousand feet he turned off the starboard engine. The women were frightened. Adrenalin fired through their blood in a way they'd never before imagined it could. The propeller of the starboard engine stopped with one of its blades pointed straight up. Out of thousands of years of woman's submissiveness to man came a realization to both women. They were completely at Hud's mercy in this moment. If he chose to turn off the second engine they could only pray that their reunion with their maker would be a joyful one. They depended on Hud for their safety. They depended upon him for their lives and any hopes either of them had for procreating offspring. They needed him to care for them no less than the herd of elk cows depended on their champion to defend them and procreate them.

The moment transfixed Hud's passengers no less than it transfixed him. In this reflective moment he realized that he also depended upon his own good faith and skills to keep these women safe. They were in his care now. Feelings of duty and honor owed toward them swept over him. It was not unlike the call to stand and fight that the herd bull felt when he stood there in defiance of his airborne enemy, prepared to sacrifice himself for his cows.

"Do you feel frightened?" Hud asked calmly.

"Yes" said Sheila; "Hell yes," said CC.

"Don't be," commanded Hud. "You are perfectly safe with me and this aircraft. I keep it perfectly maintained. It can fly all the way back to Calgary on just one engine. Each of these engines has enough power to go it alone. That's why I use a twin engine plane. I would never have turned off that engine if I thought for a moment that any harm could come to you. I use a twin engine plane not because it needs both to power it, but because if one should go out I can trust the other one to get us home. I'm a firm believer that two is better than one. Wouldn't you agree?"

"Yes, of course," said Sheila. Her voice relaxed. Her trust cemented itself to Hud in a way she had not felt since she was a child riding with her father on his tractor or in his pick up truck. She found a place inside herself that told her she could join her life with this man's life and not be afraid of her decision. She noticed a glow arising in her tummy. She wondered if he felt the same toward her, and somehow she knew that he did. A woman's intuition told her they would some day marry and have children. But, as she breathed deeply, she knew that all good things came in due time.

"Oh, absolutely, two is much better than one. It must be marvelous knowing that either engine can power the plane on its own, but with both engines you really can have the ultimate experience, can't you, Hud?" CC's reply to Hud's question was boldly nuanced. Hud inferred from her hint that the ultimate erotic experience was somewhere in his future. He was falling in love with these two beauties and feeling committed to their happiness and their shared goals, whatever they were.

They hadn't told him the entire reason why they were here. That didn't matter at the moment. He sensed they would divulge everything to him in a manner and at a time of their choosing. He restarted the idled Lycoming. The Baron surged forward with renewed power. It was like a stallion chomping at the bit, eager to run and anxious to flex its muscular power. Hud pointed out the rivers and lakes and circled stunning Lake Louise before they returned to the Calgary airport for a perfectly smooth three point landing.

Hud stood on the tarmac to assist his passengers deplane. Sheila stepped to the edge of the wing and let herself fall. Hud's strong hands gripped her waist and pivoted her softly to the ground. What happened next is not found in any flying manual or etiquette book. Sheila felt herself drawn to Hud. Stepping away from his grasp or shaking his hand just wouldn't be sufficient to thank him for the delightful experience.

She moved a step closer to him. She felt safe as his hands tightened their grip on her waist. Their closeness pulled her feelings into acceptance and desire. She sought to hold fast to the feeling and keep it suspended in time. She clasped Hud's arms with her hands and forthrightly kissed him. It was an unapologetic, honest kiss on the lips.

She held her kiss longer than a kiss given as a mere thank you and looked deeply into his eyes when she gave it. With it she communicated her acceptance, love and commitment to this magnificent human monarch. In her heart she knew the kiss was right. It signified for her that here was a man every bit as good a man as her own father, only stronger of mind and body; and here was a man who evoked more yearnings for his passions and companionship than Johnny ever did; and here, possibly, was *that* man, the one she willed would liberate her from virginity and father her children. Yes, she knew in her heart's soul, that her kiss conveyed all those things.

Hud lost every sense of his past when Sheila graced him with her kiss. Suddenly here she was. She could be *that* girl, the one that was fated to find him, according to the spirits. Her kiss was a crossing over. He felt something inside him move from his present life alone into eternity alongside her. He prolonged the hold he had on her waist and just stared at her. He knew what had just happened and he knew these feelings would never leave him. Then he realized that Cecilia was standing on the wing smiling at the two of them and that she, too, needed a lift down.

He lifted his arms from Sheila's waist and outstretched his arms to receive Cecilia. Cecilia bounded outward with a motion like a gymnast's pose before she launches into her tumble routine. He captured the airborne nymph with his huge hands, also clasping her by the waist, but her momentum propelled her body into his. Suddenly Cecilia was there, pressed close against him. She then wrapped her arms tightly around his waist, gave him a crushing hug and kissed him on the lips. Her kiss was full and moist and with it she communicated her uninhibited yearning to be intimate with him. The kiss was an innocent, honest offering of her passions and eternal love, for Cecilia also recognized that Hud was their special *that* man.

Hud was shocked. He felt a torrent of passion and undeniable love for Cecilia. Her kiss left him speechless and craving intimacy with her. He felt a sudden ache in his heart. His feelings didn't want to wait another second to hold her bountiful beauty in his arms and cherish her forever. Sheila's kiss left him feeling a burning intensity of love and commitment, and now he had identical feelings for Cecilia. His heart was pounding with passion for both of them.

To become a lover of both women would be to defy conventional morality, yet he couldn't imagine favoring one over the other. He couldn't conceive of denying either woman his love and devotion, nor could he imagine himself inflicting hurtful feelings upon either woman if he spurned her affections. He couldn't live with his guilt if he denied either of them. That would only blight his relationship with the one he chose. Also the two women seemed inseparable and possibly intimate with each other. He rubbed his jaw while pondering his peculiar dilemma. He struggled with the thought that he was human and supposedly more rational than a herd bull mating his cows, but the emotional flames that coursed through him made him understand that he wasn't different at all.

"You ladies run on ahead to the terminal. There's a coffee shop in there. Go get your espressos and claim a table while I get our things together and tie down the plane," Hud said while trying to regain his emotional bearings. His mind was reeling and his heart was racing. He needed a few moments to himself to sort through his feelings.

The women walked gracefully and their strides were measured in unison. Their backsides floated seductively away as they walked from the plane. He mused about whether he had the emotional fortitude to be a lover to both of them, but looking at their heavenly anatomy convinced him that whatever the possible emotional tolls, being their companion and lover would be wonderful and worth it. He grinned to himself and wondered how much stamina, protein and rest he'd need to keep them both satisfied.

He got to work, now feeling eager to join them. He tied his rope loop hitches close to his wing hooks then placed slack hitches in his lines closer to the ground. Then he tugged both lines to make sure they had some slack play in case a strong wind arose. He was very loving to his Baron and took all measures to ensure it was always safe. When he finished tying the plane down he smiled at it and patted it on the engine cowling. "Things are going to be a little different from now on. You'll need to get used to them flying with us, old boy," he said affectionately to his Baron.

CHAPTER TWENTY-EIGHT

RICH ESPRESSO

Sheila and Cecilia wanted to taste a jolt of espresso before they returned to Lake Louise. They got their single shots, anchored a table and waited for Hud to join them.

"I love him," said Sheila.

"He's Mr. Perfect," said CC. "I love him too."

"Do you think he'll understand us?" asked Sheila.

"Of course he will," said CC. "I could tell that by the way he looked at you when you kissed him, and I could feel it by the way he kissed me. He's going to love loving both of us. And we will be so good to him he'll never want things any other way. I'm sure he'll accept us. He's even carrying our day bags for us."

"This is so wonderful, CC. It's my dream come true, and with you, the three of us, it's everything I've ever imagined and more. I hope this is the beginning of something wonderful. I hope we'll both carry a child of his. I love you, CC."

"We will, Sheila, we will bear his children. I love you too, Sheila. And I think you should be the one to explain things to him."

"Like why we've come here or how we feel about each other?"

"Oh, tell him about both, Sheila, why hold back? He's going to be our lover and confidant. We should never keep anything from him."

"I agree. Okay. I'll explain everything."

Hud arrived to find the women seated and sipping their drinks. Hud ordered a medium coffee and dumped a quarter cup of cream into it. Then he joined them at their table. No sooner had he sat down than two big men approached their table.

"Hey, George, look who we got here!" sang out a once familiar and friendly voice to Hud's ears.

"Well, I'll be a wolverine from Panama," barked out the second voice. "It's Hud, and he's got women with him! Hud, what in hell are you doing back here in Canada? We thought you'd be on a South Sea island somewhere." The two men were rugged outdoor types. They rushed to the table. They lifted Hud to his feet and hugged him and slapped him on his back like they'd all survived a war together. "Who are these raving beauties, Hud? Are they traveling with you or just seeing you for a real short time?" winked the first interloper.

Hud wrapped his huge arms around the waists of his two long lost acquaintances.

"Pete Johnson, George Burnett, I'd like you to meet my two dear lady friends, Sheila and Cecilia. Ladies, meet Pete and George. I've known Pete and George for many years. We go back a real long way. It's great to see you guys. What are you doing here?"

"Hell, we live here, Hud. We just got back from a cruise. Our wives are nearby shopping someplace. We'll find them later. We just had to stop and see you. But, the bigger question is what are *you* doing here?" asked Pete. "We figured after you sold the Little Cow you'd never be back in these parts. What *are* you doing here, anyways?"

"Well, boys, I confess. I would never keep secrets from you two. I've been rocking up in the Golden Triangle. I remembered some color shows from years back and got to looking at claim maps; then I put some claims together. And, before I knew it I was back on a mountain. Nothing big, not yet, just a drop camp with another geologist, not even a cook. He died in a chopper crash about a month ago. I'm working it all alone now. I've just finished some recon with a chopper and my prospector's picks. I had a rig up there a few weeks ago and took some shallow cores. They showed color but I haven't gotten results back yet. I decided to go back to the States for the winter and come back next thaw." Hud seemed overly modest.

"You ladies keep an eye on this one. He don't sit still long. He's a workaholic nut case he is," said George with a wink to Hud.

"You prospect for minerals?" asked Sheila. Her inquiry was directed to Hud.

"Hell, lady. This Hud here is the greatest gold finder in the history of rock cracking. Didn't he tell you? He found the Little Cow Creek!" Pete sounded shocked that the ladies didn't know who Hud was.

"Okay, boys, I can see this is some kind of inside joke," said Cecilia. Would one of you tell us what a little cow creek is?"

"Lady, where have you been?" boomed Pete. "Everybody in British Columbia who is anybody knows about Hud and the Little Cow!" Pete had an emphatic look that said the women should know all about the Little Cow too.

"Well, boys, please enlighten us lower forty-eighters. We've never even been to B.C. before," said Cecilia looking very lady like and a little miffed.

"Oh, Jesus, Mary and Joseph," said Pete. "Hud here found her. We was with him. George here cooked. I hauled supplies and ran mules. We were both near dirt poor, but Hud gave us work. He didn't pay much, but he paid us with some stock in Golden Hud Exploration. When we proved up the Little Cow Hud sold her to a biggie mining company from Toronto. Me and George here became multi millionaires! Does that enlighten you?"

Cecilia's jaw dropped. "So, you're telling me that the three of you are all millionaires?" She sounded thrilled to be in the presence of deities.

"Hell yes, Lady, me and George here is multi millionaires, thanks to Hud here; but Hud ain't no millionaire." Pete put his hands on his hips as a way of saying something matter of fact like.

"He's not?" Cecilia's face went crestfallen. Her budding hopes for a rich lover just had cold water thrown on them.

"Hell no, he's not a millionaire, lady. Hud here's a billionaire." Pete then launched into a brief history of their venture. "The Little Cow belonged to Hud and his sister. The Cow was one of the richest, most profitable high grade gold mines ever found anywhere in the world. Hud and his sister is both billionaires. And they're mighty fine people, yes maam, never uppity or braggers about it. Hud's good, honest and humble, ain't you Hud? You ain't gotten much different from us, your old buddies, has you Hud?"

"Well boys, I try to stay true to my roots," answered Hud. "I haven't changed much. I have a nice modest home in Plaintown now and a good man who keeps after the place and cooks; and I bought myself a Baron airplane and a Land Rover that I keep at a garage here in Calgary. But I still keep my old CJ 5 Jeep and tools at the garage in Stewart for when I go rocking. You know that's my passion. I still love rocks. They talk to me and tell their story. So, no, I ain't changed much. I still come up here with the spring thaw and work the peaks and I still run legal checks on who's got what claims."

"Hud, if you ever want to go again we'd like to go with you," Pete said suddenly standing erect like a statesman. "I mean if you was ever getting a hankering to put a scratch exploration company together again we'd like you to consider us. We'd be honored to throw in with you again, Hud, just like the old times, wouldn't we, George."

'Sure I would. I never had so many good times in my life. I'd throw in with you in a hot New York minute, Hud. Say Hud," George's voice dropped into a conspiratorial tone, "would these girls happen to be from one of them saloons in Stewart? They seem kind of like upgrades from the ones we used to———"

Hud cut George off in mid-sentence. "These aren't camp girls, they are very classy ladies," he said protecting Sheila and Cecilia. "They're career women who work in offices, not the types we used to have drinks with. Anyway, with wives nearby you boys should pay better mind to your P's and Q's.

"And, yes, my answer is yes. I've put together some geology since you've seen me last. If the color I'm looking at has a good shear zone with plutonics, chlorites and chalcopyrite stringers and if I get good results from my lab cores showing some path markers I'll be ready to put a company together and I'll be calling you. We'll cut trails and set up drill platforms and drill until we find the intrusive where the mantle bulged into the host formations and pushed up the gold.

"I'm ready to go again, not for the money this time, mind you, but just for the love of finding another deposit. I'd love to bring in another big one. I feel it in my blood. She's still up there, waiting for us to find her. I think this one will even be bigger than the Cow. By the rocks I'm seeing, I believe I'm on another big one."

"Hear that George? Hud, we love you, man. We'll follow you anywhere. Just call us. You know we're good help," pleaded Pete.

"We're the best," chimed in George.

"I know it. I said I'd call," said Hud as he shook both their hands.

Everyone then hugged everyone else in the impromptu party at the coffee shop. They said their goodbyes and swore their promises to stay in touch. Then George and Pete left to find their wives. Sheila and Cecilia looked at each other, speechless. These men were different than any men they'd ever met. These were rough and tumble, hearty adventurous risk takers. They were man's men. They feared nothing, not man nor beast nor the elements. Both women felt the electricity of the men's excitement rubbing off onto them. Their joyful can do anything spirit and camaraderie was contagious. The women's jaws went slack. They stared into each other's eyes. Their world was suddenly flying through clouds like the Baron. They were speechless and amazed at their good fortune.

CHAPTER TWENTY-NINE

YUMMY

During the return ride to Lake Louise Hud called ahead for dinner reservations for three. He insisted the threesome close out their spectacular day with a spectacular dinner. He chose the Fairview room and vouched that their rack of lamb was outstanding.

No arms needed twisting. Sheila and Cecilia, dressed in elegantly casual skirts and jackets, joined Hud at his table just as the sun was setting over Lake Louise. The views of the lake and mountains were spectacular.

"Hud, there's something we need to tell you. It's about why we're here," began Sheila. "Please don't think we're crazy, but we've stumbled onto a dastardly plot to murder a million Americans and overthrow the government."

Hud dropped his desert fork and took a long slow sip from his coffee. This was not what he expected. He thought they would possibly propose a ménage a trois, or suggest that he join them in their room for an after dinner drink. He was shocked to hear that these two lovely women had knowledge of something sinister and deadly.

Sheila saw his surprised look. It was all to be expected. "We're not involved in the plot, Hud. We believe there's a way to prevent it, and that's why we came here," she rallied his attention quickly. He leaned into the table and began to relax a bit.

"Forgive me for being just a little curious. What are you two beauties doing that you came to learn of such a plot, and how in the world does coming to British Columbia somehow help you save the lives of a million Americans?"

Then Sheila spilled the whole story to him. She divulged all the secrets she knew about Bear and Otter consulting, the taped conversation of the banker plotters and the general, the drone program she was laboring to solve, and the strange dark presence that appeared to her and CC.

"Okay, I get all that; but you still haven't told me why you came here to defuse this evil plot. Why are you here?" Hud's eyebrows lifted and his brow furrowed. He looked at the two women in a different way now. He thought he might be in the presence of a couple of wackos.

"Okay, I know this will sound crazy to you, but it's all we have to go on and we desperately need to find someone who lives here," said Sheila.

Hud relaxed his skepticism slightly. "So, who are we looking for? He asked.

"A woman named Rosemary. All we know about her is that she wrote a couple of steamy romance novels about some murders and that she lives in a log cabin somewhere in B.C. with a cat named Bud. CC sometimes hears Rosemary's spirit voice when she works on her drawings of the dark. The voice told her that a Spirit comes and talks to Rosemary at a place near where she lives. It told her secret rocks exist nearby that have compositions from fifth generation stars. CC is on to something. I believe this spirit thing is happening to both of us. We must find these rocks."

"Are fifth generation stars and their rocks even possible?" Hud's imagination recalled his own experiences. He was visited by the spirits at his drop camp, and there was the matter of his company's mining claims. Someone was willing to pay twice what they were currently worth. Could it be the rocks Sheila was talking about were on one of his claim groups and somebody else already discovered them? He decided to trust a little further what Sheila and CC were telling him.

"Yes, if they were from fifth generation descendent stars formed in the first few billion years after the beginning of the universe," said Sheila. "It's even possible that there were civilizations in solar systems around those early stars. It's conceivable that they did the same math that Tesla and I did. But they would have had to wait until the universe produced fifth generation stars. If a civilization formed during the time of second, third or fourth generation stars and if they knew the math, they may have existed for billions of years and may have found planets from fifth generation stars. It's possible those civilizations existed at the same time fifth generation stars with their planets came into existence. It all proves out in my math work on Tesla's theories. I proved that through electromagnetic resonance, using elements with much denser nuclei, you can harmonically amplify their magnetic resonances to speeds infinitely greater than light speed. You can travel anywhere in the universe almost instantaneously." Sheila was excited and breathless when she finished.

Hud sat with his jaw agape. There it was! The spirit thing, the Tesla connection, his own encounter with the spirits and the visit from Tesla's spirit that night along with the spirits of his mother and father and his beloved grandfather. He intuitively knew these women were for real, that their experiences were real and that everything Sheila said was the truth. He wrestled to find the right words. He didn't want to sound flippant or cynical. He knew that no matter how preposterous Sheila sounded she was a highly intelligent mathematician and she and her friend Cecilia totally believed everything she said.

"There's something else, Hud," Sheila continued. "We brought along a tape recording of a conversation and a set of earphones. Just listen to this and you'll see why we need to find these rocks."

Hud listened to the recording that Sheila made of the conversation that took place in the conference room on the dark fortieth floor. He learned of the plot to kill a million Americans. He learned that BASE bank was involved somehow through Walter Black, its chief executive. He also learned that a woman named Sandra was at risk of being murdered and that a man named Santifalo had already been liquidated. And, he learned the plotters were looking for some mountain man expert marksman traveling with a woman because they had a map. He noted that General Porter of the plotters essentially hated Walter Black. He quickly surmised that the map had profound significance; and possibly it was a map that led to the fifth generation rocks. Hud intuited that such rocks would be worth untold billions. Whoever possessed the rocks would control universal travel and possess amazing powers likely far greater than nuclear energy. Essentially the possessor of these rocks would control planet Earth and likely much more.

He needed to throw in with Sheila and Cecilia one hundred percent or get up from the table and run away. But he couldn't just get up and run away. He was a man who loved adventure. Sheila's babblings about fifth generation elements existing at the same time our fourth generation sun exists intrigued him. He wondered about the implications of her theory for the composition of rocks somewhere, anywhere, in the universe. Then there was the matter of this woman named Sandra who worked for Walter Black at BASE bank. Clearly her life was in danger. The chivalry in his soul could not turn away from her, knowing there were these wicked plotters who could kill her. He was raised to help those in need when he knew he could make a difference.

He had another compelling reason for not running away. He had fallen in love with Sheila and Cecilia. It was a sensational feeling that took root in his heart when he first met Sheila and glimpsed Cecilia at breakfast, and the feeling continued growing stronger. The more he was around them the closer to them he wanted to become. He broke into a huge grin. "So, you want me to go on a mission to find this reclusive lady with her cat and she'll tell us how to save the world. Am I getting this right?" he finally signaled his interest. "Just how much time do we have left to save the world?"

"The plot will be executed in two months time. We need to find a way to stop it before they kill all those football fans," said CC with a hint of consternation in her face and desperation in her voice. "Will you *please* help us?" CC's pleading eyes and puckered lips captivated Hud. When she turned on her disarming charm no man with red blood in his veins could say no to her. He sat back in his chair and tugged at his chin, as he always did when making a big decision. Then he broke into a wide grin. "I'm in ladies. In as in 'in for a dime, in for a dollar!' I've discovered I simply can't say no to either of you. You've completely captured my interest, and honestly, my heart."

"Do you have any idea where we could start looking for this Rosemary woman?" asked CC.

"As a matter of fact, I do. Pete, the Pete you just met, mentioned her to me one day at camp. He said he met her while he was getting groceries at a small country general store. He used to go there for supplies because it was closest to camp. The store is on a back country dirt road. I know the place. He saw her buying cat food and talked with her a bit. If I know Pete he tried to hit on her, but she's a recluse, like you said. About all he got out of her was that she believed in spirits and lived in a cabin somewhere near Roger's Pass. That pass isn't much of a stretch from the store. Pete thought your Rosemary was a nut case."

"We don't care what Pete thought of her. Would you know how to get to that pass?" asked a hopeful Sheila.

"Sweetheart," he spoke confidently, feeling they were bonded together in purpose. "I like the idea of getting to the bottom of this mystery and finding the reclusive Rosemary woman. If her cabin is in B. C. I'll find it. I know that country like I know the back of my hand. I own a lot of mineral rights there. We'll find your Rosemary woman all right. We should start out tomorrow morning. And tomorrow morning one of us must call that BASE bank and locate the woman named Sandra who worked with a Mr. Santifalo and tell her that her life is in danger. It's the right thing to do, and who knows, she may be helpful to us in some way. She knows this Black fellow and he's up to no good. You never know where something like this will lead you. But, what would you both say about coming up to my room for a nightcap and we'll start off after breakfast tomorrow?"

"Oh, we say yes and double yes, Hud. If you hadn't asked us, we'd already planned to ask you to our room," said Sheila.

"I can't wait another minute to be in a room with you, Hud" said CC., her voice communicated a depth of pent up passions eager to be unleashed. She felt herself becoming moist with anticipation. "Please take us to your room," she whispered.

CHAPTER THIRTY

LIFEJACKETS

C onnie opened the landside door of the boathouse and peered into the blackness. In a moment her eyes adjusted aided by of the shimmering reflections of moonlight on the lake. Dim light from the waning quarter moon played on the wave ripples that broke below the boat house's lakeside doors allowing her to make out shapes in the darkness. She slipped into the boathouse and closed the door.

"Paul are you in here?" she whispered.

A noise of Paul's shifting body upon a pile of kapok life jackets preceded his reply. "I'm here. I'm on the other side of the boats. I found the life jackets. They're on the old sofa where you said they'd be. Just stay there by the door and I'll come to you."

"No, Paul, don't be silly. I'll come to you. Just close your eyes. I'll find you," Connie spoke in an audible whisper. It wasn't necessary to remain silent because no one in the Lake House could hear what was happening in the boat house. She kept her voice low because she wanted to heighten the mystique of their rendezvous. She slowly felt her way past the boats to Paul. He was lying on the life jackets looking up at the moon through the boathouse's skylight windows. "I'm here, Paul. Can you see me? She whispered.

When Paul shifted his body to lay on his side he saw Connie standing next to the sofa. Less than a foot of deck separated her from the water. She was naked. Paul stared at her in wonderment. She was beautiful. The dim moonlight peeking in and out of passing clouds played across her face and breasts. He stared at her body taking in its inviting sensuousness. Her hips were lower than the side of the sofa so his imagination had to supply what his eyes could not see.

In the years since his divorce he'd been celibate. He'd not even made any effort to date a woman out of concerns that even the slightest liaison could have an adverse effect on his little Margaret. The divorce traumatized his daughter and he desperately wanted to give her some semblance of stability. But Connie understood human nature. Thankfully she sympathized with his daughter's terrified position and made every effort to ensure that Margaret felt secure and loved. Connie was astute, caring and patient in matters of the heart. She very quickly recognized that the way to Paul's heart was to befriend his daughter. She had done that. Margaret felt safe with her. Connie made the Lake House the little girl's home away from home, complete with her own bedroom. It was obvious to Paul that Margaret now preferred to be with him and Connie at the Lake House over being home with her mother.

"You're naked, Connie," Paul spoke in a soft voice.

"You're not afraid of me are you Paul? She asked as she took his hand in hers.

"No, not afraid, it's just that it's been so long since I've been with a woman. My former wife, that was over three years ago. I'm not sure I know how to, you know, make a woman happy. I don't believe I ever pleased my wife. I'm pretty focused on my research. You saw me that night————."

"Shhhh, Paul," Connie knew he was feeling afraid that he wouldn't please her and that he feared their first time would be awkward for him. "You don't need to apologize for anything.

You're a wonderful man and a wonderful father. You already make me happy, Paul. Just relax. Love is the most beautiful thing two people can know, Paul. I am in love you. I love the way you are with Margaret and I love you as a man. You can't do anything wrong when we're together as man and woman. You'll see. We'll take our time."

"Come; let's get you out of your clothes. Let's just touch for a while. Tonight will be beautiful. It's time for you to stop having regrets about your marriage and divorce. You didn't do anything wrong, Paul. You are a good person. You have nothing to feel guilty about. You have nothing to be ashamed of. You can let all your pain fade into the past. It's okay. You don't need that past anymore, Paul. You're not going to be hurt anymore. I'll never hurt you and I'll never let your ex hurt you again, either. You have Margaret and me now. You are very much loved. We both love you with all our hearts. We all have a wonderful time together and we'll have a wonderful future together. Let's know each other as a man and a woman. Let me help you remove your clothes."

Connie slowly unbuttoned Paul's shirt and removed it; then his belt and pants. She helped him slip out of his shorts. She slowly climbed onto the life jackets and lay side by side with him, their naked bodies touching. Then she began her kisses. They were soft loving touches on his face and lips. Between kisses she spoke softly.

"Intimacy is a wonderful thing, Paul. When two people love each other there's no greater happiness on earth. Can you hear the frogs and the crickets out there? That's nature saying we're doing the right thing,"

Connie moved her hand to his chest and rubbed it in a soft circular motion. She felt his body relax as if it felt a woman's touch for the first time. 'Your wife must have been one colossal idiot.' she thought.

"I love your body, Paul. I love touching you," she said as she continued kissing his face and lips. Her kisses were touch kisses designed to arouse and stimulate. Connie loved foreplay and the nuances of love making. She was extremely patient. She preferred long and slow sex, not the wham bam, thank you maam sex that Mole offered, nor the savage animal, exhausting fuck fest marathons that she'd experienced with George. The last few times with George were terrible. He made her feel dirty, like she was a pig thrown onto a pile of dirty jock straps, and then fucked until she was too sore to stand up. She wanted no more of it.

She breathed in and savored the inviting smell of Paul. He used a manly after shave and deodorant that aroused her. He had the smell of a man that came from a cultivated man's shower, very unlike the smells of the locker room she associated with George. Connie never considered herself to be a nymphomaniac, but before Paul came along if an attractive man wanted to take her for a tumble, she made herself available. Now everything was different. She wanted her love with Paul to be permanent. She wanted her days of experimenting with different men to end.

Her father kept an old cotton quilt at the foot of the day bed. He often slept under it here in the boathouse on cool summer nights. Connie reached down to the foot of the bed and found it. She covered herself and Paul with it. The damp fall air incentivized them to cuddle and enjoy each other's body heat. Their heads peeked out from the quilt that covered their bodies. Under the quilt she put her hand on his chest and continued rubbing him with slow soft rubs. She wanted to engage him and share his mind. She learned from watching her mother's management of her father that a shared experience or a shared conversation was the best doorway to intimacy. She knew it was important for Paul to get his concerns about the banking system out in the open and she wanted to hear him talk about them.

"Paul," she whispered, "tell me about your spread sheets. I want to know what you found that disturbs you so much. I want to trust your research and I need you to help us get through this problem, whatever it is. I know it's on your mind and I want you to tell me about it. I want you to offload all your worries to me; will you do that, please? I think sharing that with me will help us get closer and I want that very much." She approached Paul using the same loving technique her mother used to unlock her father's thoughts.

Her mother understood when her dad was troubled. She knew when he needed her. It was during those times that Mother came to Father and gave him a listening post. Other than that her mother pretty much left her father alone, unless he was in his Billy Goat Mood, as Mother called it. That's when her dad was cantankerous. Mother would take him by the arm and walk him into his den. Then she'd seat him in his big leather chair, remove his shoes, and rub his feet a little. Then she'd promise to bring him a cup of tea and a cigar if he wanted one. Those actions took his mind off his troubles. Lying here next to Paul, softly rubbing his chest under the quilt, Connie silently thanked her mother for her example of how to deal with a workaholic male. As her hand patiently glided over his chest she knew having a life with Paul and babying him the same way Mother babied Dad was her destiny. She loved the feeling of security and wholeness that life with a man like her father offered her.

"Yes. You need to know what I'm finding," said Paul speaking easily. He was in his element now. "I believe your wealth is at stake and I don't want to see you get hurt. The stuff you saw on my desk that night was just the tip of an iceberg. My work goes back way further than the present condition of the banks and the financial markets. You need to first understand, by way of background, why President Wilson allowed the Federal Reserve and the Income Tax to come into being. It was a way for the government to spend more money than it was taking in through its fees. It made it possible for the country to loan money to the French and British companies that were buying war materials from us for World War One. It guaranteed that the banks would get repaid on those loans because the Kaiser's troops had France and Britain on the ropes. That's background information you need to understand, okay?"

"Okay. I'm following you," she purred. "I know big things like the creation of the Federal Reserve happen for a reason. So, you say that making sure our bankers got repaid because Wilson was going to get America into the war and he needed money printing to do that was the reason?" Connie kissed him submissively on his cheek.

"Yes, that's what I think."

"Okay, go on."

"Well, it seems that the bankers have had one overriding agenda that's stayed true ever since the creation of the Fed. And that agenda is to expand the power and influence of banking into society on a world wide basis. Their agenda leads them to place the interests of banking and bank profits above the interests of any one nation's peoples. That's as simple as I can state it.

"They will lend to low cost sources of material and labor and install political policies through their influence that further that objective. They do this to reap greater profits, which is logical. In a financial way their activities propagate the spread of communal poverty in nations that have greater wealth, and greater prosperity in nations that have lesser wealth. Americans could see the Fed as the agent of a world wide banking network anchored by the Bank for International Settlements, the International Monetary Fund and the World Bank, as proponents of communism; while China could see the Fed and it's cohorts as proponents of capitalism. Are you following my thinking?"

"I am," she said while moving her fingers to touch his lips. "This is why we did the Bretton Woods accords where we rebuilt Europe by agreeing America would lend in return for the great powers agreeing that the dollar was as good as gold, right? And it worked all peachy until Charles DeGaul demanded gold for France's excess dollar balances, right? " Connie continued to softly rub his chest, careful not to allow her hand to rub him lower than his breasts, although she had it in her mind that her hand would eventually work its way much lower in due time.

"You know your history, don't you?" Paul's smile showed in the moonlight. Connie could tell she was establishing camaraderie.

"Well, I tried to stay awake in class," she whispered softly, sexily. "So where does this bring us to now?"

"My work says we are at a major crossroads. Now I need to give you some background for that."

"Okay, shoot it to me," said Connie as she kissed Paul on the cheek. She wiggled a little under the quilt like she was a happy puppy about to get a dish of warm milk.

"You need to understand China," Paul continued, although his thoughts were increasingly about holding her in a warm embrace. He soldiered onward with his banking theories. "Historically China has seen itself as the Middle Kingdom and all other regions were inferior, subservient, and required to pay tribute, or Kowtow, to China's rulers to gain the benefits of trade with China.

"Today China is ruled by ruthless thugs. I believe they see the world as an extension of the way the Han dynasty did, meaning that they have not changed their view that other nations must Kowtow. The Chinese have amassed a vast hoard of gold. I believe they are doing this because they want a new world monetary order that is gold backed. That places them in contention with the Western world's fiat based banking order.

Both the thugs that rule China and the closet communists that rule the world banking system want to be in control of the world economy. They both can not be in control unless the world banking system capitulates by devaluing the dollar relative to gold and then works with China using the Chinese gold hoard to create a new currency and banking order based upon the Chinese Yuan. Getting this?" Paul turned to look at her face. Her brown eyes invited him to make love to her whenever he was ready.

"Yes. Men are power crazed. I get that," Connie softly kissed him on the cheek again. "So, when will the fireworks start? What's a poor little rich girl to do; and will you help her do it smartly?" She feigned to be pouting in distress over needing to make a decision.

"The fireworks have already started. The Americans have had enough of fiat based world central banking. They are sick and tired of seeing their standard of living drop while other countries take their jobs away. They are sick and tired of phony schemes to corral their wealth and set it up to get slaughtered. That's why they elected the Orangejob President, the guy with the crazy hair. He promised to change things."

"What do you mean by phony schemes, Paul?" Another kiss on the cheek followed this question. This time the kiss lingered a while.

"I'm talking about the tax breaks that are given for investments in pensions so that the financial planners have an easier sale. They give an implied guarantee that if you put money in the plan you will get a tax deduction, 8 percent growth each year over time and you'll have a house on the beach with income for life." Paul was speaking freely now. He was on a roll.

"Not true?" No kisses followed her question this time. Paul's reasoning was finding its mark.

"I highly doubt it, not with long bonds around three percent or even six percent and governments' unfunded liabilities exploding. This is where my spread sheets scream that we have a problem.

"But let me conclude the thought about China's power struggle with America." Paul stretched his arms above his head then locked his hands and rested his head on his hands. He was looking up at the skylights in the boathouse again. The moon was shining brighter now and his face bathed in its light.

"China, I believe, is willing to use force to maintain its status as the middle kingdom of the world; but they are clever about the way they use force. They support North Korea, a dictatorship aligned with theirs, but a lesser kingdom that poses no real threat to them. The Chinese have facilitated the ability of the North Koreans to rain down nuclear bombs on American cities and on our allied countries, South Korea and Japan. Now, my premise is that, unless our government, our European and Japanese allies and our current fiat based international banking apparatus acquiesces to a change in the world monetary order, a change that places the Chinese Yuan currency in supremacy to the U S Dollar, the Chinese will instruct the North Koreans to send a nuclear bomb into San Francisco."

"Why San Francisco, what did those people ever do to China or North Korea?" Connie seemed stunned. She propped herself up and lay on her side facing him.

"I get there by the process of elimination. They wouldn't hit Washington because they want our politicians in place. They know our politicians can be bought off and made to screw the American public, just like they sold their souls to put the Federal Reserve in place, just like they sold out the public when FDR devalued gold. No, they will not kill off the rats that will betray their own people.

"Also, they will not destroy the middle of the country because they will want to have the agricultural production and they want to repopulate America's heartland with Chinese. There's no benefit to be gained by hitting Arizona or Florida, either. They are valuable states for minerals and agriculture. The old people who live there will naturally die off anyway. They will not hit the great Sacramento valley or the South either, again for the agricultural considerations. But they will destroy Silicone Valley and San Francisco. They have stolen most of our technology already, so that would be no great loss to them.

"Also, that whole area is populated by leftist liberal lunatics. And it includes Berkeley, the seething hotbed of irrational liberalism. China's totalitarian regime has no use for people like that. They do not like dissent, so they'll just kill everyone in the Bay Area at the get go of a war. Technology is the only thing America has going for it, besides agriculture, so if the Chinese destroy the Bay Area America will be badly crippled."

"Paul, this is heavy stuff," she said, again placing her hand on his chest. How do you think it will all come about?" Now Connie gently massaged his chest with her finger tips. She could feel her stimulation working. He was having goose bumps. That signaled she could arouse him sexually by moving her hand lower.

"You've heard about false flag events, haven't you? It's when a government manufactures a crisis and then uses it to tighten controls on its people. There's precedence for it. The Tonkin Gulf attack on the Turner Joy and the Maddox, two Navy destroyers, never actually happened, but that was the excuse the public was given for the Vietnam War. Saddam Hussein never had a weapon of mass destruction, but that was the excuse the public was given to invade Iraq. The main beneficiaries of these wars were the bankers. Their influence and profits grew."

"Do you think they'll do another false flag attack again?" she asked as she nuzzled her face against his neck. "I mean, don't you think the public will get wise to this tactic?" She adjusted her head lower resting it on his chest and moved her second hand to touch his forehead and rub it softly.

"History tends to rhyme. Behaviors follow a pattern. Bankers have more power today than they've ever had, so yes, I believe it's likely that the bankers will insist on our government creating another false flag attack. That will give them the excuse to have more war, to spend more money, to plunge America deeper into debt and to crush the Dollar currency. Then the bankers will flip their allegiance to the Chinese. It could be one or all of those things, but likely a false flag will weaken the dollar and strengthen the hands of the bankers and the Chinese.

"The public will not figure it out. The American public has been so greatly dumbed down by our educational system and the media that the American people are no longer capable of reasoning anything out for themselves. The media is also in the pocket of the bankers, so the media will spew propaganda telling the public we need to have more war. We will take the path that most benefits the bankers, not the people. We will be humbled badly in our next costly war. We will lose our currency supremacy and we will succumb to China.

"Face it Connie, the American public has lost its way. They are completely absorbed in mindless television talk shows, idiotic sit coms, dancing shows and sports programming. Americans have been so dumbed down they don't even try to think anymore. Over half the voters alive today never even heard of the World Wars, Korea or Vietnam. We have a defunct educational system that teaches self esteem and bull shit instead of math and science. The communists in the teachers' unions have completely destroyed their students' futures and produced a nation of dunces." Paul shook his head at the hopelessness of it all.

"What do you think is their goal for doing this, and how will it happen?" she kissed his chest as she asked. Her mind was engaged in thoughts about what Paul was explaining as well as her quest for intimacy with him. This visit to the boat house was presenting her with a challenge to digest it all. Now she wanted to understand those who would destroy her wealth as much as she wanted to make love.

"I expect another false flag like the Tonkin Gulf incident or a cyber security attack will be used to draw us into conflict or into an outright surrender of our currency. It will be expedient for the bankers to shut down the banks and ATM machines, flip their allegiance to China, use their gold for a new banking system and expand Chinese currency based bank credit lines world wide. Then they'll reopen for business using Chinese money. Every American will become a vassal slave working for the Chinese except those who have gold and silver."

"Can you predict what the next false flag will be, Paul?" Connie leaned her head over his and looked into his face. Her concern was real. Their engagement in conversational intercourse was real, and their relationship was solidifying.

"No, it's hard to think like a world power grabber; but it will have to be big enough to tell people that they need to give up control of their bank accounts because the false flag, whatever it is, has caused a nationwide banking crisis. Maybe there will be an attack on the national sport of football or a concert will get blown up, something like that. It will have to be scary enough to make it sound plausible to the public that there is the need to shut down the banking system, bail in the banks, which is a bureaucrat's way of saying it's legal to steal everyone's deposits and asset accounts, stop all pension plan payments and shut down the banks.

"When they reopen the banks there will be a lot of fan fare about how the Chinese have saved our sorry degenerate lives and we'll be so grateful to them that we'll agree to use their gold backed money. Then there will begin a prolonged depression in America and the entire western world, during which the

Chinese will buy America's farms and real estate. Americans will be so broke and so devastated they will take any offer, even a piddling one, to get grocery money."

"Okay, Paul. I get your thinking, but does your spreadsheet work indicate when all this will happen?" Again, Connie kissed his cheek. It was a warm, loving honest kiss that conveyed her feelings of love and respect for him. Their minds had joined as one now. They were becoming a team.

"It's imminent. My work shows that there is scant liquidity in short term treasuries to collateralize the leveraged derivatives that prop up the stock and bond markets. America's corporations and banks are more leveraged now than ever in history. Any shock will cause a downside runaway in the markets. Asset values will crater and dividends will be eliminated, bonds will stop paying interest and markets will go no bid. Real Estate will crater for all the reasons that real estate should never be viewed as an investment in the first place. People will not have money saved or cash flow to service interest and tax costs or even pay for garbage collection. Houses that sell for a million will eventually sell for delinquent taxes when local governments need their money. They'll dump their tax foreclosures onto the market and crush the artificial price structure.

"Gold and silver will do the opposite. They will go no offer because they are not leveraged in the physical market. Their paper futures markets are presently negatively leveraged to keep their prices suppressed, which the bankers need to do to maintain the public's confidence in the Dollar. That game will all fly apart. We know it's a nasty game they play because a big bank already pleaded out guilty to criminally artificially suppressing the prices of gold and silver; and now there's a federal civil case with eighty yet to be named defendants. Likely, many of them are banks. So, I'm not the crazy one when I tell you these things. The bankers are dogs with derivative fleas. They've overexposed their balance sheets to a leverage unwind. They're the crazy ones, but they are wily and they own the political system. They will not get screwed or jailed for what they've done. They'll quickly slip away like all cockroaches do. The public will never expose them to the light of day. They own the politicians and the judges. They'll walk away with slaps on the wrists. It's the public that does not own gold or silver. That's who will get screwed."

"So, Paul, when should I start buying gold and silver?" She kissed his the tip of his nose in a most endearing gesture of love and trust. Connie was ready to act.

"Yesterday would have been a good day to start. When imminent danger is staring you in the face it's time to take action. And, you want to be the first mouse out the door with your cheese." Now Paul reached his arms around her and pulled her body close to him. She could feel his need and his love. She relaxed and lay against him while he continued explaining.

"You see," he said, "the entire fiat system is based upon the central banks of the various nations having equal confidence in each other, and that is based upon all of them having confidence in the International Monetary Fund and The Bank for International Settlements, and this entire pyramid of confidence depends upon one little guy at the bottom of the pyramid, the American citizen. That guy who only has his mind on the NFL must have confidence in the system. And he does. He'll get up every day, put his pants on and go to work because he believes in the system. He'll believe until the false flag occurs. That's when he'll have doubts whether or not the government can control events. When he realizes he's on his own he'll stop trusting the system or the banks, but by then it will be too late.

"There's a statistical term for what he's going through. It's called normalcy bias. A good example is the turkey chick and the farmer. Every morning the farmer brings a handful of grain to the chick. The chick gobbles up the grain. This goes on for a whole year. Every day the farmer brings more grain and the turkey eats it. The turkey gets fatter day by day. He depends on the farmer and trusts him. He looks forward to getting fed every day. He loves the farmer. He can't wait to see his farmer friend every morning. Life is good for the turkey. Until that one day in November when the turkey comes for his grain and the farmer grabs his head and cuts it off. The turkey had normalcy bias. The bird thought things would never change. He didn't know he was getting fat because the farmer was feeding him for a reason. The American public also has normalcy bias. They don't understand that the banks are giving them credit lines for a reason. Like the turkey they are also living fat dumb and happy. They will soon have their heads handed to them, their financial heads, that is."

"Okay, Paul," whispered Connie. "I'll start making calls tomorrow, but now it's time for us. Let's not talk for a while." She assessed Paul as a man who once experienced a manipulated form of intimacy with his former wife, but with no one else. That posed an opportunity and a challenge for her. If she and Paul became intimate it would be unlikely that he'd ever stray from her; but if she frightened him tonight or caused him to feel guilty about betraying a misguided notion of fidelity to his ex wife, then she could lose him. Everything would be awkward and awful and they'd leave the Lake House after a strained weekend.

She thought about her mother's tactics with her father. Like Paul, her dad was absorbed in work. Mother often went to him in his den to get him for dinner, but mother never just called him to dinner. She never just grabbed his hand and yanked him out of his big leather chair either. Mother always used persuasion. She was patient, loving, and affable toward

Father whenever she wanted him for anything. She shamelessly babied him like he was her infant.

When Mother wanted Father to come for dinner, she'd stand behind him as he sat in his big chair. Then she'd rub her hands down over his chest and rub his chest and breasts. She'd even tickle his nipples and kiss his ear. When she could tell he was starting to smile and setting his reading aside she'd whisper, "Is Papa ready to come to dinner?" Father always responded well to her encouragement. He always got up and followed her like an obedient puppy dog to the dining table.

And when Mother was having a party for friends she would always have the family cook bake five pies instead of the necessary four. The cook would place the pies on the pantry shelf to cool the night before, and Father would always come and claim one pie all for himself. He would eat a good part of it and put the remainder in the refrigerator. Mother would tease him the next morning about some mysterious pie eating mouse making off with one of the pies, but she never scolded him. She always gave him what pleased him before she took pleasures for herself. That was Mother's genius. She was the only person who knew how to have her way with Father.

Connie softly touched Paul's nipple with her fingertips. She played with it while snuggling close to him, her face against his cheek. "I've often wondered why men have nipples. I mean, could a man breast feed a baby if the mother died and the world ran out of baby formula? Have you ever wondered about that?" Paul's head turned toward her face. She didn't expect that. She thought for a moment that the weirdness of her question might make him think she was some kind of crazy person, but then he moved his head back and continued looking up at the skylights.

"I have no idea. I've never thought about it," he said, chuckling.

"But there must be a reason, don't you think?" she persisted now that he signaled he was willing to engage in her whimsical thoughts. "Mother Nature wouldn't put nipples on a man if there was no purpose for it, would she?" Connie teased, and then moved her hand and fingered Paul's other nipple. "Do you like the way it feels when I touch you there? I've always wondered if a man feels the same way a woman feels when her nipples are touched. Do you like me touching you like this? I hope you do because I like touching you like this." Connie sought to gradually soften Paul's inhibitions for intimacy much like her mother softened her father's reluctance to leave his chair.

"I like how it feels. You're giving me goose bumps. You are one very playful woman aren't you?" Paul's face was smiling. Connie knew she was pleasing him.

"I love to have my nipples touched," she whispered seductively, "I feel these tingles all over my body when I'm touched there. I like it so much I often touch them myself. I wonder if we feel that way because we're supposed to feel pleasure when we feed life into a baby. Mother Nature is wonderful the way she thought everything through, don't you think?" Connie moved her hand a little lower and began rubbing Paul's stomach and the side of his torso. "Touching feels nice wherever we're touched, but there are special places where touch produces a stimulus that's especially sensuous. Don't you find that fascinating?"

Paul's thoughts momentarily slipped into his past. He grew up poor. But his mother was a loving woman and there was love and harmony in the home. He had never before encountered a woman who experimented with sex and intimacy like Connie did. His only sexual experience was with his ex wife and all they ever knew was simple maiden position sex. He naively had assumed all women were pleasant and loving, like his mother, but it never occurred to him that a woman might expect him to please her sexually.

His wake up call came when his ex wife got interested in acting. She played the role of an adulterous wife in an amateur play. He never saw any of the rehearsals. He just stayed home with baby Margaret. After the play was going for about six weeks he finally went to see it.

That's when he got an eye full of his ex wife's true character. It was a revelation that he never imagined existed. During one scene she lay on top of the lead actor and kissed him passionately. Obviously she was thrusting her tongue into his mouth and sexually writhing all over him. Then, in another scene she wantonly kissed another actor in an identical way. She lustfully squeezed his ass and pulled his pelvis hard against her sex. That actor was supposed to be her secret lover. Paul couldn't recall his wife ever kissing him like that. He felt jealous and he complained to her about his unequal treatment afterwards. Her reaction was a shock to his essence as a man. She told him he just didn't light her fire like those other men did, that she was tired of living with him because he was so dull, and that she wanted a divorce.

A few days later when he was served with divorce papers she told him to get out of her house, the very house that he had recently bought for the two of them. Then she told him that looking at him made her sick to her stomach and that she wished he'd fall down the steps and die and be eaten by rats. It was after those events that Paul deduced that he didn't understand anything about women. His family life growing up never prepared him for the hell that his ex wife unleashed upon him. Her behavior was a revelation that some women are vicious, nasty predators, like ferrets that relentlessly attack and kill mice.

Unfortunately he married a weasel type personality instead of a cuddly bunny sort of woman like his loving mother. He paid a heavy personal price for his misplaced assumption, not just a financial price. He became withdrawn in matters concerning the opposite sex. He buried himself in work and involved himself in his daughter's life the best he could with the limited times the court system allowed him to see her. Paul lived in a shell as a part time father and part time hermit. But, like Connie's father, he was a brilliant analyst.

Now he felt Connie pulling him out of his shell. She was touching him and he was enjoying it. He felt joyful but timid about his inexperience. Tears came to his eyes. She was unlocking his self imposed prison. Connie was setting him free.

"Yes," finally his well considered answer came. "Nature seems to know more about us than we know ourselves. Wouldn't you say that's true?"

"Yes. It's a truism I wonder about," Connie suddenly gushed in her lowest most husky seductive voice, "All I can conclude is that when I'm in the moment having those sorts of feelings I want more of them. I just have to let myself go and experience all of those feelings nature has to offer. There's nothing like it in the world. That's why I very badly want to share those feelings with you. Will you please let me, Paul? I want to share them with you very much."

Paul's hands held her face and he kissed her softly with a child's like wonderment kiss. "Yes. I want us to share those feelings," he confessed. "I want to know how it feels to be in love with you. I mean I am already in love with you, Connie. I do love you. I feel it deep inside me, but I mean I want to know how you feel and how I feel when we make love. I mean I want it to be all right for you and———."

"Paul, shhh," she whispered convincingly. "It's going to be all right. It will be beautiful. Let me take the quilt off you and wrap it around me. Tell me if I'm stimulating you, okay?"

By now the quarter moon had risen to near its apex. Its faint light streamed through the skylight and played softly swaying shadows of the boats on the boathouse wall. The boats rose and fell with the wave ripples, moving the night along and overtaking the earlier darkness. The frogs and crickets quieted down as different pairs found each other and mated, but there were still some male crickets chirping intermittently in hopes of attracting a female.

Connie proceeded by first kissing Paul's stomach while still touching his nipples. After a short while she rested her head upon his stomach. She felt safe there and closer to him than before. Her hands returned to rubbing his chest. "This feels wonderful. I love feeling your stomach moving up and down and I love hearing your heartbeat," she whispered. "I'm going to touch you now in a very sensitive place. Just relax. I won't hurt you, I promise." Connie then slid her hand over Paul's stomach and brought it to rest on his testicles. As she kneaded his gonads with her hand she moved her head down until her lips found the tip of his penis. Paul had never experienced fellatio. She heard him let out a gasp of pleasurable surprise followed by a moan of surrender. She soon coaxed Paul into a full hard erection.

She lifted her head up and marveled at Paul's penis. It was huge, very robust in girth and easily eight inches long. It was a masterpiece compared to George's or Mole's. 'Paul, you ex wife was truly a fucking idiot,' she thought to herself as she beheld the huge organ. It was a magical living obelisk, standing before her at full attention in the moonlight, casting its own faint gray shadow on the boathouse wall. She felt her wetness gathering. For all her experiences she never was as eager to mount a penis as she was this one, this night.

"Paul, do you hear those crickets? She asked.

"Yes," he answered.

"Do you know what they are doing?"

"They're chirping."

"Well, what I want you to think about is what those little crickets are chirping about," she said softly while gently stroking his penis. "Right now, somewhere out there in the grass, a girl cricket has heard the chirps of a boy cricket. She has climbed up on top of him and she's rubbing her abdomen upon his back. He loves the way he feels when she rubs him like that. That makes him want to give her something special.

"He opens a tiny slit in the shell on his back. Then, because she keeps rubbing him he pushes his tiny tube up above the top of his back shell. He feels so wonderful because of her rubbing that he shoots a tiny droplet of white sperm paste out of his tube. Her abdomen sucks up the sperm paste while she continues rubbing him. A few days later she lays a hundred tiny eggs that hatch next year and become baby crickets. Isn't that wonderful, Paul? I mean isn't it grand the way nature makes the female want the male and how nature makes the male want to please the female, and they end up making baby crickets?" She smiled with mischief in her eyes and kissed him, this time pushing her tongue into his mouth.

"Let's pretend we're a couple of crickets, Paul, okay?"

"All right, but I don't know how to chirp. Is that okay?"

"Yes silly. You just lay there for now and I'll be Mrs. Cricket. Lay your head back and relax."

"Okay," Paul did as her was told.

Connie sucked Paul's penis a second time. It became so hard her lips felt its blood vessels pulsing. She smiled in anticipation of the joy his huge cock would bring. She reminded herself that his first time since his divorce could be hard for him. She hoped he wouldn't have feelings of guilt or shame. And she promised herself to remain patient.

She slowly straddled him and gently rubbed his penis against her outer vaginal lips. The size of his penis made her tremble inside. She watched his face relax and begin to smile slightly. He was finally ready to leave his former wife. The cock's touch caused her to moisten. The two sex organs were signaling they were ready. She guided his shaft past her inner lips and slowly lowered herself until it was deeply into her vagina. When its tip touched her cervix she lifted up slightly thinking how good their sex was going to be once she became accustomed to his size.

"Paul, we're doing very well. Now I'd like you to pretend that we're just like a pair of crickets. Make believe my knees are one set of legs and our arm pairs are the other two sets. We'll pretend that we each have all six legs. Now, you place your hands on my breasts. Squeeze them and stimulate my nipples like I stimulated yours. I'll put my hands on your breasts and do the same with you," Connie instructed him, smiling a winsome smile the whole time. She believed sex should be fun filled. Her libido was ravenous and she imparted a contagion about it to Paul through her easy manner. She felt his entire body relax through her hands. She could feel she was getting him familiar with her body at just the right pace.

Her thoughts soared to how wonderful it was going to be to have him as a partner for years and years to come, but then she reminded herself that tonight she must be patient. Tonight she must not give any hints that she liked to do kinky things like having him lick whipped cream from her pussy; or tickling her with feathers; or slapping her ass before he entered her from behind; or that she loved to mouth a man's balls and feel the testicles making sperm as they rolled against her tongue.

No, tonight she would not be an uninhibited wildcat. She must be maiden vanilla pure. She must be the loving innocent helpmate who was making a good life for him and his daughter. And she vowed to herself that, even above her own pleasures, she would be dutiful to Paul and Margaret, and put their needs above hers. She made a silent pact with herself that she would never be unfaithful to Paul, for that would devastate him and little Margaret after what the ex wife put them through. She would honor him always as her mother did her father.

Paul did as he was told. Both felt their passions building. "There, now I'm going to gently rock my pelvis forward and backward and push my pussy hard against you, and I'm going to wiggle my ass slightly sideways from time to time. I'll make some ooh and ah sounds. That's okay. It won't mean you're hurting me. It will mean that I love feeling the different sensations of your big penis touching and rubbing all over inside me. Will you be okay with that?"

"Yes, sure, do you want me to continue touching your nipples?"

"Oh yes, absolutely. I love that," she frowned and pouted a little and gave him a look that said he was being a silly man. Then she twisted her body slightly and smiled again. "If you want to stop for a while to kiss me and hug me close to you while I'm fucking you, I'd like that too. In fact I'd like it very much if you expressed tenderness once in a while."

Paul did as Connie coached him. He was eager to please her and he felt his confidence growing with each moan she uttered and with each thrust of her pelvis and every rotational grind of her ass. He no longer stared up at the moon through the skylight. Her face fascinated him more. He studied her every facial movement as she alternately pursed and pulled back her lips in pleasure. He adored her every smile as their fucking lifted her spirits to a serene other worldly place. Watching her and feeling her body he knew she was completely different from his ex. He felt loved.

His ex avoided sex as much as possible. When she did copulate she did it quickly and sparingly and likely out of a sense of duty to him or some notion that it was necessary for her to still be a woman. He belatedly understood that now. His ex never once had an expression of sensuous pleasure glowing from her face as Connie did now. Connie, he could tell, loved sex a great deal. Fucking was the centerpiece in her smorgasbord of life's experiences. She studied sex diligently and practiced its many permutations of pleasures with her passion for new eroticisms. Her intensity and fervor about the intimate art surpassed the most ardent florist's compulsion to experiment with arrangements.

As Paul stared into Connie's face he became lost in the wonderment of her. His penis was alive with feelings of erotic sexual pleasures it never knew before. Connie's pussy was velvety soft and slippery wet. It devoured his cock and anchored it deeply inside, fastened it in place with her squatting abdomen directly above it. It executed an undulation of its wall muscles in an upward pulling Kegel movement. He saw in her face a goddess of the night endowed with extraordinary sexuality. He was being immersed in her world and becoming beholden to her. And he wanted to give her pleasure.

"Now, Paul. Remember how Mrs. Cricket rubbed on Mr. Cricket and got him so excited that he opened his sperm tube for her?" she asked with the smile of desire.

"I remember," Paul replied grinning. "Is Mrs. Cricket ready to receive sperm from Mr. Cricket?"

"Oh, yes, Mr. Cricket. Mrs. Cricket would love to have Mr. Cricket's sperm very much. She wants him to give her all that he has."

"Has Mrs. Cricket considered that she could become pregnant if Mr. Cricket doesn't pull out of her very soon?"

"Yes, Mr. Cricket. She has considered that and she has decided that she would like it very much if Mr. Cricket made her pregnant."

"Are you sure," Paul hesitated and froze.

"Yes I'm sure, Mr. Cricket. Mrs. Cricket would like to produce a little brother or sister for Miss Margaret so that when Mr. and Mrs. Cricket are gone from the Earth little Miss Margaret will still have a family," she nodded her head showing confidence that she knew exactly what she was doing. "Mrs. Cricket would love to be the wife of Mr. Cricket if he so chooses; but regardless of that Mrs. Cricket wants very badly to have a child of his and urges him to impregnate her." She continued to nod her head. Her face smiled broadly. It conveyed to Paul that conceiving his child tonight, having a family of her own, was her primary goal in life.

After her proclaiming her desire for pregnancy she accelerated her thrusts and Kegel contractions. Surprisingly, Paul's penis stayed erect while she began to orgasm.

'He amazes me,' she thought. 'He's staying hard while I come. My clitoris is rubbing his shaft like I'm a frenzied mink and he's still hard. He's my Mr. Wonderful. He's smart, like Father. He's better looking than Father; and he's very sensitive and caring. I love him. Oh, now he's grabbed my ass with both hands and pulled me down hard onto his cock. Oh, gosh, I just let out a gasp! He's as big as any black cock I've had inside me, and he's staying hard. They didn't stay hard like this. What do I have here? He's amazing.'

Connie rapidly rubbed her clitoris over Paul's shaft as her orgasm gushed from her dam with opened floodgates. Paul's penis stood no chance of holding anything back in the face of her sexual onslaught. In short order it was shooting semen filled with millions of its sperm deeply into her vagina. It pulsed over and over again and repeatedly shot streams of its microscopic egg seekers into her. They flooded her vaginal cavity and raced upward through her cervix toward her fallopian tubes. Like a battalion of determined infantry they charged forward until one sighted an egg and launched itself firmly into its target.

Then Paul sat upright and held her in his arms. His penis was still inside her. She wrapped her legs around him and clenched her hands around him, pulling their bodies close against each other. Their bellies touched. They both felt the warmth of each other as if they were one unified being. It was the most wonderful feeling of closeness to a woman Paul had ever known. Connie felt the completeness and happiness of Paul's feelings flowing from him to her. Neither of them knew that a new life had begun in her womb.

"You spoke of marriage, Connie, but your father wants you to go to graduate school at Cornell where he endowed a chair. How can you do both?"

"Paul. It's what you want, not what Father wants that is important to me now. It's our life, not his. Would you like to have me for a wife or wouldn't you?" Connie sounded a bit impatient. And her face assumed a coquettish look.

"Oh, yes, I would like that. I'd like that very much," he stammered. Paul knew he was being overtaken by events, but he also knew he loved her and decided that, like a good Mr. Cricket, he needed to do whatever she required to please her. And that look she gave him erased all misgivings and second thoughts. She was marvelously beautiful, charming, witty and sexy beyond anything he'd ever known in his limited experience. He was smitten and he was hers.

"Then you must ask me, Paul," she responded peevishly. "A woman loves to hear her man ask her to marry," she pouted slightly, miffed that she had to instigate her invitation to marry him.

"Yes, of course. Connie, will you please marry me?" Paul's face showed a tinge of fear that he might possibly have offended her by being slow to speak.

"Do you love me, Paul?" Connie again put the coquettish invitational plea on her face. She could be a brilliant tease.

"Yes. I love you. I love you more than anything in the world." Paul's eyes looked deeply into hers and touched her mind with their sincerity. He was certain of the truth of his words and it showed.

"Then, I shall marry you, Paul," she declared with a triumphant smile on her face. "Will you marry me?" Connie was quick to assert that marriage was a joint commitment. She wanted to make it clear that he was also marrying her.

"Yes. I will be honored to marry you." Paul said as a glowing continence appeared on his face. Tears flowed from his eyes. He was the happiest man in the world at this moment.

Connie had her man and the life she wanted now. The actual wedding that would follow was a mere formality as far as she was concerned. She knew they made a bargain that would withstand any challenge.

Their eternal vows were first said in the old boat house that night. The newly engaged couple hugged each other tightly and shared kisses while the night outside fell silent. And thousands of mating creatures also made new life happen that magical night by the lake house. The earlier chirpings of crickets subsided as the night lengthened. The cricket pairs parted from each other now. Instinct drove them to find shelter from the night chill.

One by one they retired into their dark hiding places and under old decaying leaves. Until warmed by tomorrow's sun they would rest and gather their strength. Tomorrow evening they would again play chirp and seek—rub and mate. Many females would successfully achieve a hundred fertilized eggs. Frogs, toads, centipedes, and birds would feast on many of those eggs before winter drove these predators into dormancy or migration. But, like sperm, the crickets were a relentless army of millions. Through sheer numbers some would overwhelm predation's perils. Their species would survive.

The romantic night frogs also retreated into the darkness. The shore of the lake had several inlets where the still water harbored lily pads. The lilies tethered their stems to the moss strewn lake floor and provided homes for many frogs. Legions of these frogs returned to the same pads they had inhabited since birth. Others swam to the offshore platform dock, where children played by daylight and where sailing crews tied up their boats. Those frogs grew fatter there than most other frogs on the lake. They had a good thing going. They learned to sip mosquitoes from the surface as those insects first stood upon it before opening their wings to dry, after rising as nymphs from the lake floor. By attaching one hind foot to a dock pillar a frog could rest comfortably under the dock, sip its fill of mosquito nymphs and grow fat, unseen by predator birds above.

Unfortunately, tonight would not go well for some of these frogs. Smallmouth bass routinely patrolled the lake's shores by night in search of small fry fishes and errant frogs. These bass had voracious appetites and frogs with fatty legs topped their menu. Tonight a few bass cruised further offshore than they usually did. Their changed course brought them good fortune this night. They discovered the secreted frog hideaway. One by one a hapless juicy frog was seized by body or leg and pulled below the surface to be devoured by a hungry bass.

Of all the mating pairs at the lake that night only the two humans left their mating place together as a couple united for life. Each frog and cricket went its separate way. Some of these animals went to lay eggs that would be eaten by fishes; some of their surviving eggs would grow into frogs that would eat crickets and fish eggs; and some hapless dock dwelling frogs would be eaten by bass. These animals' cycle of mating, eating, being eaten and living would continue as it had for millions of years.

And the darkness of the night overcame all creatures that mated. The far shore became an indistinguishable blend of darkness and uncertain shadows that were foreboding to any late returning craft to its mooring or dock. Off in the distance on the forested lands beyond the opposite shore coyotes yelped a joyful chorus. The darkness of this pale moonlit night favored their hunting. And the moon slowly made its way below the horizon.

The sky was black now and filled with shining sparkling stars when Paul and Connie walked back to the lake house. Connie held Paul's hand but now her thoughts were of her father, Howard. He was a giant of a man. She recalled those many times as a little girl when she walked beside him holding his hand. And she recalled those times when she sat between Mother and Father in church. She didn't understand the services then. The priest was always talking about some man who was a salvation and a right hand of a father. She thought this savior man somehow saved things and gave them to the Salvation Army man who rang the bell in front of the supermarket at Christmas time. She didn't understand how he could be at the right hand of the Father when she was the one who always held her father's right hand. It was all so confusing to her then, but now she visualized Paul and herself going to church with their children and having their children sit between them in a pew just like she sat between Mother and Father.

She imagined Paul and she would join a country club just like Mother and Father did. They would meet all the right people that way. She would join the women's groups and do the good things for the charities; and she would use her influence to gain contacts and influence for Paul and in her subtle ways she would help push his career along. She understood, through Mother, that a successful man is that way because he has a good woman behind him. And she knew, after the years of watching her mother, that was a truism and not a mere cliché. And she would be a good woman to Paul at home. She only hoped that Paul would be a man of the same commanding stature as her father. Father gave orders and companies marched to his tune. Only Mother could approach Father as an equal. But no one, not even Mother, ever dared to defy Father. That is before tonight. Connie knew that tonight she did defy her father. And she defied him shamelessly right there in his boathouse, next to his precious boat. Connie's memories recalled many things about Daddy's lake cruiser.

She had made love to Paul in full view of it. Much like she was Daddy's living pride and joy, that boat was Father's inanimate pride and joy. It was his favorite toy. He coddled it and loved its company. He loved that boat with its varnished hardwoods and polished brass. It was his respite from those grueling, bruising corporate battles. It had chronic engine and pumping problems, but Father kept it in original condition regardless of the trouble or the costs. Old Smiley Johnson, a mechanic in the village, was often called out to repair it. Father proudly said the boat's motor and pumps no longer had one single original part, but he kept the cantankerous boat with its finicky engines despite its astronomical repair bills. Connie had often thought that Father kept it because he wanted to keep Old Smiley employed more than for any other reason. But tonight she realized that Father kept that old classic boat because he liked things to stay just the way they were. Dad was like his boat, proud, serviceable and determined to fight on against all challenges and against age. Father, that fierce indomitable lion who had fired scores of chief executives and changed corporations, resisted all attempts to change himself or to allow changes to be made in his own world.

But tonight she had done what she'd never dared to do before. She defied Father. She'd made love to Paul right there on Father's life jacket pile on his old day bed, his favorite sleeping place in his whole private solitary world. She had committed a sacrilege against Father in his lion's den. She had invaded his holy place. Her shadow had moved sensuously, sacrilegiously on the hull of Father's precious boat as she lifted her pelvis and rocked it back and forth upon Paul's penis.

Her shadow had played mischievously, sensuously on the boat's high white hull when she pulled Paul's hands to her breast. The source of that shadow knew that the boat was a great source of joy to her as a young girl. Her father took her along on it for many spins on the lake. She would snuggle her tiny frame next to his giant one and he would place his huge arm around her shoulder while his other hand tended the steering wheel. She felt safe and unafraid then when she was Daddy's little girl. They would motor out to his favorite fishing cove. Daddy would stop the boat, reverse its aging motors and release one of its huge anchors. Then Daddy would cast a popper lure close to the shore and slowly retrieve it. She would look innocently up into the heavens and wait patiently for the strike. Then it would happen, predictably as it always did. A huge bass would emerge from the weed beds and thrust itself skyward. It would savagely slam into the lure and shoot itself out of the water, its mouth hopelessly hooked by the lure. Then Daddy would play out the fish until it surrendered itself into his net. Then Daddy would start up the chrome capstan and slowly retrieve the anchor. And they would return to the boat house. Daddy would prepare the bass for Mother to cook. And that once proud monster of the lake, that had terrorized and eaten many frogs, would be eaten for family dinner that very evening.

She had arched her back in front of Daddy's boat, breathed deeply and lifted her contented face to the skylight. She loved sex most when she was on top. Her love making with Paul was beautiful. Her lungs still felt the wonderment from taking in their full measures of the cool air while she was making love with her future husband. She had all these thoughts and feelings as she and Paul walked back to the Lake House. The heavens were dark now, except for the quarter moon and some dim stars' twinklings. Father's big lake cruiser had yawed like an airplane up and down, its bow and stern rolling with the wave motions beneath its hull. It did that patient rolling motion silently without voicing its objection to her and Paul lovingly copulating beside it, their motions in rhythm with its own. She felt like she had showed an old friend that there was now someone more important to her.

That old boat captured her past feelings. She knew it still held those precious feelings dear to it, and she still loved it as well. But her love for the boat was all different now. That little girl's memories were tinged with guilt. She'd showed the old boat that it had been downgraded to second place in her heart. It floated all alone in the boat house now, a silent floating fossil of her past. She wondered if it felt that she was saying goodbye to it tonight or if it felt sad that she was no longer the little girl it so proudly carried. She looked up and fixated her dreamlike gaze upon the quarter moon and thought all these private thoughts. She was in control of events now. Father was only with her in those warm childhood memories. But she would be going onward with Paul as the main man in her life, not Father.

She accepted the truth that she would never fully understand the financial matters that troubled Paul. She didn't share his passion for analysis like her father probably would. Possibly she would live to regret her decision to trust Paul but her inner voice told her that she must trust him. In many ways Paul's mind was more encompassing than Father's and his passion for the truth equaled Father's. She thought that possibly her own mind's capacity for matters of finance became handicapped because it was overshadowed by her father's dominance. She fixated her stare on the moon. She wondered if it ever felt her similar feelings. Just as she was always dominated by Father, the Moon, too, was likely frustrated that planet Earth was impossibly large for it to ever equal.

She anticipated that her father would disapprove of her behavior tonight. But her intuition told her that her actions were the right thing to do for her own life, and for Paul's and Margaret's. She knew herself. She understood her feelings and trusted them. Daddy would not be there to protect his little girl forever. Paul was a man with Daddy's same strength of conviction and keenness of mind. That same safe feeling she knew with Father expressed itself through Paul.

Men often can not understand things they can't objectively quantify or see. They are simply much less complex than women. But that was not her concern anymore. What Paul thought about becoming her husband was irrelevant now. The business of marriage is properly a woman's craft. Her mother's behavior convinced her that was true. A man's duty is to accept the woman who chooses him, adapt to his fate, learn to love the woman with all his heart, mind and body; and never complain about it. And that is as it should be, for a man without a woman to guide his life is generally a pitiful specimen of humanity. Those were Mother's sentiments and as the events of this evening played out she found herself in full concordance with Mother.

Connie had contemplated patiently. Paul's penis had been deep within her. She had slowly ground her pelvis into him, lulling his shaft to reach ever higher and deeper into her. She had searched her deepest feelings of love and her commitment to mothering his first child and his second child that she hoped to birth. She had shared his penis's yearning as it reached ever upward toward the deepest reaches of her womb. Everything felt right. Everything was right. She had not hurried Paul. A male lover is much like a testosterone charged bass, she thought. She understood the patience needed in trolling for a bass to strike. How ironic it was that seeing Father's fishing tactic prepared her to hook her man's heart.

She had slowly worked her irresistible velvet lure over Paul's anatomy. Like a bass losing its mental faculties before the strike, Paul had panted and moaned. His throbbing penis had strained to ejaculate. She had felt his yearnings for her. It was all good. It was beautiful. It was much like that of a furious madly passionate bass desperate for the lure. Then Paul's body had shuddered and trembled. The man who had no sex for over three years finally exploded. Paul's penis had pulsed repeated shots of semen into her, attacking her sex like a magnificent angry bass thrashing itself upon a lure. Her sex muscles clamped down hard on her catch and squeezed his sex tightly. She had clamped onto him then and vowed to never let him go.

Mission accomplished, her thoughts transfixed into a dreamy nether land of beautiful tomorrows, where she would have the life she wanted with the man she wanted; and she would have his children. And she would fuck him this way and in many differently positioned ways. And she would forever fascinate him with her sexuality. And they would fuck often and in many different places. He was like a wild bass gathered into her net now. And she would savor him and devour him thousands of times with her insatiable appetite for sex.

She knew her father's boat saw everything she did and knew all. Paul was a mere accomplice to her deed. He had no way of knowing he was enabling her to slip her tether lines to her father, but he did participate in her transgression. If Father ever found out what they did this night his outrage would mark Paul as an equal offender. Connie silently vowed that where she and Paul first copulated and the promises they made to each other this night would be their eternal secret. She came to an adult's reality that the inanimate lake cruiser could never say a word. And she smiled.

As they entered the Lake House Connie thoughts vacillated back to the way a little girl might think. She silently wondered if they left a clue by the wooden lake cruiser that might reveal that they made love in its presence. Then she snapped out of her little girl thoughts. They'd gathered up all their clothes and the boat could not talk. They had nothing to fear and nothing to feel ashamed about. She was an adult now. She wanted a married life with children and she wanted a family with her Paul.

Father was simply not going to deny her the life she wanted. She was not going to go to Cornell just because he did. Howard Rockman, lord of his companies and his family, would have to get used to the fact that the world really did change. She was a living, growing, loving woman. She was not some old boat that was never going to change because Father decided it suited him to never let it change. She was in love with Paul now, and that love was a much stronger pull on her heart strings than her love of Father and all the nostalgia she connected to him.

She knew from now on things would be different between her and her father and for her and Paul. Life had changed for all of them. She would soon need to deal with her father's indignation much the same way her mother did. He'd huff and puff and bluster about her decision, and then he'd act like a wounded lion. After a few days, or possibly weeks, of roaring and pouting his bellowing pain would stop. He'd face reality. He loved Connie deeply and would do anything to please his daughter. He would, with some hesitation at first, eventually take Paul into his confidence, share with him his thoughts and tactics, and accept him as family. Father was at his core a very good hearted and loving man. And he would forever be her lion and her king.

Tonight and every night from now on there would be another major change. She would no longer live as a single woman. She would no longer sleep alone. She and Paul would sleep in the same bed and they would make love often. She silently promised herself that their love making would never be dull or routine. Paul would always find her inviting and intriguing. She loved sex and erotic pleasures and was unashamed of expressing her wants to her husband to be. She would continue to educate Paul in the ways of giving a woman pleasure. She would explain the beautiful eroticism of oral sex and teach him to expertly perform cunnilingus with her.

As they made their way to her bedroom that first night of sleeping together she imagined all the times she would suck him and bring his delicious sperm paste into her mouth; and she imagined all the thousands of orgasms she would have with him in all the different positions she would teach him. She vowed to herself that their sex life would never be dull. She would keep him guessing. Sometimes she would be demure and teasing, persuading him to give chase to her. Other times she would be as aggressive as a shameless bitch dog in heat. And she would keep him off balance by sometimes being impeccably clean tasting and perfumed; other times she would approach him when she was lusty, sweaty and raunchy like she felt right after playing tennis. But at all times she would be loving and endearing and sincere. And she would never take him for granted or ignore his needs.

She closed her eyes and thanked God for her great good fortune. She fixated upon that first instant when she saw his splendid penis. She marveled now, as she did then at how huge he was. 'Oh, I am so lucky, lucky, lucky,' she thought to herself, 'that huge cock is going to ravage me so many times I'm going to feel like my head is popping off. I'm such a lucky girl! The men I knew before Paul had either a brain or a cock that attracted me. Paul has both, and he's all mine.' She felt smug now and considered herself blessed anticipating their many future conversations and the many thousands of times she would joyfully hold his cock in her hands and guide it inside her.

As she undressed before sleeping naked with him this first night she remembered the troubling things he told her about the future of the country. Paul's explanation of the precarious position of her investments disturbed her. She followed his logic and also instinctively knew he was correct. There were more and more signs of civil unrest in America.

People's incomes were not keeping pace with the rising costs of everything needed to live and the peoples' trust in President Orangejob was flagging. His key conservative aids were forced out by communist bankers in his inner circle, and some of the people who elected him felt betrayed. Some were openly calling him a scam artist and a swindler. Their hopes that the country would return to a precious metals backed currency by a gradual increase in metals' backing of the currency were dashed. It now appeared that the only way to restore power to the people and truly wrest it from the banker controlled central government would be through some sort of systemic shock or default.

Meanwhile, as any central government will do when threatened, measures were put into place to arrest dissenters and send them to concentration camps. Violent clashes broke out between those who wanted limited government and those who wanted communism. The political class of both major parties was siding with the communist factions because they saw themselves as the survivors of the struggle, the elite bourgeoisie. They had no particular aptitudes at anything productive. Their main successes were as political con artists and dutiful lackeys of the central bankers and special interest lobbyists; nevertheless they believed they were ordained to rule over the country's peoples and enslave its proletariat class. They reveled in the peoples' miseries. They snickered and giggled and openly flaunted their contempt for the people as they rigged the economic and political system against them and as they stole from them and left their noble men for dead by horrible betrayals in hell holes like Bengasi, Libya. President Orangejob was opposed by these vilest of the vile.

Reports began leaking out that the major banks were short a record number of derivative contracts on gold and silver. It appeared likely that their artifice dam of confidence in fiat currency was about to break. China was demanding that oil be traded in gold backed trading certificates redeemable in either Yuan or gold, but not dollars. America's standard of living was about to drop significantly promising to spawn yet more unrest. North Korea, China's proxy state client, held nuclear threats to America's head if President Orangejob dared to defy China. Architected by former Secretary of State Kissinger, the artificial privileged petrodollar construct that facilitated the Dollar's world reserve currency dominance was now unraveling.

Connie sensed an urgency to act. She trusted Paul's advice about making the necessary phone calls. She made a mental note that she also needed to warn her closest friends as well. She would call her three associate friends first thing in the morning. She would insist they hold an emergency girls' night out meeting next week to discuss fast moving financial events.

She turned her bedside light out then rolled over onto Paul. She gave him a long soulful kiss and told him she deeply loved him. Then she curled up to his body, her back against his chest, so that she could feel his breathing. His arm draped over her, capturing her closeness; and his body cradled hers as a spoon holds a tempting morsel. She was unafraid of the future now, whatever it may hold. She and Paul would face it together. As she fell asleep she felt her vagina's muscles still faintly pulsing from the wonderful sex she had in the boathouse. She knew with all her mind and body that she had made the right choice for her life. She smiled a contented smile and she was at peace with her world.

"I want intimacy with you, Paul," she whispered before falling asleep. "All my life I've searched for the right man to be my partner. Now that I've found you all I want to do for the rest of my life is make our life together a happy life." Then she fell asleep.

CHAPTER THIRTY-ONE

MEETING HASTILY CALLED

C onnie insisted that they meet Wednesday evening at Tee O"s. She told her friends there wasn't enough time to wait until their customary Friday get together. No wine was ordered this evening, for tomorrow they all needed to be at work. Each woman ordered coffee and the waiter was instructed to leave two full coffee pots on the table. Tonight Sebastian, the guitarist, was absent. A piano player softly tickled the ivories producing romantic melodies. But this meeting was more of a gathering of a woman's war cabinet than a discussion of social matters, except matters that were mentioned incidental to the purpose of the meeting.

"I called this emergency meeting to inform you that our country and our assets are in imminent danger. Paul, the analyst, has done research work that confirms what Mole was saying about liquidity drying up in the treasury markets to collateralize derivatives. Paul took a hard look at the commodity markets and correlated the off balance sheet disclosures of the major banks with the increases in open interest short positions in gold and silver on the world's commodity exchanges. He discovered that the banks' equity could easily and quickly be wiped out by a ten percent move upward in gold and silver prices. The banks are suppressing the metals' prices to keep their balance sheets from blowing up."

Connie went on to declare that they all needed to buy physical metal and precious metals mining stocks and dump their positions in the general stock, bond, and real estate markets.

"We've heard this crap for years," said the ever skeptical Pattie. "It has not happened yet. What makes you think it will ever happen?"

"Because, as Paul explained to me, it has indeed happened before. It happens every time the bank credit expansion grows so much that the debtors can't service their loans. Then there is a financial collapse, like in the nineteen thirties, the nineteen seventies, which was a slow motion one, and the one we've entered now. Each time the price of the metals is revalued upwards relative to the fiat currencies." Connie's voice was strained from asserting her belief.

"But this isn't the thirties or the seventies. Everything is different now," Pattie persisted.

"No, according to Paul everything is the same. He means peoples' belief systems haven't changed. They never change. People always want to believe that the government or the central bank has their back, but it never does. He says that people don't understand the game because they are the game. They are the ones that will be screwed."

"Wait a minute," responded Pattie. "You're in research now, right?"

"Right," Connie stared at Pattie's skeptical face. "What are you getting at?"

"What I'm getting at is what I predicted a few times ago when we met," began Pattie's rejoinder. "I said that by the end of the summer you'd be fucking Paul's brains out. Remember my prediction? Well, are you?"

"Am I what?" shot back an indignant Connie.

"Are you fucking his brains out? Are you fucking Mr. Drop Dead Magazine Cover Gorgeous? That's what you called him last time. Well, are you?"

"Yes," answered Connie a bit sheepishly. "I am fucking his brains out every single night. We fell in love over the last two months. I got to know him and his daughter, I mean our daughter, Margaret, very well. I love him and the child. We got married by a judge yesterday."

A round of oohs and ahs, congratulations and well wishing broke out at the table. Each woman rose and went to Connie and kissed her cheeks. "Please keep it secret," Connie requested. "My parents don't even know it yet. We want to wait until this weekend when Father is home from Europe to tell them." The other three women swore their secrecy and looked at Connie with a newly found look of admiration.

But then Pattie, ever the one to look at negative possibilities, chirped up her doubts. "But, Connie, sweetheart, he doesn't have any money. He went through a nasty divorce, and he has another woman's kid." Her comment was meant to be a reality check and a general rain cloud on an otherwise happy group.

"Please don't lose any sleep over us, Pattie," said Connie as she leveled a gaze on her antagonist. That cold piercing stare was of a woman defending her man. It told Pattie that Connie might plunge a dagger into her heart, "I have plenty of money on my own. Besides, I know how to handle my father. I've watched Mother handle him for years. He's really just a puppy dog although he pretends to be a Billy Goat Gruff. And get it straight, Pattie. I love that little girl as if she were my own child. She's precious to me and I don't want to hear anything more from you about her being a burden to me. She's a joy."

Pattie was not through with her cold water shower. "Well, that's all well and good. And good for you and Paul! But, frankly, I vote that your judgment in matters of finance is now clouded. I can't see how you can reach a logical conclusion about what your husband says when, frankly Connie, you are once again thinking with your sex crazed cunt just like you always have. Why should we believe there's anything different to consider here?"

"Because she's absolutely one hundred percent right," interjected Sandra. Ordinarily Sandra was the meek one of the group who never spoke out except to vote on issues that came before them. It was hard to pry out of her before that she was sleeping with Walter Black, the president of the bank. Now she spoke with a shaky voice, but she was determined to be heard. All heads turned to the buxom blond, the pretty silent mouse among them, in astonishment that she would dive into any controversy.

"I wasn't going to say anything to any of you about this," continued Sandra. "I wasn't sure what to do with it. I thought about going to the police, but then I got afraid because Mr. Black has so much power in this city I thought he might find out I went to the police and————."

"Oh, for God's sake, spit it out, would you?" voiced a frustrated Linda. Linda was a woman of few words, but a barracuda when it came to decisiveness and taking action.

"Okay, okay," stammered Sandra. "Remember Mr. Santifalo who was murdered a couple of months ago?"

The others sat frozen, paying rapt attention to Sandra's hesitating utterances. Murder has that effect on most people. They nodded their heads in encouragement for her to continue.

"I received the strangest call on Monday morning. It was from a man in British Columbia named Ehud Burke," began Sandra in a low whisper. "He said that he had information and proof that connected Walter Black to the murder of Mr. Santifalo. Then he played this audio tape for me over the phone. Walter Black's voice was on the phone and he was with this group of men that were planning a terrorist attack. They planned to use drones to drop poison nerve gas on ten National Football League stadiums right during a football game.

They expected to kill maybe a million football fans right there on television so everybody could see their murders.

"Then they plan to seize all the media communications throughout the country. Their discussion was about how they would shut down the government and the banking system and call it a national emergency, make it sound like it was a necessity that they do that. They had this Army or Marine Corps General Porter with them and he was going to take care of all this shut down stuff. He sounded like a real nasty control kind of guy and he kept threatening to kill Walter if Walter screwed up anything more.

"They have some kind of deal or understanding with the Chinese government to let the Chinese just come into the United States and take over the whole country. Then the Chinese were going to round up all the dissenters to the occupation and kill them; and then the Chinese were going to round up all the racial minority people and kill them too, because they considered them to be inferior, but the other people who accepted the occupation could become slaves of the Chinese if they didn't want to be killed; and they were going to kill all old people who were over sixty five." Sandra held her head with her hands as if to emphasize just how mind boggling the plot was. Then her eyes began to water and she started sobbing. "I am so terrified. I don't know what to do and I am so afraid," she confided.

"Was this guy some kind of nut? Is this a joke," asked a stunned Pattie.

"No, he's not," sniffled Sandra. "At first I thought he was, but then I checked him out. He is who he said he was. He's a very successful geologist who found a lot of gold and he and his sister and her husband own a successful investment advisory form as well. I know this is all true because Walter has been trying to buy their firm. I know about that from being with Walter. I don't know what the connection is, but I'm sure he is for real. He said that I was somehow involved in something called a plan B and that he knew Walter was romantically involved with me, but that I couldn't trust Walter not to kill me because I'd heard about Plan B.

"And here's the part that has me terrified. The general wants Walter to kill me right now because I know something. I don't know anything except that I heard that one phone call where a man told me they were executing Plan B. Remember that?"

The others nodded their heads. Sandra had mentioned this Plan B business on a previous time when they'd gotten together.

"Well, this fellow said to call him Hud. This Hud fellow asked me if I knew anything about some map that was involved in this Plan B business. By now I'm going out of my mind. I have this stranger telling me stuff that has to be true, otherwise how would he know I was Walter's secret lover, and how would he know about Plan B? And, I checked him out. He told me Walter was trying to buy their little firm and willing to pay an outrageous price for it, but the only reason he could imagine why Walter would pay that kind of money was that one subsidiary of their investment firm was this Hud fellow's mining company. It has huge mineral claims in British Columbia and this Hud fellow told me he believes there is a connection to the claims and the map and Plan B and Walter's offer to buy their advisor.

"He pumped my memory hard to see if I knew any details. I told him that I could confirm that I'd heard the voice that spoke of Plan B. Then Hud said that could be enough to get me killed. Now, I'm very scared. I believe this man should be trusted. How else would he know about Plan B and the details of Mr. Santifalo's murder and Walter's efforts to buy his advisory firm? I'm afraid to be alone. I'm also very afraid to be with Walter because he might kill me, like he had Mr. Santifalo killed.

"Hud told me that he was traveling with a couple of friends, and I thought I heard two women talking in the background, so I believe that was true also. Now get this. He said he was trying to find a certain person who might provide the missing link to all this. He said he thought this person would know why Walter would want to buy his advisory firm. He also thought this person might know what it was that was on one or more of his mining claims that Walter was so interested in. He said this person lived somewhere near Roger's Pass in British Columbia and that I should go there and find an old general store on a country dirt road near the pass and tell the owner who I am. Then the owner would get in touch with this Hud fellow and he'd come get me. And he said once I was with him and his friends I'd be safe."

"Sounds like a crazy wild goose chase. Is there some other way he could have heard about Plan B? Did either of you, Connie or Linda, ever mention it to anyone? Sandra, did you ever mention it, because I'm sure I didn't." Pattie, ever the fact checker, was covering her bases. When the other three women solemnly shook their heads she had to concede that Sandra's narrative and this Hud fellow had the ring of truth.

"I need to reveal something," spoke Linda. "It's time I laid my cards on the table, but first I must have each of you sworn to me, on our fellowship and sisterhood pact, that you will reveal what I say to no one."

The other three all nodded their heads and agreed to be sworn to silence.

Linda continued. "You remember Sebastian, the guitar player who was here a few months ago?"

"How could we forget," sighed Pattie. "He was quite the hunk. Tall, very dreamy eyes, adorable face and hair, and that chest! He was real eye candy. I wondered where he was when I came in tonight. What about him?"

"I'm involved with him. I've always felt guilty about beating up on little people who couldn't pay back their loans, forcing them to lose their businesses and homes, especially when it was because Walter's loan committee decided to raise their variable rates above our cost of funds raises," Linda began.

"What's this got to do with Sebastian," asked Pattie. "Am I the only one here who's kept her panties on this past few months? What is going on with your guitar player, Linda?"

"He's more than a guitar player. He's a lawyer and a highly educated Spaniard from a wealthy family that had their plastic extrusion plants in Venezuela confiscated. They were screwed out of a fortune by the socialist government there," Linda began to explain.

"So what, everybody in this world is getting screwed by somebody else. Who gives a shit?" Pattie was getting tired and cynical; and she was perplexed that she wasn't getting any sex while everyone else seemed to be screwing like a company of minks.

"Let me talk, damn it," barked Linda. "Carlos is a revolutionary. He's actively working as one of the ringleaders of a group to overthrow the Venezuelan government. His group wants to end socialism and the Hacienda System in Latin America once and for all. They want to establish constitutional republics all across Latin America modeled on the U. S. Constitution, with gold and silver backing for their currencies. They have a secret currency pact to back a new pan American currency with gold. They're going to call it the Amero; and they'll have a smaller denomination silver coin too. They'll call that one the Amigo, because silver will raise the living standard of all Latin Americans. It will be the peoples' new best friend.

"He showed me their plans and I believe they will succeed. Already they have thirty thousand fighters enlisted to their cause across Latin America. Venezuela and Argentina will fall into their hands first, and then Mexico; and then the others will fall into line, even Brazil. They've done exhaustive research. People are fed up with the corruption and the drug violence. They want peace and governments that work for them instead of screwing them. This revolution is different from all the others because the peons will have honest money and their standards of living will rise. They will not just replace one corrupt strong man with bull shit promises with another strong man with his variety of bull shit promises. This revolution is spreading like wildfire. Men are willing to die for monetary freedoms."

"So, you got hot for a cause. What does this mean for you and Sebastian?" It was Pattie again. The skeptical workaholic was up since 6AM and now she was fading fast. She poured another coffee.

"I decided to finance their revolution," whispered Linda in a conspiratorial tone.

"You did what?" The question was sounded simultaneously by all three of the others.

"I opened a secret credit line from our bank's International Monetary Fund swap lines to a sympathetic bank in Barcelona, a small provincial bank that provides a Euro credit line to the revolutionaries. They are using it to buy arms. They are getting automatic weapons, mechanized artillery, fighter jets and foreign pilots, bombs, rocket propelled grenades, the fastest ocean going patrol boats with mounted torpedoes and fifty caliber machine guns, anti aircraft cannons, high frequency radar directed fire control systems, and lots and lots of hand held grenades. We're getting the latest and best stuff on the international arms market. With my help, Sebastian, or may I call him by his real name, Sebastian Carlos de Carmella, or Carlos for short, and I will change Latin America forever and I will become the Mother of the Revolution!" Linda smiled.

"You'll get yourself thrown in jail for life. This is way over the top," remarked a stunned and caffeine awakened Pattie. "How do you think you'll get away with this?"

"Oh, I'll get away with it all right. I already have. The credit line went out over Walter's secret authorization codes, the ones he's using to get unlimited credit to finance the coup against America that Sandra here was just talking about. If any agency looks into those authorizations under Walter's codes, they'll hang Walter, not me. I won't know anything about it." Linda was a true barracuda, ever willing to slice through a rival. It was no big secret in the bank that she hated Walter's guts. There are few things on Earth more dangerous than a woman who has a cause in her mind, a love in her heart, and a notebook full of secret pass codes to the world's banking system.

"How big is the credit line these revolutionaries have, asked Sandra? She suddenly seemed pleased that someone was screwing over Walter's evil plans and was forgetting her own danger.

"It started at 200 billion dollars, with automatic increases to five trillion dollars, as long as they service it at one percent interest."

"That's easily serviced and it's more than the gross national product of Russia and most European countries," remarked Connie.

"Yeah, well, wars aren't cheap you know," smiled Linda sheepishly and nonchalantly shrugging her shoulders. All her table partners blew up with roaring laughter. They enjoyed knowing Walter would eventually get fingered for the chaos that was bound to ensue. "And," Linda continued, "When you love a guy, you're supposed to help support his dreams, right? Can I help it if the guy I fell in love with has big dreams? I'm just a poor love sick secretary, right? How could I possibly concoct a plot to overthrow all of Latin America?" Linda was at her coy, cynical best and smiling like a cat that swallowed a canary.

"Do the three of you understand what this means?" asked Pattie. "It means we all know too much about Walter, about this Plan B, about Linda's revolution, about Mr. Santifalo's murder; about this blood thirsty General Porter. It means we all need to get the hell away from this bank before it's discovered that any of this stuff is known by any of us. It means we all need to go to someplace safe. We all need to get our asses to that general store in British Columbia.

"Connie; you also need to bring your new husband along. You'll be lost without his penis. And, he could be in danger too. Maybe we'll all need to seek political asylum in Canada. If these people are as ruthless as Hud says they are; if they are trying to overthrow the U. S. government, they won't have second thoughts about killing us." It was agreed that all five, including Paul, would call in sick the next morning and meet at the airport where they would purchase one way tickets to Vancouver, Canada. By the time evil Walter figured out that they were on to his plot they'd be off!

CHAPTER THIRTY-TWO

ROAD TRIP

F all was bringing change to North America. The crickets and frogs of summer were in hiding now, sealed away for the winter in their long wait for warmer times to return. Leaves on the deciduous trees were in their blazing colors of reds, oranges, tans, browns, golds, and blues. Nuts of the pines, oaks, beech and walnut trees offered their bounty to the squirrels and chipmunks that scampered about in a fevered pitch to gather and store the trees' produce as insurance against winter's freeze. In the high country marmots gathered and stored roots and grasses as the thirteen thousand feet mountaintops were receiving dustings of early season snow. Lower elevation creatures such as ground hogs, mice, voles, and the like accelerated their pace of gathering. Their conditions were never as harsh as their high altitude brethren, but slackers were never spared by the elements. And thus they busied themselves. The survival urge was instinctive. It swept over every living creature like a chilled wind.

It was time to store calories and put on fat, and for many species, to breed. The varied males of the ungulate species pawed earth, locked antlers and butted heads for dominance, while their herd females watched and judged the competition. And berries of Hemlock, Juniper, Yew, Bitter Cherry, Boysenberry and Currants burst full with color, attracting birds of all sorts. And the air was clean, clear and invigorating to inhale deeply.

There were three vehicles traveling to a place called Roger's pass, British Columbia this fall season. Each bore people with their own set of circumstances. And each traveler believed their quest to locate an old country store on a dirt road somewhere near the pass was of paramount importance.

Hud's Land Rover started out two hundred miles from the pass. He drove with Sheila in the front passenger seat with Cecilia riding in the back. As they drove, Cecilia massaged Hud's neck and occasionally kissed it; Sheila placed her left hand alternatively on Hud's leg and his penis. The three had become an intimate threesome by now and they were absorbing their newfound feelings of intimacy.

During their dinner the night before a male Clark's Jay lighted upon the window sill outside their table. It surveyed their dinners and carefully examined the glass barrier that prevented him from joining them. It plainly wanted to steal some food but could not see how to get at it. Then from a near by fir two female Jays called to him. He looked in at what he could not have and then looked away to what he could have. The two females plainly demanded his company. He vacillated, not sure what to do, hopping back and forth on the sill. He repeatedly looked in at the table and then looked away to the females. Hud, Sheila, and Cecilia were amused at the conflicted bird and began laughing at his predicament.

"That poor bird," said Cecilia. "Two women want him and he wants to finish our dinner for us, but they seem anxious to have his company. He doesn't quite know what his priorities are. It must be difficult for him. I wonder when he'll come to his senses and go to them."

"He'll soon forget about food. The females will keep him busy. He'll eat pine nuts instead of our left over's. That's better for him. The poor fellow has confused his priorities." Hud's comments signaled that his own priorities placed women's company above food at the moment.

"Oh, let's leave this silly bird and let him figure out what he's expected to do. We are wasting precious moments we may not have for some time. Let's retire to your room, Hud, and have that nightcap and, may I say, satisfy our own needs?" Sheila's smile was mischievous and infectious. Soon the threesome found themselves in Hud's room. They were in a hesitant awkward hurry this first intimate night. They each self consciously undressed themselves then sat side by side on the huge king sized bed. Hud was between the two women. That's when Sheila confided to Hud that she was still a virgin and informed him that she had selected him to free her from her condition. She told him that she would feel honored if he would do so.

Cecilia said she thought it appropriate that an acceptance prayer be said for their union. Then she whispered a prayer to the spirits before their intimacy. "Oh Great Spirit, please accept us as we are. Please help us understand your love and help us all to know love for each other. And please let us feel the wonderment of love, and please make our love making be long lasting, filled with understanding and free of guilt or regrets. Bless us now in our love for you and for each other." It was a simple direct and honest request to her spirit guardian; and it had the effect of lifting away all of their inhibitions and feelings of awkwardness.

Thus a triangle was formed. Sheila first assumed the maiden position. An agreeable Hud performed her first penetration and broke her hymen. Cecilia watched while alternatively kissing Hud and Sheila. After Sheila's baptism to sex she felt soreness and after a short while she and Hud thought it best that he withdraw. Then he proceeded to copulate with Cecilia. The next morning, before they set out, Sheila was feeling better and Hud had full conjugation with her. Now both women had felt the full measure of his sex, both had received a full ejaculation of his semen, and all three of them felt an acute awareness that they had crossed a foreboding barrier.

Motoring over the road that morning each of them had their thoughts about the night before. Hud remembered the extreme sensitivity and tenderness with which Sheila approached sex. He realized that the act was wonderment for her, an entry into a new world. He could tell she loved her experience. Her body and gentle hugs told him that, but the soreness that accompanied her first time tempered her joy. He needed to be gentle with her.

Cecilia, by contrast, was an explosive wildcat. She'd dug her nails into his back and writhed wildly. Sex with her was like riding a wild tornado. She had unbridled enthusiasm that lifted him skyward to his limits and then brought him down with a quick violent collapse on top of her after he came. This morning Sheila had needed him again. And she tolerated her residual soreness very well. Their sex was slow and sweet. She winced a few times but spoke confidently to him to continue until he ejaculated. He could tell that both women accepted his relations with the other; and he believed that this new world he had entered would long endure.

Sheila had her private thoughts of belonging and fulfillment. She finally knew how it felt to have a penis inside her. She felt that making a life with Cecilia and Hud would be wonderful. She thought about the many future times when Cecilia would lick her pussy, and she would lick CC's; and how she could learn to give blow jobs to Hud. She looked forward to more experimentation with each of them. And she felt a warm glow inside her that she had not known since she was a child on the farm with her parents.

Cecilia was very pleased with her bi sexuality and had been for several years. She salivated with her thoughts of the sensual pleasures that lie ahead. In her deepest being's most fervent wish she discovered herself silently asking her spirit to please help her become pregnant with a little girl baby. She asked that the spirit not put her through any more bad relationship times. She asked that her times with Hud and Sheila be filled with goodness and happiness. She reminded the spirit that she had had more than her fair share of heartbreak with the loss of her son, Frank. She prayed silently that the love she felt for Sheila and Hud was reciprocated from each of them and both of them to her, and that the love and wild passions she felt last night would endure forever.

And Cecilia thought that, since the three of them were now embarked upon an unconventional relationship, she would need to invent some new rituals to sanctify their new order so that it would be accepted in the broader world. She thought that, surely, the Spirit had heard similar pleas before from others who, in their own time, sought to have society at large accept their new understanding of how they fit into the world.

She reflected that these same thoughts must have come to Abraham when he made his famous bris with God by cutting the animals and birds in half and placing himself on one side of the severed carcasses and God on the other side. He and God struck their bargain that day. The Hebrew tribe would worship as monotheists, differently than the polytheistic ways of others. And now, five thousand plus years later, the world, albeit in some quarters begrudgingly, accepts the Hebrews.

And she thought it was, likely, too, that when Jesus and Judas invented Christianity they must have thought long and hard to devise their ritual of the body and the blood of the Christ. She shuddered at the devotion those two men must have had to their concepts of love of fellow man, forgiveness and the beatitudes. What a change that thinking was from the uncaring way humans regarded others before! She admired the duo's deep commitment to furthering mankind's humanity by giving up their lives. That took commitment to a fledgling concept if ever there was one. She reflected that what they did was pure genius. Whoever at the time of their creative concepts would have imagined that from such modest beginnings would grow religious dynasties that swam in riches and influence? She prayed silently for something much more humble and simpler for herself, Sheila and Hud.

She asked the Spirit to help her devise a heartfelt honored ritual that would achieve respect and acceptance in broader society, but not something that would require them to give up their lives to initiate it. She loved sex and life itself too much to die for any cause. She sought help to create something small and innocuous that moved societal norms toward understanding acceptance. Priests and the like would no doubt label her as a witch or a harlot if her thoughts and rituals were revealed to them, and that concerned her. She understood that no established entity, including religious ones, liked to yield market share, and in generations past such usurpers to established powers were met by torture, death and damnation. As the Land Rover approached Roger's Pass she felt hope rising in her breast that their lives would be accepted, her prayers would be favored and the inspiration she sought would be delivered to her.

Meanwhile, a second car, a rental sports utility vehicle Jeep with Colorado plates was also approaching Roger's Pass. Gibby and Jo Anne were near the end of the journey they began on the mountaintops above Ouray. They had outfoxed General Porter's death patrols and they still had the old prospectors map.

Gibby figured the general expected them to traverse the high mountains and would have placed sentries to spot them. Gibby surmised that the general would not expect him and Jo Anne to reappear in Ouray, but that's what they did. After crawling hundreds of yards in a cloud heavy night, the two made their way off the high tundra into the pine forest. If infrared reading satellites detected them, their image readers likely would conclude they were a pair of cougars or lynx moving stealthily on four legs. Once in the pines they stood upright. Then they walked very close together, Jo Anne with her arms around Gibby and walking bent forward. They traveled downward, meandering slowly during the night. The image readers would likely mistake them for an elk moving lower to feed, and then sleep at a meadow's edge when the sun rose. When the sun rose they skirted the meadow and continued slowly lower by day, stopping frequently under large pines. They thusly avoided detection. When the streets of Ouray were busy with tourists they emerged from the mountainside and walked among them to Sam's Bald Eagle Bar. Once inside they slipped into a storeroom unseen and waited.

When Sam opened his bar that day, two rifles, two service .45 pistols and a knapsack full of ammunition was lying on the bar. Gibby and Jo Anne sat on bar stools in front of the guns.

"I see you found him, Jo," said Sam with a knowing chuckle. "I knew you two couldn't stay apart for very long. What'd I tell you, Jo? Old Sam knows people like the back of his hand. I'm glad to see you both! What are you doing back down here in town, Gibby? I would have thought that, after you sold your place you'd have gone away for good."

Some men laid their cards on the table, Gibby laid down his guns. It was Gibby's way of laying it all out there and holding nothing back. He explained to Sam all that had happened since he last saw Sam. He told Sam that he and Jo Anne desperately needed help, but that anyone who helped them would be putting his own life in danger.

That didn't deter Sam. He was a red, white and blue flag waving patriot. He, like Gibby, saw action in Vietnam and Sam didn't much care for generals. The idea of duping a rogue General appealed to him.

Gibby and Sam hatched a plan. Then Sam made a phone call, and put a 'closed today' sign outside the bar. Shortly after that a man came to the bar and knocked twice. Sam admitted him. He had photographic equipment. He set up his camera and background screen, and then took Gibby's picture. He had make up and a wig of black hair for Jo Anne, which he arranged very neatly on her head. She looked like she'd never been a redhead. Then he took her picture too. The man left and promised to return in two hours. When he returned he brought with him fake driver's licenses and passports for Gibby and Jo Anne. Sam drove Gibby and Jo Anne with their new fake identities in his pick up truck to the Telluride airport. There he rented them a new Jeep SUV and gave them ten thousand dollars in cash.

Jo Anne gave Sam a big hug of thanks. "Aw shucks, Jo," he said blushing. It's the same you and Gibby would do for me. What's friends for anyways. All I ask in return is if and when you two ever find what's at the end of that map and if you live through whatever this general is trying to do, you come back to the Bald Eagle Bar in Ouray and sit on my bar stools and tell old Sam all about it. When Gibby shook hands with Sam he placed into Sam's hand a good sized emerald. Then the two men hugged. "Gibby," said a choked up Sam, "you didn't need to do that."

"Yeah I did," said Gibby. "I wouldn't of felt right if I didn't. I'd do the same fer you, Sam. What's friends fer anyways?"

Two weeks later Gibby and Jo Anne were near Roger's Pass. They'd traveled state maintained side roads to the east coast then driven north and crossed into Canada at Magoog, Quebec. They drove west until they reached northern British Columbia. They asked local Tlingit Indians about an old woman who traded with the Tillamook to the south. After two days of driving and asking they found the woman who had traded for the map from the old prospector. They learned that the prospector's cabin was about fifty miles west of Roger's Pass. The Tlingit woman thought the prospector's wife still lived there. Gibby and Jo Anne went there next and luckily they found her. They explained to the old woman that finding the area where her late husband was when he made his crude map was now a matter of life and death. She sat bewildered, searching her memory.

"I remember some things," she said. He was always excited about what he found. He was even more excited when he showed me these unusual rocks. I still have them here, see." She pulled back a curtain in her cabin and revealed a pile of rocks.

They looked ordinary until Gibby picked one up. When he did a small film from it soon covered his hand and the rock began to glow in many different rapidly changing colors. Gibby was amazed and frightened, for he'd never seen rocks such as these. "They have unusual powers," said the old woman. "I am afraid to touch them, although they did not hurt me when I did touch them. I have noticed that when I set one of them near my electric generator it changes colors even more rapidly than it just did when you touched it. It lifted from the ground and spun around until I turned the generator off. I can not imagine what anyone would want with such rocks. If I put them near the garden they make my plants grow sideways to try to get away from them; and when the deer come near them the deer startle and run away. I don't like the way they frighten the deer. I like the deer. I fence my garden so the deer won't go into it, but I like them to come near the cabin. They are good company."

"Yes, maam, but please forget about the deer and your garden for a while. It is very important that you remember where your husband was when he found these rocks."

"Oh, yes, my husband, he wasn't here much," the old woman's voice trailed off and she looked far away. Jo Anne decided she needed to intervene, woman to woman.

"When my man is gone from me I feel very lonely. Is that how you felt when your man was away from you?" She sat next to the prospector's wife and placed her hand on hers. The old woman looked into her face and cried a little.

"Yes. It was terribly lonely for me when he was away," she nodded her gray head.

"And when he came home to you, I'll bet he was real excited to tell you where he'd been every time he came back to you, wasn't he?" Jo Anne looked into her eyes and nodded along with her. "And I'll bet that when he came back to you that last time he was more excited than he'd ever been, wasn't he?" Jo Anne was recreating the moment in the old woman's memory.

"Yes. Oh yes! He was so excited. He said he'd gone further east into the forest than he'd ever gone before. He said he had to walk all the way to several miles far beyond a mountain pass called Roger's Pass; and then he said he went north for a few miles through some very thick timber. He said he did not think any white man had ever been there before because the timber was so thick. Then he went east a little further until he collapsed from exhaustion and fell asleep. When he woke up the rocks were there across a drainage cut from him. They looked out of place, he said, like they came down from a landslide but that was impossible because the terrain had no high point from which they could slide. He said he went to them and picked one up and it made fire colors in his hand. He knew he had something, but he didn't know what."

Gibby wrote down her narrative as she recalled it. He now had the approximate location where the old prospector found the rocks. They graciously took along a few rocks that the old woman offered them. They declined her invitation to stay for coffee, said their goodbyes and were off!

Once at the Roger's Pass area they began asking if anyone knew the forest to the north of there very well. They arrived at an old general store that had an old basset hound lying on the front porch. They went inside. A gray haired man, bent over with age, came out from behind a curtain that separated the front from the back of the store.

"Ken I help yas?" He had a distrusting look on his face.

"We're here looking for somebody but we don't know who we're looking for," said Gibby.

"Well, then he ain't here," said the proprietor. "Maybe you'd like to buy something?"

"Yeah, I'll buy something all right. But first you need to help us. We need to know who it is around these parts that know the woods around these parts."

"Well, everybody and nobody, depends."

"On?" Gibby sensed the information was soon forthcoming.

"On how far into the timber you want to know about depends on how far into the timber anybody's gone and come back to talk about it. There's wolves and bears and cougars in there you know. Not just everybody goes off for walks to get themselves lost or eaten, ya know."

"Okay, I get it. But there must be somebody around here that's familiar with the deep forest. Doesn't somebody go in there?"

"Well, yep, matter of fact somebody does," The proprietor was scratching his beard and looking about at his stock of overpriced and stale dated shelf goods.

"Okay, well, I'd like to meet him and take him some groceries. Can you tell me who he is and where he lives?" Gibby betrayed some impatience.

"Yep, I can. I think he'd like it if you took him some groceries though."

"How much groceries?" Gibby betrayed a little anger this time, but the man had him at his mercy and Gibby had no choice but to play along with his game of extortion. Gibby suspected it was a game the owner of this desolate store played very well.

The man sized Gibby for a possible fight and realized Gibby would easily take him. He didn't want to push it too far. "How about you take him three hundred dollars worth of groceries? That's U. S. dollars, mind ya. You's is 'Mericans, ain't ya?"

"Yes. We are Americans. Here's your three hundred U. S. dollars. You pick up what he'll want or give him a credit chit that I can take to him and we'll be going. Now, who is he and where is he?"

"Okay, just a minute," the man took out a pencil and paper and made out a chit for one hundred dollars worth of groceries to a Rosemary Bitner and handed the chit to Gibby.

"You got three hundred dollars, said Gibby. This chit is for one hundred!" He was about to go to his fists, but he needed this troll's cooperation.

"Yep, that's right. There's a two hundred dollar information discount in the three hundred. Agreed?"

"Agreed, now where is this person? Is it man or woman? Is this Rosemary his wife?"

"Ha, ha," the man laughed. "Hell no, she ain't no wife. Rosemary ain't the marrying kind of woman. That's too bad, too. She's easy to look at, you know. But she's more in love with her damn cat and the forest animals than she is with any man. She lives alone in a log cabin. Ya goes up this dirt trail that starts behind the store. Wait, ya got four wheel drive?"

"Yes, Jeep." Gibby's patience was wearing very thin, and it came through to the man who noticed Gibby snarled between his teeth.

"Okay, you're good then. Ya goes up this trail exactly three miles, then go left for six and three tenth miles, then right for one half mile and ya'll see Rosemary's place."

"How will I know which cabin is hers?"

"It's the only one. There ain't no other place for a good half mile from her. She's a real loner."

"And what makes you think she knows the deep forest?"

"Oh, she knows it all right. She comes in here once in a while when she needs something real bad. She tells me she takes these long walks and has these secret places she goes to and she talks with the animals and the spirits. If ya ask me, she's a bit off. Some gets that ways from living alone like she does, ya know. Say, what are ya two doing here anyways? I mean why do ya want to know about who knows the deep forest?" The proprietor had his curiosity tickled.

"Would you really like to know?" Gibby's face lit up.

"Why sure. A fella likes to know what's goin on in his back yard, so to speak."

"I'll tell you," said Gibby, "but that'll cost you five hundred U. S. Dollars.

"All you 'Mericans are greedy sons of bitches," the old man's head snapped back indignantly. "Nope, I ain't gonna pays you a dime. Get out of here now. Our business is through." The old man bristled at being trapped in his own game. Gibby and Jo Anne climbed into their Jeep SUV. Gibby fired up the engine and they were off!

Not more than two hours later a second vehicle, a GMC four-wheel drive Suburban, pulled into the old general store near Roger's Pass. Four women and a man crawled out of it and stumbled past the old basset hound into the store. The dog drooled and slowly lifted his head this time. He hadn't noticed so many people in one afternoon in all his years. He watched everyone's feet carefully. He didn't want his body or tail getting stepped on. Paul rang the little bell on the counter. After a while the proprietor came out. "What can I do for you nice folks?" he smiled.

Paul spoke for the group. "We're curious if you'd be kind enough to help us," he said. "We're looking for someone who knows these forests real well, who can help us find our way around here."

"Rosemary," said the proprietor. "You're looking for Rosemary. What do you need her for?"

"I can't tell you why, old timer. How do we find her?" Paul was matter of fact, but not curt.

"I can tell you," replied the proprietor slyly, but it will cost you. Information around here costs money."

"How much," asked Paul.

The proprietor hesitated to think a bit. Obviously something important was going on and this was his chance to milk it, but if he charged too much these people might just go knocking on cabin doors until somebody told them for no charge. He felt emboldened to up his price.

"That'll be five hundred U. S. Dollars," he declared straightening his back.

"Here," said Connie as she pulled a huge money clip from her purse and peeled off five one hundred dollar bills. That did not make a dent in her huge clip. The old man realized he could have charged twice that. But, a deal was a deal and once made he kept it. He gave them the same directions to Rosemary's as he'd given Gibby and Jo Anne. The four women and Paul climbed into their Suburban and they were off!

Less than a half hour later a man and two women pulled up to the general store in a Land Rover. Hud, Sheila and Cecilia got out. "Nice doggie," said Hud as they entered the store. This time the dog yawned and put his head back down on the wooden porch of the store. The basset hound thought to himself, 'This must be what it's like to sleep in the doorway of a supermarket.' Hud rang the counter bell. After a minute the owner came out from behind his curtain.

"Let me guess," he said. "Ya's Americans and ya's looking for an old woman named Rosemary, right?"

Hud decided to play for information. "What makes you think we're looking for Rosemary?" he asked.

"The others were looking for her too," he answered matter of fact. By now he figured that something about Rosemary must be connected to a scavenger hunt.

"What others?" Hud, Sheila and Cecilia looked dumb-struck. Sudden fear showed in their faces. They worried that General Porter might be ahead of them waiting for them. They couldn't let the general get the old prospector's map first. Now they looked anxious. "What do you know about it," asked Hud.

"About what?" the old man was genuinely confused. What were these people after? He wondered.

"Listen mister, I don't have time for games. This is a national emergency. If you don't tell us where these people were going and we don't find them in time a million people are going to die." Hud had the voice of authority about him. The old man suddenly wanted nothing more than to be left alone. He gave Hud the directions to Rosemary's cabin.

When the Land Rover reached the cabin a Suburban and a Jeep SUV were already there. They walked to the door and Hud knocked. A small comely woman, well figured, very pretty and with a hint of gray hair answered.

"Well, well, come in and join the rest of us. You are also Americans, I presume?" She had a pleasant smile and was very cordial.

"Yes, said Sheila. We are running out of time. We must find a map that an old prospector made. We hope you can help us. We need to get to the location on his map where he found some fifth generation star rocks. I need to get some of those rocks and take them back to America with me or a million people will die."

Gibby stood up from the sofa. "Wait here, lady," he said to Sheila. When he returned from his Jeep he held a rock in his hand. It changed colors and deposited a thin film on his hand. "Is this what you are looking for?" he asked.

"I think so. I'm not sure. I need to run some tests to be sure." Sheila was excited and her eyes fixated on the rock.

"Everybody just hold your horses," said Rosemary. "Let's all get on the same page. That's what you American people say, isn't it? Let's all talk one at a time so we all know the same things and we all know why each of us came here. Now, one by one you are all going to explain what this is all about. I can't help any of you if I don't know why you're here or what you need." Rosemary looked at each face in the room. Her own face was honest and sincere. Everyone could see she was a woman who wanted to be helpful.

One by one, her visitors told her everything. Paul explained to her why the United States was on the brink of financial collapse and how that was giving rise to opposing political factions. Sheila and Cecilia explained their secret projects and how they needed some kind of special material from fifth generation star rocks that could be fashioned into an electrical transmitter that would instantaneously reprogram the software in hostile drones and send them back to their origin point to unload their payloads on the evil plotters. They revealed that renegade General Porter and his banker accomplices would kill all of them if they figured out that these rocks could foil their plot.

Gibby spoke next and explained how he acquired the map, how they tracked down the old prospector's wife, and the ordeal that he and Jo Anne went through to get here. He confirmed that the rock he had was from the prospector's cabin.

Linda then explained how she was financing a Latin American revolution and how her fiancé, Carlos, was going to put all of Latin America on a gold standard; and then invite the United States to join them in a unified gold backed currency to make the Western Hemisphere financially sound again.

"Well, now. Wasn't that much better? Now we know why we're here and what we need to do, don't we?" Rosemary smiled upon her guests and offered them some tea. "All of you find some bedding in that closet over there and make do as best you can. The bathroom is over there," she said, pointing to another door. "And there's a privy outside behind the cabin if you can't wait. Now, we're all going to have some tea and some biscuits and some of my moose stew and then we'll all get a good sleep and start out in the morning."

"Then, you do know where the rocks are?" asked an anxious Sheila.

"Oh, no dear. I don't know where they are. I can take you close to where they are, but after that you'll need to follow Bud."

"Bud? Who's Bud?" asked Connie.

"Why, he's right here sitting next to me on the floor, dear. He's my cat. Every time I go to my secret place in the forest Bud here runs off by himself for a while. He always comes back to me with this thin film with pretty colors on his paws. I never knew until today what that was about. I thought he might have scratched his claws on some colored chalk that someone left in the forest. Come to think of it, that was very silly of me because I don't believe that anyone other than me ever goes back there. Now I see that Bud has found the rocks. The flashing pretty colors must have excited him. He's very playful you know. So, we'll take him with us tomorrow as I always do and he'll lead us to the rocks you seek. Won't you, Bud?"

And with that Rosemary picked up her cat and hugged him and Bud began to purr loudly. "Isn't he a wonderful purr fur? Oh, Bud, you are so wonderful! You are going to save the United States of America from some big bad general! Imagine that, Bud. A big superpower country like that is now depending upon you, my wonderful kitty, to save it from destruction. Oh Bud, you will be famous! But, listen, people. I like my privacy very much. After we get your rocks you must promise me that you will tell no one where you got them and that no one will ever know that Bud knows how to get to them. We wouldn't want anyone to get after my Bud, now would we baby?" She hugged her cat as she spoke to him.

CHAPTER THIRTY-THREE

EXPLORER

The group started out fresh in the morning from Rosemary's cabin. The path indicated by the map took them near the Trout Pool. Rosemary told her new friends that there was something they should see and it would only take them an hour out of their way. She led them to the Trout Pool and told them to sit and be quiet. Then she edged herself out onto the rock ledge over the pool and sat there with her eyes closed. At first the members of the group thought that Rosemary had lost her mind and that this jaunt had to be a waste of time. But then the spirit came.

Out of the air above the pool a shimmering figure of a beautiful woman appeared in a white gown. She walked on the air and stood suspended in air before Rosemary. "Hello, Great Spirit of all Living Things," Rosemary addressed the woman. "May I please present to you some good people who seek to save the United States from a terrible murder plot by evil men?"

"You may, dear," said the Spirit in a sweet melodious voice. She approached Rosemary and lifted her up with her outstretched arm and held her to her bosom over the pond. "Come join us," she said to the others. Hesitantly the others walked onto the overhanging ledge and inched their way to the edge of it. There they stopped. "Walk onward over the pond. You will not fall in. I have you safely with me now," she spoke with confidence. "Be not afraid. You can walk in the air above the water."

One by one, Sheila going first, they walked off the ledge into the air and then they stood there suspended over the trout pool. When they were all together over the pool Rosemary spoke. "Spirit, would you please give my friends a glimpse of the spirit world and explain to them that death is not to be feared. These people all know love, Great Spirit, and it would give them peace in their souls that there is eternal life for those who love, and that they can travel instantaneously among the planets of the universe."

"Yes, for you, Rosemary, I will show them; but this is something reserved for the spirits to understand and I do not wish this place or our discussions to become a tourist attraction for humans."

"You have my word, Spirit; this will be the only time."

"Very well, now all of you look into the pool." With that, the Spirit stretched out her arm over the water and then raised her hand up toward the sky. As she did that the waters lifted up and disappeared into the sky and the sky was opened for them to see beyond the sky into the spirit world. And they saw many people coming and going before them. Hud's father, Bob Burke, or Big Horse, appeared and he held a woman named Marty in his embrace and they had their child with them; and then Hud's mother, Barbara, or Little Sparrow, appeared and she too was locked in a tight embrace with his father, Bob. And they had two children with them. And then the spirits of the people who were with Rosemary appeared. First appeared Hud, and with him was Sheila and Cecilia and with them there were two children. They were Cecilia's little girls. And then the spirits of Connie and Paul appeared with their four children; and then spirits of Linda and Carlos appeared and they had three children; and Sandra appeared with a man no one recognized with two children. Next came Sandra again, this time with George, the stock trader, and they had three children. Pattie's spirit also appeared along with a nasty looking barking dog. And then with blinding speed more spirits appeared; Big Chief, Little Sparrow, Marty again, many times, in different dresses with each of her many lovers from *The Secret and the Butterfly*, the twins, the four J's, the two football players, her school teacher, her many orgy partners, and Muscle.

And the appearance of spirits came forward many times from the air and receded back into it before the visitors at the trout pool. The spirits sometimes appeared somewhat different in their ages and in the appearances of their children. Then, the Great Spirit of all Living Things lowered her hand and the opening in the sky closed; and the waters fell back into the pond and all was still. The visitors were all left breathless for they had seen wonders they could never have imagined. "Why did I see my father's spirit twice at first and then many times afterwards," asked Hud.

The Spirit answered, "Because I wanted you to see for yourself that when your body dies your spirit lives on forever, and it will take many forms. Hud, your father also has another life now besides the ones you saw. He is also with Rose who he loved as a teenager. In his Earth life he and Rose were denied by Rose's father; they now live happily together with their children on another planet. And so it is with all of you and your parents and their parents before them; and so it will be with your children and their children to come.

This is the way of the spirit world. The feelings of love are a spirit that seeks life; and after physical death it reforms into another corporeal body on another planet in another time, past or present. It is the continuum that is eternity. There is neither a beginning time of it nor an ending time of it. And the lives that all spirits know in other worlds are real lives with real flesh and blood embodying their spirits as your own flesh and blood embodies your own spirits here on Earth in this life."

After her explanation the spirit told them to walk back onto the ledge. When they safely returned to the ledge the Spirit walked away from them into the air and disappeared. Each member of the group was shaken by the miracle they had seen and their bodies shook and trembled for they had been in the presence of a power greater than any they had known before.

Then they held and hugged each other to comfort each other. They were unable to speak for they had no words for what they had witnessed. And they believed all that the Spirit showed them and told them. And each one of them had private inner thoughts about the meaning of what they had seen.

Cecilia's thoughts were confused. As a child she was taught to believe the priests and their stories of Jesus and the resurrection. When she was older she began to doubt whether those stories were true. She wondered if Christ really did walk on water and turn water into wine and multiply the fishes and the loaves of bread and heal the sick and the blind. Now she was more uncertain than ever about what to believe. Should she now believe the priests again as she had as a child? Just because she did not see the miracles of the Christ did not mean they did not happen exactly like the priests said they did. She saw miracles today and she knew if she retold them many people would not believe her either, just as many people do not believe the priests. Perhaps, she thought, what she saw today meant that what the priests said was only partly true. Perhaps the Spirit showed her the real truth of eternal life and that was all a simple person such as herself should need for proof of what to believe.

All the others had similar thoughts. Whatever feelings of love they felt for one another was something blessed by the spirits and wonderful and accepted by the spirits. And many anxieties about events in their lives were allayed. They discovered a new courage about being in love and a good feeling came over them. Pattie, the one of the group who doubted all things before today spoke directly to Rosemary.

"Why do you think the Spirit showed us so many versions of Marty's lives and lovers compared to the others?"

"The Spirit and I have had many discussions about Marty," began Rosemary. "I knew Marty as a friend by a different name years ago and decided to write about her horrible conflict. She had many lovers and fell into true love with all of them. She was a nymphomaniac with an incurable addiction to sex. But, she valiantly struggled to break free of her addiction to mere sexual love when she met a man who truly loved her just for herself, for her goodness and her open heart.

"I wrote a book about their love and her struggle called *The Secret and the Butterfly*. While writing her story I discussed many aspects of her loves with the Spirit. I believe that today the Spirit was reassuring me that my friend has many happy lives with each of her many lovers. I believe it was the Spirit's way of telling me that my friend, who was an unrepentant sinner here on Earth, is understood and accepted by the Spirit despite all her faults and misdeeds." Hearing that, Pattie simply nodded in understanding. She recalled all the many times she was critical of Connie and her other friends and silently thanked the Spirit for opening her mind to accepting others.

"Well, my dear friends, shall we proceed along the path shown to us on the map," questioned Rosemary, after she felt everyone had enough time to reflect upon what they had witnessed. After a moment to fully return their senses to the present world, the group followed Rosemary on the trail indicated by the map. It meandered through a deeply wooded pine forest and thick ground ferns on a narrow pathway that skirted moss covered downfallen trees and mossy ground patches. The scent of fresh pine filled the air and little ground squirrels scampered about before them. They eventually came to a small clearing and Rosemary stopped walking. Everyone looked around them for the special rocks, but there were no rocks present. Concern broke out. Someone muttered that they could be lost.

"Are you sure we followed the trail correctly," asked Cecilia. Everyone milled about in the forest near the clearing looking for the rocks but finding none.

"There's one way to find out," said Rosemary. "Come on, Bud. It's time for you to do some exploring." She put Bud down onto the ground. For a moment he just stood there as if he was in a daze, as cats sometimes do. He repeatedly stared out ahead of his face and then looked back and up at Rosemary. This went on for a minute while Bud made up his mind about what he wanted to do.

"Find the rocks, Bud!" commanded Rosemary.

Then, suddenly, Bud took off running into the forest. Everyone followed him. He ran for about thirty yards until he came to the bank of a dried up stream. He paused and looked for the longest time at the dried stream bed and then he crossed it. He walked up the hill on the opposite bank and there before him was a field of rocks. They looked like ordinary rocks but they were far from ordinary. They were peculiar rocks from a fifth generation star. Bud approached a rock, then batted at it as if to play with it. When he did that the rock came alive with rapidly changing colors.

Sheila rushed across the dried stream and picked Bud up and hugged him. "Oh, you good boy, you. You are a very special cat, you know. He likes to play with these rocks, doesn't he? Rosemary," asked Sheila turning to her hostess.

"What is it about them?" Rosemary was no scientist, but she was curious.

"These rocks have special properties that have come to us from a different universe. I've worked out mathematically what they are capable of doing in my theories. Now that I know they exist I can run tests on them and design some circuitry for them. When I coat them with gold I will cause them to activate harmonically from airborne electronic signals. I can program the circuits that encase the rock material to reverse the signals and send hostile drones back to their points of origin. I should be able to instruct a terrorist drone to unload its lethal payload upon the terrorists." Sheila was breathless with excitement.

The discovery was one for the ages. Her genius mind was already thinking about how she could use the rocks' elements to amplify harmonic resonances between the sun's and earth's gravities. Once she accomplished that she could design a spaceship that would move millions of times faster than the speed of light.

Sheila moved to pick up one of the rocks. When she lifted the first rock three dark irregular shapes suddenly appeared from out of the air and levitated before her. Each shape reconfigured itself into a human like form shaped in solid blackness. They were all twice the size of average humans. One was a man, another woman, and the third a child. Each form held hands with the other forms. The forms smiled at Sheila and then bowed low before her. They then made soft musical sounds as if they were each playing stringed musical instruments. The sounds came from their heads although their mouths were not opened. And the sounds resembled sweet chorus singings of gospel songs from a far away distance with background sounds of ocean waves crashing upon a rocky coast and, alternatively a babbling brook. The humans observing them were dumbstruck for the second time this afternoon.

"They're trying to communicate with us," said Connie. 'I believe they are trying to tell us they are from some place far away and they have water there. They have oceans and running streams like we have here on Earth."

"But why are they telling us anything? Why are we seeing them?" Pattie questioned the motives of the black shapes.

"I think I know," said Cecilia. "I have seen them before when they were only irregular shapes, the same as they were here today when they first appeared to us. I think those irregular shapes are the spirits of real people who live on a different planet in a different universe. Somehow when the universes intersected these rocks brought the spirits of the people from the other universe to us here on Earth."

As soon as Cecilia spoke the three spirits rushed to her and surrounded her. Then they lifted her up into their arms and hugged her and passed her back and forth between them hugging her. This entire spectacle took place in mid air. None of the spirits or Cecilia touched the ground. Then they did the same warm greeting ritual to Sheila. When they finished their hugging they stepped backward in the air and bowed profusely to the entire group. Then they arose several feet higher into the air and rearranged their shapes into wavy columns; and then the columns descended into the rocks and disappeared, thus becoming affixed to the rocks and entombed in them.

"Sheila," cried Cecilia, "they were telling us that they came from a place much like Earth, and then they thanked us for finding the rocks. It must mean that by going into the rocks they have a way to get back on their planet, even though part of it is here on our planet! They have sort of gone home. They were appearing to us as irregular shapes months ago because somehow they had superior intelligence. They were able to understand that you would somehow find the rocks. It's like they had a precognition or a telepathic power because they have a superior intelligence. But now their spirits are home in their rocks. Maybe that means that somewhere in another universe there are people whose lives have been reunited with their spirits here in these rocks. This is what I have been trying so hard to draw in my studio. I finally see what the spirits of the dark shapes were telling me. They were trying to tell me they wanted to go home! I feel a sudden uplifting of my soul within me. Do you feel it?"

"Yes, I feel it too. Their spirits are home now. Somehow we have done a good thing for some beings on another planet in another universe. When I design a spaceship using the rock materials' new elements, they will have a way to travel the stars and they will have a way to get home. Now, quickly," urged Sheila, "We must each of us gather up all these rocks and carry them back to our vehicles. Then we need to get to Washington as soon as possible."

"Why Washington," asked Pattie.

"Because, implored Sheila with her sense of urgency, "I must see the President immediately. There is a terrible plot to overthrow the elected government of the United States. I do not know who all is involved in the plot, but I do know that he can not be involved because he is our elected President. We must explain what we have in these rocks to him and help him foil the evil plotters. We must make haste or people will die!"

Everyone pitched in to help Sheila gather rocks. Together, they picked up three hundred pounds of the rocks and returned as quickly as their legs would carry them to Rosemary's cabin. When they got there Rosemary once again made everyone tea and biscuits to fortify them for their journey home. With everyone sitting in a make shift circle she turned her attention to Hud.

"Hud, you've been very quiet the whole time. What's your interest in all this and these rocks?" Rosemary tilted her head to encourage Hud to speak.

"Well, since you asked," he spoke softly, "I want to do all I can to help Sheila. I believe she's our best hope to save our country from this scourge of terrorism. And, I have another interest as well. You see, this entire area for around sixty miles around here sits on my company's mineral rights. In other words I own those rocks."

"I see. How did that all come to happen?" Rosemary had a penchant for discovery and details.

"Well, first I discovered the Little Cow Mine. I put every dime I had into some initial drill holes; then I calculated I had a pocket of very high grade. I took my company public and did a bought deal financing for ten million, giving investors ten percent of the company. Then we drilled more and hit sensational grades. The rest is history. My sister and I sold Little Cow for five billion dollars and kept a royalty on it. So, we invested in mining claims and mines since then and here I am."

"But, what got you interested in the Little Cow and why did you buy the mineral rights around here?" Rosemary wanted details.

"Well, you'd have to appreciate geology. To some people it's just dull rocks, but to me it's much like sex. You see, there are processes called subductions where tectonic plates slides beneath others. Well, it gets exciting if you see the subduction plate as a giant three hundred mile wide and two thousand mile long penis. As it goes into and under the receiving plate, lava shoots out the top of the penis into the host rocks of the receiving plate. Some types of host rocks fracture in ways that allow gold bearing fluid to come up into the receiving plate. I look for the right kind of rocks in areas like the Golden Triangle where the right kinds of rocks exist. Those rocks are here."

Jo Anne got up and sat on Gibby's lap. "Gibby," she said, "I want you to know your penis works fine. Like you say, it shoots hot lava out of its muzzle. That's just the way I like it. I don't want you letting this fellow putting notions in your head. I like your penis just the way it is and I don't want you going and poking holes in the top of it to try anything crazy, okay?"

"Okay," said a dumbfounded Gibby. "You don't need to worry about that, sweetheart." The rest of the group tried to hold back their giggles.

Connie got up and sat on Paul's lap. This rock talk was making her excited. "You know, my love, this kind of makes me think maybe when we get back we should look into taking some courses in geology!" She wriggled her ass in his lap. "I've never felt sexed up over rocks before."

"I like rocks a lot," said CC. It was hard to know what she was thinking when she said that.

"Well, obviously, so do I," said Hud. "What fascinates me is how I can make money knowing about rocks." He stood up and went over to Sheila, lifted her from her chair and kissed her. "But, I've got to say, I've never had extremely valuable rocks fall into my lap before. This trip has been wonderful for me in so many ways."

After tea and biscuits the group said their heartfelt good-byes to Rosemary and drove off to the Calgary airport.

Hud phoned ahead to a charter service based at the airport and explained their immediate needs. When the three vehicle caravan arrived at the Calgary airport, there was a Gulfstream G650 fueled and ready for them. He made another call to the Canadian Prime Minister's office, informed him of their situation and the terrorist plot, and asked him to call the President of the United States to alert him to their arrival.

"Are we going in that? Are you going to fly us, Hud? Can you pilot a plane that big?" Cecilia's questions were rapid fire. She was agape at the size of the jet compared to the Baron.

"Sweetheart," Hud referred to her in this affectionate way now, "there isn't a plane made that I can't fly. Relax. We'll be at Washington Dulles in five hours. Just everybody load your rocks in the cargo bin and climb aboard." Everyone did as instructed. As soon as their seat belts were fastened, Hud started the powerful twin Rolls Royce turbofan engines and they were off!

CHAPTER THIRTY-FOUR

MEETING IN THE OVAL OFFICE

Two F35 Air Force fighter jets escorted the Gulfstream from the moment it entered American air space until it touched down at Washington Dulles. A Marine Corps helicopter picked up Sheila's group, along with their cargo of precious rocks. A half hour later they landed on the White House lawn. Secret service agents carried the rock boxes and escorted them directly to the Oval Office. President Orangejob greeted them warmly and invited them to sit on the sofas and chairs arranged before his desk. Then he seated himself behind the desk. Sheila stood and introduced everyone, then held up one of the rocks. The President saw it change colors and his eyes widened.

"Young lady, can you please explain why these rocks do what they do, how they do that color change thing and where you got them? What am I looking at?" the President demanded.

"They are the product of fifth or possibly sixth generation supernova star explosions, sir," Sheila answered. "They have heavier atomic weights and contain elements that rocks on Earth do not have. Earth rocks are from younger fourth generation star bursts. The stars that created the heavy elements contained in these rocks existed five billion years or more before our own sun was born. They are a priceless discovery, Sir. They can enhance electromagnetism, boost harmonic frequencies, and enable space travel at millions of times faster than the speed of light. They are not natural to Earth. We stumbled onto a unique find. I don't know how they came to be deposited on Earth, but I think there are at least two ways they could have come here."

"How do you think they got here? And you are, I presume, the brilliant woman from MIT that the Canadian Prime Minister told me about?"

"Yes Sir. These people who are here with me all had a role in the discovery of these rocks. We are all committed to foiling the terrorist plot against America, and the coup plot to overthrow you and your government, Sir."

"Very well, great to have you with me! Now, how did the rocks get here, your opinion, please?" The President's face projected a serious frown, as if his mind was struggling to reach a decision about the rocks before he had time to digest any facts about them.

"I can think of two possible ways. They may have been ballast or cargo that was ditched by an alien spaceship; or possibly they were deposited here when our universe intersected a parallel universe. Earth may have randomly brushed against a planet or comet from that universe, and then the universes separated leaving those rocks behind."

"Can something like parallel universes even exist, young lady? Can an intersection of different universes even be possible?" The President looked skeptical.

"Yes Sir, to both your questions. I have worked out the math for that."

"Oh, there's math for something like that?" The President's tone implied doubt.

"Yes Sir, the math *is* there. It's infallible. There are many dimensions beyond our own, and we do occasionally intersect with them."

"There's more than math, Sir. These rocks have spirits in them, spirits from people who live on another planet in another universe. We all saw those spirits didn't we?" It was Gibby speaking. The others in the group nodded their heads in agreement.

"Do tell. This sounds like science fiction." The President was openly dismissive.

Sheila was accustomed to male skepticism about her competence. Men naturally assumed their opinions and reasoning powers were superior to a woman's; and the duty always fell to the woman to set them straight by placing facts before them. In the domain of male attitudes she accepted her place as a woman. She understood that men tended to blindly follow their erroneous assumptions into wars and all sorts of misguided follies, even when women knew the outcome of those adventures would lead to ruin. She realized she could never fully understand men, just like she never understood why her younger brother disobeyed her father resulting in his untimely demise, or why her father could not accept change but opted for suicide instead.

She was a highly intelligent woman, finding herself in the position of not just educating the President but needing to break through his skepticism as well. She drew a deep breath, knowing that she had to accept the situation and do her best.

"It's not only possible; it is highly likely that at least a million times or so in the last thirteen billion years other universes have intersected with our own. Exactly where they intersected is unknowable. Whether or not the intersections resulted in planetary rubs or bumps with our planet Earth, and whether or not matter from another universe crossed over the horizon boundary to our universe is a random chance occurrence. But, it does happen. The math does not lie."

The President looked at Sheila with a dumbfounded facial expression. He rubbed his jaw as if in deep thought before he spoke. "And, now young lady you are telling me that there is some plot to kill a million Americans who want to watch a football game on a Sunday afternoon. Is that right?" Do you have any proof of this?" A skeptical frown appeared on the Chief Executive's face. Plainly, he was wondering if he was in a room full of lunatics.

"Sir, if I may," Cecilia spoke up.

"And who are you again, Miss?" The President's eyebrows rose up displaying his umbrage for having his thoughts interrupted by a woman speaking out of turn.

"I am Cecilia. I am a sergeant in the United States Marine Corps. Before you ask another question, Sir, you need to listen to this recording." Without waiting for permission Cecilia played the conversation of the conspirators for the President and the others.

"And this recording has not been doctored in any way?" asked the President after hearing the conspirators for himself. He was clearly shaken by what he'd heard.

"No Sir," averred Cecilia, "I swear on the oath I took as a Marine that it is the original and only recording of the plotters' conversation."

"And who is this General Porter and this Walter Black fellow, can anyone answer that for me?"

"I can help you Sir," spoke Gibby. "General Porter was the mastermind of the assault team that tried to take my map from me."

"What team, what map are you talking about, and what was your name again?" asked a puzzled President looking bewildered at Gibby.

"Sir, I am Gibby, Navy Seal trained Marine Corps expert marksman with sharpshooter credits and thirty-seven confirmed enemy kills. I bought a map from a Tillamook Indian woman. The map was made by an old prospector who first discovered these magical rocks. General Porter sent five men in two separate teams along with a helicopter to take the map from me. I know that because I heard one of his men mention his name."

"And where are those men now?" The President felt himself getting drawn into the narrative of this bearded salt and pepper haired man with the piercing blue eyes and square jaw.

"I kilt 'em, Sir."

"All of them? You killed all of them single handed?"

"Yes Sir. Every one of 'em. I also killed a man who guided their best sharpshooter and I killed the pilot of the chopper when I destroyed the chopper, too."

"You shot down a helicopter, with a rifle?"

"Yes, Sir, Mr. President, Sir. I nailed it damn good with a kill shot to the rotor assembly. Big fireball, ya shoulda been there, Sir, better den Fourth of July, ha, ha, ha!" Gibby waved his arms wildly in the air and looked a bit crazed. "It was some good shootin, wasn't it, Jo?"

"Oh, it was, Mr. President, it was," said Jo Anne, sitting wide eyed and nodding her head as if she was seeing the event all over again, "You shoulda been there, Mr. President. It was awesome. There was this great big explosion. It went boom when it crashed; and it made a real big fireball like Gibby said. I never seen nothing like it. I got myself so excited and hot when I seen it that my Y eye got real slippery wet."

"Your what?" asked the President.

"You know, Sir," blushed Jo Anne, "my special woman part, you know the part Gibby likes kissin before he plugs himself in. It's that little horny spot where a woman needs to put a ———"

Gibby interrupted her. "I'm good at killin, Sir. I'm one of the best. That's what I do. If you want somebody kilt, you call Gibby. But if you want to save money on your car insurance, you need to call somebody else." Gibby couldn't resist touting and joking about his skill set.

"Okay, okay, Mr. Gibby. I think our Defense Department, our CIA, and some other agencies we have in the government can get all our killing needs taken care of without your help, but thank you for your kind offer." The President looked disparagingly at Gibby. "Now, I'm starting to understand that this plot business is serious. Thank you Cecilia and you as well, Mr. Gibby. Now, what are the rest of you doing here?"

"Sir, I can answer that. I'm Connie Rockman. I work at BASE bank where Walter Black is the Chief Executive. Linda, Sandra and Pattie here are my co workers at BASE. We can attest that Mr. Black is up to no good. He killed Mr. Santifalo, the Assistant Research Director of the bank because he thought Mr. Santifalo had stumbled onto the terrorist plot. Sandra here is the woman the plotters discussed killing on the tape you just heard."

The President shook his head. The information was coming too fast for him to absorb. "All right, now hold up a minute. Will somebody tell me why anyone would want to kill this pretty woman here," he nodded his head toward Sandra.

"Sir, because I am romantically involved with Mr. Black and the plotters became paranoid that I might have heard about the plot while I was in bed with him," blurted out Sandra.

The President eyed Sandra as a man might eye a tasty plum. "Your Mr. Black must be quite the man, huh Sandra?" his curiosity piqued.

"Sir, actually he's a creep. I regret what I've done. Mr. Santifalo was my boss and he was a very good man."

"I see," voiced a now somber President. "Now, before I have General Porter and Walter Black and the others arrested and charged with conspiracy to commit treason, can anyone tell me why this plot to kill Americans was hatched in the first place?"

"Mr. President, my husband, Paul here, has his theory about it although we have no conclusive proof," said Connie.

"Hold off on that a minute," barked the President. He picked up his phone and instructed his chief of staff to have some secret service men, his National Security Director, and the Vice President join him in the Oval Office. He wanted all of them to hear Paul's theory. After the room filled up with the President's men he told Paul to present his theory.

"It's simple business economics, Sir." Paul stood to speak when everyone was assembled. "The rest of the world, the Chinese, Russians, the Arabs, and many others have amassed huge reserves of gold. They believe, rightly or wrongly, that America has sold off all its gold and has little or none left. They see our stock, bond and real estate markets manipulated upward by actions of the Federal Reserve and the bankers to keep asset prices artificially inflated. That creates a wealth effect where those who already have assets see their assets appreciate in value, but those who do not have assets see their incomes failing to keep pace with the asset inflation. Thus, the rich who already had wealth keep getting richer and the poor keep getting poorer.

"To continue world acceptance of the U. S. Dollar as a viable currency our Treasury, working with the FED, operates in the markets to artificially elevate the value of the dollar. And, to keep other countries from trading in gold, an asset which, unlike the dollar, carries no risk of government default, the Treasury and the Fed, along with our European and Japanese allies, artificially suppress the prices of gold and silver as measured in dollars.

"Now, these market conditions have created fertile grounds for treason against our country. General Porter is likely just a front man for either the Chinese or Islamic terrorists who would benefit if your government is overthrown, Sir. The bankers will flip their allegiance to which ever nation has the gold. The plotters' new government would likely stop the artificial dollar and market supports and the artificial gold and silver price suppression. That government could package America as a vassal state and deliver our nation to our foes; and the traitors would be well rewarded for their deed." Paul sat down and stared at the President, waiting for any questions.

"Yes, I am aware of the precarious condition of our currency and the ambitions of our adversaries. Thank you for your eloquent summation. I have pondered at length what, if anything can be done about it, and I remain indecisive. I———."

"Mr. President, you may remember my father, Mr. Howard Rockman?" Connie stood up and interrupted the President mid-sentence.

"Yes, young lady. I do remember him. I had business dealings with him when I was in the business world. What is your point? What does he have to do with the condition of our country? " Obviously the President was miffed at the impertinence of his young guest.

"He has everything to do with the condition of our country, Mr. President. My father is decisive. Once he understands a problem, he takes action. He does not vacillate. He moves fast. He roots out obstacles to his success and crushes those obstacles. Well, Sir, you need to do the same thing. You need to address the problem we face." Connie stamped her foot, folded her arms, and then stood there, shaking slightly from her assertiveness.

"Well, young lady, what would you have me do?" The President tilted his head and raised his eyebrows, and he smiled. He was enjoying this group and now he was engaged. Thoughts of throwing off the yoke of business as usual appealed to him.

"Let *me* answer that," said Linda as she stood to speak. "Mr. President, I am a lending officer at BASE. I see first hand how banks screw the little guy and bend over backwards to bestow favorable terms and credit to their rich and powerful friends. I've listened to your speeches. You are right. The system is rigged. That rigged system has moved the nation toward a civil disorder like that which preceded the Civil War. As Paul here explained, the economic pie for most Americans is shrinking. You need to identify the problem correctly and rip it out by its roots, like Howard Rockman would. The problem is not Republicans' and Democrats' animosity towards each other. That's the symptom of the problem. The problem is the nation no longer has honest money.

"We have lost our honesty, our morals and our way. We are even losing our national identity and our historic culture. Look at the movies of today compared to those you saw as a child, Mr. President. Innocence is absent from today's films. We now have mentally ill directors using mentally ill actors and actresses to make movies about people with psychiatric disorders committing criminal deeds. Is it any wonder our population is numb to societal disintegration? We have been on the downward slippery slope since Woodrow Wilson authorized the Federal Reserve and the Income Tax. To save the nation as it was configured to be, a Constitutional Republic, the mistakes of Wilson must be corrected."

"Give me specifics, young lady!" The President barked at Linda. His adrenalin was surging. He leaned forward in his chair like an attack dog poised to bite. He was a man who craved action but needed to be pointed in the right direction.

"It's simple to do the specifics once you grasp the problem, sir," continued Linda. "You must first eliminate the Federal Reserve. Lock their doors. Send all their employees home without a paycheck. Tell them their charade of phony money printing, blather nonsense speeches and high priced lunch junkets all over the world is over. Then bulldoze their building on Maiden Lane and start over from scratch. Erase the abomination of fiat money from the nation's memory so no future demagogue fool will seek to resurrect it. Build something useful in its place. Just visualize it, Mr. President, where their building was bulldozed you could build a skyscraper twice as high as the Washington Monument. You could see your new skyscraper going up as you look out from the White House. And, when it's completed, you could slap the name ORANGEJOB on top of it in big bold letters."

As Linda spoke a big smile came over the President's face and he began rubbing his hands together. For a moment in time he thought he was a toddler again. He was playing with modeling clays and building blocks on the floor of his parent's family room.

Linda continued, "Then you should do the same thing to the lobbyists' hangouts on K Street, Sir. Bulldoze them and put up a second skyscraper even bigger than your first one. Slap the name ORANGEJOB on all four side of it and all around the top of it. Let the entire world know who the boss man is in this town!"

Now the President smiled even broader. His eyes sparkled and he began to chuckle out loud. He smacked his lips and rubbed his hands together vigorously. In his mind he was no longer America's chief executive dressed in a business suit. He was now a young boy playing with his stick building toy kit making even bigger structures than he made when he was a toddler. He was about to show all the neighborhood kids that his structure was built taller and better than theirs. Linda's recommendations were resonating in his heart.

"Start a new Bank of the United States," Linda continued speaking, "owned in equal shares by each one of the fifty states. Void all dollar currency bills in circulation, default on all our debt, issue a new gold backed dollar, and open the nation for honest trade, without government subsidies for favored companies represented by lobbyists. Next, eliminate the Income Tax completely. Restore money to what money was before 1913. Charge fees for essential government services and tax the state governments for their representative shares of national defense. Eliminate foreign entanglements completely. Walk away from them. Refuse to allow another single American boy or girl to bleed for a foreign sovereign's defense. And that would be a good first start. Sir, the nation hurts and we are broke. And we are divided. There are still many who believe the Civil War had nothing to do with slavery but everything to do with the theft of States' rights by a central government. Your people hurt, Mr. President. Other countries see that and we are no longer able to fool these other countries about our financial condition. They know we're broke and they don't want to take our money anymore."

Linda stopped and stared at the President who was still chuckling and rubbing his hands together. It wasn't clear whether he was paying attention to the discussion or whether he was lost in his thoughts of building skyscrapers in Washington with his name on them. "Mr. President, Mr. President," Linda repeated herself to snap the President out of his daydream.

"Huh, oh yes, yes," the President recovered as he looked up at her. "Now then, who would run this new Bank of the United States?" The President shook his head and recovered the train of thought from the discussion. He had multitasked.

"I will, Mr. President. It doesn't require thirty years of academic gobbly gook studies to understand what needs to be done here. I will form currency agreements with our neighboring Latin American nations to use a unified gold backed currency." Linda spoke in rapid fire. She had ready answers.

"And, what makes you think you can do all that? What makes you think you can get our country some gold?"

"Sir, Sebastian Carlos de Carmella is leading a revolution to take over the Venezuelan government as we speak. I know he will succeed. I got him the financing and he is well financed. Once he is in power he will forge Pan American alliances to establish a unified gold currency. In exchange for access to U. S.

markets he will agree to supply gold to us on favorable terms." Linda folded her arms and tilted her head back. She held the pose of a supremely confident woman.

"And how do you know he will do this?" The President looked up at Linda with his mouth agape.

"Because, sir, I am his wife, I am the Mother of the Revolution. He will do as I ask to please me. We have also reached certain understandings," she said with a confident smile. "I hold his revolution's finances, as well as his sex life, in the palms of my hands." Linda spoke with the unabashed assurance of a woman who often dealt with men on a business level.

"And who will preside over the dismantling of the Federal Reserve?"

"I will, Mr. President," said Paul as he rose to speak. "I will, with the help of my father in law, Mr. Harold Rockman. We'll get it done in less than two month's time, sir."

"But there are all sorts of currency agreements, swaps, complications, trade agreements, and the petro dollar deal where we exchange oil for dollars."

"Sir, with all due respect, the petro dollar deal that Henry Kissinger put together has outlived its usefulness. The Arabs are about to scrap it anyway and trade their oil for gold or Chinese currency. As far as the swap lines, I'm confident that I and Mr. Rockman can unwind all of them in short order.

"And, while we're at it we'll get legislation going to repeal the misguided laws and regulations that put derivative holders ahead of savers and investors in bank bail in liquidations. Most Americans think that their savings are their money, and not just unsecured liabilities of a bank holding company; and most Americans believe that their investments and retirement plans with these big brokerage sponsors are only subject to market risks. They have no idea that a bad derivative bet by their bank holding company can take away everything they have. These banks are all set up to pay their executives big bonuses and pensions and golden parachutes; and the little guy and the government are required to pick up the mess of their failures. That's just wrong, Sir, real wrong. The public is sick and tired of being gutted by these bastards. We'll get that fixed too."

"Well, I knew I inherited a mess, and none of this will be easy. Listen, you are all young people with high ideals. But you do not have the experience that I have. I have met many times with the congressional leadership of both major parties. It's like hitting a brick wall. Every time I want to get something accomplished they tell me that I do not understand how things are done here in Washington. They tell me that the way I want to do things is not how things are done. They talk about making sausage and how complicated it is. They explain to me that that's the way the Constitution set up our constitutional republic and I must get used to it."

"That's just it, Mr. President," Paul held up his fists for emphasis to his words. "You do not have a constitutional republic anymore. These congressional leaders are blowing smoke up your ass, Sir. When they say that's the way things get done here they are just spewing bull shit. Our constitutional republic was founded in the Constitution's Article One powers of the people, that they should always have honest gold and silver money. That honest money power guarantees that the government works for the people, not that the people work for the government. The Article power of honest money is the key that gives power to the people. It was a stroke of genius by the founding fathers.

"Mr. President, do you understand what the patriots did?"

"Oh yes, yes, of course. A great team, a great owner and terrific coaching and management, great players, wonderful people, great run they had, terrific Super Bowl game."

"No, no, Mr. President, *not* the football team Patriots" Paul said. "I'm talking about the original patriots of the revolutionary war. Those men walked miles and miles on their bloody feet through snow in freezing cold to take the battle to the enemy. They faced the greatest military in the world and they *beat* it. They took bullets, they froze to death; they lost their homes and families and their very lives for a government *for* the people. They did not sacrifice everything they had for a government of snakes, rats, lobbyist lice, special interests and bankers. That government for the people was taken away from us by Woodrow Wilson and given away to the snakes and the bankers. Sir, you *must* honor the sacrifices of those great patriots of the American Revolution. Your nation's people elected you to do no less. The people elected you so you would get them their country back."

"Oh yes, I remember the original patriots. I studied history, you know. Well, it's easier said than done, people. I watch the conservative news shows and I listen to conservative talk radio. The anchors on those shows rail about how nothing is getting done and they make these lists of things I promised I'd get done, but I can't get either party in congress to get behind my legislative initiatives. I can't get the Unaffordable No More Health Care Act repealed. I can't get them to see my way on tax cuts. I can't even get money for my border wall."

"Sir," Linda interrupted. "You don't need to ask congress for the money for a border wall. Just bypass them."

"I don't? How do you come by that?" The President was all ears to any suggestion that would rescue a campaign promise.

"By thinking outside the box, Sir! You have the U. S. Mint in your executive branch," Linda began. "You have the power to coin gold and silver. Mexico mines lots of silver. Simply order the U. S. Mint to pay double the market price to Mexico for all the silver they can dig. Make your purchases contingent on Mexico remitting half of the above market overage back into a fund to build the wall. Then contract with the Mexicans to build the wall right alongside American companies. Have a grand ceremony of cooperation with our southern neighbor.

Have a five ounce silver coin minted with your face on one side and the Mexican President's face on the other. Be bold and just go ahead and build your wall. Build a really big wall and put your name all over it. Have ORANGEJOB in bold lettering and in neon lights placed every mile on the wall. The Mexican economy will boom. Drug traffic will drop drastically. Immigration will be easier to regulate and control. A wall will make both countries better."

"But that would be a side deal. I'd be going around the congress to make a side deal with the Mexican President."

"So what?" retorted Linda, "the whole city of Washington runs on side deals. Every congress person has them. That's why the country is in such a mess. The side deals put the special interests ahead of the peoples' interests. It's high time the people had their own side deal, the side deal of honest money. It will be the side deal that ends all the side deals. It'll end the FED and all the corruption that goes with it. It'll put the people back in charge of the government and give them their Article One Constitutional power back. And, Sir, with all due respect, why would you even waste a thought about offending congress? They have lower popularity ratings than vultures, rats, flies and lice."

"She's right, Mr. President," shouted a wild eyed Gibby standing up again. "Ya just gotta build that wall. There's ten billion Mexicans right up against our southern perimeter and they's itchin to come across the border and grab back Texas, New Mexico, Arizona, California, Nevada, and Colorado. We can't let 'em overrun us, Sir. We can't let ten billion Mexicans in here. They'll piss in our streets and steal our groceries. You need a big wall, Mr. President," said Gibby widening his arms, "bigger even than the one they got in China's Russian Gulag; and you need it guarded every hundred yards with blockhouses and three man teams with thirty caliber and fifty caliber machine guns. That way, if any fuckin wet back gets within a

thousand yards of us, we'll just waste that little fucker, Sir."
Gibby was salivating at the idea of killing so many people.

"He's right, Gibby's always right!" screamed Jo Anne,
standing up next to Gibby.

"And who, again, might you be, Miss? And what do you
do?" asked the President.

"I'm Jo Anne, Sir. I carry Gibby's ammo for him and I
keep him good and warm at nights, too, don't I Gibby? We are
patriotic Americans, Sir."

Gibby nodded and smiled at the President.

"Are there many like you out there, Gibby?" The President
seemed a bit concerned.

"Oh, you bet, Mr. President. There's millions of guys just
like me. We's USA all the way, yes Sir, USA and NRA!"

"Well, Gibby and Jo Anne, I'll take your thoughts and
offers about this to my Chief of Homeland Security and the
people who are doing studies on the wall. Thank you very
much for your valuable ideas. Now I'd like to get back to what
Miss Linda was saying.

"Young lady, said the President, now addressing Linda, "if
I did your silver deal and minted coins like you suggest the talk
show hosts would scream that I've violated the constitution.
They'd say I took power from the congress. I'd face a shit
storm. Right now congress has lower approval ratings than I do,
but if I did as you suggest my ratings could plummet. The
leading commentators on the conservative news channels keep
screaming that the congress is to blame for all my woes, but
when I talk to these congressmen and senators I get lots of
mush talk and delays. The conservative commentators blame
leaders of both parties. I actually kind of like that. I'm not sure
I want to change their view of things. I don't know what to
think!" The President's frustration was obvious.

"Mr. President," said Paul as he took over the conversation. With all respect, Sir, you of all people should understand

that those conservative commentators are only about snagging ratings and advertizing dollars. They are going to forever rail and whine about how their base, the Republican voters, are getting short changed by this or that perceived evil threat or this or that no good son of a bitch. They need to keep people stirred up. They need to constantly shove some enemy in their audiences' face so the audience will keep watching the shows. They need to deliver red meat to their lions. The leading liberal commentators are no better. They pretend they are interviewing deep thinkers all the time. And their audiences lap it up. They rail about how misguided conservative thought is. They extol liberal thought.

"Think about it, Mr. President. These media outlets all play to their base. I'm not even beginning to talk about the fake news outlets. The liberal outlets throw red meat to their liberal watchers. Now stop and think for a moment. What do you think would happen if any of these outlets aired out the real problem that plagues us, which is the problem that we don't have honest money? What would happen if there was thoughtful discussion with these network anchors and key congressional people and yourself? What would happen to all the divisiveness in the country if there was an agreement forged to gradually return to an honest money standard of gold and silver backing of the nation's money?

"Let me answer my own question for you, Sir. If you were successful in turning the nation back to the constitutional republic it once was, built upon a solid foundation of honest money, the dissent and bickering level would drop, the government would work for the people again like it did before the banker snakes got their hold on it; and, guess what else would happen, Mr. President?"

"What, pray tell?" The President barked out. Now he wanted answers.

"The television ratings for the television and radio talk show anchors and all the fake news channels would drop and most would just fade away and go off the air. The FED, which prints the phony money, which the favored few have access to, is the glue that holds the deep state together. The deep state swamp would lose its power over the people. The people would be less agitated and calmness would settle over them. They'd be more secure in their money and their futures. Acrimony between conservatives and liberals would cease and discussions would be more productive and solution oriented. Why, the people might even relax so much that they'd watch more baseball and less football, like they did back in the early nineteen hundreds. And you, Sir, you would be the most revered President the nation has ever had since Abraham Lincoln! The people would love you and they'd vote you a second term! These other people are right, Sir. Just go ahead and build your wall!"

As Paul stood speaking, the President noticed Connie looking up at the young man as a young girl might look while admiring her own father. Obviously the young lady had a great respect for the man who just addressed him. The President's thoughts returned to what he had just heard.

"Do you really believe it could all be that simple?" he asked with a perplexed look on his face.

"Sir," said Gibby. Paul's right. My paw always told me that when something makes sense that's 'cause it's right. Dem fuckin bankers never made no sense to me, no how. I been listening to all what's said here, Sir, and you've gotta listen, too. Dem TV guys just give out a headache ever time I listen to 'em. Fuck 'em, all of 'em I say. Stop listening to the television, Mr. President. Sir, at least stop listening to any of these commentators until they stop playing the blame game and they correctly define the problem. The problem is the FED and the banking system. You simply need to tear it all out by the roots and bulldoze it like you do a condemned property. Then rebuild the country right. You alone can do it. Do not let the deep state snakes buffalo ya. I've been listening to Paul and Linda here and they make sense to me. My paw always said when something makes sense it's probably right and when something doesn't, it probably is wrong."

"Well, this is so simplistic. But I have this North Korea problem too. The Chinese are using this little despot to threaten us if we try to resist the new world order the Chinese seek, with the Chinese being in charge. If I start a war, it won't look good. If I do nothing, the Chinese will get a new world currency order and we'll be just a marginal country going forward. What will the Chinese have the North Koreans do if I default on our government bonds and back our new currency with gold?"

"Likely, the Korean man child will strike first. The Chinese may have him start a hot war someplace to make our currency appear risky," Paul spoke.

"Then what?" asked the engaged President.

"Then attack that fat little fucker and kill the little sons a bitch," rudely interrupted Gibby. He was in lock and load mode, clearly a veteran who craved action. "Some guys just needs killin, Mr. President. Killin 'em is the only thing that gets 'em to pay attention to what you's tellin 'em."

"But that will start a war, possibly a big one, possibly World War Three," glared the President.

"Then bring it, Dink muthar fuckers," responded Gibby, open eyed and calm. He had the look of a man who'd seen a great deal of combat and had faced death many times without fear or reservation. "Don't you worry yourself any about any war, Sir. We'll win it, Sir, we're Americans. We're the 'A' team. But you gotta do war right from now on, Sir."

"What do you mean, Gibby?"

"Sir, that Vietnam war was lost because of the American media. The media is communists, sympathizers with communists. They rooted for the communists to win. They falsely reported that we was losin when we was winnnin. They got the American home folk all mixed up nuts with bad information. They glorified people who was hippy traitors and that was bull shit on us men who was doing the fightin. Next time America does war, Sir, you need to keep reporters out of the war zone. That way the home folk don't get fake news. Then you can unleash the military, Sir. When you'se in war you needs to turn loose the dogs of war."

"You're recommending I go all the way, aren't you?" The President seemed fearful.

"It's their way or our way, Sir," said Gibby. "That's how war is. I get it. I done it. I done it lots. I know war involves dying. And that gets a little personal. But, Sir, they's no good sons a bitches. War is the only thing they understand. They cheat us. They steal our technology. They sneaky walk around a deal and find ways to not keep it. So, like my paw said to me when I was a boy, 'If it looks like a skunk and smells like a skunk, you needs to shoot it 'cause it's a skunk.' You can only make a fair deal with people like that after you kill 'em dead." Gibby had that unmistakable wide-eyed thousand mile stare of a man afflicted with severe post traumatic stress, but he wasn't about to succumb to it. He was ready to invade North Korea all by himself.

"Okay, that's enough war talk," the President first shook his head, then stopped shaking it and began thoughtfully nodded it. His thoughts vacillated. He realized these people, as impetuous and simplistic as they spoke, had a grasp of the nub of the greater problem, the money problem. He recognized that they were not like the polished loquacious orators and bull shitters that he dealt with in the Congress. They were ordinary Americans. These people represented his core constituents, each a uniquely separate personality and each the product of a great and free society.

And he felt affection in his heart for all of them, even the mentally damaged ones like Gibby, as he did for all Americans, even the ones who did not vote for him. "I'll take up your perspective, Gibby, with the Joint Chiefs. And I thank you for your service to our country." He eyed Gibby warily and wondered if this maniacal professional assassin had managed to get into the Oval Office with a hidden weapon. He shook the notion from his head then turned to the group to get the conversation back on track. "I see you young people have defined the central problem; but what about this immediate problem of the terrorists and the plotters? That's what brought you here, isn't it? How do you suggest I deal with them?" The President spoke now as if this impromptu group was his sounding board, a kitchen cabinet of sorts.

"Mr. President!" Cecilia leaped to her feet shaking her fists and shouting. "*You are the people's President!* You must stand up! You must be a *man!* You must be a strong man. You were elected to lead the people, not to be a popular television personality or a poll taker. These plotters are traitors to America. There are times when a leader must be a mean ass son of a bitch!

"You need to round up these traitors and have them tried for treason. You *must* enforce equal justice under the law. That is your duty, Sir. It is the oath of your office, the peoples' office. The Republic will dissolve without equal justice for all. While you are at it, Sir, have your treasury stop paying congress members' salaries until they stop being treated differently than the people they serve. Make it illegal for them to do insider trading. Make them subject to the Unaffordable No More Care Act for their health care like everybody else. We elect these people to represent us, not to be Gods with different treatment than the rest of us. Level the playing field. You are America's last best hope to save its Republic. You need to remove the blinders from the American people and level with them about the real problem of fiat money. They *can* handle the truth, Sir." Cecilia sat. She was so overcome with emotions she began crying.

"But to do as you would have me do, to go back to honest money, we could have a depression."

"Sir," spoke Paul mildly but with a matter of fact authority, "with all respect; we are going to have a depression no matter what you do or don't do. The debt service costs guarantee it. My numbers don't lie. The sooner you act the easier it will be for the country to climb out of its decline. What's a depression anyway, compared to your peoples' never-ending bleeding from dishonest money? Linda is right, Sir. Your people are being hurt.

"Have faith in the people who elected you, Sir. Have faith in Americans. They can handle *anything*. Family and church will step in to ease the sting of hardship in places where government pulls back. To restore America's greatness, you must lead boldly, Mr. President. The people look to you with heavy hearts and tired eyes. They need you to lift their burdens of monetary unfairness and to thwart their enemies. You must be strong. You *must* lead us, Sir. When you lead them the people *will* follow you." Paul nodded his head as he sat. The President stared across the room to look at some place far, far away and said nothing.

Sensing the moment, Cecilia rose and walked behind the President's desk and kissed him on his cheek, leaving her signature crimson lipstick mark upon him.

"Mr. President, I just gave you the kiss of the Crimson Mariposa. She is the butterfly of freedom. She carries the love and well wishes of all the people for you. Wear it proudly. It is the symbol of the peoples' love for you."

Cecilia's kiss had an exhilarating effect. The President lifted his head high. He suddenly felt a charging surge of power and a sense of urgency. A far away visionary glow came into his eyes that no one had seen for many months. He was more energized and spirited than a thoroughbred racehorse. He sprang to his feet to speak.

"I want to thank each of you for coming here today," he said while carefully looking at each one of his guests, "you are all great and wonderful people. You represent the finest product of America's freedoms and its greatness as a country. I love each and every one of you. You are fabulous, loving, good hearted patriotic Americans. You are courageous people of high morals."

When she heard the President say high morals, Pattie cringed and brought her hand to her mouth to contain herself from laughing. She looked at her sorority sisters, Linda, Connie, and Sandra. They squinted, winced, pursed their lips, looked at Pattie and gave their heads short rapid shakes. If the President wanted to believe they had high morals they did not want to disabuse him of his fantasy. They lifted their faces to him and smiled sweet innocent sorority smiles. He continued speaking without interruption.

"By bringing this problem to me you did the right thing. I like solving problems and I like building things. That's what I do.

"And that reminds me of a man I knew. He was the skipper of a Navy destroyer during the Vietnam War. And his ship shot lots of rounds into Vietnam and killed lots of bad people. He killed more enemy than all those B 52 strikes we put on those bastards, combined. And he had this credo that he told his officers and men. He told them that if there was a problem on his ship he wanted to be the first to hear about it and he wanted to hear about it right away. That's how he became so successful at killing so many bad people. Now, that gives me another great idea.

"As the People's President, I want the people to be able to get their problems directly to me. I want to know what their problems are and I want to know right away. I like solving problems and I like building things. That's what I do. So, I'm going to have a big suggestion box placed outside the iron fence on Pennsylvania Avenue. I'll have it guarded by Marines. They are great at guarding things, you know. They are great, wonderful people. And then any American who has an idea, like the ideas that you people have brought to me here today, then that American can write the idea down and put it into the suggestion box. Pretty neat idea, huh? Is that a great idea or what? It's a great idea, believe me."

Everyone in the room nodded their head in approval. The President continued speaking. "I want you to know that I'm going to look into this Federal Reserve issue you brought to me. I remember from reading my history book that President Andrew Jackson had problems with bankers and he got that issue straightened out on his watch. He was a great President, Old Hickory was. He was too harsh on the Indians, though.

"The Indians are a great people and a great part of out heritage and culture. They are just like the men who fought for the South in the civil war who are also an important part of our great heritage and they should never be forgotten, either. Just because their side lost doesn't mean that they had no value as people or that we should pretend there is nothing worth learning about their beliefs in States' rights. It's all part of our history, the good and the bad of it. History has a lot of good and bad in it, believe me. I know that's true because I read it in a magazine once. And, slavery was bad and it still is bad believe me. And I heard your point about how the Federal Reserve is making slaves of all of us. I will solve that problem too. I like solving problems and I like building things. That's what I do.

"Thank you all, again, for coming. You are the very finest, most loving, wonderful and best of all people on Earth. You are good Americans. Together we will make America safe and strong and more beautiful and better and richer and better and greater than ever before. We will make America really great again, believe me! I love all of you. A lot! You are terrific people. I love terrific people. It's wonderful to have so many terrific people here in this room with me. And don't pay any attention to fake news. Those guys are bad people, bad, bad, bad, really, really bad people. And do not lose any sleep over these terrorists and their drone plot. I am on that problem as of right now. I'm going to get rid of those bad people real fast, believe me. They are going to get hit so hard and so fast, believe me. They won't know what hit them, believe me.

"And remember to vote, people. I need you to get out there and vote for candidates that support the idea of making America great again. No more swamp people! We are voting them out. Out! We're going to throw them out! I'm going to crush the opposition in the next election cycle. Absolutely crush them, believe me. Those dirty, filthy crooked swamp lovers, those rats, those flies, those lice, those nasty bad people are going to get booted out of office, believe me. Their days of screwing the American people are over, believe me!" Then the President smiled a broad smile and waved good bye to his guests. He appeared to be clear headed, purposeful and up to the great tasks that lay before him.

And he was. He could feel his destiny mapped out before him. As he looked ahead into the future he envisioned the American people coming to him and rallying behind him in their new cause of honest money. He saw how his Presidency could weather the gathering storms and the foreboding depression that loomed ahead. He gritted his teeth, seethed angrily at the nation's traitors, and he was determined to destroy them. And he had confidence. He believed he was destined to go into the history books as one of the greatest Presidents America would ever have.

The President walked forward. Beneath his white and orange frowning eyebrows his squinting blue eyes looked ahead with a piercing fire. He looked far away as if he lived in another world. He excused himself from his guests, and walked from their Oval Office to disappear into the vast corridors of the White House. He walked taller now. Everyone noticed his chest was puffed out, his head was held high and his jaw jutted forward. His guests felt there was a renewed sense of purpose in him. From a distant corridor they heard him bark out an order to get a suggestion box placed on Pennsylvania Avenue. And they echoed his confidence within themselves. They believed that he would not rest until he fully restored the key foundation of the Republic. They felt his boundless energy. It electrified them and they believed in him like they believed in no other. No other politician made them feel this way. He was one of them now. He was a man on a mission more so than ever before.

He was blessed with the kiss of the Crimson Mariposa, and he was off!

EPILOGUE

I n the days that followed the meeting in the oval office the traitors were rounded up and tried for treason. Some who had conspired to murder America's diplomats and trade its security secrets were executed. The others were sent to Guantanamo Bay, Cuba for confinements ranging from ten to one hundred years.

Sheila designed the circuitry that instructed her fifth generation rocks to reverse the instructions the drones received from the terrorist plotters. Each NFL stadium was protected with a pole that rose above the stadium. When the deadly drones approached the stadiums they were sent back to their launch sites where they released their nerve gas and killed the terrorists who sent them. After that Sheila designed a space craft that flew millions of times faster than the speed of light. She and Hud and Cecilia formed a space travel company and made a huge fortune.

In the weeks that followed the Federal Reserve Bank of the United States was replaced by the Bank of the United States. Its shareowners were the fifty states of the American Constitutional Republic, with each state owning one equal share. Its charter forbids the sale of its shares by any state to any other person or entity. The new bank promptly defaulted on all government obligations incurred under the previous Federal Reserve banking system, declared all dollar notes in circulation to be null and void, and established a new gold backed dollar currency, redeemable at any bank chartered by the new Bank of the United States in gold coins.

The United States ceased being the policeman of the world. Its citizens no longer paid income taxes and the Internal Revenue Service was abolished. A new agency titled the Agency for Fees and Tolls was created to raise the necessary revenue for minimal government services. Each state was assessed its proportionate share for the national defense based upon its population.

Sheila, Cecilia and Hud returned to their domestic lives as a happy threesome. Cecilia eventually gave birth to her first baby girl. Sheila began a period of introspection to try to understand her feelings.

Connie and Paul were married and had a boy and a girl of their own. Little Margaret became big sister Margaret. She was very happy with her life in the family.

Sandra was discovered by a very successful money manager who married her. They bought a big house with a white picket fence and filled its six extra bedrooms with children.

Linda became the driving force of Latin American unification. She and husband Carlos eliminated the hacienda traditions throughout Latin America, established a Pan American gold backed Amero currency, and dramatically raised the living standards of all Latinos. Linda was adored throughout Latin America as the Mother of the Revolution. She had coins struck in her image and she and Carlos had three children.

Pattie became the warden of the federal penitentiary at Ricker's Island Prison, New York. No one ever escaped from her prison and there were no more instances of inmate against inmate violence at the prison during the thirty years while she was in charge. She married a former inmate of Ricker's and they had two children together, a boy and a girl. She kept three Doberman Pincer dogs as her house pets.

Gibby and Jo Anne moved back to southwest Colorado. Gibby operated a rifle range and hired out with a government consulting company for wet work assignments which entailed assassinating persons hostile to the United States. Jo Anne worked as a waitress. The two married and adopted a young orphaned boy from Vietnam.

The President was reelected in a landslide victory. He had long coattails. The people loved having honest money. There was a new sense of pride and a blossoming work ethic in America. The people gave President Orangejob an even larger majority in the House and Senate than he had during his first term. He appointed three conservative justices to the United States Supreme Court.

And, as a result of his landslide reelection victory, President Orangejob got the votes in congress that he needed to build his great border wall. And he built the wall because he liked building things and that's what he did. And the wall was truly the greatest wall the world has ever known. It was greater than Hadrian's Wall that the Romans built across Britain, and greater than the Great Wall of China. Every mile along the wall there were placed huge neon signs that said ORANGEJOB because the President's company built the wall and he wanted people to know that it was he who built the wall. And every mile along the top of the wall there were huge fortified blockhouses built that housed men armed with machine guns. And every time someone got within a thousand yards of the wall, one of Gibby's wall guards shot that person. But, oddly enough, after the wall went up nobody tried to cross the border anymore. After all, when you think about it, no one in their right mind actually tries to break *into* an insane asylum.

And in the two weeks following his meeting with Sheila's group in the Oval Office the President did not shave or wash off the lipstick on his cheek from Cecilia's kiss of the Crimson Mariposa.

OTHER NOVELS BY
ROSEMARY NESS-BITNER

THE SECRET AND THE BUTTERFLY
Unmasks the poorly understood illness of nymphomania.

WHEN THE BUTTERFLIES COME
Explores the conflicted emotions and bizarre mindset of a psychopath who runs a financial institution.

SECOND SEGMENT
Chronicles a woman's journey to understand true love.

www.ingramcontent.com/pod-product-compliance
Lightning Source LLC
Chambersburg PA
CBHW020506020726
47493CB00001B/209